The Chemistry of Love

OTHER TITLES BY SARIAH WILSON

Stand-Alone Novels

Cinder-Nanny

The Paid Bridesmaid

The Seat Filler

Roommaid

Once Upon a Time Travel

The End of the Line Novels

The Friend Zone

Just a Boyfriend

The #Lovestruck Novels

#Starstruck

#Moonstruck

#Awestruck

The Royals of Monterra Series

Royal Date

Royal Chase

Royal Games

Royal Design

The Ugly Stepsister Series

The Ugly Stepsister Strikes Back

The Promposal

PRAISE FOR

The Seat Filler

"Wilson (*Roommaid*) balances the quirky with the heartfelt in this adorable rom-com."

—*Publishers Weekly*

The Friend Zone

"Wilson scores a touchdown with this engaging contemporary romance that delivers plenty of electric sexual chemistry and zingy banter while still being romantically sweet at its core."

—*Booklist*

"Snappy banter, palpable sexual tension, and a lively sense of fun combine with deeply felt emotional issues in a sweet, upbeat romance that will appeal to both the YA and new adult markets."

—*Library Journal*

The #Lovestruck Novels

"Wilson has mastered the art of creating a romance that manages to be both sexy and sweet, and her novel's skillfully drawn characters, deliciously snarky sense of humor, and vividly evoked music-business settings add up to a supremely satisfying love story that will be music to romance readers' ears."

—*Booklist* (starred review), *#Moonstruck*

"Making excellent use of sassy banter, hilarious texts, and a breezy style, Wilson's energetic story brims with sexual tension and takes readers on a musical road trip that will leave them smiling. Perfect as well for YA and new adult collections."

—*Library Journal*, *#Moonstruck*

"*#Starstruck* is oh so funny! Sariah Wilson created an entertaining story with great banter that I didn't want to put down. Ms. Wilson provided a diverse cast of characters in their friends and family. Fans of *Sweet Cheeks* by K. Bromberg and Ruthie Knox will enjoy *#Starstruck*."

—*Harlequin Junkie* (4.5 stars), *#Starstruck*

The Chemistry of Love

SARIAH WILSON

This is a work of fiction. Names, characters, organizations, places, events, and incidents are either products of the author's imagination or are used fictitiously. Otherwise, any resemblance to actual persons, living or dead, is purely coincidental.

Published by Montlake, Seattle

www.apub.com

ISBN-13: 9781542039246 (paperback)
ISBN-13: 9781542039239 (digital)

Cover design by Philip Pascuzzo

Printed in the United States of America

For Rian Johnson—
For making the best Star Wars and because I know you would have made sure Ben Solo lived

CHAPTER ONE

There were three things that I really despised—being late, the color orange, and having to clean my beakers after making an anhydrous product (because those hardened waxes were nearly impossible to remove).

Today I was late for work, and the only thing that could have possibly made that worse would have been to arrive at the lab and find out that my next assignment would be to create a lip balm. An orange lip balm.

My boss was going to freak out. And he was going to make a scene while I had to stand there, quietly taking it . . . I shook my head. No. Maybe I could sneak in, and Jerry wouldn't even notice that I'd come in late.

Even as I thought it, I knew it wouldn't come true. Something was going to happen. Again.

The guard at the front desk waved me through the security gate without me showing him my badge. Normally I would stop and chat with Daniel, but instead I was too busy doing my White Rabbit from *Alice in Wonderland* impersonation.

I was so, so late. And I was never late.

Daniel furrowed his brow, as if he sensed that something was off. I wondered if he'd tease me, but instead he just smiled. "Good morning, Anna!" he said as he buzzed me through.

"Good morning!" I replied, trying to retain some semblance of dignity as I power walked to the elevator bank.

I could still hear my grandma's words in my head as the elevator doors finally opened and let me inside. She had noticed my tardiness and said, "Being late is disrespectful to you, and it is disrespectful to your colleagues. Even if you're not working at a real lab."

The memory made me sigh heavily. It was a real lab, despite what she thought, and I hadn't been trying to disrespect anyone. I'd accidentally slept in on my first day back at work after my company's two-week holiday break, which somehow just zoomed by. One day I was leaving the office with nothing but time in front of me, and the next it was New Year's Eve, where I sat with my grandparents on their couch and watched the ball drop on their ancient television. My grandpa's favorite parrot, Feather Locklear, had repeated, "Happy New Year! Happy New Year!" in the room behind me, and I realized that I wasn't actually happy with my life.

My vague sense of dissatisfaction was also due in part to my grandmother's constant, pointed comments about me being a cosmetic chemist (or as she liked to call it, wasting my college degree by becoming a "makeup lackey") instead of choosing an important job, like being an environmental scientist.

Which was what she did for a living.

I was extremely happy with my chosen profession. I was less happy with the lab I worked in. Still a real lab, but it had drawbacks. There were definite bright spots, like my fellow chemist and best friend in the world, Catalina Diaz. She'd been here for six months (compared to my four years), and being the only two women in our division had quickly cemented our friendship.

That, and our devotion to Lord of the Rings and nerd culture in general.

But working at Minx Cosmetics hadn't turned out quite how I'd hoped. I had so many ideas, things I wanted to work on and try out, but my boss, Jerry, shot all of my proposals down.

He was the kind of guy who wore a three-piece suit under his crisp, pristine lab coat instead of comfortable clothing like the rest of us and always smelled slightly of formaldehyde. His sporting that particular scent should tell someone everything they needed to know about him.

Radical innovation wasn't really his thing, despite the fact that we were in the research and development branch of the company.

The branch that was headed up by our yummy vice president, Craig Kimball.

Thinking of him made me sigh, my stomach fluttering. Tall, with light blond hair and smiling light eyes, he was kind and funny and charming—and I'd fallen in love with him.

Catalina was a little too fond of pointing out that Craig and I had never had a conversation that had lasted longer than ten minutes, but that wasn't a deterrent. I knew we could have something special between us—I just had to find the courage to talk to him again.

Maybe I could tell him about how I wished I could start my own makeup company where I'd be free to experiment and try all sorts of new chemical combinations.

Like neurocosmetics. I loved the idea that there could be an interaction between the nervous system and makeup—that it could possibly influence moods, soothe or inflame, all while making your skin radiant.

That was the reason I was late—I'd stayed up too late reading a paper by a German biochemist about transient receptor potential cation channels and how stimulation of those TRP channels could heal wounds faster and cause skin regeneration.

Seriously fascinating stuff.

The elevator doors opened, letting me out into the lobby of our floor. I walked down the fluorescent-lit hallway, heading toward the lab.

The more I had thought about it, the more I wanted to dabble in neurocosmetics. I wished I could experiment in my home lab, but I still needed to get a high-shear mixer, and the cheapest, smallest one I could find was three thousand dollars.

Which I did not have.

I'd considered asking Jerry if I could stay after work, but I knew he would never let me conduct personal experiments during off hours.

Last night after I finished reading the article, I'd felt inspired. I'd thought about the fact that the New Year had just begun, so I figured it was time to make some resolutions.

First, I resolved to figure out a way to start my own company. I'd take business classes, learn how to find investors, whatever it took. I was personally terrified of change, but I wanted this enough that I hoped I might actually do it.

The second thing I wanted to do was tell Craig how I felt about him. Another terrifying thought, but I'd been in love with him for two years, and after another holiday season spent with my grandparents and their menagerie of birds, I was ready for something more.

A real relationship with the perfect man.

I scanned my badge at the sensor and heard the door to the lab unlock. I walked quickly to my station, ignoring the stares of the other chemists. I hated this uncomfortable feeling.

That was my third resolution. To never be late again.

To never put myself in a position where Jerry might coldly berate me.

I got to my workbench and put my backpack in my bottom drawer, on top of my folded-up lab coat. I remembered that I was chewing gum, as I often did when I felt anxious or needed to concentrate, and I tried to be discreet as I leaned over to spit it out in my trash can. Another thing Jerry hated. Gum chewing while working.

I sat down and had just nudged the drawer shut when I felt someone standing next to my stool.

"Anna! Finally. Here." Catalina placed a beaker down on my workbench. It was filled with an odorless clear liquid. Which made me remember that in my rush that morning, I'd left my Hydro Flask at home.

I grimaced. I tended to get caught up in my projects and would skip lunch and all fluids—I would definitely dehydrate myself if I didn't have some water at my table. "What's this?" I asked her.

"I brought you some cyclopentasiloxane."

"Why?"

Catalina looked at me like I'd flunked Basic Analytical Chemistry. She was the only person in my life who had ever looked at me that way. "Because the project you were working on before the holidays? The mythical lipstick that's all-natural and chemical-free, made of the tears of a unicorn and pixie dust? The one that crumbled after you baked it?"

Right. I'd been working on a new formulation that had been requested by one of the product developers. A long-lasting lipstick that the company could market as organic and sustainable, without any of the -ites or -ates that consumers told us they didn't want / were afraid of. Which always struck me as a bit strange, considering that cosmetics was one of the most regulated industries in the entire country. "Cyclopentasiloxane is a chemical," I reminded Catalina.

She rolled her eyes. "Barely."

I got her annoyance. It was something she and I had discussed often. The kind of makeup we were supposed to create—it was a little like somebody bringing you the most moist, delicious cupcake you'd ever eaten and then saying, *Now make me something exactly like that, only it has to be gluten-free, vegan, no sugar, and nonfat.*

There was no way.

Although my goal was always to make as close an approximation as I possibly could.

"But it still counts as a synthetic substance," I said.

She shook her head as if she disagreed with me. "Adding this to your mixture will make the lipstick go on smoother and prevent the crumbling."

Catalina was right, but I'd have to figure out another way.

The crumbling lipstick hadn't happened solely due to lacking a silicone element. I'd been extremely distracted that day. I'd almost smacked face-first into Craig in the break room.

I'd never seen him there before—it was a bit like being out for a hike and coming across a wild horse on the trail. Yes, that animal belonged in the outdoors; you just weren't expecting to see such a magnificent creature on one of your daily walks. It took my breath away.

And even after I blinked slowly several times, Craig was still there, all cute and tall, and it was like my brain couldn't compute that we were sharing the same space. That he was in the room where (when I remembered) I ate my greek yogurt.

He smiled, nodded, and then left. While I stood there feeling like I'd been hit by a delivery truck.

"Duck me," Catalina said, looking at me. Her resolution was to not swear, and so she'd been using the substitution word my grandpa had suggested. "You're thinking about him again, aren't you?" Catalina put one of her hands on her hip. "You get this goofy look on your face whenever you think about that waste of space."

I didn't know whether to deny her true accusation or defend Craig's honor. For some reason, Catalina didn't like Craig and tried to find his flaws.

"He's not a waste of space," I protested.

She rolled her eyes. "Look at his hair. Too much gel. Like he fell in a vat of boy bands. Hair should not have the same consistency as piano wire."

"That's not—"

"Not to mention, he drives a truck, which is a definite red flag."

"What? That's not a red flag."

Catalina shook her head. "If it's not red, it's at least orange. Because the size of a truck is inversely proportional to the size of his manhood."

"Untrue."

"Anecdotal maybe, but I have personally conducted a thorough study on the subject. It's true. And Craig's truck is enormous. I'm just saying."

Now I really had to defend his honor. Not that I had any firsthand experience, but it seemed like an unfair accusation. But from the look on her face, I knew that I wouldn't be able to bring her over to my side. She didn't have to like Craig, but at the very least, she could be supportive. "I wish you'd get on board with me being in love with him."

"I'm sorry, but I can't. I'm on the dock, watching you head for that giant iceberg."

My relationship with Craig was not the *Titanic*. Before I could respond, there was motion at the edge of my peripheral vision.

It was one of our colleagues, Zhen, getting up from his workbench at the far end of the room. Catalina followed my line of sight and sighed happily. She had had a huge crush on him for a long time, and he was one of the few guys in the lab who was nice to both of us.

"He and I are going to have the smartest babies," she whispered to me as he started walking toward us. I wondered if he had any idea that he was about to be totally conquered. Any time my best friend set her sights on a man, she got him.

It was an ability that we did not share.

"Wait. I thought you were dating that Steve guy."

"*Dating* is a strong word. We were more dating adjacent," she said. "Whatever it was is over. I've decided I'm done dating hot guys. They're awful."

"Me too." I mean, I never actually dated a hot guy. I had hopes of that changing in the not-too-distant future, though.

"Zhen is good looking, but not in that you-need-to-activate-the-tracking-app-on-his-phone kind of hot. Plus, he's smart and nice. I could use some of that in my life."

Yes, she could. So could I.

Catalina flicked her long, dark hair over her shoulder, positioning herself into a dramatic lean against my workbench. I moved the beaker she'd given me to my left so that she didn't accidentally knock it over while she was, as my grandpa would say, showing off her plumage. She understood all the intricacies of a mating dance, while I was helplessly inept in that particular area.

To my surprise, Zhen didn't stop to talk to us and veered off to the left at the last second. He did manage to mutter two distinct words, "Lab coat," in passing.

Uh-oh. Catalina and I exchanged worried glances. It was a code phrase. That meant Jerry was in a terrible mood. He generally tolerated what he considered to be our lack of discipline and respect to the lab by not wearing our lab coats. They were so annoying. Impossible to keep clean, and the sleeves were so baggy that they constantly got in my way so that I might have, on some occasions, spilled some not-so-safe materials all over the countertop.

Catalina scurried off to her workbench while I pulled the bottom drawer back out to grab my coat. All the other chemists were donning their own coats as well.

My lab coat was definitely dirty. I tried to scrub at one of the more obvious stains from a bright red pigment. I grabbed a beaker and filled it with water from my sink and dipped my fingers in it, applying it to whatever color I'd managed to permanently imprint on my lapel, but no luck.

I dumped the water out and then, reconsidering, filled it up again so that I could get a drink. I pulled a long swig and had just set the beaker down when I heard Jerry's door open.

When I'd arrived earlier, I'd deliberately not looked toward his office, using some childhood logic that if I didn't see him, he somehow magically wouldn't know that I had been late. As his highly polished shoes crossed the epoxy-resin-sealed concrete floor, my heart started to beat a little faster.

I was definitely in trouble.

I stood up slowly, hoping that he might stop at some point and call me into his office. But his stride never faltered and instead he made a beeline to my workbench.

I groaned. I should have known. With me, it was always public humiliation.

He glared down at me. "Miss Ellis? You and I have a problem."

If I'd been paranoid about everyone staring at me before, there was no question that it was happening right now. For some reason, I was the only chemist who Jerry disciplined in the middle of the lab. Everyone else he dealt with privately in his office. But me?

My suffering would be seen by all.

He seemed particularly angry today, though. Was it just the tardy thing? I'd done other things that weren't great. I'd thrown out my fair share of beakers that were too hard to clean, claiming they'd been chipped. But everyone did that.

My boss didn't know about that, did he? Were there security cameras in here? My gaze darted to the corners of the ceiling. Had someone been filming us the entire time?

Okay, I was overreacting.

But so was Jerry.

"Problem?" I echoed his last word. I hated this feeling. I'd never been great with confrontation, and talking to Jerry always gave me this icky feeling, like I'd been coated in a soap residue that couldn't be rinsed off.

"Yes. I don't appreciate you coming in late." His words were clipped, furious. Again, I didn't know why I seemed to elicit so much venom from him. Other people had been late; I certainly wasn't the first. Jerry usually seemed annoyed when other people did it, but this wasn't just annoyance.

He always made me feel like a little kid who'd been called up to the teacher's desk to be made an example of in front of the rest of the class.

I hated it. Really, really hated it. I could feel my face warming—wishing I had the courage to say something back, to call out the inequality in how he treated me in comparison to my colleagues. Catalina shot me a sympathetic grimace, but I was on my own here. My pulse felt wonky.

There was a moment when I really let myself savor the prospect of standing up for myself, but I took the meek route. "I'm sorry about that. It was—"

But Jerry cut me off. "Your work is often subpar, forcing your colleagues and me to cover for you."

That made me rear my head back in surprise. I knew I was one of the best chemists in the lab. I was always given the most difficult assignments because the product managers knew I could deliver. I opened my mouth to say something, but he went on.

"Everyone else managed to get to work, again covering for you. I don't understand why we keep having issues."

It was bad enough that he'd accused me of doing subpar work, but was he really going to keep harping on the tardy thing? I had never been late before, not in the entire time I'd worked here.

I wanted to defend myself but realized it wouldn't do me any good. He seemed to genuinely dislike me, and I wasn't sure why. I did do good work. Despite his assertion to the contrary, I hardly ever messed up.

This felt so personal, and I didn't know how to take it. Some part of me desperately wanted to quit. To be honest, I always wanted that—to strike out on my own. But I knew that wasn't the right decision. I didn't have a safety net. I was stuck here. I swallowed the lump in my throat. "It won't happen again."

"Be sure that it doesn't. At this point, your job is in jeopardy. I don't want to keep having these conversations with you. We have an inspection this morning, and I can't—*we* can't afford to look bad in front of upper management."

He gave me one last glare and then walked away from my workbench. An inspection? Upper management?

Did that mean Craig was coming here?

My emotions shifted so quickly from humiliation to giddy anticipation that I felt a little nauseated. This situation needed to be discussed. Which members of upper management was Jerry referring to?

After Jerry closed his office door again, I inclined my head toward the supply room, sending Catalina a message. We kept all our materials and supplies there and in the walk-in fridge and freezer.

She met me in the refrigerator, closing the heavy door shut behind her. Virtually soundproof. She gave me a quick hug, asking if I was okay. I nodded.

"What was that?" she asked, her eyes flashing in anger. "He was so completely out of line! I've never seen Jerry be so—"

But that wasn't the thing I wanted to discuss. I'd shove those angry feelings down deep so that I could keep my resolution and focus on the things that might make me happy. "An inspection. Who do you think is coming? Did Jerry say something before I got here?"

She frowned at me. "No, our illustrious leader didn't say a word. And I know you want me to guess that it's going to be Craig, but I think it might be Loch Ness *GQ*."

Catalina and I had nicknamed the CEO of Minx Cosmetics Loch Ness *GQ*, because we hadn't ever seen him in real life, much like the Loch Ness Monster, and he was ridiculously handsome in the one photo we had seen in the quarterly report, where he looked like a model on the cover of *GQ* magazine. I assumed he had an actual name, but we'd been calling him Loch Ness *GQ* for so long that I had no idea what it was.

There was a rumor he was somehow related to Craig, but I figured it had to be a distant connection. They looked nothing alike.

"Why would he come here? He has other things to worry about." Loch Ness *GQ* was apparently good at his job because the company's earnings increased year to year in a highly competitive market. "But Craig, on the other hand, he has to concern himself with what our department is doing. He's more of the hands-on type of leader."

"Yeah, I know what you want him to put his hands on."

"Ha ha."

Then she put her hands on my shoulders, turning me toward her. I was a head taller than her, but I felt a little intimidated. "You don't know Craig. I've heard some things. I think you should steer clear."

"I can handle it," I said, not willing to believe bad things about my future husband. "Rumors are just that: rumors."

She didn't look convinced. "If even a fraction of them are true, I would blow up this whole lab before I'd let him date you."

"I appreciate your willingness to choose violence on my behalf, but I'm a big girl. You don't have to protect me," I said. She had told me more than once that I was like a newborn lamb, walking around on wobbly legs, and that she felt compelled to protect me from harsh reality.

While I loved her for it, I really could make my own choices.

"Don't say I didn't warn you," she said, letting her arms fall.

"If you're right, I give you full carte blanche to tell me I was wrong and you were right."

That got me a smile. "I'll remind you of that."

"I know. But we should probably get out there and go back to work," I said. Technically, I hadn't actually done any work at all yet, and I did not need to make Jerry even angrier by staying in the refrigerator. Especially when she didn't have any useful intel.

As if she could read my thoughts, Catalina stopped me, putting her hand on my arm. "Are you sure you don't want to talk about Jerry?"

That icky soap-residue feeling was back. I pushed my glasses back up the bridge of my nose. "No. I was just trying to gather data about the inspection. You know how much I enjoy doing that."

I opened the fridge door and gasped.

Standing there, in the middle of the supply room, as if I'd conjured him up, was Craig Kimball.

CHAPTER TWO

"Hello," Craig said with a smile. The sun shone down on his light blond hair, and his pale blue eyes somehow gleamed. He looked like an angel come to rescue me. My heart bubbled with excitement.

I tried to speak.

Nothing happened.

Just me standing there, gaping at him, my mouth partially open like a fish that had just been yanked out of the water.

"Hi! I'm Catalina Diaz, and this is Anna Ellis." My best friend came rushing to my rescue, and I had honestly never adored her more. Although why she felt like she had to introduce me, I wasn't sure. We'd met. He knew me.

"Craig Kimball," he said, as if we were unaware. Like I didn't think about him every single day.

As if I didn't remember what he had done for me two years ago.

And my memory of it had me making a strange gagging noise in response.

Now my face was flushing for a second time that day but for an entirely different reason.

"You're our two lady scientists," he said with a wink.

Catalina bristled beside me as she responded, "Actually, we're just scientists. No qualifier necessary."

I felt completely off kilter. There was still that lingering feeling of dread and embarrassment from Jerry's mini-lecture, and now I couldn't quite catch my breath with Craig standing in front of us, his arms folded, smiling at me.

At. Me.

I could sense Catalina was aggravated, but I wasn't sure why exactly. I was too busy focusing on the way Craig's mouth moved, how he seemed to caress the words coming out of it.

I forced myself to pay attention.

"Oh, I hope you didn't take that the wrong way," he said. "It's just so impressive that you two are succeeding in what's typically a male-dominated field."

Ah. That's why Catalina was annoyed. I wanted to give him the benefit of the doubt and assume he didn't mean any harm by what he'd said, but I also understood why she felt defensive—we were often treated as "less than." Not only here at work but at conferences, too. As if we didn't have the same level of education and skills as our male colleagues.

Craig cleared his throat, as if he finally realized that he'd stepped in it, and changed the subject. "What are you working on?" he asked.

My tongue still felt too big for my mouth, but if I didn't say something soon, he might think I was weird.

Weirder than he probably already thought I was. "Uh, we were, um, getting supplies."

I had spoken! Actual words had been said!

Never mind the fact that I hadn't answered his question. I could only stand there, grinning at him like a demented jack-o'-lantern.

Catalina shot me a look that very clearly said, "Why do you like this guy?" and I shrugged in response. There was no way to make her understand. She just didn't know him.

Technically, neither did I, but I could personally vouch for the fact that he was a good guy.

She shook her head and announced, "I'm going to head back to my workbench and make a little nitroglycerin."

I got her intent, even though her concerns were misplaced. She left the supply room, and I was alone with Craig.

Alone—and talking to him.

"Did she say nitroglycerin?" Craig repeated, sounding amused.

"Vegetable glycerin," I said, not wanting to explain what my best friend had meant. "She's making an organic moisturizer. Personally, I like working on makeup better. It's my favorite thing to create. Like now, I'm working on this lipstick that will be long-lasting and totally natural. Really vibrant colors, too."

His gaze shifted, and he glanced around the room. Was that . . . boredom in his expression?

I thought we'd bond over a love of cosmetics. This was my fault. I was nervous and saying things he didn't care about. I had a tendency to do that sometimes.

Time to trot out a story that people usually enjoyed. "You know, speaking of nitroglycerin, I had a lab partner in college who wanted to see if he could make it himself and blew out all the windows in our lab."

It worked. I had Craig's attention again, but now he looked concerned.

"It's okay—he was fine. It burned off his eyebrows and the front of his hair, but he was far enough away when it blew up."

That was the one exciting story I had in my past. I knew how sad that made my life, but I was just happy that I'd succeeded in getting his attention back.

"Is that the sort of thing that goes on here after hours? Are you guys busy making black-market explosives?"

Had I implied that somehow? "My lab partner, that wasn't a money thing. He was just curious. But no, we don't make explosives here. And we won't. Not unless someone figures out a safe way for people to use them in order to diminish wrinkles and fine lines."

I hoped he'd laugh, but he just nodded. "You wanted to show me that lipstick thing?"

"The formulation? Yes. Just follow me. I have it on my computer."

Somehow I managed to make it all the way to my workbench without tripping over my own feet. I was keenly aware of him walking just behind me, and I wanted to pinch myself. We'd been having our second-ever actual conversation!

I got to my laptop and pulled up the formulation. He stood to the right of my workstation, and the fact that we were breathing the same air made me unbelievably happy.

He picked up a sparkly, golden eye-shadow sample that I had on my workstation. "Newest blush?"

Had he not seen the gold and glitter? You'd only wear that on your cheeks if you were going to disco night at the club. "No, it's an eye shadow. Marketing says it's creasing, so I'm going to . . ."

My voice trailed off when he did the worst thing imaginable.

He started cracking his knuckles one by one. Loudly, each sharp popping sound fracking my soul and making my ears want to bleed. I loathed that sound with every fiber of my being.

A little voice whispered that my soul mate would never crack his knuckles around me. That was silly; I couldn't believe I'd even thought it. I was about to ask him to please stop with the stomach-turning noise but realized how odd that might sound.

"Here," I said, handing him my computer, hoping I could distract him.

Thankfully, taking my laptop stopped him from messing with his poor, abused knuckles. He made me so flustered, and I realized just how much his opinion on my project mattered. I wanted him to see how smart I was, to be impressed by me. I knew looks-wise that I'd never win him over, so he had to get to know me so that he could fall in love with my sometimes-winning personality.

But he wasn't saying anything, and my stomach was starting to fill up with hard knots. I found myself wanting to explain my thought process to him. "I have to be careful with the formulation to meet all the vegan parameters, to make sure I don't get impatient and raise the pH balance too quickly. I mean, all cosmetic chemists are guilty of that."

"Yes, we've all been there."

Was that sarcasm? I shifted on my stool. He had that bored expression back on his face. I pushed my glasses up my nose, worried that I might accidentally fog them up as I was breathing harder than normal. I told my brain that this moment was not as important as my central nervous system apparently thought it was. Needing to calm down, I reached for my beaker of water and took a drink.

Nope, not water. *Not water.* Cyclopentasiloxane.

I leaned forward and spit the entire mouthful into the sink. I grabbed the beaker that I'd filled up earlier with water and rinsed my mouth out, two, three, four separate times.

"Are you okay?" Craig asked, and I was touched by his concern. I was also thinking about the safety data binder in the bottom drawer of my workstation. I didn't know if there was something else I needed to do in this situation, but I felt fairly certain I wasn't going to die. I knew cyclopentasiloxane could potentially disrupt hormones, but I hadn't actually ingested it.

If I pulled that binder out, though, Craig would know what I had just done.

"Fine. I'm fine." I might have permanently damaged part of my endocrine system, but all good. "I just . . ." I didn't want to confess to my colossal mistake. I was trying to win him over with my wit and smarts, not make him think I couldn't distinguish a chemical from water.

Which was true, but still.

He set the laptop down. He didn't say anything about my formulation, and I again felt the urge to fill in the silence. "I know it's not all that exciting, but it's what they assigned me. I'd love the chance to work on some of the things I've pitched to my boss. I think I have a lot of potentially good ideas."

At that, his expression shifted. "Really? Have you shared them?"

How could I tell Craig that Jerry was a buffoon who wouldn't know a good idea if it climbed up on his face and suffocated him like one of those alien larvae? "Not yet. We have a long list of things to accomplish, and I try to focus on that."

I hoped that was diplomatic enough.

That anxious feeling returned while I waited for him to respond, and I reached across my desk until my hand landed on a thermometer. I picked it up. If someday I became famous and my biographer asked about this moment, I would never be able to explain why I made a dad joke. "Hey, what did the thermometer say to the measuring cylinder?" I paused. "You may be graduated, but I have several degrees!"

Craig blinked at me slowly, and the total and utter humiliation that filled me up, from the tips of my toes to the roots of my hair, made me want to climb under my workstation and wait for the heat death of the universe.

Then he spoke, skipping over my world-ending joke, and I didn't know if that made things better or worse. "Those ideas of yours, you should stop by my office and share them with me. I'm looking for the next big thing. Something that will put Minx Cosmetics on the map."

Obviously. We all wanted that. That's why we were here—to come up with the next great innovation that would change our industry.

Craig kept talking, almost like he was reading my mind. "I know every executive at every makeup company around the globe is looking for the same thing. Easier said than done, right? It's just that my father . . ." His voice trailed off and he sighed. "I need to find something that will make him and KRT happy with me."

I knew Minx Cosmetics was a subsidiary of a much larger conglomerate, KRT Limited. Was his father involved with that company?

Putting that aside, I wondered how anyone could be unhappy with Craig. It seemed impossible.

He added, "So if you do come up with something great, I want you to bring it straight to me, okay?"

Something in his tone felt . . . off. And he must have seen that in my face, because he suddenly leaned forward on my workstation, so close that if I had moved slightly to the right, we'd practically be kissing.

The thought of that made my brain short-circuit and forget what I'd just been worrying about.

His eyes lit up, a flirtatious smile flashing across his lips. "Are you going to the party tonight?"

"The company party?" I asked breathlessly. Of course the company party. What else would he be talking about? Minx Cosmetics always had a big event in January after everybody returned from the holidays to celebrate the previous year's successes.

I'd had zero plans to go. I hated parties and being around a bunch of people. My idea of a perfect evening was sitting at home watching movies and/or playing board games. Standing around and being forced to make small talk felt like something the Geneva Convention should outlaw.

He nodded. "I hope you're coming." Somehow he managed to move even closer, and when my nerves started shorting out, I didn't know if it was due to him or the possible cyclopentasiloxane ingestion. He murmured in a low voice, "It really is too bad that the company has that nonfraternization rule."

I drew in a sharp breath. Nonfraternization rule? What? Since when? I'd never heard of it. That seemed like something Jerry would delight in reminding us about, over and over.

And a microsecond later, I understood Craig's implication, and my heart leapt with excitement into my throat. That if there wasn't a rule . . . that we . . . that he and I could . . .

It was like a dream come true.

I didn't break rules . . . but maybe this one time I'd be willing to make an exception.

"Yes! I'm definitely going. I love parties!" I hoped he couldn't hear how fake my words were. I'd always been a terrible liar.

Jerry's door opened loudly, startling me. In my haze of excitement and hope, I'd totally forgotten about my disapproving boss.

What if he came over here?

What if Craig witnessed Jerry treating me like an incompetent idiot? That would be horrific. My intelligence had always been the trait I was most proud of. I didn't want Jerry to make Craig look at me differently. That would be a total nightmare. I actually checked with my tongue to make sure my teeth were still in my mouth.

I was torn between the desire to have Craig stay close so that we could talk and wanting to tell him to flee before my boss ruined everything.

Even though I was doing a pretty good job scaring him off all by myself between my staring at him and drinking chemicals.

Jerry cleared his throat, and Craig glanced over his shoulder. "I should go." He turned back toward me. "You'll have to save me a dance, and we can talk more about those ideas of yours. Deal?"

"Yes!" He wanted to dance with me? I couldn't imagine anything better.

"See you later," he said with a wink, and my heart nearly exploded with delight. I watched as he walked over to join Jerry, and they went into Jerry's office, closing the door.

I said a quick prayer to whoever the patron saint of cosmetic chemists was that I would not be the main topic of discussion between Craig and Jerry and then pulled my safety data binder out of the drawer as discreetly as I could. I quickly flipped to cyclopentasiloxane and saw that I needed to rinse my mouth out (done) and make sure I was still breathing (also done). I was good.

Catalina came over with a box that she set on my desk. "I've got some stuff for you to try out. A new mascara, this amazing organic face mask with honey and blueberries, a self-tanner that won't streak, a long-lasting lipstick that's supposed to be kiss-proof and sulfate-free."

I blinked at her, my brain not shifting gears fast enough. I was still freaking out about Craig and what he and Jerry were talking about and whether I'd accidentally caused my own sterility, and she was bringing me stuff to test? To be fair, though, trying out each other's products was something she and I did regularly—it always struck me as ironic that in our industry it was mostly men making women's beauty products and that they did not personally test their own creations. Catalina and I were unique in that regard.

But testing lip glosses and eyeliners did not mean that I knew how to do makeup. Creating it and applying it were two completely different skill sets, but everybody expected me to be able to do both.

I picked up the lipstick and then put it back in the box. It was too bad that whenever I tried to do my own makeup, no matter how many tutorials I watched on YouTube, the end result often reminded me of Picasso.

"Just let me know what you think when you get the chance," she said.

"Are you really not going to ask me about my conversation with Craig? We just had a really important talk. Life-changing."

She made a noise like she didn't believe me.

"It was! You would know that if you'd been there."

"Counterpoint—the only other person who was there ran off."

"He didn't run off," I muttered. "He has a job. He's working. You just don't understand."

Given that Craig was currently distracting Jerry, I used this opportunity to fill her in on everything. Maybe if I gave her all the details, including the humiliating ones, she would see how momentous this talk with Craig had been.

But she didn't react the way I'd hoped she would—matching my excitement with her own encouragement. Instead she asked, "Does that mean you, Little Miss Introvert, are actually going to the company party tonight? Should I be on the lookout for four horsemen?"

She was making a joke, like she didn't understand that this was a big deal. "Of course I'm going. Craig basically asked me to be his date."

"I don't think so. You might be reading too much into it."

If I was, I planned on reading too much into it until further notice. Instead of telling her that, I responded, "Well, if nothing else, I think it was significant, him wanting to dance with me. I think things between us are going to change tonight."

"Anna, I love you, pero no hablo delusional."

Catalina usually only slipped into Spanglish with me when I was particularly exasperating her. Her statement felt like a shock. She'd never said something like that to me before.

"Sorry," she quickly added. "I don't want to rain on your parade. You're not delusional. I shouldn't have said that. And I should be more supportive. But I think you deserve better than Craig. I'm just looking out for you."

"I know," I said. "I appreciate it. But we should probably get back to work before Jerry fires us both."

She nodded and went back to her own workstation. I slid the sleeves of my lab coat up my arms and then opened my laptop. The laptop that Craig had just been holding. My fingerprints were touching his fingerprints. It was almost like we were holding hands.

Even I had to groan at that. My late mother's adoration of romantic comedies had warped my brain.

I glanced at my screen and saw that there was an email icon. For a second I entertained the hope that Craig might have sent me a quick note, but I knew that wasn't possible. He was in a meeting, and he would have to make some effort to find my work email. He'd probably have that battle-ax of an assistant, Gretchen, find it for him.

Not that I could blame her for being so protective. If I was Craig's administrative assistant, I'd guard him, too.

But that meant if I did get an email from him, there would be a good amount of effort behind it. The thought made me smile.

When I opened my work inbox, I saw that it was a message from Jerry. My smile fell off my face while I suppressed a groan. That annoyance quickly turned to anger when I saw that his email was full of critiques of my current formulation. I hadn't sent it to him. Which meant that he'd gotten on my laptop, pulled it up, and was now criticizing all my hard work.

I knew for a fact he didn't do this to anyone else, and in that moment, it was infuriating. I knew I was onto something with this formulation, that it would work, and Jerry had all but written SEE ME in big letters all over it. I was not a child and I was tired of being treated like one.

My hands shaking, I barely glanced up when Jerry's office door opened and Craig left.

I thought of all the little injustices Jerry had committed, how he'd said no to my pitches without even looking up from his computer screen, how he hadn't let us utilize this lab and these materials the best way that we could, the way he'd repeatedly embarrassed me in front of all my colleagues.

I was being held back here. I remembered how just a few nights ago, I'd resolved to be happy and admitted to myself that nothing in my current situation was making me happy. I wished I was stronger. But the only way to be strong was to . . . just be strong. Make a choice.

I was the person who got to make decisions for my life and my potential happiness. Wasn't I the master of my fate? The captain of my . . . I wanted to say starship, but that seemed wrong.

Right phrase or not—the only way to make things change was to change them.

As my body finally realized what I was about to do, my heart started to pound hard and my limbs felt heavy, like they wanted to force me to stay in my seat.

Instead of heading straight for Jerry's office, I veered left and stopped at Catalina's workstation. And whether I wanted her to talk me out of it or cheer me on, I wasn't sure.

"I'm about to do something highly irrational," I said.

She was in the midst of pouring a dram of olive oil into a beaker. "Something worse than drinking cyclopentasiloxane?"

"Yes." I gulped. "As you like to say, today I'm choosing violence."

She paused and raised both her eyebrows at me. "You're not going to slip tetrahydrozoline in his coffee, are you? Because you know that putting Visine in someone's drink won't actually give them diarrhea. That's an urban legend. Although Jerry deserves to spend a day on a toilet."

There was a visual I did not need.

"No. I'm not going to drug him. I'm giving him my two weeks' notice."

CHAPTER THREE

I had honestly expected Catalina to argue with me. To tell me this was a terrible idea and that I should be a good little worker drone and head back to my desk.

But to my surprise, she said, "You should. If I had more practical experience, I'd leave in a heartbeat. Any lab's got to be better than this one. There are dozens of makeup companies in the Los Angeles area. You can get another job. A better one."

I could get a better job. I was routinely contacted by headhunters via my LinkedIn profile. There had to be something waiting for me out there.

Not only that, and much as I didn't want to admit it even to myself, this meant that I'd be able to get over that pesky nonfraternization rule. There wouldn't be anything to stop Craig and me from being together. I loved him, he seemed interested in me, and I was going to clear the pathway for us.

I'd never tell anyone else that I'd thought that, though. The Craig thing was not my primary motivation. This was about how badly I'd been treated by Jerry. This was going to be my moment where I triumphed over my terrible boss. Living out my quitting fantasy. Taking back my life.

"Wish me luck," I said, forcing my feet to move forward.

"Good luck!"

Every step felt like walking through quicksand with iron shoes. The old me didn't want this—it was better to sit back and hope for better things instead of making it happen.

That's what I'd always done, and it was how I'd ended up here. Time to shake up my life.

Jerry's door was still open, and I walked into his office without knocking. He glanced up briefly and then looked back at his computer screen. "What?"

If he'd been even a little bit courteous or human in that moment, I might have reconsidered. Instead I screwed up all my courage, repeated the word *happy* as an internal mantra, and then said, "I'm giving you my two weeks' notice."

That got his attention. He said, "What?" for a second time, as if he hadn't heard me.

So I repeated, "I'm giving you my two weeks' notice."

There. It was out in the world. There was no taking it back now.

I envisioned the next few minutes in my head. He would ask me why I was quitting, and I would get to tell him about all the awful things he'd done, how much he'd undervalued me as an employee these last four years, and how Catalina was right—I did deserve better. I queued up all my potential responses in my mind, ready to go.

Jerry leaned back in his chair, studying me. Like I was a butterfly he'd pinned to a board, still trying to flap my wings while being stuck in place. "Well, I don't think there's any reason to prolong this. If you're quitting, you can clear out your desk today."

Now I was the one saying, "What?" This felt too sudden. I mean, quitting spur-of-the-moment was definitely high on the spontaneous scale, but I thought I'd have time to ease into my new, brighter life. Look for another job while still holding on to this one.

I also thought I would get the chance to finally (FINALLY) speak my mind but was so flustered by his words that I couldn't think of anything to say.

"Give me your badge and pack up your things," he said, emphasizing the first sound of each word. He went back to his computer, as if I didn't matter to him at all. "I hope you're not expecting to get a reference."

I'd expect to solo a trek up Mount Everest before I'd expect a reference from this terrible man. I unclipped my badge from my front pocket and put it on his desk. Realizing that my moment to speak up had come and gone, I went back to my workstation. *My ex-workstation,* I mentally corrected myself.

I didn't work here anymore.

Packing up the few things I had in my desk drawers took a surprisingly short amount of time. I was on autopilot, and then Catalina was there, asking me questions, but there was just this buzzing noise in my ears and I couldn't really make out any distinct sounds. I grabbed the box of products she'd wanted me to try. I could still help with that.

"Anna, what happened?" Her words were finally clear.

"He told me to go home. To not wait the two weeks and be done today," I said, for both my benefit and hers. So she would know, so I would register what had happened. My voice sounded muffled to me.

Then Daniel, the security guard, was there with a very apologetic look on his face. I shouldn't have been surprised that Jerry would call security on me, but I was.

"I'm sorry about this, Anna," he said. "I have to escort you from the property."

"Right. I get it." He was only doing his job. Something I was no longer going to be doing.

I was unemployed.

Catalina asked, "Are you okay?"

"Yes. I'll call you later," I told her. For some reason, it was right then I realized that I wasn't just quitting Minx Cosmetics—I was also leaving Catalina. Tears filled my eyes. "I'm not going to see you every day!"

"We will talk and text every day, just like we do now. And when you start your own successful business, you can hire me. I'll be your right-hand woman."

If I'd been able to laugh, I would have. That was such a pipe dream. One that I wanted but lacked the ability to turn into reality.

"Anna, we do have to go," Daniel said, still sounding very sorry.

"Okay." I didn't want him to get in trouble. I hugged Catalina. "We'll talk soon."

"Definitely."

I felt the stare of every other chemist in the room as I walked out for the final time. My throat was hot and tight. I would not cry in front of all these people. The least I could do was not give Jerry the satisfaction of making me break down in the middle of the lab.

Daniel walked me all the way down to the parking lot, opening all the locked doors in the building for me with his badge.

"You'll find something else," he said when we reached my car. "Take care, okay?"

I nodded, still not trusting myself to speak yet. When he went back into the lobby, I unlocked my car and put the box into the passenger seat. I headed over to my side and climbed in, locking the door behind me.

What did I just do? What did I do?

This was so unlike me. I was not impulsive! I had never quit a job before. Granted, this was the only real job I'd ever had, but until today, I hadn't ever quit it!

As the adrenaline and shock started to wear off, I leaned my forehead against the steering wheel. My hands were still trembling as I wondered whether I'd made a huge mistake. I seriously considered running back inside and telling Jerry I didn't mean it. That I had overreacted and would do anything to get my job back. Even take a pay cut if I had to. Although I didn't know how they could pay me any less—I was pretty sure I made the least out of all the other chemists, including the recent hires. I'd never even had a raise in the whole time I'd been there.

And I hadn't been brave enough to speak up, to advocate for myself. Look where that had gotten me.

No, I was right to quit. I had to go home and figure out my next steps. I started the car and put it into gear, backing slowly out of my spot. I had a quick revenge fantasy of reversing my car into Jerry's BMW, but I refrained.

I was almost out of the parking lot when I slammed my brakes so hard, I was surprised I didn't make the car flip completely over.

In all of this, I'd forgotten one very important thing.

What was my grandmother going to say?

~

I spent several hours running errands to distract myself, going to lunch and trying to time my return home when I knew my grandparents would be gone. In the afternoon, my grandma had office hours at her university, and my grandpa was out with his bird watchers' club. His menagerie of rescue birds greeted me when I arrived home. Feather Locklear informed me for the millionth time that the "Yankees suck!" but offered no commentary on me being home early. None of the birds would care whether or not I was employed, so long as they were kept flush with birdseed.

My grandma, on the other hand? I was not looking forward to telling her.

I went into my room and was so frustrated and annoyed by everything that had happened that morning that I seriously considered cleaning it. But things had never been quite so bad that I'd felt motivated to pick up my clothes off the floor.

I threw the box with my personal effects onto the floor, and then I collapsed backward onto my bed, my arms akimbo like I was going to make a snow angel. Exhaustion seeped into my brain, crowding out my other thoughts. I figured it was all the out-of-control emotions I'd been experiencing, along with staying up so late last night to read. I'd had some very low lows today, but maybe tonight would turn out differently. The highest of highs. Craig and I dancing at the company party, in front of everyone. I closed my eyes for a second to imagine his arms around me and next thing I knew, it was dark outside.

Groggily, I turned to look at my alarm clock. The party was starting in half an hour. I was going to be late.

Again. For the second time today.

I ran over to my closet to go through my clothes. I remembered that it was a cocktail party. I didn't know what that entailed but figured it probably meant a dress.

I didn't own a dress. Literally, not a single one. I'd never had an occasion to wear one. My grandma had a personal vendetta against the fashion industry, dresses in particular, and I'd always preferred pants anyway. They had pockets.

There was no time to go buy a dress, not to mention that the last time I checked my bank account balance, I had three dollars and twenty-seven cents. I flipped through my clothes, as if pushing each hanger aside would suddenly reveal a dress I'd forgotten buying.

I got all the way to the far end when I did find a dress.

A dress I'd bought to cosplay as Arwen, the half-elven character from Lord of the Rings.

I couldn't. Could I?

Grabbing my phone, I called Catalina. She answered without saying hello. "I was waiting for you to call me. How are you? Are you doing okay? Did you get online at all today to look for a new job? Because I found a couple that I think would—"

"I need your help," I said. "The party's starting and I have nothing to wear and I'm pretty sure there's not going to be an old magical lady showing up with a pumpkin carriage and some talking mice to help make me a dress."

"The party?" she echoed my words. "You're still going to the company party? Even though you quit?"

"Yes." I said it in a tone that hopefully would shut down this line of questioning. Technically, I no longer worked at Minx, but I had to find Craig and tell him about my feelings. I would have much easier access to him at a hotel than I would in the office. The office where I no longer had a way to get in the building.

Plus, like I'd already told her, he'd basically asked me to go with him and I wasn't going to miss out on that opportunity.

She took the hint and shifted back to the reason I'd called. "Not a single dress? A prom dress? Something you wore to graduation?"

"No proms, and I wore jeans to both my graduations."

"You'll have to go buy something," she said.

"My bank account has an echo," I told her, holding the outfit up against me as I looked in the mirror. "The only thing I have is that cosplay dress."

She hesitated. "The pale green Arwen one?"

"Yes."

"Okay, okay, we can just accessorize it to make it look more modern."

"That's a lie, and you know I have no accessories."

"I know!" Catalina said with a groan. "No accessory would help. I was trying to make this better. Hold on, I'm pulling the costume up online. I'd offer you something of mine, but that won't work."

She was right—she was a good eight inches shorter than me. It would be like me wearing a Band-Aid around my hips and saying it was a skirt. Maybe I could make something. I glanced over at my sheets, but there was no way. It was this costume or nothing.

"The bell sleeves have to go," she said. "That's the part closest to your wrist. I think if you remove the bottom half, the top lacy part that goes to the elbow would be okay."

"Okay. Hold on." I tried to rip the two sections of the sleeves apart, but nothing was happening. "I can't get it! I think they stitched this thing together with titanium."

"Do you have a seam ripper?"

"Do I seem like the kind of person who would have a seam ripper?" I looked at the clock again. I was running out of time, and this entire thing was stressing me out.

"Find a pair of scissors and cut the thread holding the two pieces together. Do not cut the fabric. That will look terrible." She said that like she knew the entire thing would be awful and it would be hard to make it much worse than it already was.

I opened the top drawer of my desk and sifted through the heap until I found a pair of scissors. I did as she instructed, and it came undone. "It worked! But the lacy part looks frayed."

"I'm guessing asking you to hem the edges would send you over the edge?"

"It's fine. I'll fix it. It will work. Right?" I was sure she'd be able to hear the desperation in my voice.

"People are probably still going to wonder what's wrong with you, but it won't be as bad as if you had the bell sleeves."

"That's the spirit!" I said, pushing a pile of clothes off the top of my desk until I found what I was looking for. I grabbed the stapler. "I will take *not as bad as it could be*. I'll see you later and let you know how things go with Craig. Who might be my new boyfriend."

"You still think that's going to happen?" she asked. "What's your plan?"

"I'm going to go up to him, make some small talk, maybe a joke or two, and then I'll tell him that I quit my job for him and that I like him."

She gasped. "Do not say you quit your job for him. That's . . . too much."

"Technically that's not the reason I did it." Right? It had been a noble thing about how I was being treated. It wasn't about Craig and the nonfraternization rule. Like, at all.

But then why had I just said it? "Don't you think he'll find that romantic?"

"I do not. Also, don't tell him you like him. You have to let him make some moves here."

He already made moves. He'd asked for a dance and had stood very, very close to me. I decided to ignore her advice. I was going to go with what had worked nine times out of ten in my imagination. The tenth time it was him kissing me as soon as I walked in the room.

Which probably wasn't going to happen, but I had faith in trying to do what I thought would make me happy.

With the mess I'd made of the rest of my life, I couldn't think about whether or not things would work out with Craig. They had to.

"Okay," I said, more to get her off my back than anything else. Catalina could be extremely persistent.

"Have fun. And if that free-range douchebag likes you while you're wearing that costume, then he's a better man than I've given him credit for. Good luck!"

I threw my phone on the bed and started doing my best to fix the edges of the sleeves. I could do this. I was an actual scientist. I could make a pattern that would hold two edges together.

It turned out to be considerably harder than I'd anticipated, given the lacy material had too many holes, but I did it.

Slipping the costume over my head, I tugged it into place. It was okay-ish. It could have been worse. This wasn't too bad.

Or maybe my best friend had been right and I really was kind of delusional.

I considered leaving my hair down, but there was a line across the middle from the rubber band I'd used earlier, so I threw it up into a ponytail. I put on a pair of flats and studied my reflection. I turned around and saw the box on my bed, the one with all my stuff from work. It was a brief, ghoulish reminder of how I'd managed to upend my entire life.

Ignoring that sensation, I dug through it to find the prototype mascara and lipstick that Catalina had given me and put them on. I figured it couldn't hurt.

Until it did, when I accidentally poked myself in the eyeball with the mascara wand. Not once but four times.

After I'd done all I could do, I put my glasses back on and headed downstairs. Grandpa was having a conversation with Parrot Hilton, and by the acrid stench hanging in the air, my grandmother had again attempted to make dinner. She'd been doing this for decades now—I wondered at what point she was going to give up and admit defeat.

I wanted to sneak past them, but I forgot about the third stair, and it creaked so loudly, it was like it was deliberately trying to get me caught.

"Anna?" my grandma called out.

Attempting to head off the Spanish Inquisition that was coming, I said, "I'll be back late. I'm not sure what time."

Maybe Craig and I would have a late-night stroll. We'd walk hand in hand along a waterway (never mind that we were nowhere near a pier or river) until we found an adorable park bench, where we would sit and talk until the sun came up. That made me sigh happily, and I realized that Catalina was right. I did watch too many romantic-comedy movies.

My grandma narrowed her eyes at me. "You have responsibilities. A job you have to go to where you pretend to do actual science."

"Not anymore! I quit!" The words exploded out of me. I slapped a hand over my mouth. I hadn't meant to say that. Because I knew what was coming.

She was going to take way too much pleasure in this, and there would be a lot of crowing at my expense. Like when Crow DiMaggio had gotten the sling off his wing.

To my surprise, instead she demanded an explanation. "What do you mean, you quit?"

"I mean it in the usual sense of the word. You know how I usually get up in the morning and go to Minx Cosmetics? I won't be doing that tomorrow or any other day in the foreseeable future." Something about talking to my grandma always made me revert to a sixteen-year-old girl, and I hated it.

Instead of lecturing me about not taking care of my responsibilities, my grandmother pivoted again and managed to look slightly pleased. "Does this mean you decided to take your career more seriously and dedicate yourself to a real job that will use your degree and intelligence?"

My grandmother was an environmental scientist, specializing in soil (a pedologist, as she was fond of reminding us. Which was, as I had learned at eight years old in school, not to be confused with a pedophile. My parents got a very interesting phone call that day).

"I was already using my degree and my intelligence and I will again. I'm serious about my career as a cosmetic chemist. I will find a new job in the same field."

She pursed her lips together and then launched into a mini-lecture about me paying my dues, which I had done in full, thank you very much. Then it was on to how much harder it was for women in STEM and that we had to work twice as hard as men to be considered half as good (she wasn't wrong, but no way was I giving her the satisfaction of agreeing with her) and how I had to hold the door open for the women coming up behind me. Again, she was right, and I was already doing that.

And if I ever did get to start my own company, I'd hire every woman cosmetic chemist in the greater Los Angeles area.

Part of me wanted to tune my grandma out, but given that she was a professor, I worried that there might be an actual quiz later.

When she paused to take a breath, I said, "I know, Grandma. I have to go. I'm headed out to a party."

"A party?" She looked more shocked at this than she had when I told her I'd quit.

It hurt my ego just a bit that she was so incredulous. We didn't have a warm and fuzzy relationship, mostly because she wasn't a warm and fuzzy person. She was very serious, very focused, and very, very into dirt.

I knew she loved me and that she pushed me because one, she didn't want me to "fail" the way she thought my mother had, and two, if I was successful, then she would feel like she'd done right by my parents and that she and Grandpa had done a good job of raising me.

My grandfather came into the room with Parrot Hilton on his shoulder. Parrot Hilton let out a long string of curse words that adequately conveyed my internal feelings at the moment. Feather Locklear was the one who had taught her to swear, a behavior we were trying to extinguish, and my grandpa cooed at the bird, redirected her, and got her to stop. Sometimes I thought my grandpa was part bird. I didn't realize that *birdbrained* was an insult until I was a teenager. The ability to relate to birds so well always seemed like a superpower to me.

"You look lovely," my grandpa said to me, kissing my cheek. He couldn't be more opposite from my grandma if he'd tried. He was an ornithologist who spent most of his time either teaching or helping with a local bird rescue foundation. My grandmother was literally fixated on the ground and he was always looking to the sky.

It was actually how they'd met. Grandma had dug a big hole to take various soil samples, and Grandpa had been following a California least tern, and because he wasn't watching where he was going, he fell into the hole, breaking his leg. They got married six weeks later and had my mom a year after that.

"Thank you, Grandpa. Okay! I'm off!"

"Wait," Grandma said. "We have to discuss . . ."

Whatever else she said was lost when I closed the front door. I should have climbed out my bedroom window to avoid all that nonsense. Now I was definitely going to be late.

Putting my grandmother and her expectations out of my mind, I focused on what was ahead of me.

Tonight was about possibilities and finding a new way forward. It was all going to change.

I was going to have a bright, happy new future.

Hopefully with Craig by my side.

CHAPTER FOUR

The event was being held in the ballroom of a nearby hotel. When I arrived at the party, it was in full swing. I felt terribly self-conscious and like people were staring at me. I didn't know if it was because of the dress or if Jerry had spread the word about me quitting.

I briefly wondered whether my former boss might throw me out if he saw me. I was going to have to keep a low profile and avoid him. I had to focus on finding Craig, telling him my feelings, and we would hopefully leave together.

The thought of actually doing that made my stomach lurch. A waitress walked by, holding out a tray of champagne flutes. Liquid courage would be very helpful. I reached for the drinks and took two.

"For a friend," I said. Why did I do that? Feel like I had to invent some story? Like how I'd call for Chinese takeout and tell the restaurant that my order was for a family of four when I planned on eating the whole thing myself and spending the entire weekend in a food coma.

Maybe I should try a little honesty along with my other resolutions. "Actually, they're both for me."

"Good for you," the waitress said with a nod. "Whoever he is, you deserve better."

She was gone before I could protest. If I were a superstitious person, I would think the universe was trying to warn me.

I saw Craig standing in a corner with a group of people. I downed both glasses quickly and placed them on a nearby table. I would have to make sure to eat something later. I hadn't eaten anything since lunchtime, and I didn't want to get sloppy drunk.

Craig walked away from the group, and I saw my opportunity. He walked out onto a large patio, and I followed him. He was on a phone call, and I wondered how long I could stand here before it got creepy.

I ran over in my mind what I'd practiced to say to him, wringing my hands together. It was cold outside, but I barely felt it.

He ended the call and turned as if he planned on heading back inside.

My heart thudded hard in my chest. Now or never.

"Craig?"

He looked at me expectantly, and I waited a moment in case my tenth imaginary scenario came true and he would kiss me before I said anything.

Nope.

"Hi," I said, not sure how to start despite all my rehearsing.

"Hi." He hesitated, and then his eyes lit up. "Wait, I remember you! The lady scientist. Catalina, right?"

That felt a little like being stabbed. "No, that was my friend. I'm Anna."

I expected him to say something else, but he didn't.

His phone buzzed. "Sorry, give me a second." He smiled, and I wished I was the reason why. He started texting, his thumbs flying across the screen. "This is a buddy of mine who went to USC, and he thinks he can trash-talk my alma mater."

"Like me!"

Craig looked confused.

"I went to USC. Remember?"

His confusion deepened.

I tried again. "You jumped me?"

Now he looked worried, and I realized that the other connotations of those words were negative. "Two years ago. My car died in the parking lot. You brought your truck over and gave me a jump."

I'd stayed late that night, and my cell phone had died. I thought I was the last person there, but then Craig had come by in his truck and asked if I needed help. He had been my knight in a white Ford.

He could have called for someone else to come and assist me, but he'd stayed and made sure that I got off safely. He had asked where I'd gone to school and I told him USC, as they had a great cosmetic chemist program. He had made an unfunny and semi-inappropriate joke about USC's mascot, which I'd felt obligated to laugh at because he was being so nice. We had a great conversation after that, and I'd fallen fast and hard for him.

"Oh! Right!" he said, but I saw in his eyes and heard in his voice that he had no idea what I was talking about. It had been a seminal moment for me, and he hadn't registered it at all.

My heart squeezed painfully, and I put my hand against a window for support.

His phone beeped this time, and he looked at it. "I have to go. I've got to find someone. I hope I don't get lost. It's pretty dark in there!" He said it in a teasing tone.

I should have kept quiet. I already felt like such a fool, but I had to go and make it worse. "May the light of Eärendil guide you."

Craig gave me that look, the one I'd seen so many times throughout my life, and I wanted to kick myself. Still not able to stay quiet, I added, "You know, to be a light for you in dark places when all other lights go—"

But he was already walking away, throwing a "bye" over his shoulder. So much for that dance. And when was I going to stop making Lord of the Rings references to people who had no idea what I was talking about?

Part of my imaginary scenarios had included Craig loving the movies as much as I did. At the very least, I'd hoped he'd watched them.

None of this was going how I'd planned. I stood there, shivering slightly as the cold started to seep in against my skin, wondering what I should do next.

A few minutes passed, and I finally went back inside, feeling very unsure. Someone tapped on the DJ's microphone. It was Craig.

And he was standing next to a woman who looked like she'd been drawn by a very randy fifteen-year-old boy. She was perfection. Blonde hair, perfect curves, gleaming skin and teeth.

Craig had his arm around her. They looked like Ken and Barbie.

My stomach dropped to my knees.

"Excuse me!" he called out. "If I could have everyone's attention!" The dull roar of the partygoers quieted down.

"Thank you! This will only take a moment. Since both of our families are here, and the employees of this company are like my second family, I just wanted to let everyone know that I've asked Leighton to be my wife and she said yes!"

The whole room broke into applause and cheers, but I just stood there.

Craig was engaged.

Engaged.

The waitress from earlier walked by with an entire bottle of champagne. "Can I have that?" I asked her.

She handed it to me sympathetically, but I made my way through the ballroom doors and looked for the closest bathroom. I went in and collapsed against the far wall, sliding down to the floor. I took a big swig of alcohol.

Craig was engaged. I was too late. I was also pathetic and very, very ridiculous in this stupid costume. I had really thought he'd see me and swoon. That we'd get our happily ever after.

Then the tears started, and the mascara Catalina had made was most definitely not waterproof. Not tearproof, anyway. Although she probably hadn't anticipated somebody trying to cry out all of their internal fluids through their eyeballs. I'd have to tell her to increase the amount of dimethicone copolyol to make it more moisture resistant tomorrow when I—

I wasn't going to see Catalina tomorrow.

Taking off my glasses and putting them in my lap, I drank and cried, drank and cried, until I was very thoroughly wasted.

Which was another thing to add to the list of stupid things I'd done today, because I didn't know how I was going to get home. I couldn't exactly call an Uber given my lack of funds. I tried to call Catalina, but my phone wasn't working properly, and I couldn't dial her number. My grandparents were out of the question.

The bathroom door swung open, and I heard a man's voice say, "Are you okay?"

"Do I look okay?" I cried. That seemed like a dumb question.

There was a pause. I couldn't really see him because the dripping mascara was blurring my vision. That and I was not wearing my glasses.

"Are you aware of the fact that you're in the men's bathroom?" he asked.

"I'm in the men's bathroom?"

"The urinals didn't tip you off?"

I hadn't been paying attention to anything other than the fact that the love of my life was about to marry someone else. "I didn't see them. I'm very drunk!" I protested.

"I can see that. One too many?"

"Yes," I agreed. "One or a whole bottle too many."

He didn't respond right away and then asked, "Do you want me to go and protect the door?"

Trying to blink, I asked, "Why does the door need protection?"

Another pause. "I mean, I could stand outside and keep people out. So you can . . . cry in peace."

"I don't want to be alone," I said and realized that it was true. I usually preferred being solitary, but right now it wasn't what I wanted. I couldn't call Catalina, since my fingers weren't working and because there would be so many *I told you so*s all over the place, and my grandma would tell me how disappointed she was and that I had to stop living my life for a man, which wasn't even what I was doing. My grandpa would tell me to pet Meryl Cheep until I felt better, but that wouldn't help.

"That's . . . a lot," the man said, and I realized I'd said everything out loud instead of in my head, like I'd intended.

"Yes, it is a lot. I'm a mess. I just want to tell someone about it who won't judge me or him."

Another pause. "I've heard it's easier to talk to strangers. You could tell me."

"Pull up a gross floor tile," I said, patting the ground next to me. I lifted my hand back up as I registered how disgusting this was. I was going to have to burn this dress and sterilize my skin when I got home.

Instead of sitting next to me, he went into a stall. A moment later, toilet paper was being pushed against my hand. I was a mess of snot and mascara and tears. I blew my nose several times and then used some dry toilet paper to wipe the mascara off my eyes. I probably looked ridiculously bad.

He sat down on the floor next to me, and I noticed that he smelled . . . good.

And it suddenly occurred to me to care about who he was. I hoped he was a kindly old grandpa. As I continued to wipe my mascara off, I internally chanted, *Please be a sixty-year-old man. Please be a sixty-year-old man.*

I blinked a couple of times and then put my glasses back on. It took a second for my eyes to focus. He was not a sixty-year-old man. He was young and hot and very broad and all of this was bad.

"Why is your face so symmetrical?" I whined. He had dark hair, and I couldn't tell if it was a dark brown or black. High cheekbones, a jaw I could cut hardened silicone with, and dark eyes.

"I'm sorry?" he said, sounding bewildered.

"Symmetrical?" I repeated, as if he hadn't heard me. "Don't people tell you that?"

"Oh, you said *symmetrical*. Yes, I get that all the time," he said in a teasing tone.

"Really?"

"No."

I let out a sound of disbelief. "You should. Everyone you meet should tell you that. You're annoyingly handsome." Even though I was highly inebriated, I could tell that he was a perfect male specimen. Then I realized that I might have been influenced by that inebriation and maybe in regular life he was far less attractive. I had a hard time believing it, though. "You're hot in a you-should-be-studied-in-a-lab sort of way. Maybe they could make little clones of you. A whole platoon."

"What would you do with that clone army?"

"Not execute Order 66 and exterminate the Jedi, I can tell you that."

He smiled, and it was a brilliant smile, like the kind a toothpaste model would have. I realized that he'd understood my joke. It was such an unusual sensation, to feel like I'd been seen. Usually the only person who got my jokes was Catalina.

But that smile . . . it seemed awfully familiar.

It was then that I realized who he was. "You're Loch Ness *GQ*," I breathed.

"You may be drunker than I thought," he said, sounding concerned.

I grabbed the lapel of his suit. The observant part of my brain noted that it was a very nice suit and probably expensive and that he had the kind of shoulders that filled it out in a satisfactory way. "You're the CEO of the company. There were rumors that you existed, but none of us had ever actually seen you. We thought you were like a missi . . ." That wasn't right. I tried again. "A mifi . . ." Nope. I coaxed my tongue to form the right sound. "A mythical creature. And the *GQ* part was because of the face symmetry. You're Mark something."

"Marco, actually. Pleasure to meet you." He offered me his hand, and it looked big and strong and I thought I might really enjoy shaking it.

So I said with a laugh, "Oh, no thank you." Whew. That was a close one. Didn't want to be disloyal to Craig.

Who is marrying someone else, my broken heart reminded me. I could hold hands with whomever I wanted.

He put his hand down, and I felt a pang of disappointment as he prompted, "And you are?"

"Drunk?" I said, then I figured out what he meant. "Oh. I'm Anna. That's short for Anastasia."

I didn't know why I was telling him that. I never really shared my full name with anyone.

"After the Romanov princess?"

It surprised me that he asked this question, like he'd peered into my brain and my past and knew the exact right thing to ask. "My mom used to tell people that she had chosen it because of her love for Russian literature. She was a librarian. But that was a lie. She named me after one of her favorite makeup brands."

"Good thing she didn't name you Urban Decay or Hard Candy."

My eyebrows shot up my forehead. Look at this guy naming off 1990s makeup brands like he'd studied the subject in school, while Craig couldn't tell the difference between blush and eye shadow.

That feeling of being disloyal returned again, and I tried to brush it aside with an actual wave of my hand.

"Were you planning on going to a costume party after this one?" he asked.

What kind of weird question was that? Who had a costume party in January? "No, this is the only dress I own. Which I recognize as being very sad."

"Are those staples on the sleeves?"

I clapped a hand over the sleeve closest to him. "Listen, Irritatingly Handsome Man, my dress is fine. Just fine!"

"Is that why you're crying? Did someone say something to you about your dress?"

"No." My eyes widened in sudden paranoia. "Did someone say something to *you* about my dress?"

His eyes shifted away from me, and I realized with despair that they had. I was trying to keep my humiliation private, and apparently I'd unwittingly exposed myself to a very public variety. I cleared my throat. "That's not why I'm crying. Although it's kind of making me want to cry more now."

"Please don't," he said. "Why were you crying before? If you don't mind me asking?"

If he meant to distract me from breaking into sobs, it wasn't a good idea to circle back to what had gotten me here in the first place.

"There's a lot of things. I'm no longer employed because I quit my job today. From your company. I used to be your employee and I'm not anymore. I'm a cosmetic chemist. A good one. Which you would know if you had better management who respected their employees and recognized their work."

"A chemist? That's too bad. Your department typically turns out excellent work. Did we lose you to a competitor?"

Had he not heard my tirade about Jerry? "No. My boss was a sexist, disrespectful jerk who treated me badly. I also quit because of the company's nonfraternization rule." It might have taken me two or three times to say *nonfraternization* correctly.

Marco frowned slightly. "There's no nonfraternization rule. You only have to disclose your relationship to HR."

That couldn't be right. I was drunk, but not so drunk that I was misremembering events from earlier. I knew what Craig had said. "I think you're wrong."

"I'm usually not. CEO, remember? I know the company's rules."

I blinked slowly at him. He might be right. But then what had happened in the lab this morning made no sense.

When I didn't say anything, he asked, "Is that the reason you're upset? Did you have someone in mind who you wanted to date and thought you couldn't?" He didn't say it, but I could hear his implication—that I'd made a huge mistake if that had been the reason I'd quit.

I decided to ignore his question that might have hit a bit too close to home. "I was crying because the love of my life is marrying someone else."

"Craig?" he asked incredulously.

"Yes, Craig." Why did he have to sound so shocked? "Craig Kimball," I added, just in case he was talking about another Craig who had also announced his engagement tonight.

Marco's dark, penetrating eyes were making me feel a little lightheaded. But that sensation ended when he asked, "You're in love with my younger brother?"

CHAPTER FIVE

His brother?

What?

How was that even possible? They did not seem to have any visible genetic connection.

"Half brother," Marco said, and I realized that I had again said aloud the words that I meant to keep in my head. "Different mothers, same father."

"Oh." I didn't know what to say to that. So of course, I came up with something meaningless. "I guess that means you're going to be the best man at his wedding."

He tipped his head back against the wall and straightened out his legs. I noticed that he had a very nice Adam's apple. That wasn't something I'd ever noticed on a man before. He responded to my statement by saying, "I don't think there should be a wedding."

"You don't?" Why did this give me hope? It was probably because Marco seemed like the kind of guy who got stuff done. Maybe he knew a way to keep it from happening.

"No, I don't. I'm against that whole thing."

"Why? Are you in love with him, too?"

"My brother? No. I'm not in love with my brother."

Duh, I obviously knew that. My face was flushed, but that could have just as easily been because of the alcohol. "I meant *her*. Are you in love with her?"

"No. But two months ago, she was my girlfriend."

At that, I gasped loudly. Loud enough that it echoed off the tiled walls. "Did she cheat on you with your own brother?"

He ran one hand through his hair, brushing it off his forehead. "I hope not, but I don't actually know."

My mind made the important distinction that it was Craig's fiancée who had cheated on Marco. Not Craig. He might not have even known that Marco and Leighton were together! This could not possibly be as bad as it was sounding.

Craig wasn't like that.

I still felt bad for Marco, though. "Wow. I'm sorry."

"Why? You didn't do anything."

Shrugging one shoulder, I said, "Maybe if I'd convinced Craig to fall in love with me sooner, it wouldn't have happened."

That made Marco smile again, and I noticed sparkly tingles inside my stomach. That effect was clearly because of the bubbly champagne, and not for any other reason.

While I was trying to convince myself of this fact, Marco said, "Quick question. Was Craig the one who told you about the nonfraternization rule?"

I didn't like his tone. Like he'd just figured something out that I wasn't going to like.

Trying to defend Craig, I said, "Yes. He said we couldn't date." That wasn't exactly what he'd said, but I figured it was close enough.

"Because he's engaged."

"No," I said. Although you would think that sort of thing would come up in a flirty conversation like we'd had. "Because of the rule."

"But you don't work for Minx Cosmetics anymore. And there never was a rule."

"Exactly!" Some tiny part of my brain worried about the fact that there never had been a rule when Craig had said it like it was known, like it was something I should concern myself with. I ignored it and tried to connect the dots for Marco. "I sort of quit my job for Craig. It's the grandest of gestures. That will have to mean something to him. I know it. Do you see where I'm going with this?"

"Into the men's bathroom with a bottle of champagne?"

"Yes! I mean, no. You're not understanding. Craig and I have a special connection." One I'd had to remind him of earlier, but it was still there.

"I think he has a special connection with Leighton, too."

"Leighton," I scoffed. "Even her name is pretty. I want to make fun of it, but I'm too drunk to think of a way to mock it. Plus, it would be mean to do that, and by all accounts I'm not a mean drunk. Just a talkative one."

"You don't say?" He sounded amused.

"It's kind of gross that both you and your brother dated the same girl."

"Grosser than sitting on a bathroom floor in a hotel?" he said with a smile that didn't remind me at all of Craig. I had a hard time believing they were brothers.

And somehow I'd also forgotten that I was in a bathroom. I was enjoying talking to Marco. "It's surprising that no one's come in here this whole time."

"I locked the door. You seemed like you needed some privacy."

This might have been the champagne talking, but that just seemed like the sweetest gesture. "That was really thoughtful of you."

Our gazes locked, and there was something in the air, like I was standing on the precipice of an important moment. I didn't know what that was and I didn't want it. I needed to back away from whatever was happening right now.

Marco seemed to have the same impulse and brought Craig and Leighton back into the conversation. "Dating the same woman happens. Especially in our circle."

My brain felt a little fuzzy, and I wasn't sure what he meant by *circle* because the only kind I could think of were concentric and orthogonal.

"You don't seem like a CEO," I announced.

"You don't seem like a cosmetic chemist," he teased back.

"I think I'm insulted."

"Me too."

But it was hard to feel too upset with him smiling at me like he thought I was delightful. Maybe I should add that to my list of traits for Drunk Anna. Talkative and delightful.

Also, prone to crying and dripping a lot of snot.

A green haze of nausea swelled up inside my stomach. "I'm not feeling too well."

He immediately got to his feet and offered me his hand. "Let me help you up."

I weighed my options—I was going to have to touch this sexy man or crawl like an undignified idiot across this floor to reach a toilet.

I settled for the lesser of two evils. When he took my hand in his, it was like that time when I was eight years old and performed an experiment with a wall socket, a screwdriver, and a nine-volt battery. A massive electrical shock slammed into me. I was glad I was still sitting down, because his touch would have floored me.

Trying to ignore the sensations singing along my nerve endings, I cleared my throat and said, "I was right. Your hands are nice and strong. Are they symmetrical, too?"

Dumb. That wasn't going to help anything. *Don't talk about the man's body parts being sexy!* I told my brain, but it didn't seem to be in the mood to listen.

"Probably. We could grab a ruler and get some exact measurements if you'd like." He pulled me up slowly, and when I got into a standing position, my body swayed toward him. With his other hand, he reached for my waist to hold me still.

I stood there while those champagne bubbles fizzed around inside me. He was a big man. He towered over me, and that was no mean feat. *Mean feat.* I repeated the words internally. That seemed wrong. Fean meat? No. What was that phrase again?

"Careful," he said as I tried to make my limbs hold firm. "You don't want to fall and hit your head. That would be a lot of paperwork."

"In case I do injure myself, please tell the EMTs that I'm O positive."

He turned me then, putting an arm around my waist and helping me toward a stall. "If that happens, I'm telling the EMTs to keep you away from any open flames. Because your spilled blood would ignite like a Roman candle right now."

"Good idea. Now, I think I'm ready to vomit."

That made him hurry and help me to a toilet. And as I crouched down, I realized that I hadn't thought about Craig at all for the last five minutes.

~

I woke up in my grandparents' living room the next morning with no recollection of how I'd gotten there or why I was wearing a costume. Jimmy Talon and Dame Judi Finch were singing loudly, and I let out a groan as I realized that my head was pounding and my mouth felt like it had been recently filled with soggy, vomit-covered marbles. I pushed myself up into a seated position and quickly saw that was a mistake. I rested my head against my hands and wondered why I'd never realized just how noisy the birds were. It was a background noise that I'd learned to tune out, apparently except when I had a crushing hangover.

Something was on my forehead. I reached up and grabbed a Post-it Note. I looked at it and saw my grandma's handwriting. "Need to talk."

I did not need to talk. I was twenty-six years old. I could stay out late on a school night and drink if I wanted to. She didn't need to lecture me on the dangers of getting drunk. I was well aware of the chemical reaction and how my liver broke down alcohol into acetaldehyde and then into acetic acid and that I hadn't been able to outdrink my body's ability to break it down properly. Thus, drunk and hungover.

My head throbbed as I wished again that I could move out and get my own place. I could probably do it if I stopped buying used lab equipment.

Or if I had an actual job again.

Grabbing my purse from the floor, I started for the stairs, and the events of last night came rushing back so fast and so hard that I collapsed against the wall for a moment.

Craig. Engaged.

Me, drunk and crying and pouring out my heart to his brother, Marco. Every single embarrassing and dumb thing I'd done filled my brain, and I had to relive it for a few seconds, including Marco driving me home in his car as I ate fistfuls of french fries in the back seat while slurring out my address.

Good thing I never had to see him again.

I made it into the bathroom and dry heaved a few times, but nothing happened. I smelled so disgusting. It was a good thing I hadn't slept closer to the birds or one of them might have gotten a contact high from all the fumes I was sure I'd been excreting.

I threw my purse on my bed and peeled off my dress. I started the shower, downed what was probably an alarming amount of acetaminophen, and then hopped into the shower and stayed there a long time.

When I got out, everything didn't hurt quite as much as it had earlier that morning. I glanced at my alarm clock. It was already eleven thirty. I couldn't remember the last time I'd slept in for so long. I'd obviously needed it.

I changed into my comfiest pair of pajamas. Part of me thought that I should get on my laptop immediately and start looking for a new job, but I overruled my logical side and would spend the day wallowing in my mistakes and sadness and start the job hunt tomorrow.

The box on my bed was still there, and I decided I should do at least one productive thing. Like trying out Catalina's face mask. My skin probably needed some rejuvenating.

I pulled out the mask, took off my glasses, and applied it. Hadn't Catalina said something about the natural ingredients? Blueberry? I couldn't smell it.

My stomach growled, and I wondered how it was possible to be both nauseous and hungry at the same time. I went over and opened my closet. I reached up on the shelf to grab the container of my secret stash of junk food. My grandma would lecture me about unhealthy eating and my grandpa would sneak some if they knew about it. I took a bag of Sun Chips and settled on my bed.

I heard the birds get riled up and my grandpa soothing them downstairs. He was home? I was very unaware of their daily schedules because I was usually at work. He was probably grabbing some lunch and might be administering some medicine. I wondered if he'd come upstairs. A minute or two passed, and he didn't.

My cell phone was in my purse and I got it, plugging it into the charger next to my bed. There were a couple of texts from Catalina asking how things were going from last night. I owed her a phone call.

She picked up right away. "You're not with Craig right now, are you?"

"What? No. I'm eating Sun Chips and trying out your face mask. By the way, I'm not really picking up blueberry as one of the ingredients." Not by smell and not by sensation.

"Good note," she said. "I'll look at that later. So how did last night go?"

"Craig's engaged." There was no way of saying it other than to just come out with it. Thinking about the fact that Craig was engaged to another woman sent a lance of pain through me. It was like someone had yanked a tooth out of my mouth. It hurt and hurt, my jaw ached, and I kept probing the spot with my tongue like something should be there but wasn't. Since I wasn't keen on dwelling on that pain, I tried to change the subject. "I cried about it in a bathroom when I found out and, more importantly, I met Loch Ness *GQ*."

"You did?" she said with a gasp, thankfully ignoring my information about Craig. I wasn't really ready to discuss it yet. "What's the elusive Nessie like?"

"His name is Marco and he was . . ." What was the right word? He was kind, funny, and helpful. "Nice. He let me vent and listened. Oh! And get this! He's Craig's brother."

"What?" she shrieked, and it was so loud that I actually heard the birds downstairs call out. "They're related? Not possible. The CEO is actually competent."

I rolled my eyes. "Craig is competent. He's good at his job or else he wouldn't be in that position."

"There's a little something I like to call nepotism," she said. "You should look into that."

What was she implying? That Marco had given Craig a job?

"I can't believe they're brothers," she continued on. "This has got *switched at birth* written all over it."

"Same dad, different moms." There was a knock at my door. "What?" I yelled, not wanting to get up.

The door opened, and a human-shaped blur I didn't recognize walked into my room.

It was not my grandpa.

I had a moment of sheer panic while I reached over to my nightstand, fumbling with the contents in an attempt to retrieve my glasses. Catalina's voice was in the background. "What's going on?"

My fingers found the frames, and when I slammed my glasses onto my face, I saw that it was Marco Kimball.

He was so tall. My drunken memory had apparently blotted out that information. That didn't seem like something I'd forget about; being a very tall person myself, I tended to notice it in other people. He was so, so tall. And broad. It was like he took up the entire room by just standing there.

For a second, I didn't know what was going on. My brain couldn't comprehend this reality. "What are you doing here?" I asked.

He looked sheepish. "Your grandpa let me in and said I could come up here."

A heads-up would have been nice. My grandpa probably thought he was helping me, sending a strange man upstairs while I was in my jammies, sporting a face mask and covered in Sun Chips crumbs.

Catalina said, "Anna, you are freaking me out. What's happening? Did Wolfgang Duck throw up a bunch of caterpillars again?"

"Marco's here," I said faintly. "I have to go."

She made an unintelligible, high-pitched noise. "Holy duck! You better call me back right away," she said. "I want every ducking detail and for you to explain why the CEO of Minx Cosmetics is standing in your bedroom! Anna, do you hear me? I'm being serious! Or you could just leave your phone on so that I can listen to what's going on. Don't hang up. Just set the phone down and—"

"'Kay, bye," I said and then hung up the phone with her still giving me commands. I shoved my cell into my pocket. Marco stood near the door, as if he were afraid of what he was seeing and might bolt at any second.

Not that I could blame him. Everything around him was probably fairly terrifying. It was easy to forget what your house looked like to an outsider. I was accustomed to the mess and the smell and how old everything was. Then some obnoxiously attractive, rich, seemingly nice dude came over and suddenly I had to be embarrassed by the fact that I was poor and a slob. It made me uncomfortable, but strangely enough, I didn't feel like Marco was judging me. Just taking everything in.

I was judging myself enough for the both of us.

A voice inside me whispered, *And what would Craig think about your room?* That made the uncomfortable feeling about a thousand times worse.

I tried to suppress that emotion while studying the man in front of me. Seeing him here in daylight, he was honestly more handsome than I'd imagined him to be in what had felt like an alcohol-induced fever dream.

My pulse raced, and I couldn't explain why exactly. Or why my stomach flitted with delight when he smiled at me.

I was in love with Craig. None of this made any sense.

While I was trying to sort out my strange reactions, he gestured toward me. "Pajamas in the middle of the day?"

That insult/joke jolted my system, especially given my body's strange response to his arrival. "I know what time it is, and I can do without the judgment. I am having a well-deserved me day and I am comfortable."

"I'm sorry," he said with a self-deprecating grin that made him look . . . endearing. "I shouldn't have said that. I'm a bit nervous."

Marco was nervous? What could be bad enough that it would make someone like Marco Kimball, CEO of Minx Cosmetics, nervous?

That in and of itself was anxiety inducing, and a sense of foreboding flooded my nervous system.

I had the feeling that this was not going to be good.

CHAPTER SIX

He was about to say that Craig had eloped. He had come to my messy bedroom to personally wreck my life. I just knew it. "Are you here to tell me that Craig's married now?" I asked in a small voice.

Marco frowned slightly and said, "No. He just announced his engagement last night. He's not married yet."

I breathed a sigh of relief. Marco was looking around, almost like he was taking an inventory, and I wanted to ask him if I could help him find something.

Before I could, he cleared his throat and said something obvious. "So this is your room?"

Uh-huh, the place you entered in my house where I sleep is my bedroom, I thought sarcastically. I kept that part to myself and said, "Yes, this is where the tragic happens." We stood there staring at each other until I realized my mistake. "Magic! This is where the magic . . . you know what? Never mind. You've seen that I live with my grandparents and their birds and witnessed me in my natural habitat. Tragic was right."

"Freudian slip?" he asked.

"Freudian truth."

His glance flicked over my face, and I remembered my mask. "I just need to wash this off," I said. I'd forgotten to set a timer and didn't know how long I'd had it on. Twenty minutes? Thirty? "You can have a seat."

He looked around. "Where?"

It was very polite, still personally humiliating, but a good question to ask. I jumped off my bed and cleared a path for him on the floor. I grabbed a pile of clothes off the chair. "I've heard there's an armchair under here," I told him, trying to joke but failing. I handed the pile to him. "You can throw those in the closet." I'd sort them out later.

I mean, probably not, but he didn't need to know that.

The closet door squeaked open and he asked, "What's that?"

I had been so focused on Marco being here and the mess that I'd forgotten my closet secrets. Maybe he didn't have very good peripheral vision and hadn't seen anything humiliating. "To what are you referring?"

"The TV big enough to use in a movie theater and the life-size cutout of Legolas. Either one."

The actor who'd played Legolas in Lord of the Rings was practically old enough to be my father now, but back in the day? He was delicious. "I think the cutout is self-explanatory. Big Legolas fan. It was a present for my sixteenth birthday from my grandpa."

Marco raised one eyebrow at me and looked like he was trying not to laugh. "Blond and blue-eyed. I think you have a type."

"Craig doesn't have pointy ears."

"He kind of does."

I shook my head. "He doesn't—" I cut myself off as I pulled up a mental image. Maybe he did, just a little. Huh. "That's not the point. Craig's not an elf and he doesn't shoot arrows." I knew the difference between reality and fantasy.

"He does. Did. We both trained in competitive archery when we were younger."

Why did that make him hotter?

By *him* I meant Craig. Not Marco.

Right?

"And the TV?" he prompted as I took the clothes from his arms and threw them on the closet floor.

"My grandmother doesn't believe in television."

"Oh, it's a real thing," he assured me. "I've seen it."

"Ha ha. I mean she thinks it rots your brain and didn't want me to watch it. The black-and-white set she has downstairs barely even works."

"I saw that—the one that looked like it was built during the Eisenhower administration."

"They bought it at a garage sale before I was born, so possibly." I got the rest of the clothes off the armchair and threw them in the closet, too, pushing them over with my foot so that I could get the doors shut. "I got a part-time job in high school, and as soon as I'd saved up enough, I bought that TV and hid it in my room. I love watching movies, and they're so much better in high definition."

I waved my hand at the armchair so he could sit down. Then I turned to close the closet doors, having to shove them hard with my shoulder.

"What kind of movies are you covertly watching?" he asked as he took a seat. "I'm guessing Lord of the Rings and Star Wars."

"Two for two," I told him. "I'm also a sucker for romantic comedies." I almost sat down on my bed but remembered the mask. "Hang on. I'll be right back. Make yourself . . ." I was going to say *at home*, but he looked very out of place in a sea of mess.

I didn't finish the thought and ran for the bathroom. I closed the door and took in a couple of deep breaths. What on earth did he want? Why was he here? We were out there making small talk about inconsequential things, while there was something important enough to bring him to my house. I set my glasses down on the counter and turned on the faucet to rinse my face. After I'd finished, I grabbed a pale gray washcloth to dry off my face and glanced down at the towel.

It was covered in brownish-orange streaks. My stomach lurched sideways.

Nooo!

Putting my glasses back on, I looked at my reflection.

I hadn't used the facial mask; I'd put on the self-tanner Catalina had sent home with me.

And left it on about twenty minutes longer than I should have.

I'd never seen this shade of orange in the wild. I looked like a freaking Oompa-Loompa. I let out a groan of disbelief.

Marco's voice was muffled, but I could hear him. "I know you probably shouldn't ask someone this while they make that sound in the bathroom, but are you okay?"

I should have turned on the fan. I didn't want him, or anyone else, to see me like this. I wondered if I could send him away. The problem was, I still wanted to hear what he had to say. Obviously he hadn't come to my house to ask about Legolas. I didn't want him to leave until I knew what was going on. My intense desire to know things wouldn't allow it.

Seriously, better to look like a fool in front of him than to always be wondering what he might have said.

I cleared my throat. "Uh, so I didn't use a facial mask. It was a self-tanner. It wasn't labeled and I didn't double-check."

"A common mistake." Sarcasm or support? I couldn't be sure without seeing his face.

"I'm hungover!" I reminded him.

I half expected him to say something jokey, but there was just silence. Then he said, "You can use an exfoliant to lighten it. Or you can put on a combination of baking powder, lemon juice, and water as a paste and that will help."

Walking out of the bathroom, I came back into my room to stare at him. I already knew all that. How did he?

He blinked several times when he saw me, but he didn't smile or laugh. "It doesn't look . . . uh . . . that is to say that you . . . wow."

"I know. It's bad." I walked over to my personal chem lab and pulled off the big sheet I used to protect the equipment and the table. "I don't have any exfoliant on hand, but I have the ingredients. It shouldn't be too hard to make."

Marco got up and came over to stand next to my shoulder. "Your own personal chem lab. This is some setup. And it's so . . . clean."

"I take good care of my workstations," I told him. It was a necessity in my line of work.

"It feels very out of place in here. Like that game of 'one of these things is not like the other.'"

His nearness was affecting me in a way I wouldn't have expected. I opened a bin where I kept supplies and grabbed one of the containers on top. "I guess I'm one of those people who is better with my professional needs than I am with my personal ones."

"I get that," he said.

I opened the container, and it was not the finely ground sea salt I was expecting. It was glitter.

Marco took a step closer to me, as if he wanted to see what was in the jar, and his yummy smell and unexpected warmth unnerved me. One second the glitter was in my hand and the next it was all over the floor.

"Oh no," I said with a moan. "I'm going to be finding glitter for the next ten years. That stuff metastasizes."

"It is the herpes of beauty supplies," he agreed. "And now it kind of looks like a drunk fairy threw up in here. Good thing you have that layer of clothing to form a protective barrier over the carpet."

That was funny, but I couldn't laugh. The glitter was somehow still falling, shimmering in the air around us.

Had it been Craig standing here, it might have felt like a magical moment.

It still kind of did, right up until Marco spoke. "Were you planning on making an exfoliator with glitter?" he asked, sounding interested.

"No. I was looking for sea salt. I'm not always great with labeling things correctly."

He gave me a pointed look that said, "Clearly," but he was polite enough not to say anything out loud about my face and the self-tanner. His gaze narrowed to my mouth and he said, "You have some glitter on your lips."

Then he reached out with his finger and barely brushed my bottom lip, and the entire world stood still. I felt a jolt of electricity that sparked in my lips and zinged through my body to light up my nether regions.

I gasped softly at the sensation and backed up.

Marco looked surprised and then apologetic. "Sorry, I didn't mean to—"

"No, it's okay," I said, shocked at my own reaction. I had honestly thought I could write off my responses to him last night to my inebriation. It turned out that wasn't even a little bit true. Although, to be fair, there was probably still residual ethanol in my body that I hadn't gotten rid of yet. Not to mention that I might have possibly damaged dendrites in my brain by overindulging, and it was making it harder for my neurons to communicate correctly.

So the champagne might still be to blame.

He cleared his throat and offered with a weak smile, "I hope that was edible glitter."

"Technically, all glitter is edible."

I had been shooting for light and funny, but somehow that made the air between us feel charged and even weirder.

"Do you want me to help you clean up?" he asked, breaking the tension.

"No. I would like you to tell me why you're here." A topic he'd successfully evaded so far.

"Right. I wanted you to come to lunch with me."

"Lunch?" I asked, surprised. "Don't you have a company to run?"

"Yes, but I let myself take a break every day to eat. I let all the other employees do it, too. I'm generous that way."

I was kind of digging the snark, but I was still uneasy about the whole why of the situation. "This feels like some kind of joke or setup."

"No," he said with a concerned tone, and I couldn't blame him. Most of the women he asked to eat with him probably didn't automatically assume it was a joke.

"Or . . . do you want me to make you something?" That was a typical occurrence in my life. The ladies in my grandfather's bird-watching club had me whip things up for them all the time. That half an ounce of moisturizer that cost three hundred bucks online? The materials to make it cost less than six dollars and a little bit of my time. I was normally happy to do it, but if Marco was after something like that, he was going to be disappointed.

He didn't qualify for the friends and family discount.

"No, I'm good on both exfoliant and self-tanner," he told me.

The only other reason that came to mind as to why a guy this good looking would want to take me out was, "You don't have any homework you want me to do, do you?"

He must have been able to hear my serious tone, because I saw the way he pressed his lips together, as if he were trying not to laugh. "I'm twenty-nine years old. I don't have homework."

"But why do you want me to come eat with you?" It couldn't just be the pleasure of my company.

"I'll tell you that at lunch."

"I don't go to lunch with strange men." Even though I kind of knew him already.

He called my bluff. "I'm not a stranger. Last night you confided in me that you're in love with my brother. Your deepest, darkest secret. If that doesn't make us friends, I don't know what will."

"I told you that under duress!" I protested.

"From me?"

"No, from the bottle of champagne!"

He smiled at that. "Regardless, I think you'll find what I have to say intriguing."

"I don't know. I'm kind of feeling like I'm stuck in a battle with the second law of thermodynamics today." I noticed that intelligent men tended to back down once I used a term they were unfamiliar with.

"Then let's get you to stop from falling into entropy and make you not be an isolated system by coming out with me." At that, I gawked at him, fully in shock. One, how did Marco Kimball know about the laws of thermodynamics well enough to throw them back at me and two, why was he pushing this so hard? I obviously wasn't interested.

I mean, I was interested in what he had to say. Just not in him as a person. Or a potential romantic partner.

"But if I were you," he continued, totally oblivious to my train of thought, "I'd be more worried about Newton's first law of motion. A body at rest staying at rest and all that."

"You are really going for the hard sell here." What with his quoting science at me.

"I am. And I'll explain everything." His voice was edged with exasperation—not enough to make me think he was really unhappy, but it was probably because women didn't generally turn him down.

I wanted to tell him no. Maybe I'd even be the first woman to ever do that. I wished I could say that I wasn't interested in his mystery box. But my curiosity had always been a driving force in my life, and it was hard to resist the invitation.

"I'm not really dressed up to go anywhere." I could only imagine the kind of restaurants Marco Kimball frequented.

"Okay. Tell you what," he said. "I drove your car here. I'll call a rideshare and meet you at the restaurant in an hour. If you want to come, do, and if you don't, well, it was nice having met you."

"You brought my car?"

He handed me my keys, and I was careful to make sure that no part of him touched any part of me. If I got another electrical shock like the last one, it was going to stop my heart. Cardiac Arrest City, population me.

"Yes. Why do you say it like that?"

"Because it's suspiciously nice," I said.

"Or it's just regular nice."

"You're too good looking to be that nice." I still felt like he was up to something major, and I couldn't live with myself if I didn't know what it was. Why was he making me go out in public to find out?

Catalina was right, and hot guys were the worst.

Especially ones who get engaged to women they've only known for two months, that inner anti-Craig voice said.

I ignored it, but it did make me think that whatever Marco had to say was about Craig, and that pushed me to want to say yes.

He didn't respond to my jab at his niceness and instead said, "Here. I'll text you the address of the restaurant." He took out his phone, and I felt my own phone buzz in response.

"How do you have my number?" I asked.

"You gave it to me last night."

I pulled my cell from my pocket and saw that I had added him to my phone as "Hot Bathroom Guy." Lovely. Too drunk to remember his name, but not so drunk that I'd forgotten where I'd met him or how he looked. "Why didn't you just call me instead of coming over?"

"And miss the orange face and glitter?" When he saw that I wasn't laughing, he shifted gears. "I thought this was more of an in-person situation. I also thought you'd say no if I asked over the phone."

"I might still say no."

"You might," he agreed, but his tone indicated that he thought I wouldn't.

While I stood there, trying to decide what to do, I heard the front door shut, the birds call out, and then my grandmother's voice.

Fan-freaking-tastic. That was all I needed. Growing up, there had been a rule that I couldn't have a boy in my bedroom. I didn't know if that rule was still in effect. I'd never had an occasion before to test it.

"You have to go. And if we get downstairs and anybody I'm related to tries to invite you to dinner tonight, your answer is no. As Admiral Ackbar says—"

"It's a trap?" he finished, and again that feeling from earlier returned, of being understood.

"My grandmother thinks she can cook, but what she makes is like what Satan would serve in hell if he was trying to torture people. And I tell you this because you do seem like a reasonably nice man, and I don't think anyone should be subjected to it. And my grandfather thinks that it's rude not to eat the food set in front of you, so you'll be stuck eating it out of politeness. I have an iron stomach from many years of that kind of cuisine torture. The second I turned sixteen, I did my best to never be home during dinnertime again."

"That was a pretty long explanation for 'don't eat dinner here.'"

"Brevity has never been my strong point. Come on."

I didn't really want to walk him to the door. He'd found his own way upstairs; he could do the same going out. But I couldn't risk a Grandma confrontation. I hoped she would stay in her study and we'd make a clean getaway.

"Don't step on that one." I pointed at the third stair. "It creaks, and I'd like to sneak you past my quasi–parental units. The questions will be endless."

"It's nice that you have people who care about you."

The way he said that was so heartbreaking, so familiar, that I stumbled on the last step. Marco reached out and grabbed me, keeping me upright. The electricity returned, slamming into me and shorting out my breath.

"Are you okay?" he asked.

"Fine," I said. "You can, um, let go."

He released his hand in surprise, like he'd forgotten it was there. I didn't know that I'd be able to forget, given that I was pretty sure his light handprint had made a permanent electricity-based imprint on my upper arm.

Residual alcohol effects, I reminded myself. It didn't mean anything.

I had just put my hand on the front doorknob, rejoicing in my ability to get him out of the house without being caught, when my grandpa came strolling down the hallway toward the door. He beamed at both of us and said to Marco, "I see you found her okay."

"I did, sir. Thank you."

"Good, good." He glanced at me. "Anna, sweetie, you have something on your face."

"Thanks, Grandpa." As if I could forget. I hoped orange masked bright pink cheeks.

He whistled a tune as he left us and headed into the living room. He sat down with his newspaper (he was possibly the last person in America who not only received a newspaper but read the whole thing front to back every day). Feather Locklear was squawking up a storm about the worst baseball team ever, and I opened the door for Marco.

"I'd say thanks for stopping by, but this has all been really bizarre."

Marco walked out onto the porch and stopped to smile at me. "I'll see you soon."

I begrudgingly replied, "Maybe."

"I'll take a maybe," he said, sporting an endearing grin that made my heart melt. Was he kidding me with this? How could he be handsome and that charming? It really was unfair. God should have saved some of the good stuff he'd poured out on Marco for the other men on the planet.

My grandma said something from the other room, so I quickly shut the door. Not fast enough, though—she'd either seen Marco or my grandfather had tipped her off.

"Who was that?" she asked.

"Just a guy from work."

"The work you don't go to anymore?"

Point made. I deserved a medal for not rolling my eyes. I would not revert to my teenage self, no matter how much she annoyed me. "Yes."

I stepped on the first stair to go back to my room, but she asked, "What did he want?"

"For me to join his harem and give him a dozen children and to never, ever be a chemist again."

"Anna! Be serious!" she exclaimed, just as my grandfather turned a page of his newspaper and said, "If that's what she wants to do, that's what she should do. Whatever makes you happy makes us happy, Stinker."

I was pretty sure he hadn't even heard what I'd said, but he had always played the peacemaker between the two of us.

That made me feel bad, him thinking he had to interfere on my behalf, so I decided to be the bigger person and answer her question. "I don't know what Marco wants. But I'm about to go find out."

CHAPTER SEVEN

I checked Marco's text, copied the address he'd sent into my map app, and saw that the restaurant wasn't far from the house. I went upstairs to do as much damage control as I possibly could on my facc, which meant another shower. After that close encounter with Marco, it was probably warranted. He definitely made me a little sweaty. Again, I refused to closely examine my reactions and just dismissed them.

I went to my home lab and threw together a quick (glitter-free) exfoliant and headed to the bathroom. I turned the shower back on and considered calling Catalina while I waited for the water to heat up. But she would demand answers that I didn't have yet. I couldn't even formulate a hypothesis—Marco had dismissed all my suspicions. It was better to gather the relevant information, observe for myself what he wanted, and then talk with her so we could evaluate and draw our conclusions as a team. Right now, it was all just speculation and guesswork, and there was only one way to uncover the truth.

My phone buzzed, and there was a text from Catalina ten minutes ago asking for an update. She texted again shortly after that and reminded me that if I was interested, although she knew I wouldn't be, that I was welcome to join her monthly D&D game. She said some of our coworkers would be there.

That's all I needed. To be around chemists from the lab I'd just quit. Because that wouldn't be at all awkward.

I disrobed and put baby oil on my face. I let it soak in and then got into the shower to exfoliate. I spent a long time there, hoping it was working and wondering what Marco had to say. I stuck my head out of the shower, cleared the steam off the mirror, and checked my face. Eh. Good enough.

I was too impatient to wait any longer.

~

My grandmother had once told me to always be the first person to show up to a meeting. That it was a power move. I arrived at the restaurant about half an hour early, not knowing whether or not Marco would come. The paranoid part of my brain still worried that this, despite his protest, had been some kind of setup and he wanted me to come to the restaurant all orange and sad to make fun of me. My irrational fears were quickly dispelled when I saw him waiting for me in the lobby. I had come here specifically to find him—so why did I feel a jolt on seeing him again?

"Hey, you made it. I knew you would," he said.

That was annoying. I liked my science to meet my expectations, but nobody liked the idea that they might be predictable.

"I thought we'd sit in the back, if that's all right with you." We were in a pizza place—not quite the French froufrou fine dining I had anticipated. We were even seating ourselves.

"Sure."

I followed behind him, the smell of toasted garlic and tomatoes making my stomach rumble with anticipation. All I'd had to eat so far today was chips.

He gestured toward a little booth. "Is this okay?"

I nodded, and he waited for me to sit down before he joined me. A few seconds later, a waiter approached, did a bit of a double-take when he looked at me, and then handed us menus and promised to return with water.

There was an awkward pause because I felt like Marco was staring at me. As if everyone had been looking at us since we arrived. This might have been because he was so uncomfortably good looking that they were all wondering what he was doing with someone like me.

It might also have been due to the self-tanner.

"You're kind of staring at me," I told him.

"I'm sorry. I'm having a hard time figuring out how to look you in the eyes without staring at you."

"It's okay," I said. "We've both acknowledged the five-hundred-pound self-tanner in the room."

"It seems like you might be mixing a few metaphors there, but you're right. Does this kind of thing happen to you a lot?"

"More than I'd like to admit," I told him. "Chemistry is sometimes full of surprises."

He nodded. "True. And your face does look better. Less like an orange and more like a . . . dying orange? I don't know. I can't think of anything that is a paler orange."

Shrugging one shoulder, I said, "A few more scrubs and I'll be back to normal. Well, normal-ish."

Our waiter returned with water and said he'd be back in a couple of minutes to take our order. When he left, Marco smiled at me and asked, "Do you know what you'd like to order?"

I hadn't even picked up the menu. "Not yet." We both looked over our menus in silence until I admitted to him, "This restaurant wasn't what I expected."

"What did you expect?" he asked, as if he already knew the answer to my question.

"Something expensive with portions too small for a bird. This place is . . . homey." Much more me.

"I was in the mood for pizza," he said. Also surprising, because given that he didn't look like he had an ounce of fat on him, I had a hard time believing that he ate carbs at all, let alone pizza. "Do you want to split one?"

"I'm lactose intolerant, and I didn't bring any pills with me," I said.

"They have a cheese-less pizza here."

"Which is basically just bread with sauce on it, but okay."

"You can put pepperoni on it, too," he offered cheerfully.

As if that would solve the issue. "I suppose I could." I probably wouldn't, though. All those pepperoni slices would just slide around. I knew that from experience and the first-degree burn I'd gotten on my arm.

"They have really massive salads here. We could split that, if you'd like. Do you want one?"

Hadn't he just said the whole reason he'd come here was to have pizza? "The only way I'd order salad is if the world ended and it was the only thing left to eat in order to survive."

"You're not into salad?"

"I'm also not into splitting things." Why did he keep asking me to do that? "Why do you say things like that with so much surprise in your voice?"

He shook his head. "I've just dated a lot of women where that's the only thing they eat."

Honestly, I wasn't even a teensy bit shocked. That was probably where the offer to split everything came from, too. "I guess I'm not like someone you would typically hang out with. You should know that when you can find me not working out, I will also be making very unhealthy food decisions."

"Noted," he said, an actual twinkle in his eye. "I guess that means the 5k hike after lunch is out of the question." He laughed at my expression. "I'm teasing. Vegan pizza for you, then?"

"Yes, I'm getting the vegan pizza, but only because there's no cheese. Not for any other reason. You can't trick me into making healthy choices."

"Do you know the hardest part of making a vegan pizza?" He asked me the question seriously, and I wasn't sure what he was trying to ask.

I blinked a couple of times. "Literally nothing?"

He shook his head. "Skinning the vegan."

That was a joke that reminded me so much of my father I felt a physical twinge of longing. "Huh. I thought they had a thin skin."

That made him grin at me, and then I added, "I could be a vegan."

His eyes widened. "Are you?"

"I'm not. And I think vegan jokes are only okay so long as they're not cheesy."

At that, he laughed, his voice deep and rich, and I found myself wanting to join in. It had been a long time since I'd sat around and traded bad jokes with someone. I felt all warm and fuzzy inside and enjoyed the sound of his laughter more than just an acquaintance should.

Because deep, drunken confessions aside, we didn't really know each other.

"Okay, so now that we have the food all sorted—what would you like to drink?" he asked.

Was Marco trying to take my order? Like, we had a waiter who was going to ask me all of this. Or was he just trying to make conversation? It made me think he was nervous and this was how he was coping with his anxiety.

"Something strong? Hair of the dog?" he asked.

"What?" I was so disoriented by all of this and the magical quality of his laughter that I didn't understand what he was asking.

"You know that saying, about when you're hungover you should drink more alcohol, so you should drink the hair of the dog that bit you?"

"Oh. My grandpa always says drink the feather of the bird that pecked you. Which makes more sense, because odds are higher that you'll get pecked by a bird."

"I've never been pecked by a bird."

"Do you want to be?" I asked. "I can easily arrange that."

"No thanks," he said breezily, as if I'd offered him a dish he didn't want to taste. "But . . . drinking feathers?"

"Drinking hair?" I countered.

"I feel like hair would go down much more easily than feathers."

"Depends on the size of the feather," I said, wondering how we'd ended up at this point. "But the shorter answer is no, thank you, I don't think I'll be drinking again for the next century." One night of crying on a bathroom floor with the CEO of my former company was quite enough for me. "Plus, it's the middle of the afternoon and I'm not really much of a day drinker."

"You're not much of a night drinker, either," he said with a grin that was so adorable, I'd be willing to bet a lot of money that he had never been in trouble once in his entire life. All he would have to do is flash that smile and all would be forgiven.

It was like a weapon. Somebody should make him register that thing.

Our waiter came back, and we gave him our orders—a Diet Coke and medium vegan pizza for me, just water and a medium meat lovers for Marco.

When the waiter left, Marco folded his hands on the table and looked at me very seriously. "It's come to my attention that the Yankees suck."

Again, I felt a little bewildered at the direction of our conversation. "What?"

"The bird in your house? The one who keeps saying 'Yankees suck!'"

"Feather Locklear. She's a gray parrot. She used to be at an outdoor aviary, but she kept teaching all the other birds to curse. They asked my grandfather to rehabilitate her. When he brought her home, she immediately taught Parrot Hilton and Parrot France to swear, but Grandpa's working with them. It's 'Yankees suck' now, but it used to be much worse. He uses replacement words with her."

"Interesting. If she were my bird, I'd probably teach her to say, 'Help! I've been turned into a parrot!'"

That made me laugh, and he grinned in response. "She's mostly over it now. But every now and again, she curses in a way that would make a sailor blush."

"So why all the Yankees hate? I'm assuming your grandpa doesn't like them. What if I was a fan?"

"We are a Dodgers family. If you are a Yankees fan, then I think my grandpa might slap you across the face with his glove and demand satisfaction. For all I know, he has those birds do his bidding, and you might find yourself in a scene from a Hitchcock movie."

"You like Hitchcock?"

"Who doesn't?" I asked.

"It seems like he would fall outside of the Star Wars / Lord of the Rings / romantic comedies you said you typically enjoy. Not to mention that most people our age have never heard of him."

"Well, then they don't know what they're missing."

"Agreed."

Our waiter, who I realized wasn't wearing a name tag and hadn't introduced himself, came back with my drink. I thanked him, and he said our food should be up soon.

"Speaking of the birds, that wasn't quite what I was expecting at your house," Marco commented.

I felt my spine bristle in response. "And just what were you expecting?" Cats? Had he thought I was some sad, lonely woman with only feline companionship? I told myself to calm down—I was putting words in his mouth. Just because a man had once told me that I seemed like the type of girl who lived with eighteen cats didn't mean Marco was the same.

"You still live with your family. Is that cultural?"

"What culture?" I asked. "The bird people / scientists / nerdy girl one? I live at home because I can't afford to move out."

"I didn't want to assume . . ." His voice trailed off.

"You can assume anything you'd like. They'll probably be true."

He frowned slightly. "Our chemists are paid well."

"I think I was paid below entry level. At least according to . . ." I nearly said Catalina's name and knew how jumpy C-level executives got about people sharing salaries and didn't want to get her in trouble. "A former colleague. But I guess it was okay, considering." Considering how much my boss hated me, it was surprising I got paid at all.

Marco looked irritated, and I knew it wasn't directed at me. I wondered if Jerry and Craig were about to get a talking-to tomorrow. Marco struck me as a man of action.

Would that get Craig in trouble? I didn't want that. I felt compelled to explain that my salary wasn't the only reason I was broke. "My grandparents' home is pretty old. About six months ago, the water heater died, and we discovered that all the pipes in the house had to be replaced. They didn't have the money to cover it, and since it was due to age and not an accident, insurance wouldn't help. I emptied out my savings to fix the house. My grandpa insisted they could take out a loan, but I paid the plumber. They've said they'll pay me back, but they're part-time professors and volunteer for nonprofits. They won't be able to, and that's okay."

He stayed quiet for a moment and then said, "That is . . . exceptional. I don't know many people who would do that."

"They're my family. I love them." I felt wiggly, a bit awkward, at the expression in his eyes, and I shifted in my seat. "Plus, I have a taste for expensive lab equipment. I have my eye on a used high-shear mixer.

It's three thousand dollars, so I might be my grandparents' age when I can finally afford it."

Especially if I didn't find a job soon.

The food arrived then, and our waiter slid it onto the table in front of us and told us to enjoy. We both thanked him.

My pizza looked very hot, and I wasn't eager to burn my mouth (or my skin accidentally). I expected Marco to dig in, but he was still studying me carefully.

"So, I wanted to talk to you about something. But first . . . last night seemed pretty terrible for you."

We were finally getting to the question I'd had on my mind since he'd shown up unannounced in my room, but I still didn't quite understand what he was getting at.

"Oh, I think it would be number three on my Worst Days Ever list." I pried apart two pieces of my pizza, grabbed one, and lifted it to my mouth.

"What was number two?"

"In high school, I was helping the cute quarterback with his chem lab project. He had missed the deadline, and he knew I had a key and could get him into the lab to help him do the experiment. He was very distracting, and I made a mistake—instead of pouring a base into a burette . . ." Better to explain so that he'd understand the story. "A burette is a long glass tube that you use to—"

"I know what a burette is," he interrupted me.

"Oh." That was surprising. He seemed to be full of surprises. Like a handsome jack-in-the-box. "Anyway, I was distracted and accidentally poured sulfuric acid into the burette, and my hand slipped and it got all over our clothes. We had to disrobe and shower, and the janitor caught us and thought we were doing something else, and he called a bunch of people . . . Anyway, that story ended with me losing my chem lab key and being suspended. Which was torture, because I really loved school. I was worried it might go on my permanent record and keep me out of college."

He fiddled with the straw in his glass. "Your worst day on your list. Was that when your mom passed?"

His question surprised me so much that I held still, my mouth wide open, momentarily unable to move. I set the pizza slice back down.

"How did you know that?" I whispered. His question shocked me, like being pierced by an icy stake. I might have said a lot of things while drunk last night, but I was positive I hadn't said anything about my parents dying. I didn't talk much about them. Even Catalina had very minimal details and knew not to press me for more. Had he done a background check on me or something?

"Last night, you mentioned your mother, and I just heard something in your voice that I understood. That kind of loss causes the sort of pain that's easy to recognize in others. I don't know why they say time heals all wounds when years later, the wound still hurts just as much. The only difference is other people expect that it won't."

That so perfectly encapsulated how I felt about my parents' deaths that I was again stunned for a moment. "Who did you lose?"

"My mom."

"How did she die?"

Marco continued to mess with his straw, not making eye contact with me. "Cardiovascular complications due to anorexia. She was a model who thought she had to be perfect. She was the first face of Minx Cosmetics."

"Your mom was Giana Ricci? The original Miss Minx?"

He nodded as I took that in. She had been very beautiful. The company had used her image recently in a throwback campaign when they'd reissued some 1990s makeup.

"She was gorgeous," I told him. I imagined that it was probably hard to be that beautiful and have to stay that way at all costs. Feeling like you had to turn to disordered eating. It was much easier for women like me. Maybe not so much in the dating department, but the guys who fell for us wouldn't expect us to look like supermodels for the rest of our lives. It must have been so hard for her.

And so hard for poor Marco to lose her. "I'm so sorry. How old were you?"

"Four. I don't have many memories of her." He paused a moment and then cleared his throat. "What about you? How old were you?"

And even though I didn't usually share this part of myself, given that he knew exactly what I'd gone through, I found myself saying, "Twelve. And it was both of my parents. A car accident. The man who hit them was doing the trifecta of bad driving decisions—drunk, texting, and ran a red light."

Now it was his turn to say, "I'm sorry."

That pang of overwhelming grief, the one that as he'd pointed out never really went away, pushed down against my chest. "It's fine. I had my grandparents. I've done okay. And you still had your dad, right?"

"Seven weeks after my mom died, he married Tracie, my stepmother. Craig's mom. And my dad is the CEO of KRT Limited." That was Minx Cosmetics' parent corporation. I remembered Catalina's claims of nepotism. Was this what she'd been referring to? Marco continued. "So he was working nonstop and left me with a woman who wanted to replace me as his heir with her own son."

There was something in his voice, something that sounded angry and hurt. I wanted to know more, but Marco gave me a slight smile and added, "Speaking of my half brother, that's why I asked you to meet with me. I need your help."

What kind of assistance could someone like him need from someone like me?

He answered my unspoken question. "I want to break up Craig's relationship, and I think you're the person who can help me do that."

CHAPTER EIGHT

Again, he'd shifted gears so quickly that it was hard to follow his thought process. One second he was telling me about losing his mom and his distinctly not fun childhood and the next he was saying something about me being able to help him wreck his brother's engagement.

"Did you want me to be your lookout while you seduce Leighton or something?" Nothing else made any sense.

Not that anything he'd said so far made much sense.

"No, that relationship is definitely over. For a lot of reasons. She and I don't have feelings for each other. While you . . ." He trailed off, arching his eyebrows at me.

"While I what? Am in love with Craig?" It seemed like Marco had forgotten one teeny-tiny fact. "Craig's in love with someone else. I think this may be what is formally known as a lost cause."

"Nothing's a lost cause," he said. "Plus, I have a plan."

"Oh, this should be good." I'd meant to keep that as an internal thought, but I couldn't keep it inside. Especially since I was envisioning one of those evidence boards detectives used with note cards and strings to link all the parts of a complicated crime together.

But then I realized that I didn't want to hear all the details until I understood the reason he was doing this. So I asked, "Why?"

"Why do I want to break up their engagement, or why do I think you're the person who can help me?"

"Yes." I wanted answers to both of those statements.

"Craig's engagement is going to be bad for Minx and possibly KRT. Leighton is what they colloquially refer to as a gold digger."

"How do you know that?" It seemed like a big assumption on his part. Which might be fair, considering he was the one who had dated her.

"Personal experience."

"So what if she is?" I asked, finally grabbing a piece of my pizza. It was starting to get cold. "Plenty of wealthy men marry women who are after their money."

"Leighton's family owns Reflection Cosmetics. They want to merge with Minx."

I chewed and swallowed the bite in my mouth. "Again, so? That's not too unusual." Cosmetic companies were constantly buying each other out.

"It is when Reflection is deeply in debt. I suspect they're cooking their books and expecting Minx, and by extension KRT, to absorb their losses. It could ruin Minx financially. I know that Leighton's family intends to do this because it's the reason I broke things off. She accidentally forwarded paperwork her family's attorneys had drawn up to merge the companies, along with a detailed letter about why she should insist on us not having a prenup."

I opened my mouth in surprise. Hadn't he said they'd only been dating for a short time? And the lawyers were talking marriage? It sounded like Leighton's family had seriously jumped the gun there.

So when Marco ended things, she went after Craig instead? Who did propose after a few weeks? The whole thing seemed . . . gross.

Marco was still talking. "I won't let Craig destroy it because he doesn't know when he's being played and can't keep it in his . . ." He trailed off and then said, "Because he's so easily distracted by shiny things."

Leighton was definitely shiny. I took another bite. Reflection Cosmetics was one of the companies I'd planned on applying to. I supposed that was out the window.

"You remember I just quit Minx, right?" It seemed a little odd that he would be counting on a former employee to help out his company. Of course I didn't want to see Minx Cosmetics fail, but why me?

"I do, and you said it was because your boss was a jerk. I did some research on you this morning. Got your file from HR and I pulled up some of your projects." That felt off, like something he shouldn't have done. I reminded myself that technically I had been his employee and he had a right to it. He must have seen my facial expression shift as he hurried to add, "Your work was exceptional. Meticulous. I saw your cover letter when you applied four years ago and how much you wanted to work for Minx."

"It was one of my mom's favorite makeup brands," I said quietly. "I wanted so much to work there to honor her."

"This company is my mother's legacy," he said. "So I get it."

Again there was that feeling of being seen and understood, of a shared connection with him. I didn't want to feel that way, so I circled back to what we'd been talking about. "What does it matter what Craig wants? Last time I checked, you are the CEO of Minx. You don't have to merge anything just because Craig and Leighton are, uh, merging."

He let out a short sigh. He loosened his tie and shrugged off his suit coat, letting it lie on the bench next to him. "Craig . . . is very good at getting our father to agree with him. So is his mother. That's the reason he's VP of product development right now, even though he doesn't have any training or experience. His last job was as a DJ in an Ibiza nightclub."

That couldn't be right. Craig seemed much more reliable and capable. Responsible.

The same guy who got engaged to a girl he dated for two months? my contrary inner voice asked, and I told it to shut up.

"And when Leighton and I *casually* dated," he said, for some reason emphasizing the word *casually*, "she repeatedly brought up the fact that she wouldn't marry a man who insisted on a prenup. Whether that was her idea or her attorney's, I don't know. What I do know makes me concerned, as you can imagine."

He sat quietly, letting me absorb all of this information while I ate. There was something that bothered me. Honestly, there were a lot of things bothering me about this conversation, but one more predominant than the others. "Is this why you asked me all that stuff about my tragic childhood? Were you trying to make me feel vulnerable in an attempt to butter me up so that I'd listen to your request?"

"What? No!" he said forcefully. "That wasn't my intention. I asked about your parents because I recognized a kindred spirit and wanted to know more about your story. I find you interesting and easy to talk to."

Well. That made me feel good—pink-champagne-bubbles-floating-inside-my-veins good. Interesting. Easy to talk to. If he was trying to butter me up, those were good things to say. I felt very flattered.

Marco continued. "I didn't mean to lose sight of what I wanted to ask you. You can be distracting."

When he said this, his eyes kind and sparkling, his mouth twisted mischievously, his jawline ready to cut through time and space with all its sharpness, hitting me with the whole force of his charm, how could anyone be expected to be immune to a full-frontal attack like that?

I noticed that my heart was racing, and my breathing was a little uneven. The scientist in me wanted to analyze what was happening and why, but the rest of me wanted to ignore these continually weird reactions. "You're very good at this," I told him with a forced laugh. "I bet no one ever tells you no."

He shrugged one shoulder, and I didn't know if that meant he agreed with me or if he didn't. It was enigmatic, which was appealing, because I had always loved solving puzzles.

But this was one puzzle I needed to steer clear of.

Right after I found out how he thought I was going to help him break up Craig and Leighton. Because there was no way I was walking away from this conversation without finding out that tidbit of information. "So what is your great plan to destroy your brother's happiness?"

I noticed him wince slightly at my words before he said, "It's pretty simple. You and I pretend to date."

He leaned back as if this explained everything. "Say more," I instructed. My heart wasn't just racing now—it was in a full gallop, trying to get out of my chest. Date? This creature who looked like he'd been forged by fallen angels just to tempt all womankind?

Uh, no.

"Craig and I have always been ridiculously competitive with one another. His mother made sure of that." That bitter tinge was back in his voice, but he shifted his tone into something softer. "If he thinks we're dating, he will want to steal you away from me. And before you ask, I know that because it's happened before."

With Leighton? I wanted to ask but refrained because he no longer seemed like he was in an open and share-y place. Now that I finally knew what he was up to, I wasn't interested. "Okay. Well, thanks so much for your reluctant and strange offer, but I'm going to have to pass."

Even if my brain was busy conjuring up an alternate reality where I did pretend to date Marco. I inserted him into my Craig fantasy—walking along the water, sitting on a bench all night talking.

It was kind of scary how easy it was to swap one out for the other.

Another reason I shouldn't do this. I was in love with Craig.

In. Love.

Marco interrupted my stern self-talking-to. "Why not?"

"Seriously?" I asked. "This is wrong in so many different ways that I would need charts and diagrams to explain it."

"How so?" He uncuffed his shirtsleeves and started rolling them up his forearms.

His very masculine and strong forearms that made my mouth water.

That was the yummy vegan pizza I was eating, I told my body. That's what caused the reaction. Not this fine specimen of manhood in front of me.

It took me a second to remember that he had asked me a question that I needed to answer. "Do you really want to sit here and debate the ethics and morality of pretending to date in an attempt to trick your brother into breaking up with his fiancée and dating me?"

He folded his arms, and I had to actually force my eyeballs to not look at his forearms again, sitting so nicely against his chest. Which I'd bet was also pretty nice. Plus, his very broad shoulders. You could build a subdivision on those things.

My inappropriate train of thought was brought to a halt by his response. "There's no morality involved. We wouldn't be doing anything wrong or hurting anyone."

But I would have to . . . pretend to be Marco's girlfriend, keeping my apparently rebellious hormones in check (because no matter how much I wanted to lie to myself, my body was not this excited about a cheese-less pizza). I couldn't imagine how any of this would even work.

"Come on," he cajoled me. "You could help me save Minx and get Craig out of a bad situation. Let's kill two birds with one stone."

"Let's not. Nobody needs to be murdering birds. We don't do that in my family," I said reflexively.

I should shut this down. Thank him for helping me to get home and returning my car, and then go back to my regular life.

Instead I found myself echoing his words. "A bad situation?"

Marco nodded. "It's easy to see how this is going to go. Craig's trust fund is going to be depleted. His heart is going to be broken. You'd be keeping him from having to say *my first wife* and having trust issues with women going forward. That's a kindness."

It was such a stretch, but I found myself wanting to go along with it. I still protested, though. "I don't think your plan will work. It's done. They're getting married. What can we do?"

He smiled. "That's the spirit! What can we do?"

Deliberately misunderstanding my words was not as cute as he thought it was. "Even if your plan would work, which based on what you've told me, I don't think it would, I don't want to be responsible for breaking up an engagement. That seems wrong. And like it would bring a lot of bad karma into my life. Which I do not need right now." I did not want to get the universe involved. I was messing up my life just fine all on my own.

"This relationship of theirs isn't going to last. They've only been together for a couple of months. We would just be helping to speed things along."

"My grandparents dated for six weeks, got married, and have been together for almost fifty years. It can happen."

"How many decades ago was that?" he countered. "The world was different then."

"Fine." Whether or not people could be happily married after knowing each other for only a short amount of time was irrelevant to this discussion. "You should know that I'm a terrible liar. I have an obvious tell. It's that everyone knows when I'm lying."

"I'm excellent at it," he said.

"I don't know if that's something you should be proud of."

"Unfortunately, it was necessary." A shadow passed over his face, but he tried to smile through it. "That's easy enough to take care of. We'll actually date. Like, today for example. I asked you to lunch; you came." He reached into his back pocket and pulled out a wallet. He grabbed a hundred-dollar bill and put it on the table. "And now I've paid for our food. All of which makes this an official date. And we can spend time together and keep 'dating.' Being comfortable with one another, getting to know each other, that will help sell all of this. It will feel real and not like a lie."

I threw up both of my hands. Was he going to argue with every point I made? "There's no guarantee of success here. There are too many variables. It's unpredictable."

"What's the alternative?" he asked. "You do nothing—you know the inevitable outcome. A hundred percent odds that you don't get to be with Craig. But if you do something, go along with my plan, you could potentially affect the end result for the better. This is your chance to conduct a real-life experiment. Find out whether or not I'm right."

I still wasn't quite sold, but he was making a good amount of headway. "I don't like things I can't control."

"Nobody does. Although there is something to be said about injecting a little chaos into your life to change things up. We could have some fun together. And in the end, you could wind up with the guy you're in love with."

He made that chaos sound enticing. I tried my last protest. "I need to spend time looking for a new job. I don't really have the time to pretend to date you."

"I actually have a solution for that. KRT Limited can bring you on as a consultant. I checked, and they haven't used their full consultant budget for Minx this year, and we'll lose that money if we don't hire someone."

"You want me to consult on how to ruin Craig's relationship?"

"No. We can talk about makeup and facial products. You are a cosmetic chemist, after all. And our consultants get paid a flat fee instead of an hourly rate." Then he named a figure that was three times my previous annual salary.

I couldn't help it. I gasped. "Why is it so much?"

"Consultants get paid more for their expertise and because we don't have to pay benefits, given that it's a short-term arrangement," he said.

Wow. It was a lot of money. I could replace all the appliances in the kitchen that had been born before I had. It would also mean that I could buy that high-shear mixer. The red one. *My precious.*

To stop any further objection, he added, "You would technically be employed by KRT, so there wouldn't be any conflict with us 'dating.'" There was a tone to his words that indicated it wouldn't have mattered to Minx if he was my boss.

At least he didn't remind me again that the company didn't have a nonfraternization rule. That would have annoyed me.

And if I'd had any dignity, I would have told him no. That he could keep his fancy job that paid a ridiculous amount of money and the opportunity to win over the man I was in love with, no matter how improbable it all seemed.

Unfortunately, dignity had never been my strong suit.

"All I would have to do is hang out with you?" I asked.

"It would be a bit more involved than that, but essentially yes."

I tried to bring up that fantasy I had of Craig, and for a few seconds, I saw his face as we walked, holding hands, but it kept shifting to Marco. I don't know what that was about, but I wanted what I'd initially imagined. Craig and me together, having our happily ever after.

"Do you want Craig?" he asked, almost as if he could see my thoughts.

"More than almost anything," I admitted.

"Then give this a chance. We can both get what we want."

This was all so bonkers. My grandma would have so much to say about it if she knew. That kind of made me want to do it.

He must have sensed my resolve weakening. He said, "You can't think about this like you're trying to hurt people. You want to be with Craig, and you think he would be happy with you. My company stays safe. We would all be happy."

"Not Leighton."

"Leighton could move on to finding her next victim. I don't think she'd be too heartbroken."

Besides the Leighton stuff—he was right. This was a perspective I hadn't considered yet. How this might be a beneficial thing for both Craig and me. This could mean me ending up with the man of my dreams. Why would I miss out on that opportunity? Marco was also spot-on about changing the outcome of my current situation. If I didn't do something, I would have zero chance with Craig because he was going to marry someone else.

I hoped this wasn't a mistake.

"Okay," I said, rushing the words out before I could change my mind. "I don't see how it's going to work, but I'll give it a shot."

CHAPTER NINE

"Yes!" Marco said, clapping his hands together as he beamed at me. "I do think that we can do this if we work together."

I wanted to believe him, but it was difficult. Especially given how simplistic his actual plan was. It was full of holes, but I'd give it the old college try.

"We should probably keep this between us," he said. "Secrets tend to have a way of coming out."

"I have to tell Catalina. She's my best friend, and she works at Minx. She would definitely notice if I suddenly started dating her boss's boss's boss with no explanation. She's smart. She would figure it out." Plus, I had the feeling I was going to need the moral support.

"What about your family? Do you need to tell them?"

"My grandparents aren't going to care about you unless you suddenly decompose or grow a beak and feathers." Becoming dirt or a bird was honestly the only way they'd be interested in Marco.

He picked up his water. "Well, I'm definitely not telling my family for obvious reasons. Anyway, I feel like we should make this official. A handshake or a toast or something."

"A toast," I said quickly. I didn't want to hold his hand again. It seemed unwise.

"To saving my brother from himself," he said.

"And Minx Cosmetics."

We clinked our glasses together and both took a quick drink. "You should try your pizza," I told him. He was the one who had wanted to come here. I felt bad that he hadn't eaten anything yet.

He picked up his slice and did the weirdest thing ever—he folded it in half lengthwise. "What are you doing?" I asked in alarm.

"This is how you eat a slice in New York. I went to boarding school there during high school."

"Like a taco? That's culinary blasphemy."

"You need structure in your crust or else you get the flop." I wanted to tell him this wasn't New York and our crusts in California already had plenty of structure, but he gave me a mischievous grin and took a big, wolfish bite. I wanted to laugh but refrained.

When he swallowed his food, he said, "So tell me what you were working on before you quit."

I figured it'd be safe to share that information because I'd done the work at his company. We ate while I told him about all of my recent professional projects. I wondered who had taken them over and had a brief pang of regret. I kept expecting him to interrupt me or change the subject, but he didn't.

He also didn't get that glazed, bored look in his eyes. He seemed interested in what I had to say. This was nice. He would make a great brother-in-law.

One thing at a time, I told myself. I was jumping too many steps ahead. First, Marco's completely sane and totally-based-in-reality plan had to work.

After we'd both eaten half of our pizzas, the waiter brought over a couple of boxes and the check. Marco made a big show of paying the check, and I didn't offer to split it. He could afford it. I thanked him and grabbed my jacket to put it back on.

"Before we go," Marco said, "we should make plans to get together soon. We should go on a date."

"A date?" The words squeaked out of me. I'd thought we were just going to pretend to date. It just hadn't clicked that we might actually go on a real date. Together. In the same place at the same time.

Him paying for lunch didn't count.

"Yes, a date. You've seen them on TV—now have one of your very own." He was teasing, but the reality of it felt unsettling. "Like I mentioned earlier, I think we should do a couple of practice dates before we specifically spend time around Craig and Leighton." He took out his phone and scrolled through it. "It's too bad there's no red-carpet events coming up soon. We could get our picture taken together and put on some website. Craig's assistant has a Google alert set up with my name."

I did not want to know how he knew that. Totally believable, though, knowing Gretchen. "I may know a way to get his attention."

Marco looked skeptical. "Really?"

"The friend I mentioned earlier? Catalina? She's having a D&D party at her place in a couple of days. She asked me to come, even though she knows I won't."

"Then why did she invite you?"

"Duh." I almost rolled my eyes. "I still want to be invited; I just don't want to go to her parties."

"I'm confused. You just said she's your best friend."

"Yes, which is why she knows she has to invite me but that I won't be there. I never go to parties." Too many people and too many conversations. I found them so draining.

"You never go to parties?" he said in the same way someone else might ask, *You don't breathe oxygen?* His tone had me wondering if he was rethinking our agreement.

I felt a little judged, even though he hadn't said anything negative. He was just surprised, which was fair, given that most nonintroverted people seemed to enjoy things like parties. I had to stop assuming that people meant the worst when they were only being curious. I couldn't project my own personal insecurities onto others.

"No," I told him, "I never go to parties. I mean, I could have gone to one last Halloween, but instead I told people that I was dressing up as Amelia Earhart, and then I just didn't show up."

He laughed and said, "I don't really enjoy parties, either, these days. All the ones I go to are for work."

I didn't know how Marco was going to feel about the whole D&D thing, but we'd just deal with it when we got there. "If what Catalina keeps telling me is true, Minx has a massive gossip network, and there will be some former colleagues of mine at the party, so it'll be easy to get the word out about us. We can even have someone take a picture and tag the company." Old Gretchen would definitely see it then.

And she would pass it along to Craig. Would it make him jealous? Would he finally notice me and realize that we could be happy together?

Marco stood up, getting his suit jacket, and I followed him out to the lobby. I remembered that he didn't bring his car. "I can give you a ride home," I said.

The edges of his eyes wrinkled up when he smiled. "I thought you didn't get in cars with strange men."

"I think I can make an exception for fake boyfriends."

"Thank you, but I already requested a car."

I realized I didn't know if he meant on a rideshare app or if he had an actual car with a driver sort of situation happening. Our lives were so completely different that I didn't know how we were going to make anyone believe that we were falling for each other. But somehow we had to convince Craig that we were in love.

Again, one thing at a time. Right now I just needed to head home and process all of this. "Okay. Well, I should probably get going."

"If you can," he said.

"Was that a dig at Betty?" I asked, narrowing my eyes at him.

"Is that what you named that monstrosity that you drive?"

Betty was a twenty-seven-year-old Toyota Camry that may or may not have been dealing with some rust issues and pieces that were being held together by duct tape. "My grandma very much wants to save the earth and all its soil, and apparently it's bad to buy a new car. Not to mention that I couldn't afford one, even if I wanted it."

"Replumbing an entire house can't be cheap." He nodded thoughtfully. "And your parents didn't leave you anything?"

"No. They were both young, and they didn't have life insurance. And given my taste for pretty lab equipment and the house . . . there's nothing left. I did my undergrad at USC. I'd wanted to get my master's degree in cosmetic chemistry, but I couldn't afford it. My grandma told me to take out student loans, and I told her that it was much more expensive than in her day when getting your master's basically meant paying a hundred bucks and promising to fight communists."

He laughed. "Good thing your new job starts tomorrow. I'll have the contracts sent over to you. They'll be fairly standard, but you should probably have a lawyer look them over."

"I'm going to be double-checking to make sure I'm not accidentally selling my eternal soul to the devil or something."

"Don't worry. We only put that clause in the contracts of the consultants we know are headed there anyways."

I grinned at him.

He asked, "So once you get your soul-selling money, what are you going to do with it? Get that degree?"

That was a good question. "No. I think I'm going to buy my grandparents some appliances that were made in this century. I hear those ice dispenser things in fridges are pretty good."

"Revolutionary," he agreed. "It will change your life."

"I'm also going to buy that mixer."

"Don't forget you need to restock your glitter," he reminded me.

"Obviously. And then I'm going to save the rest."

"For a rainy day?"

"To start my own makeup company." Again, we were back in territory that I hardly discussed with anyone outside of Catalina. It always felt so personal, private, but I sensed that Marco wouldn't make fun of me for it.

"Your own makeup company? So . . . you'll be using my father's money to become my rival?"

"That's the dream."

"It's a good one," he said. "I also appreciate the heads-up. Most other companies lack the common courtesy to let me know that they're going to be competing with me for market share."

"You're welcome. What about you? What's your dream?"

"To take over KRT Limited from my father." But he said it with so little conviction that I had a hard time believing him. "It may not happen for a couple more decades, but it's what I've been working toward for a long time." He paused. "It's what Craig wants, too."

"Oh." For Marco to get what he wanted, Craig would have to lose out. I didn't know how I felt about that, and I was surprised that I was having complicated feelings about it. I should want Craig to have what he wanted, right?

"Are you rooting for Craig?" he asked, and I was again surprised by his perceptiveness.

"You seem to know a lot of things about me," I said apologetically, not acknowledging that he was right or that he might be a little bit wrong.

"Like how you would come here today," he agreed.

"What do you mean by that?"

"To speak your language, I formulated a hypothesis about you."

"Which was?" I asked.

"I thought that if I made you curious enough, you'd meet with me to find out what I wanted."

Scoffing, I said, "Most people would have come. Your premise is flawed."

"Most people wouldn't, given the circumstances."

What circumstances? The glittery orange ones? "If I asked you out to lunch, you're telling me you'd say no?"

He leaned in, that weaponized smile of his gleaming at me and making my knees a bit wobbly. "Anna, are you asking me to go to lunch with you?"

"We're already at—" I cut myself off. I was exasperated, and I knew he was messing with me, but his charm was too effective on me. I was worried I was going to say something I'd regret.

Of course, that was one hypothesis I had to prove to be true. "You need to shine that handsome spotlight of yours somewhere else. You're not as charming as you think you are. It's annoying." And my aggravation came not only because I felt defenseless against him but also that he'd used my curiosity against me. That was something that should only be used for good. Like discovering the perfect long-lasting foundation or lipstick that wouldn't smudge.

"Sorry about that. I'll work on improving my charm to meet your exacting standards. But not too much, because I don't want to ruin things between us."

"Ruin them how?"

"I wouldn't want you to fall in love with me."

Of all the arrogant, self-centered, egomaniacal . . . "Ha, I say. Ha."

He shrugged. "You're the one who keeps bringing up how attractive I am."

I opened my mouth to protest and had to shut it again. I couldn't object because it would be a lie. "It's just an objective fact. Like I can see that a Porsche is objectively beautiful, but it's not for me. Too fast, too flashy. I don't want to own a Porsche or go for a ride in one."

"You're saying you want me to give you a ride?"

I couldn't help blushing at his innuendo, and I found myself annoyed again. "I'll take Betty any day."

"Now you're comparing my brother to your death trap?"

"That's not . . . you're missing the point."

His grin let me know that had been on purpose.

"You are the worst," I informed him.

"I am," he agreed cheerfully.

"You also take way too much pleasure out of annoying me."

"I do," he said.

"Stop being so agreeable!" It was hard to be mad at someone who went along with your accusations.

"Sorry," he said in a way that didn't sound at all sorry.

He aggravated me, and I enjoyed him at the same time. I didn't understand the contradiction. "You're the one who said your competitiveness with Craig will make him fall for me. When that happens, aren't you worried your competitiveness will make you want to keep me for yourself?"

"No, I don't think we'll have to worry about that."

Ouch, did that smart. Not that I wanted him to be in love with me, but it still dinged my ego.

He must have seen my expression change, because he hurried to add, "We'll just make it a rule. I know how much you like those. The rule is I won't fall for you and you won't fall for me."

"Done," I said before he'd even finished his sentence. Easiest rule to keep ever.

"Can I tell you a secret?" he asked.

"I think I'm owed one," I responded, especially after everything he knew about me.

He smiled slightly and said, "I'm jealous."

For a single irrational moment, I thought he meant he was jealous that I liked Craig. That he did want me to have feelings for him instead. But I knew that was ridiculous. "Of what?"

"I don't think anyone's ever felt about me the way you do about my brother. I've never had a woman in my life who would do something like this just to be with me."

"Have you ever felt that way about someone?"

"Not even close. I'm not sure I think love even exists."

"Oh, it does," I told him. "I've seen it."

Marco recognized that I was echoing back his joke from earlier about the TV and smiled again.

"Sounds like dating you is a rough proposition," I told him, trying to tease him again, but I felt like I'd failed when his smile flattened out.

"So I've been told." That pain was there in his voice again, and all I wanted to do was hug him and tell him that everything was going to be okay. "But I know I dropped a lot on you today, and I wanted to ask you how you're doing with all of this."

It was considerate of him to ask, but it felt unnecessary. He'd gotten what he wanted from me—he didn't need to try to be my friend, too. "It's fine. I just don't like change, and this is all going to be a really big change."

"But you change things at a chemical level all the time," he said.

"That's different. There are expectations and knowledge there. Predictability."

"There are also surprises that turn out to be amazing. Teflon. Penicillin. Superglue. Plastic. Vaseline. All discovered by accident."

Had he read an article or something? "I know that, and I'm always looking for new combinations and new ingredients, but I have a background and an education. I know what I'm doing and can guess how things will turn out."

"Ah." He said that far too knowingly.

Wait, what was that supposed to mean? Were we back to him thinking I was predictable?

He handed me his phone. "Did you want to add any details to your contact info?"

I wasn't sure what kind of details he wanted. He already knew my number, where I lived, and my name. My email, maybe? I glanced at his screen. "You misspelled my name." I corrected it, added my email, and handed him his phone back.

"Two Ns in Anna?" he asked. "I thought it was short for Anastasia."

I had told him about my real name? I must have been really drunk. "Apparently in kindergarten, I insisted on two Ns instead of one, and my parents thought it was adorable, so it stuck."

He nodded. "I can imagine that you were adorable when you were five."

My heart started to pound in my chest. What kind of compliment was that? And why was I responding to it like he'd just told me I should be Miss Universe?

A car (not a limo) pulled up outside in the parking lot, waiting just beyond the lobby doors.

"That's my ride," Marco said. "Thanks for waiting and keeping an eye on me."

Ha. As if I needed to protect this very muscular and tall man from anyone. He opened the door for me, and it took me a second to move through it. It was like I just wanted to stay there and talk to him instead of going back home.

The cold January air hit me hard, making my eyes sting a little.

I walked over to the waiting car with him, and he opened the back passenger side door. "I appreciate you meeting with me. I don't want to keep you from a busy afternoon of whatever hobby you enjoy. Like maybe collecting spores, molds, and fungus."

He was teasing, but I still sputtered, "I don't collect . . . it was one time for a science fair project in sixth grade, and I won."

At that, he laughed and said, "Good luck getting home in that thing. If you get lost out there on the Oregon Trail, set up a signal fire, and somebody will come and rescue you."

With a wink and a nod, he climbed into the car, and they drove off.

"My car is not a covered wagon!" I yelled after him, but he couldn't hear me.

Marco Kimball was equal parts enjoyable, amusing, vexing, and infuriating.

What had I gotten myself into?

CHAPTER TEN

I drove home, muttering to myself the whole way about dysentery and the buffalo stampedes that I thought should befall Marco on his trip. Oregon Trail. Betty. Making fun of science and my car. Why did that wind me up so much? They were jokes. My reaction made no sense to me. I blamed it on the traumatic events of the last couple of days.

I arrived home quite safely, because Betty was a . . . well, consistent mode of transportation. What she lacked in beauty she more than made up for in reliability. When I got inside, Feather Locklear loudly announced that the Yankees sucked, with my grandfather telling her she was a good, smart girl, that they did suck, and I headed straight up to my room.

The glitter had indeed metastasized and still lay all over my floor, like a shimmering snowstorm that had been localized in my bedroom, but I had to ignore it for now.

I desperately needed Catalina's guidance. I curled up in a ball on my bed, pulled my covers up, and called her. She picked up immediately.

"I cannot believe it has taken you this long to call me back. There should be some kind of friendship fine you have to pay when you leave people hanging like that."

"Hello to you, too," I said.

"There is no time for that!" she said. "I have so many questions. Hang on a second—I need to grab my notebook."

"You took notes?" I asked.

"Yes. Why?" She said this like I was the weird one for asking.

"No reason." I paused. "Do you think I should be taking notes?"

"You're a chemist. I think you know the answer to that."

She was right. I should be taking notes. This whole thing with Marco and Craig wouldn't be much of an experiment if I didn't document all of it.

Catalina kept talking. "Okay, before we get started and you give me every single detail of your encounter with Marco Kimball that apparently lasted for hours, we have to talk about last night. First, I'm sorry I wasn't at the party. You almost died in a hotel bathroom, and I should have been there."

"I didn't almost die," I said. "Not even close. But why didn't you go? It's not like you to miss a work event." Especially given her long-standing crush on Zhen.

"So get this. I was planning on going with Steve as my date. He called last minute and told me he couldn't make it because he wasn't feeling well. I decided to stop by and surprise him with some chicken soup, only I was the one who was surprised when his pregnant girlfriend answered his door."

"Uh-oh. Is he still alive? Is that why you're telling me this? Am I supposed to be your alibi?"

"He's still breathing," she said, her disgruntled tone evident. "But obviously, we're completely over. See? This is why I told you I have to stop dating hot guys. They're all the worst. My abuela keeps telling me that I just have to wait, the right guy will find me, and this is where I end up."

I didn't think it was wise to remind Catalina that she was the one who had pursued Steve. "I'm with your abuela. I kind of hope the right guy does find you, because I got to tell you, it seems like all the wrong ones have built-in infrared homing devices designed to track you down."

"That is unfortunately true. And that's why I'm moving on. I don't believe in waiting for someone. I'm too proactive for that. Zhen is the kind of guy I should be dating."

"You're right," I said. I wondered whether she should take a minute before jumping into another relationship, but given the intensity in her voice, I figured it would not be wise to say anything in that moment.

She continued. "Zhen's smart. And he's cute without being he-will-cheat-on-you hot. And he's such a nice guy."

This I could point out. "He is. Which is why this is doomed. You don't date nice men."

"I do now," she insisted. "No more hot guys and, by extension, no more jerks."

"I'm with you on that one."

"Not if you're in love with Craig still. That guy is the tooliest tool that ever tooled."

"Catalina!" I protested.

"Fine, fine, I'll stop. But it's true. Anyways, that topic isn't actually in my notes. Well, I guess it is a little. Because I want to know why Craig was hitting on you yesterday if he was already engaged."

"I thought you said that it was nothing and I was imagining things that weren't there." She didn't get to have it both ways.

"Regardless of what I may or may not have said while I was trying to protect you and your feelings, there was something going on. He was definitely leaning toward you in an 'I'm interested' kind of way."

"Aha! I knew it!" That gave me hope that I hadn't felt since yesterday, before Craig made his announcement. And it made me think that I'd made the right decision when it came to Marco's plan. If there was a spark there, a tiny bit of fire that could ignite and turn into something bigger, didn't I owe it to myself to do what I could to make that happen?

"But the point is that he was engaged while doing whatever it was he was doing with you."

"I don't—" I stopped for a second because I realized I didn't know when he actually got engaged. Not knowing things was a feeling that I did not enjoy. I assumed he'd gotten engaged at the party, which didn't really seem like an ideal place, but my memory of his words was spotty at best due to the copious amounts of alcohol that were still making me feel achy all over.

Craig and Leighton could have gotten engaged sometime before the party and just made the announcement there. Which could mean that Catalina was right and Craig had been flirting with me while engaged to another woman.

"I don't know the technicalities of the timeframe—"

She cut me off. "There is no technical issue here. Even if he wasn't engaged while he was hitting on you, he was serious enough about someone that he was set to propose to her. Either way, he's a slimeball."

"I—" I tried to say something but couldn't find the right words. What could I say? She wasn't wrong. Either way did not look great for Craig.

And I didn't like that feeling.

I got out of my bed, wanting to pace, but the second I put my feet on the floor, I was met with glitter. I let out a groan.

"What is it?" she asked.

"There's an ocean of glitter on my floor," I said. "It's a long story."

"If it involves Marco, and if you don't tell me everything, I swear by all that is holy that when I die, I will come back and haunt you. And I believe in ghosts, so please know how serious I am when I say that. And before you do anything else—send me a picture. I want to see how that professional photo of him compares to regular life."

"I don't have a picture of him," I said.

"You forget that I have hung out with you when you're drunk. You most definitely have a picture of him on your phone. Check your gallery."

"Hold on." I took my phone away from my ear and opened the app. Sure enough, there were at least a half dozen photos of Marco. I wondered when I had even taken them. Most of them were blurry, but there was one good shot of him that I forwarded to Catalina.

"Sent."

She let out a long string in Spanish that I couldn't interpret. Then she demanded, "Tell me what this delicious man was doing in your messy room, right now. Wait! Before you do that, though—I need to tell you that I did a deep dive on him online."

"And?"

"He dates a lot, and by *a lot* I mean an exponential amount. There are like, a bajillion different photos of him with various model types."

Models, huh? That seemed about right. Sticking with his own kind.

"I tried to look up his social media accounts, but as far as I can tell, he doesn't have any. That seems both sus and refreshing at the same time."

"What does *sus* mean?" I asked.

"Go online once in a while, Anna! It means suspicious. You have accounts, even though you never post. I'm not sure how I feel about this, and I have drawn many possibly incorrect conclusions about him, so now I need you to give me the details."

I tried to shake my feet off, but the glitter was stuck to my soles like glue. Defeated, I got back into bed. I had wanted Catalina's opinion—time to share it all with her.

So I explained how Marco had stopped by unexpectedly, our weird conversation, and then the incident with her self-tanner. "Which, by the way, you should know tends toward orange when you leave it on for too long."

"How did you confuse a mask and self-tanner—you know what? Never mind. I've met you. So now your face was orange and . . ."

"And he invited me out to lunch."

"Yes, as rich CEOs do. What did he do after you turned him down?"

I grimaced slightly. "I didn't turn him down."

There was a long pause on the other end. "You went out with him . . . to eat in public . . . while your face was orange."

"It was a paler orange after I scrubbed it," I said defensively. "Anybody would have gone. You would have. You saw that he's hot."

She seemed to consider this. "I mean, his hotness would definitely be a factor in his favor. But a guy who had seen me at my absolute worst wanting to hang out and talk to me? No thanks. Plus, I would have been too embarrassed to go out in public with residual self-tanner on my face."

This meant Marco was right in his assertion that most people wouldn't have gone to lunch with him. I didn't accept that. "He wouldn't tell me what he wanted to talk about. I had to go."

"And what did he want to talk about?"

"He wants to break up Craig's engagement."

She gasped. "Is he in love with Craig's fiancée?"

"They used to date. Casually," I added, as if Marco himself were saying it. "There might have been cheating involved on her part, but I'm not sure. No, he wants to protect Craig, and he's worried Leighton's after Minx, so he also wants to protect the company."

"Wait. I'm confused. Why would he want you to help out with this? You don't even work at Minx anymore."

That was like a little knife twist in my stomach. "Apparently, Craig and Marco have a terrible rivalry. He thinks if he and I pretend to date, that Craig will want me for himself and break off his relationship."

I half expected an outburst, but to her credit, she didn't laugh. "Holy duck." She hesitated and then asked, "He really thinks you guys pretending to date will make Craig drop his fiancée?"

"Yes."

"Wow. That is some rom-com-level delusion right there," she said. "It's never going to work."

"Marco seems to think it will."

"It's a good thing that man is pretty, because he's obviously not very in touch with reality. I've seen the movies. This sort of thing never works out. If anything, it's only guaranteed to make you fall in love with him."

I pulled my blanket up over my face, glad she couldn't see me. "He made it pretty clear that that won't happen. Not that I would want it to. I'm in love with Craig."

That sounded a little weak, even to my ears.

"This is just some basic math here. I'm calculating some serious trouble ahead for you. It's coming. There's no way you get out of this without catching feelings. Because if you're the dragon Smaug, he's going to be your Dwarven treasure hoard you will want to keep all to yourself."

"That's not true. I like him as a friend. He's easy to talk to—"

"Easy to talk to?" she interrupted me. "The man who has had two assistants quit in the last six months because he's so terse and stern with everyone? He's supposed to be scary."

Scary? Marco? I couldn't imagine it. "He's not like that."

"Maybe not with you. If you had ever plugged in to the office gossip once in a while and talked to someone besides just me, you would know that."

I pushed my blanket down. It was getting hard to breathe, and my glasses were fogging up. "He's nice. Perceptive, kind. Understanding. Smart. Maybe a little ruthless when it comes to breaking up Craig and Leighton. He can be kind of annoying sometimes, too. But I don't know why anyone would say he's scary. He was telling me dumb jokes at lunch."

"Like what?"

I told her the vegan pizza one, and there was another long pause on her end. Then she said, "That's kind of graphic."

Sighing, I responded, "You're not supposed to visualize it. He obviously wasn't being serious or literal. It didn't strike me as graphic, just funny."

"That's because you have the sense of humor of a ten-year-old child. Or a forty-year-old dad. I guess if nothing else, you guys will have your dumb vaudeville comedy routine in common."

I was about to say that wasn't true, but she did kind of have a point. "Dumb or not, it made me smile."

"You like him!" she exclaimed.

I made a face. "I just told you he was nice. Yes, I like him."

"No, I mean you *like* like him. You're attracted to him."

"What? I am not!" I immediately said.

I wasn't the only one not believing the lie. "Anna!"

"Catalina!" I retorted, as strong a comeback as I could manage given the dishonesty.

"You do so. I can hear it in your voice."

"Okay, yes. You saw the picture. He's very handsome. I've been thinking about it, and I figured it out. The reason I find him attractive is because he's Craig's brother. There's got to be a genetic component there that I'm instinctually responding to."

"They're half siblings. They only share twenty-five percent of their DNA. I reject your claim. You want to science up another excuse?"

No, because that was the only one I had. I had grown up believing that there was one perfect person for everybody in the whole world. I rejected the notion that I could be in love with one man and attracted to his brother.

When I didn't respond, Catalina's tone shifted to concerned. "Based on the ancient texts, or every romantic comedy that we've ever watched together, I say again that this is going to blow up in your face. I'm sorry if I keep repeating myself, but I'm worried about you. I don't want you to get your heart broken."

I smiled a little. Catalina was the only person who could call rom-coms "the ancient texts" and sound like it was a real thing people said. "It may not end well, but maybe I'll have some fun in the middle."

"That will be good. You could bookend the tragic ending with the humiliating beginning."

"I hear what you're saying," I told her. "But I'm committed now, so I guess I'm going to see it through."

"This doesn't seem like something you would do, so I'm going to guess that Marco Kimball is a hard man to say no to."

I couldn't help myself. I laughed. She had no idea.

"I'll take that as a yes," she said. "So what now? Am I going to be getting a fake invitation from you inviting me to an imaginary wedding?"

"No, now we're going to go on actual dates as we pretend to fall in love. He thinks it'll help if we spend time together and know stuff about each other."

She agreed. "Definitely. It makes me think he's seen a rom-com or two in his day. You guys absolutely do not want to be answering questions where you give opposite answers. Getting your stories straight is a good idea. I'm against you having real dates, though. You tend to like unobtainable guys, and I don't know if there's anyone more unobtainable than Marco Kimball."

"You think I only like guys who won't like me back?"

"Sometimes I do." She sounded so sympathetic that my heart squeezed painfully in response.

Was that true?

While I wanted to argue with her, I couldn't think of a response to refute it. In my mind, I ran through all the men I'd crushed on and how I hadn't ever had a real relationship. My crushes usually never crushed back on me.

This was new information that I'd never considered before. I felt the need to examine it, test it, and make my judgment after the first two steps. Right now, though, there was too much to process and so I was going to let my subconscious work on it while I talked about other things.

Catalina cleared her throat and, thankfully, kind of changed the subject. "So when is the first date? Besides today, I mean?"

"Your D&D party, actually. Marco agreed that it would be a good idea for us to show up at an event with a bunch of people from Minx so that the word will spread back to Craig."

"Smart, smart," she said thoughtfully. "I'll do what I can to get the word out."

"No." I stopped her. "I mean, yes, tell people Marco and I are dating, but nothing else. Marco didn't want me to tell anyone, but I said telling you was nonnegotiable. In large part because I knew you would figure it out."

"You're right. I would have. And my lips are sealed. I won't tell anyone."

I knew I could trust her. "Thank you."

"Coming to my party as your couple debut . . . that seems significant. Does this mean you're finally going to roll a character?"

"No, thank you." I rolled my eyes. We had had this discussion so many times that I could predict what she'd say next.

You like Lord of the Rings; how can you not like D&D?

"I'll never understand how you can be so obsessed with the Lord of the Rings movies but not want to play D&D."

Okay, so it wasn't verbatim but close enough. "They're not even remotely the same thing. Plus, I prefer being a passive observer rather than an active participant." The truth of that statement struck me—not just about the game but how it was generally true in my life.

It felt depressing. I added, "It's going to be stressful enough without trying to play the game, too."

"I think you'd have fun. But at least you'll be there when my half-elf bard makes a move on Zhen's half-ogre barbarian/paladin."

Her ability to bounce back from a failed relationship never ceased to amaze me. Sometimes I wished I could be more like her and not fall in love with a guy for two years without even really talking to him.

Catalina's way seemed much better.

I reminded myself that I was doing something now—being an actual active participant. I was going to try to win Craig over for myself.

With Marco's help.

Again, I had to wonder how Marco was going to view this party. "A half-elf and a half-ogre, huh? At least it won't be too weird for Marco."

"I think you two will be bringing the weirdness all on your own."

"It's not that weird. Lots of people pretend to date the CEO of their former place of employment in order to get his brother to fall in love with them. Happens every day of the week, I'm sure."

At that, Catalina laughed, and our conversation shifted to what I would wear. She was pushing for something uncomfortable and tight, while I was leaning toward jeans, tennis shoes, and a hoodie.

As we talked and laughed, it occurred to me that while Catalina had been so concerned that I would fall for Marco, not once did she say that she thought Marco would fall for me.

And that bothered me more than it should have.

CHAPTER ELEVEN

The problem with our first official date being two days away was that it gave me plenty of time to overthink and regret my decision. And just how much all of this was not going to work. Catalina was right. It was doomed to fail.

Not only that, but Marco was a bad fake boyfriend. He didn't pretend to text or call me even once.

Okay, he did text once. It was to ask for Catalina's address. I sent it to him and then . . . nothing.

I wanted to text him and say, *Hey, remember me? The woman you're depending on to save your company and your brother?*

Why did I care so much that he hadn't reached out?

It was all disconcerting.

I thought a diabolical plan like ours would have more, I don't know, actual planning. Diabolical or otherwise.

The night of the D&D party, I kept myself busy creating a formulation for a new easy-glide lipstick. Lipsticks had always been my favorite thing to create, given how quickly they could go wrong in so many ways. The powder of eye shadow or blush was often more forgiving. I liked the exactness and precision of lipsticks.

An alarm sounded on my phone, and I realized that I needed to get ready for the party.

Catalina called me a few seconds after, as if she knew I was messing around in my home lab and not getting dressed.

When I picked up, she said, "What are you wearing tonight?"

"I was thinking clothes."

"Anna! Are you wearing sweatpants right now?"

"No." *Yes.*

But she didn't believe my lie. I'd told Marco I was bad at it. "Are you going to change?" she asked.

"Yes." *Maybe.* I liked being comfortable.

"I bet Marco will wear something nice."

"Probably. Because so far, all I've seen him in is a suit, but that seems like overkill for D&D."

"Poor you. I bet his best look is *out* of a suit," she teased.

"I don't know. His suits are pretty fire." I was a fan.

My bedroom door was open, and my grandpa stuck his head in. "Whose suits are on fire?"

"Catalina? I have to go. I'll see you soon."

I heard her call out, "Spit out your gum!"

She knew me too well. I spit my gum into the trash and turned my attention to my grandfather. "No one's suits are on fire. It's just an expression."

"Oh." He blinked behind his spectacles, and it had always reminded me so much of an owl. "I was just reading the newspaper, and there was an article about the death of a local ornithologist."

That made me set my mixing bowl down. "Oh no, was it someone you knew?"

"No. And apparently the police suspect fowl play."

I groaned. Only my grandpa would come upstairs just to tell me that joke. "I love you, but you are the actual worst. You and Dad are the reason I tell dumb jokes."

"Thank you," he said brightly, as if I'd complimented him. "Are you going out tonight?"

Just how long had he been listening at the door? "I am."

"With that Marco fellow?"

This felt very observant for my usually out-of-touch grandfather. "Yes."

He nodded. "He seemed like a nice young man. I liked him. And it was easy to see that he liked you, too. Well, have fun. Don't join any harems."

Huh. I guess he had been listening when I was arguing with my grandma about Marco's intentions. Maybe he was more aware of the household goings-on than I gave him credit for.

Him saying he liked Marco . . . the last guy my grandpa had approved of had been my dad, so his words seemed significant somehow.

But his declaration that Marco liked me? That was easy to ignore. Not true. A grandfather's love making him oblivious to reality.

He whistled as he left my doorway, and I refocused my attention on tonight. I tried to figure out what I should wear. Jeans? I probably should have done laundry over the last couple of days. Instead I'd been online trying to look for a new job. That had forced me to spend time updating my résumé, and Minx was my only professional experience. It had been my first job right out of college.

Again, I missed my lab.

But I wondered if another company would hold it against me that I'd only ever worked at one place.

Although I supposed now I also worked for KRT Limited as a consultant.

The contracts had arrived yesterday, and I signed them as, unlike Marco, I did not personally know any lawyers. I knew I could probably find one, but I figured there weren't many people who were willing to work pro bono on a consulting contract.

I also wanted that money before someone else snatched up my high-shear mixer.

That inspired me to look up the listing again, but when I did, it said the mixer was gone. Someone else had bought it.

My heart deflated like a leaky balloon. That was very disappointing.

I was going to be mourning that mixer for a long time. I had a tendency to do that—to get fixated on something I wanted and if it didn't go the way I'd planned it in my head, then I didn't always cope so well with the outcome.

That loss put me into a fairly bad mood. I really did not want to go out tonight, but I didn't have much of a choice.

I realized that I didn't know anything that was happening this evening other than Marco and I were supposed to go to Catalina's. I texted him.

What's up? When are you getting here?

I didn't know if he was the kind to show up early or if he wanted to arrive late to make a grand entrance. Not having a timeframe was throwing me off.

He replied quickly, saying he was running late because he was stuck in a meeting that didn't look like it would be wrapping up soon.

Can you meet me out front of her house in an hour so that we can go in together?

That made sense. Catalina's home was at the midway point between my grandparents' house and the office. It would be easier for him to meet me there than drive all the way out here to get me and then drive back.

I supposed that when I imagined this night, it was with him picking me up and the two of us arriving together. That felt more date-like, but I tried not to fixate on that initial plan. I'd meet him there. It was fine.

I put my hair up and found a clean-ish outfit on my armchair. Just jeans and a T-shirt that said BEN SOLO DESERVED BETTER and a dark purple hoodie. I wasn't really a dressy kind of person, and this felt about as formal as I'd get. Outside of Arwen dresses anyway. Catalina would probably be excited that I'd changed out of the sweatpants, though.

I wondered if Marco would expect me to dress up.

Too bad for him if he did.

I went back to working on my lipstick until it was time to go. It was a quick drive over, and I realized that I didn't know what Marco's car looked like. I found an empty spot near Catalina's house and parked Betty by the curb.

I texted him to let him know that I'd arrived. There wasn't a reply, and I was trying to figure out how long I should wait.

Your car didn't spontaneously combust? he finally replied, adding a winking emoji. I'm shocked. I'm at a stoplight—I'll be there in a few minutes.

Just as he'd said, a few minutes later he arrived and, on Feather Locklear's life, the man was driving a Porsche.

Some part of me wondered if he'd bought it just to mess with me.

I got out of Betty and walked over to where he'd parked, waving to him. He rolled down the passenger window and very innocently asked me, "Did you want a ride?"

"No thanks," I told him, and he laughed.

There was a jolt when I leaned down to see him properly. Absence had made my heart forget that the guy I was pretending to date was super attractive, and it was annoying that my body kept leaping with excitement every single time I was around him.

"I probably shouldn't invite you to join me. I have a policy of not getting in a car with strange women."

He just thought he was so hilarious, didn't he? "I'm willing to bet you've had a lot of strange women in this car."

Marco laughed as he reached across to the passenger side and opened the door. "Here, get in. See what you're missing out on."

Again, he was hard to resist. I slid into the passenger seat and closed the door behind me. The interior was warm and inviting.

It smelled like him. That delicious, expensive, probably custom-made cologne that would be a sense memory for me for the rest of my life. If I ever smelled this particular combination of . . . light citrus and amber musk and something I couldn't quite put my finger on, I'd always remember him and this moment.

"What do you think?" he asked, and it took me a second to realize he meant the car and not how good he smelled.

"It's very nice," I said begrudgingly. All shiny with a dashboard that looked like the gauges actually worked. Seats made out of leather that were still intact. "I think it's interesting that somehow I intuited you drive a Porsche."

"Psychic?"

"Or you're just really playing to type here," I said.

He smiled again. I took that opportunity to steal a glance at him. Yep, just as handsome as I'd remembered. Especially with that five-o'clock shadow on his jaw. Just a bit of roughness in the overall image of a cool, polished, collected man. He made me feel severely underdressed even though we were wearing literally the same thing—jeans and a T-shirt. It was refreshing to know that he did own something besides suits. But even in his casual wear, he looked like a model who would be paid a fortune just to stand around and look pretty, and I was wearing wrinkled clothes from my bedroom floor.

As if he sensed my thoughts, he said, "You look nice."

"Wow. You are a good liar." Even though he'd said it in a way that made me believe him. "And you look just terrible."

He laughed again, and I found that I really enjoyed the sound. How was this the guy people were scared of at Minx?

"Ben Solo deserved better?" he asked, looking at my shirt. "What is that supposed to mean?"

"Well, first, have you seen the sequel Star Wars trilogy? Because that's going to change how I explain it."

"Of course. Hasn't everyone?"

"There are so many reasons Ben Solo should have lived—"

"Wait," he interrupted. "He was the villain. The only way he could have paid for his sins was by dying."

"Says you and every man on the internet," I said. It was an argument I'd heard ad nauseam, and it was wrong. Not that I could make myself heard in the midst of online fandom fights, given that the Star Wars fandom (especially the menaces) were not kind to female fans. "No, he didn't need to die. If you'd read the canon comics, you would know that he was abused and tortured his entire life by Snoke/Palpatine. The kid never even had a chance. And even then, he still felt continually pulled to the light. All the main characters from the original trilogy, Han, Luke, Leia, his loved ones, wanted him back. They wanted him to live. And they all sacrificed themselves so that he could survive. Not to mention that he was part of a dyad, that Rey was his literal soul mate, and as the heroine, the girl who wanted a family more than anything, she should have been given her Disney prince. The first one to die after love's true kiss, by the way. People don't have to die to atone for their sins. He was the last Skywalker. He came back to the light. He should have lived."

Marco was grinning at me, like he was enjoying my rant. "I'm guessing you didn't care for the last movie?"

"I did a lot of handwaving and loud groaning. I felt personally attacked. When it ended, I actually looked behind me to see if there was an issue with the camera, because surely the movie couldn't have ended with him being dead." I let out a big sigh. "Anyway, thank you for coming to my TED Talk."

"It was very good. And all the things you brought up—I guess I never thought of it that way. You've won me over. He did deserve better. You are very passionate about this. That's good. Craig will like that."

Saying Craig's name was like Marco had just poured a bucket of ice-cold water over my head. Why was it such a shock? Had I just been really caught up in what I'd been saying, and being reminded what we were here for caught me off guard? That made a certain kind of sense.

It wasn't the reason, though.

Once again, I'd forgotten about Craig and had been enjoying my time with Marco. I looked out of the car window at Catalina's house. Now we were about to go into this party and had to convince a room full of questioning, observant scientists that we were a real couple.

It suddenly seemed impossible and overwhelming.

He asked, "Is there anything else I should know about you before we go inside? Any big surprises?"

Did I have any secrets left? I felt like he knew almost everything about me. "I think we've cleared out all the skeletons in my closet."

"In your case, it's half-elves in your closet. Are you sure I'm not going to find a Ben Solo life-size cutout in there, too?"

"No! That's a more recent obsession, and obviously I'm a grown woman so I can't go out and buy that."

"I could buy it for you."

"That's . . . interesting. I mean, no. I don't need that. I'm an adult."

"Enjoy the things you enjoy, Anna. Don't let other people make you feel bad about it."

That made a strange lump appear in my throat, and I shifted my gaze away from his. I glanced down and saw a tiny piece of glitter next to his stick shift. I pointed it out, and he nodded. He said, "I'm still finding glitter in weird places."

"Same. Plus, I'm pretty sure they've started a colony in my car." I reached out to touch it, and it stuck to my finger. Which was a little jittery at the moment.

"Are you nervous?" he asked.

"Yes."

He leaned toward me, like he was going to do . . . something, but he didn't. "Don't worry. I'm here. You have my sword."

A line from Lord of the Rings. "And your axe?"

Marco gave me a funny look, and I realized that he'd misheard me.

"Axe," I repeated, emphasizing the X sound. "I said axe. Although your, you know, is nice, too. Not that I've been looking!" How did I keep making this worse? "It's just . . . I have eyes and you—I'm going to shut up now."

He gave me that smile, the kind men like him had, where they knew exactly the effect they had on women. I wanted to hate this about him but found that I couldn't. It was almost . . . endearing? Which made no sense, because it was basically arrogance and I'd always hated arrogance.

"It will be okay," he said.

"I don't know. At the moment it feels a little like somewhere out there, a hobbit is carrying a ring to a volcano."

"Things aren't that bad. Tell me about the people at the party. What should I know?"

It was a good distraction, and I wondered if he had done it deliberately. "Okay, so Sanjit should be there. He's really competitive and spends most of their D&D games yelling about the game being rigged and/or the dice being loaded. Catalina is . . . Catalina." How could I describe my best friend in a couple of sentences? But he didn't press me to explain. "There are some self-righteous trolls who you can just ignore. There's Peter—he always comes. He's really quiet, but he is scary smart. A lot of the guys there are just like him. Shy but brilliant. Dorks of a feather flocking together and all that."

"How do you know so much if you don't go to the parties?" he asked.

"I've gone to a couple." I'd sat in the corner alone and just watched the whole night, but I'd shown up and supported my friend. "And Catalina is an 'every detail' kind of friend. She tells me everything about her merry band of nerds."

"You're making them sound a little stereotypical," he said.

"Says the rich, charming CEO to the geeky, awkward scientist."

"You're so much more than a stereotype, Anna." There was something about the way he said it—something special that pierced my heart. My pulse quickened.

Instead of responding to his declaration, I kept going as if he hadn't spoken. "Zhen will definitely show up. Catalina's had a crush on him for a long time. But don't say anything about that!"

"Not a word," he promised.

"Good. I'm pretty sure he likes Catalina, too. He has a half-ogre character that he rolled entirely to impress her. I guess you could say he's head ogre heels."

"Or that he's an ogre achiever," Marco added.

I couldn't help but smile back and realized that I no longer felt quite so anxious. "Anyway, his half-ogre character is supposed to be part barbarian, part paladin even though everyone keeps telling him he can't do that. He says he's pushing boundaries, and Catalina lets him because she thinks he's cute."

"Two classes? That makes no sense. Their alignments alone would be all wrong. You'd have lawful good and chaotic neutral at best, and that's not even talking about the armor. One wears plate and the other leather." He said this without thinking, an automatic response to my statement.

"Is that right?" I gasped with delight. "That is the second nerd reference you've made in the last five minutes. Marco Kimball, are you a secret nerd?"

He looked uncomfortable. "We should go inside."

"Wait, I have to know what you're into. Like are you a Magic: The Gathering type of guy? Into Pokémon? Avatar? *The Last Airbender* or the blue-guys one? Or both?"

He grabbed his keys and got out of the car, slamming his door shut.

I scrambled out after him. "*Star Trek*? *BattleBots*? *World of Warcraft*?"

"I may have dabbled in some things when I was younger."

"Like?" I felt almost giddy. No way would I have ever predicted this. It was too much fun to think that Marco might speak the same language as me. "Please tell me it was YA fantasy." I would one hundred percent die if Marco was a secret *Twilight* fan. Hadn't he just told me to enjoy what I enjoyed? Why wouldn't he say what he liked?

But he didn't answer, and my mind was totally racing with possibilities. There was something there—I just didn't know what yet. But I was not the kind of person to leave a mystery unsolved.

We got to Catalina's doorstep, and my mood shifted. This was it. I was about to see a bunch of people I used to work with. I wondered if it would be embarrassing—if Jerry had been bad-mouthing me since I left and everyone would stare. It had been only a few days since I'd quit—maybe it would just feel normal and I was overthinking this.

"Are you going to knock?" Marco asked.

"Give me a second."

There was a loud popping sound—he was cracking his knuckles, and I felt it at the base of my spine.

"Could you please not?" I asked. "I really, really hate that sound. Knuckle cracking, popping, whatever it is, makes me nuts."

"Sure."

He waited a few moments and then said, "You really think I look terrible?" He was teasing, and I wondered if there was any real insecurity behind his ask or if he was just trying to distract me again. "I am about to meet your best friend."

Catalina was going to love him. So much so that I might have to run interference because she probably shouldn't date the CEO of her company. Whatever he said about nonfraternization rules, I couldn't imagine that would be a good situation for either one of them.

And there was absolutely no jealousy involved whatsoever. At. All.

"You do look nice, but you already knew that." Maybe he needed a little something extra. "And you really do have a nice axe. I wasn't kidding about that earlier." There. Good deed done for the day. Reminded the handsome man that he was handsome.

"Back at you." He winked.

Did he really think that? Part of me was tempted to crane my head over my shoulder to see how my butt looked in these jeans to verify what he'd said. Although he'd probably just returned the compliment to be nice.

I hated that I couldn't tell the difference. "This is hard to admit, but I'm going to need your guidance here. I've never fake dated anyone before."

"Neither have I."

"I think of the two of us, you probably have the, um, more colorful dating history."

"Just what are you insinuating?" he asked jokingly.

"Nothing. Only that you might have more knowledge in this particular area."

"I haven't dated that many women."

I laughed. I couldn't help myself. "We must collect data and arrive at logical conclusions differently."

"Very funny. I'll take the lead here. But if there's a Lord of the Rings movie trivia challenge, I'm going to depend on your skill set."

I blinked a couple of times at him. "I know you're joking, but do you think something like that exists?"

"You never know. I'm curious, though. Do you think there's a lady of the rings?"

"Galadriel," I said immediately.

"It was a joke," he told me.

"Yeah, I don't joke about Lord of the Rings."

"Understood," he said. "By the way, we have been standing on the porch for an uncomfortably long amount of time."

"I know, I know. Do you have any gum?" That would make me feel calmer.

"No. Why? Did you need fresh breath for something?" Again with that smolder and sexy smile of his. This man was going to be the death of my ovaries.

"I chew it when I'm nervous. Or to help me concentrate. Some of my best work has been done while chewing gum."

"Sorry," he said. "Shall we?"

"Okay." I nodded.

Then he reached down and took my hand in his.

CHAPTER TWELVE

I jerked my hand back so fast that I smacked myself in the mouth. "Ow!"

"You can't keep jumping every time I touch you." He sounded frustrated, and I couldn't blame him. I knew my reactions weren't typical. "And now you're injuring yourself."

"I'm sorry," I said, although I wasn't sure why I was apologizing to him. I was the one with a sore lip. "It just surprised me."

"No one's ever going to believe that we're together if we can't touch each other, least of all Craig. One step at a time. Deep breath. That's why we're here. To practice and get to know each other. I'm going to hold your hand. Don't punch me or yourself, okay?"

"Okay," I agreed. I tried to breathe in deeply, but then I would just smell him, and I was pretty sure that was going to make everything worse.

He took my right hand in his left one, and I willed myself to feel nothing. To be oblivious to him and whatever pheromones he secreted that were currently taking up residence in my hypothalamus. Again it was like being struck by an electrical charge big enough to power a city. He was warm and strong, and the touch of his skin against mine made me feel faint.

Definitely not typical. I should probably date more.

"Are you good?" he asked.

At first I wanted to laugh, to tell him that I might never feel like myself again. Then I wanted to ask him if he felt it, too, that connection between us, but I knew he didn't, and I couldn't stand to see a pitying look in his eyes.

I could take a lot of things from Marco, but not his pity.

"I'm fine." I half expected him to call me out on it, but he didn't.

"Hey, what did one proton say to the other?"

What? I wasn't sure why he would ask me that, but my physical reaction was admittedly messing with my ability to think clearly. Talking protons?

"Stay positive," he said.

His dumb joke should have calmed me down, but I was pretty sure that I might never be calm again if he kept touching me. "My dad used to do that. He was an environmental scientist, too. He was one of my grandma's graduate students. He told me science jokes all the time."

Marco smiled. "I had a grandpa who cared about me. He liked those kinds of jokes, too."

I knew he was trying to make me relax, and under normal circumstances it might have worked, but these were not normal circumstances.

He reached up and knocked on the door, which was good because I currently felt like I was holding on to a live wire that was going to electrocute me at any moment and there was no way I could have knocked. My right arm actually felt numb. Was that the heart attack arm? I couldn't remember.

Because my entire brain was scrambled, and all he was doing was holding my hand.

Good Baby Yoda, I was in trouble.

Catalina opened the door with a big smile on her face. Her expression changed to one of complete shock before she got ahold of herself and, smiling again, said, "You made it! Welcome! Come on in!"

She stepped back to let us inside. Marco waited for me to enter first, and it was really odd to be pulling this giant of a man in after me. I told myself to think of it as passing through a portal and that I had to keep our hands linked.

Maybe if I thought of our hand-holding as some kind of safety tether instead of one of the greatest yet scariest things that had ever happened to me, things would feel better.

Instead, my hand was starting to sweat profusely. He was going to let go, and there would be a puddle of sweat that was going to form on the floor between us.

"I'm Marco." He introduced himself to my best friend, and I felt stupid for not jumping in right away. I should have made those introductions. Maybe I would have been more up on my social graces if I wasn't so busy trying to keep the molecules in my skin from spontaneously combusting.

"Catalina," she said. He offered his right hand, but she said, "Oh, I'm a hugger!" Marco released me to hug my best friend, and I tried to secretly rub my palm on the back of my jeans so no one would know that I'd been in danger of drowning Marco with my hand sweat. She hugged him for a bit longer than what might have been considered typical and then said, "Nice to meet you. I like you already."

She had to start things off by embarrassing me. I should have known.

"I'm assuming that means someone's been talking me up?" His sly smirk was aggravating.

"All good things," she assured him. "Can I get you two something to drink? Some of the guys are rolling new characters in the dining room, so we haven't started yet."

There were some people sitting at the dining room table, which was where they usually played their game. Other guests were standing around talking, eating the snacks that Catalina had provided.

Zhen passed by, and Catalina grabbed him by the arm like he was a life preserver. "Zhen, this is Marco, our boss. I'm going to get them a drink. I'll be right back."

I folded my arms across my chest so that no one would touch my somehow-still-sweaty hands ever again. "Zhen, good to see you."

He smiled at me but was still giving Marco a fair amount of side-eye. I guessed he probably hadn't been expecting the CEO of his company to show up to their bimonthly game. "You too, Anna."

"How's work?" I asked.

"Same old. We do have a lot more to do—I don't think anyone realized how many projects you handled solo. You have big shoes to fill."

It was an expression, I reminded myself. He wasn't making fun of my size-twelve shoes, but I did notice Marco glancing down in my general shoe area. He was about to make a joke about my feet, wasn't he?

"Thanks," I said to Zhen.

"Yeah. Hey, are you guys creating a new character tonight before we start?"

"I'm not," I said.

"I'd like to," Marco responded, surprising me. "It seems like the kind of thing a boyfriend would do. Roll a character to participate in his girlfriend's best friend's game."

I had an internal freak-out at his casual use of the word *girlfriend.* Like, obviously that was the plan, but I felt unprepared for its usage.

My former coworker didn't seem to notice how stilted Marco's declaration was. Instead, Zhen's eyes had gone wide, and he glanced back and forth between us like he was trying to solve a particularly difficult equation that just wasn't adding up for him.

I understood.

He cleared his throat and said, "Come on over and join us. We'll get you set up. Good seeing you, Anna." He left, and Marco was still looking down at the floor.

I said, "They're smaller than yours. By a lot."

"What?"

"My feet."

"What about your feet?" he asked, the picture of innocence.

"You were—never mind." It wasn't worth arguing about if he was going to play dumb. Or maybe I was making mountains out of molehills again.

"I'm going to go make a character. Will you be okay on your own?"

Aw. It was sweet of him to ask. I mean, most men would have assumed that I'd be fine, considering I was at a party surrounded mostly by people I knew. But Marco seemed to get it. "Yes."

"I'll be back," he promised. Then he paused and got that wolfish grin that let me know he was up to no good. "It's a good thing to know which fairy tale you wouldn't be the star of."

There it was. That was a Cinderella jab. I wanted to run my sweaty palm all over his stupid face. Well, his face wasn't stupid. It was gorgeous. But the principle still stood.

Yes, I had big feet, but I could be Cinderella! I was in love with a prince! Well, a millionaire, and in this day and age, wasn't that basically the same thing?

I could be the princess in my own love story. I mean, I didn't need a prince to rescue me. It was coincidental that Craig had money. I did want the fairy tale, though. The happily-ever-after aspect. I knew it could happen. Like it had for my parents.

He left, and all I wanted to do was find a place to hibernate for the rest of the evening. I wished I had an escape hatch, but leaving would defeat the entire purpose of coming here in the first place.

Catalina had a little nook / window seat in her living room, and I headed over to sit. I settled onto the cushion and looked at the windows. They were painted shut. Which was probably a good thing so that I wouldn't consider using them to make a potential getaway.

I flexed my right hand because it was literally still tingling from where Marco had touched me. Like some kind of phantom imprint that I couldn't shake off. Real but not real.

This was the first night. The. First. Night. How was I going to keep this ruse up for any length of time?

I currently did not have a single drop of alcohol in me, but even I had to admit that I was attracted to Marco. I tried reminding my hormones that I loved Craig, but they did not care.

I was a victim of my own biochemistry, and my hormones were trying very hard to stage a coup against my brain.

Catalina came over with the drinks. She handed me one, looked around to find Marco, and then apparently made an executive decision to keep his drink for herself. She squeezed onto the window seat next to me, her legs pressing against mine.

"First, Anna, are you ducking kidding me? Why didn't you tell me how tall he is?"

It was a fair question. It seemed like the first thing I should have mentioned—I always noticed how tall people were. I wondered if people of average height did the same thing.

Then again, maybe there was a reason I hadn't. Because I didn't want to think of Marco as a viable romantic interest. This was an arrangement, nothing more.

I didn't want it to be more. I wanted Craig.

"How tall do you think he is?" she went on, oblivious to my internal train of thought. "Six four? Six five?"

"Easily."

"I'd let him put me in his pocket," she said with a sigh.

"You might actually fit." I took a long drink and then spit it back into the cup when I realized it was just straight vodka. I did not need to be drunk tonight and knew it would take very little to get me there.

"Why are his shoulders so broad? How does he fit through doorways? Does he have to turn sideways?" she asked. "How many organs do you think he's carrying around in that massive chest? Three hearts? Two stomachs? And why is he so strong looking?"

"He does have more muscles in his left arm than I have in my entire body," I agreed with her.

"How am I supposed to feed a man that size? All I have are some chips and a vegetable tray. What does someone like him eat? Two cows?"

"So far he's eaten a regular amount. Nobody had to butcher extra animals for him," I said.

"If you didn't already like him, I would take that man down with all due disrespect."

A flash of jealousy made it hard to breathe for a second. "I don't like him."

She waved her hand. "Oh, you do. You've just convinced yourself that you're in love with that anthropomorphic bran muffin Craig." Her eyes widened, and she held her cup up. "Sorry. I'm a little tipsy. I didn't mean that."

I was pretty sure she did.

She continued. "It's just that Marco is will-cheat-on-you hot. He should be inducted into the Hall of Fine. If I had a butt like his, I would walk backward into every room." She let out a big breath as she finished listing all the ways that he was hot. "I don't know how you're supposed to resist that."

I didn't tell her that I'd been sitting in this nook worrying about the very same thing. "Shouldn't you be telling me to stay clear of him, then?"

"I'd never deprive you of the experience," she said. "Hugging him is like hugging a sexy statue. Have you hugged him?"

"No."

Her eyes got big. "That is bad." She reached into her back pocket and pulled out her phone. She messed with the screen for a moment and then handed it to me. It was a movie clip. I recognized it as being from *The Proposal.*

"Such a great movie," I said. "They don't really make them like this anymore."

"That's not the important part. Watch this scene."

It was the one where the enthusiastic grandmother had the main couple, who were pretending to date, kiss under mistletoe.

"Do you see that?" Catalina asked. "The awkwardness? The secondhand embarrassment you get from watching two people who've never kissed before? If you really want Craig to believe that you're together, he'll never believe it if you kiss Marco like this."

To be fair, the kiss did get better when the two leads both realized that they were enjoying it, but that was beside the point. Catalina and Marco were both right about Marco and me spending time together.

Touching.

Possibly kissing.

My face flushed at the thought.

"You can't be uncomfortable with each other," she said. "You have to hug him and hold his hand and do other stuff," she instructed me. "Definitely kiss the man before some rogue mistletoe or nefarious matchmaker exposes you. If you're going to commit to your lie, you might as well be all in."

"And just how far do you think I should take this?"

She took another drink and then giggled at whatever she was imagining. "I mean, if it were me, I'd run that ball all the way into the end zone."

I frowned at her. "You know I don't do sports references."

"You do what you feel comfortable with. But you can't act like strangers."

"He said the same thing earlier."

"See? I knew I liked him already. He really is great. You're living the romantic-comedy dream, my friend."

Except there was nothing remotely romantic happening, and the only comedy so far had been me awkwardly embarrassing myself at every turn.

She finished off her drink and handed me the empty cup. "I'm going to the bathroom. I'll be back in a minute."

I stuck her plastic cup under my own and then set both down on a nearby end table.

Marco sat with the group at the dining room table, and the entire scene happening in front of me was surprising. I had thought he would feel uncomfortable at the party. He was so different than everyone else around him, but he was sitting in their midst, and whatever he was saying, he had the rest of them literally sitting on the edge of their seats. If Sanjit scooted forward any farther, he was going to fall on the floor.

Then Marco said something that made the entire group break into laughter, and I wanted so badly to know what he was saying.

I remembered how he'd said I was easy to talk to. It also seemed that it was easy for him to chat with a bunch of strangers, but that was beside the point at the moment. His declaration that I was easy and nonthreatening was right—men always saw me as their buddy. The buddy who would help them with their science homework. I wasn't ever the girl they asked to the dance.

And here I'd gone and put myself in that position again. Marco had said he was too old for homework, but there was work he couldn't get done without me. Another group project where I had to do all the heavy lifting. Marco was obviously helping, but it wouldn't affect him the same way it had affected me. He didn't have any feelings for anyone involved, so he wasn't the one being hurt by having to pretend to like one man while in love with another.

Catalina joined the group a couple of minutes later and made a beeline for Marco. They were talking, and he had focused his attention from the rest of the group to her. He said something to make her laugh. She threw her head back as she laughed and touched his forearm.

Jealousy. Bright, red, sharp, flaring to life inside me.

How could I be jealous of my best friend? *You're being ridiculous,* I told myself. There was nothing to be jealous about. She was just being friendly. And if he wanted to date her, he could. I didn't have any claim on him.

My heart apparently didn't get the message, because it lifted immediately when he got up from the group and came over to stand in front of me.

"Can I join you?" he asked.

"Sure." I should have said no. There was no room, but my traitorous mouth had spoken before I'd gotten the chance to shut it down.

He accepted the invitation. It had been a tight squeeze with Catalina, and she was the size of a pixie. A giant beast of a man like Marco? He had to press up intimately against my side, squishing us both.

I found that I didn't care, though. Some part of me felt victorious, like I'd just won something.

The rest of me was luxuriating in the feel of him, all tall and strong and warm. There were tiny fizzies that started in my gut and grew in size as they spread until my entire body felt like one giant tingling nerve.

I was having a hard time breathing steadily.

He seemed unaffected, though.

I needed to talk, a distraction so that I'd stop fixating on him next to me.

"You guys aren't playing yet?" I asked, my voice sounding uneven. At least it was a valid question. It seemed to be taking a longer amount of time than I was accustomed to for them to start.

"Zhen is fighting with the group over his two-class character. Catalina's the only one on his side, so they're not starting until they come to an agreement. There may not be one, as far as I can tell."

There was a long pause, but it wasn't uncomfortable. I was just too aware of him. I started reciting the major laws of chemistry in my head so that I would stop thinking about him next to me. Conservation of mass. Dalton's law. Faraday's law. The second law of thermodynamics . . .

Whoops. That one made me think of Marco in my room and had me focusing on him being so close.

He spoke, and I was grateful for the interruption.

"Gum?" he asked, offering me a stick.

"You got me gum?" I asked, my breathing getting more labored as my heart fluttered up in my chest. It was such a sweet gesture that I felt a little overwhelmed.

"Yes. You said it would make tonight easier for you."

I took the silver-wrapped gum from his hand, doing my best to not touch fingertips again, which was stupid given how close we were pressed together.

For just a second, I let myself imagine what it would be like if he kissed me. I figured it might be like a nuclear bomb exploding.

I didn't think I could handle that kind of detonation.

Shaking off that impossible fantasy, I focused on the gum, slowly unwrapping it. I wanted this. Not the gum, but a man who was considerate and thoughtful and easy to spend time with.

I was determined to get it. "I can have the fairy tale."

He looked at the gum as I put it in my mouth and then back at me. "You lost me."

"Earlier. When you said I couldn't be Cinderella? I can have that. I can find my perfect person and fall in love and have my own makeup kingdom and live happily ever after."

His expression was odd, like he wasn't convinced. "Have you been sitting over here thinking about this the whole time?"

Other than the parts where Catalina and I were waxing poetic over his physique? Sort of. "I even have woodland creatures living in my home. All they do now is swear and eat and poop, but maybe I could train them to help me clean. But that's not even the point! I can have true love and a happy marriage."

He frowned briefly in disbelief. "You might have lost me there. A happy marriage really is a fairy tale."

"That's not true," I protested. "I've seen it. My parents were so in love and deliriously happy. My grandparents were made for each other. It's real."

"My father has never been faithful to a single woman. When he married Tracie, she was already pregnant with Craig. They had been having an affair the whole last year of my mother's life. He's cheating on Tracie now, but she stays for the perks. Marriage is a transaction of two people who usually end up hating each other."

"And what? You think all marriages are like that? They're not."

Marco kept his gaze fixed on the arguing group, Zhen's voice carrying over to us. Then Marco said, "I don't want to end up like my father."

"Then don't be like him," I said.

He turned back to look at me, and the intensity there was shocking. I felt the burn of his look deep in my gut. "Do you think it's really that easy? Don't you think we're doomed to repeat the mistakes of our parents?"

"No. Aren't we supposed to be trying to do better than the generations before us? Fix their mistakes, don't pass along their trauma? Give ourselves the best possible shot at life? If your dad is a terrible husband, then you can be better than him. Be committed."

He didn't say anything, and that only made me feel compelled to keep talking. "My grandma—she became an environmental scientist in a time when not a lot of women were doing that. She had to be tough and serious. Kept people at arm's length, including her loved ones. But my mom was softer and more open. I want to be the same way." I wasn't doing a great job of it so far, though. I needed to be better about letting my walls down.

He seemed to take in what I was saying. Zhen yelled something that had Sanjit yelling back at him. After Catalina got the two men calmed down, Marco looked at me again.

"I wasn't trying to upset you earlier. I tend to tease the women in my life."

"Maybe that's why they don't date you for very long," I offered with a wry smile. "As I just demonstrated, I'm usually the teasing kind, too. I don't know what's going on with me or why I'm being so prickly and putting up walls."

"We're friends, aren't we?" he asked.

"Yes." And as friends, we should be allowed to give each other some grief. I was taking everything far too seriously.

Somehow he managed to move closer to me, putting his arm behind me so that he could lean in. My throat closed in completely as the air in my lungs solidified. What was he doing?

He looked down at my lips, then back up to my eyes. "I know you're going to have your happily ever after, Anna. I don't doubt that for a second."

The air inside my lungs turned solid as I realized what was happening.

Marco was going to kiss me.

CHAPTER THIRTEEN

Right here, in front of a bunch of people I used to work with.

Okay. Don't freak out, I told myself. We should be practicing. This was fine. It probably would look like just a regular old couple about to share an average everyday kiss. Like we did all the time.

Only this one wouldn't mean anything, and nobody else was supposed to know that.

I probably should have let my eyes close, but I wanted to see what was happening.

I could feel myself overanalyzing and calculating and trying to figure out how I could let this happen and not lose myself completely to his touch.

But oh, his eyes were mesmerizing. Dark pools of chocolate that I wanted to dive into and live in. Something shifted between us, that electricity arcing to life and making the air around us crackle with excitement.

"Anna." He murmured my name, his lips moving closer to mine. Somehow the entire space-time continuum stopped. My heart beat quickly at first, then slow and hard. I kept telling myself I could do this. I could kiss him and not lose total control.

But every nerve ending, every hormone, every cell in my body was telling me that that was a complete and utter lie.

I also found that I didn't care. I didn't care what the reasons were behind it or whether or not I'd be able to dismiss it afterward. In that moment, the only thing I cared about was it happening.

"Marco! Marco!"

Someone was calling his name, and it was like a lightsaber cutting through that electricity between us. I jerked back, hitting my head against the wall behind me. I reached up to touch the back of my skull.

Marco looked concerned. "Are you okay?"

New rule I was going to follow—no more injuring myself around this man. It was getting embarrassing.

"I'm fine. Totally fine." I didn't know if I would ever be fine again.

Zhen called out, "Marco!"

Could they not see him? How? The man was so tall, he took up half the room. It was like I was giving off some kind of invisibility radius that shielded him from view.

Annoyed, I responded, "Polo!"

That made Marco laugh, and Zhen came over with his phone out. "Hey, I wanted to grab a picture of the group for the 'gram."

I should have been given a medal for not rolling my eyes. Was it really so hard to say Instagram? Had he saved time by omitting two syllables, or was he somehow cooler because he'd used the term?

"Sure thing." Marco got up, and it felt like he was being peeled away from me bit by bit and when he was standing up, there was a void there, an ache. I wanted him back where he had been.

That was alarming.

They formed a large group, putting their arms around each other's shoulders, and I waited for someone to remember I was there and ask me to take the picture.

Marco looked over his shoulder. "Anna, come join in." He had Peter move and then waved me over.

I got up and walked toward him, standing in the spot he'd indicated.

"Everybody squeeze in," he instructed, holding up Zhen's phone to get the whole group in the picture.

I moved closer toward him, Peter on my other side. Marco put his arm around my waist and pulled me in tight so that I was against him. Sitting next to him in that nook must have desensitized me, because I didn't feel like I was going to pass out just because his hand was on my waist, so that was good.

My pulse still beat erratically, though.

"Everyone say 'iron golem'!" Marco said, and we all said it while smiling. He took a couple of pictures and then handed the phone back to Zhen. Everybody else started walking back toward the dining room, but we stayed put.

Zhen asked, "Are you coming?"

"We're just going to hang out here for a little while," Marco said. "Thanks."

I didn't want him to feel like he had to babysit me or something. I was more than okay with being alone. "You can go."

His arm was still around me, and he squeezed me gently. "What kind of boyfriend would I be if I abandoned you at a party? We can hang out."

"Okay." The word slipped out. I did want him to stay, and that was very unlike me.

But I stepped out of his embrace and directed him to the couch. My body whimpered at the idea that he wasn't going to be holding it any longer, but I ignored that feeling. I sat down, and he sat next to me, close. I was both excited and worried at the same time. He wasn't touching me, but close enough that if either one of us shifted even slightly, we would be.

Catalina sat at the head of the table in her role as the dungeon master, announced it was time to start, and everyone gathered around her.

"Probably not the kind of dungeon you're used to, huh?" I wanted to slap a hand over my mouth. Why did I say things like that?

He grinned. "What kind of stuff do you think I'm into?"

"I don't know," I said, wishing I could take it all back. "I haven't thought about it."

He put his arm on the back of the couch, again almost touching but not, and leaned in. He asked in a low voice, "Haven't you?"

What was he doing? He couldn't be flirting with me for the benefit of the class, because nobody was paying us any attention. Was it that practicing thing he'd mentioned? To get us ready for our big reveal with his brother?

Who probably wasn't going to believe any of this anyway?

"I have a hard time imagining that you and Craig are so competitive that dating me will automatically make him interested."

That made Marco pull his head back, and he looked a little sad. "It's true. We used to be close. We were both raised by nannies, and he was my whole world. I loved him, and he loved me. That continued for years—anything I wanted to do, Craig was there with me. He was practically my shadow. And it stayed that way until I was fourteen."

The pain in his voice was hard to listen to. "What happened when you were fourteen?"

"Tracie convinced my dad to send me off to boarding school. That was the beginning of the end. I tried calling Craig, but he was never around to take my call. I sent letters but never heard back. Tracie and Dad were always traveling during the holidays, so I didn't get to go home and see him. After I graduated and moved back for the summer, everything had changed. He was a totally different person than the kid I remembered. He'd taken over my room, and all my stuff was packed away, like I hadn't ever lived there. I kept trying to get him to hang out with me, but he wouldn't even talk to me. One of the housekeepers told me that Tracie would constantly tell Craig how terrible I was, that

I had to be sent away, and how he was so much better than me. That I had hated him and resented him. She ruined everything that we'd had."

I couldn't help myself. I put my hand on his forearm. I ignored the way my fingers tingled and just wished I could help him. "That must have been so hard."

"It was. I went off to Harvard and tried to stay in touch, but if I did hear from him, it was to brag about his grades or his extracurriculars. Or how he was spending time with Dad."

That didn't sound at all like Craig. I had a hard time believing it.

But why would Marco lie about it?

"Everyone came up for my college graduation. I had been dating a girl who was a couple of years younger than me, and Craig spent the entire time winning her over. He succeeded. He can be charming when he wants to be. Same thing happened with Leighton. Anyway, that's why I know this will work. Because it already has."

That was . . . awful. There had to be some kind of mistake. Or misunderstanding.

"Do you hate your brother?" I asked.

"No. I could never hate him. I love him. I still want good things for him. I'll always see my little buddy when I look at him."

I squeezed his arm and briefly registered just how strong he was and how he could probably bench-press cars with those forearms.

"You're one of those good things, Anna. He'd be lucky to have you." That tone of sincerity, that emotion, those dark brown eyes, made it hard to not react the way my lady parts wanted me to.

So that I wouldn't plaster myself against his lips like one of those face-huggers from the movie *Alien*, I lifted my hand and shifted away.

Now he was the one who seemed uncomfortable. He turned his body forward and cleared his throat, folding his hands in his lap. "Well, consultant, what do you think is the future of makeup?"

This was the only thing he could have asked me about (besides Ben Solo) that would have made me not shut up. "Neurocosmetics."

He nodded. "I've read a bit about it, but I'm not very familiar with the concept."

Honestly, that wasn't surprising. In some ways, Minx was leading the industry with its commitment to organic, nontoxic, and environmentally conscious makeup, but in others, it didn't seem to be paying attention to trends at all.

"The types of ingredients that are used in neurocosmetics are focusing on the fact that nerve endings in our skin are sensitive to certain kinds of stimuli. Those nerves and neuron cells in the skin are, obviously, connected to our brain. We know that there are heightened feelings that can mess with the skin."

"Like when I say something that embarrasses you, how your cheeks turn pink?"

It was literally happening right now. My face was getting hotter. I was just going to pretend that I was fine. "I was thinking more along the lines of how when you're stressed, it can cause breakouts or a rash. So currently, there are scientists looking at things like frankincense extract. It has beta-endorphins to ease your stress, help regulate cortisol, and it also is an anti-inflammatory and can restore collagen."

Now he looked interested. "So it's mood enhancing and has antiaging properties?"

"Yes, it tackles both that brain/skin connection and makes a user younger-looking at the same time. Then you could add something like lemongrass as the scent because it's been shown to reduce anxiety. We do some aromatherapy with our products now, but we could be doing a lot more."

Whoops. I realized a second too late that I was talking about Minx like I still worked there.

He made the same mistake when he asked, "So why aren't we doing that?"

"That's an excellent question, Marco. I don't know the answer. I tried pitching it to my boss many times, but he said something about weird crystal-carrying hippies dancing in the moonlight with cats and shot me down."

Marco took out his phone and started typing. He put his phone back in his pocket. "Just making a note," he said.

"I think it's the future of cosmetics. And not just the way it is now—how we try to use ingredients that positively affect the nervous system. But as you mentioned, like with the way skin blushes when you're embarrassed, what if we could use the nervous system's reactions to affect the makeup a user is wearing?"

"That could certainly have some interesting applications. I hope that's something you've been working on."

The truth was, I hadn't. It was something I'd been waiting on permission for at work when I could have been doing more in my home lab. Why was I always standing aside instead of going after the thing that I wanted? I didn't need Jerry to tell me it was okay before moving forward with experimenting in a field that fascinated me.

Catalina laughed loudly at something that had happened in the game, and I couldn't help but smile. I'd always enjoyed her sense of humor. I wished I could be more like her—at ease in any social situation, with any person. Not like myself, consumed with my own awkwardness and lack of social skills.

We were basically friends because she had adopted me.

"She seems like a happy person," Marco commented.

"Definitely. Until she's not. But you won't even know it's happening. She's the kind of person who would stab you while still wearing a smile. If you piss her off, you'll never see it coming. I've told her she needs a neon sign on her forehead with her current feelings. Like some kind of face mood ring."

A face mood ring. There was a jolt and then a buzzing sound in my head. Like I'd been struck by lightning. Marco said something to me, but his voice was too far away, and I tuned him out. That was it. The neurocosmetics application I'd been looking for.

A lipstick that would show the user's mood. There were lipsticks that changed solely from outside temperatures. Mine would change with temperature, but it would also respond to the user's nervous system. I began to run the problem through my head. The obvious first issue was that the thermotropic liquid crystals that made a mood ring change colors were toxic to skin. Could I put some kind of barrier around it? But that wouldn't work—people would forget and touch their lips or eat something and swallow those crystals, and that wouldn't be good.

What if there was a way to use the crystals and make them not harmful?

I remembered reading a study years ago that I hadn't thought much about since—it had been about using thermochromic polymer materials to eliminate the toxicity and carcinogenic properties of the liquid crystals. I grabbed my phone and did a search and found the study quickly. I read the abstract. I did another search and found an additional study on certain thermotropic crystals that were not toxic to mammalian cells.

This was it. I started creating formulations in my head. I needed a computer. And my lab.

I stood up. "I have to go."

Marco also got to his feet. "Anna? What's going on? You totally spaced out there for a minute."

"I know, I'm sorry. I just had a really great idea. If I can make it work . . . I think it could change everything in our industry."

His eyes widened. "That sounds big."

It was then that I remembered Craig telling me that if I had a big idea, I should come to him. Should I tell him? Would this be a reason to talk to him?

Right now, though, the person I wanted most to tell was Marco.

That felt like another betrayal. I rationalized that I probably only wanted to tell him because I'd been spending time with him.

For now I would keep it secret. It was just for me. When I figured out whether or not it was possible, then I would tell other people.

"I want to start working on it now. Tonight," I told him.

"Then let's go."

"Thank you for understanding."

"Of course." He said this like my thanks confused him. I just knew that there were other men who would have pressed me for details or insisted we stay and have fun, that I could work another time. I knew that because it had happened to me before.

But Marco just accepted it.

"I'll tell you about it when I know whether or not it's possible." That made me feel a bit better.

"Anna, you don't have to tell me anything unless you want to. Let me go grab Catalina and tell her we have to go."

He walked into the dining room, and again I was struck by how nice he was. I probably would have just left without saying anything, caught up in figuring out whether or not this could work, but Marco was going to make sure that we didn't leave without saying goodbye to our hostess.

Catalina would have understood either way, but he was right to do it. She got up from the table and said, "Keep an eye on Sanjit!"

He protested loudly that he wasn't the one who cheated, it was everyone else, as she came over to join us.

"Heading out already?" She gave me a wink and then said, "I don't blame you."

Why was she doing that? She knew it was fake.

"Thanks for having us," Marco said.

"Thanks for coming!"

I figured I should probably jump onto this appreciation bandwagon. "Yes, thank you for the invite. It was nice to be part of a group that didn't have the word *study* in front of it."

Again, I wondered why I couldn't just stay quiet instead of saying things that were designed to make Marco think less of me.

Catalina gave me a sympathetic smile and then walked over to the door and opened it for us. "I'll see you later! And, Anna, I'll be calling you soon."

She said it like a threat, and Marco laughed at my expression. We walked out to her porch, and she closed the door behind us.

"Is there anything you need for your project?" he asked as we walked down the pathway toward the sidewalk.

I needed that mixer that somebody had stolen out from underneath me. "I haven't received that consulting fee yet, and the ingredients I'm going to need to buy will be expensive."

"Here." He pulled out his phone and texted something. "Make a list and send it to my assistant. I just gave you her email address. She'll get you whatever you need."

I knew I probably should have protested, but I wanted that stuff as soon as possible. I hated waiting. So I just said, "I will. Thanks."

"My pleasure. Let me walk you to your car. Are you going to need a jump-start to get it moving? A timing belt? A new engine?"

He laughed at his own joke, and I elbowed him in the ribs. "Don't disparage Betty. You'll hurt her feelings."

"Apologies, Betty," he said as we got closer; then he put his hand on the top of my car. We stood there together on the sidewalk. "Do you think she'll forgive me?"

I thought all Marco would have to do is bat his lashes and if my car had any free will, she would have dumped me in a second to follow him. "Maybe. But she can be temperamental."

"I'll remember that. Well, good night." He started walking away, and I realized that I didn't want him to leave.

"Wait!"

He stopped and turned around with a quizzical look on his face.

"Could I . . . give you a hug good night?" I realized how pathetic that sounded and added, "I just want to verify something." He didn't need to know that Catalina had been ready to write sonnets about his hug. I wanted to see for myself.

But if he thought my request was weird, he was polite enough not to say anything. Instead, he walked toward me, holding out his arms. I let him envelop me, wrapping my arms around his waist.

And great mother of Legolas, it was glorious.

I'd had my side pressed against him more than once that evening, but that paled in comparison to this full-frontal hug. There was warmth and strength and that delicious scent of his that made me want to melt against him. I kind of did anyway, my curves pressing against his taut chest. He was so firm and sweet.

There was a definite physical component there. All those traitorous hormones of mine were dancing with delight, making my nerve endings explode in celebration, and breathing was difficult.

But it wasn't just about how yummy it was to touch him. There was an emotional element to it.

A person could get lost in a hug like this. It had been a very, very long time since someone had held me this way. Catalina had been wrong about one thing. It wasn't like hugging a statue. He was much too alive for that. Marco made me feel safe, like nothing bad could ever happen to me as long as I had his arms around me. No wonder Catalina had liked it so much. If Marco could bottle this sensation up he'd be, well, even more of a millionaire.

"Did you verify what you needed to verify?" he asked against the top of my head, and it caused warm tingles to skate across my scalp and travel down my body, spreading as they went.

I let go of him and took a step back, worried that I'd start to shake or something if he kept whispering things against my skin. I commanded my legs to keep me upright and was glad that they listened.

"I did. Thanks," I said as I folded my arms across my chest.

"Did you do that for our audience?" He nodded toward Catalina's front window. She was there watching us, but when she saw me looking at her, she quickly shut her curtains.

"If we wanted to put on a show, I could kiss you good night. That would be more date-like and authentic," he offered.

I couldn't catch my breath for a moment, that internal warmth he'd caused heating up to more molten temperatures as I seriously considered what he'd said. "Catalina's gone. Plus, she already knows we're not really dating."

There was a hungry look in his eyes, and I couldn't tell if I was imagining it or if he was actually doing it. Like he wanted to kiss me either way.

He'd let me know repeatedly that he wasn't interested in me. I was definitely making it up and feeling stupid that I had done so. "We should save some stuff for later. No reason to jump all in now." Better to put it off for as long as I could, because I didn't know what would happen when he actually kissed me.

That was going to happen. It would be unavoidable.

The problem was that despite my protestations, I didn't want to avoid it.

Again he wore that knowing smile—like he understood exactly what I was doing and why—and it was infuriating.

"See you later, Anna. And good luck with your project."

He walked back to his ridiculous car, and I told myself that I needed to focus on two things—Craig and my mood-changing lipstick.

Nothing else mattered. I shouldn't be thinking about anything or anyone else.

The problem was that Marco had started to take up a large amount of real estate in my brain.

And I was ready to give that man a long-term lease.

CHAPTER FOURTEEN

When I got home, I sent my list of supplies to Marco's assistant. The next morning, she replied to my email and said she'd take care of it right away and have everything overnighted. I was very excited for it all to arrive.

Because I'd been laboring over the formulation, and I was pretty sure it was going to work. I was doing some research on my computer the next day when I heard a screech of, "Yankees suck!" Someone must have knocked, and I hadn't heard it.

My packages.

They were from several different suppliers, and there was a large box that was hard to lift. That one intrigued me the most, and I opened it first, right there in the foyer, because I was so curious.

There was some packing material that I pulled up, and inside I found a high-shear mixer.

A red one.

And it was brand new.

I didn't know what to do. I called Catalina. We'd already had our post-party discussion where she'd filled me in on everything I'd missed, and we talked for a very long time about the hug with Marco. I repeatedly told her that I had only been doing what she'd told me to do, to touch him and not get freaked out and to see if it was like hugging a statue, but she didn't believe my excuses. Because she was smart enough not to.

"A mixer!" I said when she finally picked up on the fourth ring.

"What?"

"Why do you sound like you're out of breath?"

"I had to run to the refrigerator so I could talk to you." Jerry hated cell phones and personal calls. I should have thought of that. I was just so excited. "Did you say a mixer?"

"Marco just sent me a red high-shear mixer, and it looks brand new." It would have cost him a lot of money. Thousands and thousands of dollars.

"Aw. That is so unbelievably sweet. There wasn't anything he could have sent you that would have meant more."

She wasn't wrong. This beat flowers any day.

"Is there a note?" she asked.

"Hold on." I put the phone down and pulled the mixer out of the box completely. I dug around the bottom and found a tiny envelope. I opened it and grabbed my phone.

"It says, 'I hope all your dreams come true' and then his name."

"Wow. It's too bad you don't want him, because that is some grade A boyfriend material right there. Do you think if I fake date him, he might get me that Tesla I've always wanted?"

Ignoring her joke, I put the note down and ran my hand along the top of my mixer. "I can't believe he did this."

"You're not going to try to give it back to him, are you?"

"No!" I exclaimed. Why would I do that? It was mine now. Forever and ever. "I'm going to be buried with this thing."

"Some people are like that. Thinking they can't accept a gift because of the implications or imbalance or whatever. Wait, I hear something. I think Jerry's looking for me. Gotta go."

She hung up, and I wasn't sure what to say to Marco. I had to thank him, though. I wondered why he'd done it but figured if he wanted me to know, he would tell me.

I decided that it would probably be best to text him. I sent him a quick note that said:

Thanks so much for the mixer. I absolutely love it.

I saw the three dots at the bottom of the screen indicating that he was writing me back, and then suddenly my phone rang and I dropped it out of shock.

It was Marco calling me.

I picked it up and said, "Hello?" as if I didn't have his contact information in my phone and didn't know exactly who was on the other end.

He didn't even bother saying who it was and quickly asked, "So you like it?"

"I kind of want to marry it. And I know this is probably the part where I'm supposed to tell you it's too much and I can't take it, but I'm not going to do that because I really, really want to keep it."

He laughed at that. "It's fun to give a gift to someone who appreciates it."

"It's fun to get a gift that you've been dying to have. Thank you so much. Seriously."

"Now you can go out and upend the entire makeup industry. I can't wait to see what you come up with."

I opened my mouth, wanting to tell him about my formulation. How I might even have a prototype this evening, if things went according to plan.

"There are a couple of things I wanted to ask you," he said. "First, if we go to a fancy party, are you okay for like, hair, makeup, clothes, that kind of thing?"

"I have all that stuff."

He made an annoyed sound. "You know what I meant."

"Okay, then, what I have is probably not up to snuff."

"I only ask because you said you just had the one dress, and I don't think an Arwen outfit is going to win Craig over. It takes a certain kind of man to respond to that."

"Yeah," I scoffed. "The kind with good taste." Not liking Lord of the Rings was definitely a detraction in my book.

"Why do you like those movies so much?" he asked, genuinely curious.

A strange lump appeared in my throat. That was the hardest thing about grief—you thought you were dealing well with things, going about your life, then you would hear a sound or smell a scent or someone would say something that brought you right back to that sadness. "They were my dad's favorite movies. We used to watch them together all the time. Rom-coms with my mom, sci-fi and fantasy with my dad."

There was a long pause. "I'm glad you have those things to hold on to. A way to keep your parents a part of your life. I wish I knew what my mother's favorite movie was."

I wished he did, too. "Can't you ask your dad?"

"I doubt he'd know." He cleared his throat. "I was actually calling to ask what your plans are for this weekend."

"My plans?" I squeaked the word out. There was no way I was telling the man who looked like he should be crowned Handsomest Man Alive that my plans involved cookie dough and binge-watching all nine Star Wars movies. "It's too bad you didn't call me earlier. My other fake boyfriend and I are going out on Friday. He's flying me to the Riviera."

Marco laughed and then said, "It sounds like I need to up my game."

"You do," I agreed.

"How about you blow that guy off and come over to my place Friday evening around five o'clock?"

His place? That sounded . . . dangerous. At least here, we had avian chaperones and two senior citizens to watch over us. He probably lived alone. In some sexy bachelor apartment where I'd be even more powerless to resist him than usual. He'd lean against doorframes and show off his forearms, and I'd collapse into a heap on the floor.

I couldn't tell him any of that, though.

Then I had a moment of panic that he was inviting me over to tell me that our experiment had failed, that it was too hard to pretend to date me and this farce was finished. In a resigned way, I said, "Yeah, okay."

"Great. I'll text you the address. See you then!"

When he hung up, I realized that it bugged me how he let my imagination run wild instead of just telling me what was going on. It was a testament to his charm that I didn't demand answers from him. Rationally, I told myself that the meeting was probably to go over our next steps, but some tiny part of me was secretly hoping that there might be another reason.

Like he wanted to see me again just as much as I wanted to see him.

~

Late Friday afternoon, the mood lipstick was giving me trouble. There were a lot of factors I had to take into account that I didn't normally deal with, and the texture and general adhesion were off. I made a mental note to add more of my solidifying agent to the next batch.

This stage was always difficult—coming up with the perfect formulation. One of my last projects at Minx had been a night cream. I would create it and send it off to marketing for review. They'd told me it was too tacky, too sticky, too thick, too thin, it needed more glide and slip, they didn't like the scent, it needed to be tinted pink . . . I'd made hundreds of variations over a year and a half, and the product still hadn't been ready when I left. I wondered which one of my former colleagues had been stuck with it.

That timeline and constant rejection were pretty standard when it came to the cosmetic industry. The good thing with this project—doing it by myself and calling all the shots. No marketing department to make happy. The bad thing? Doing it by myself and calling all the shots. No marketing department to give me feedback.

Users might not like the end product, and I didn't have anyone besides Catalina and me to test it on.

One of the bright points in my experimentation was that the high-shear mixer was utter perfection, and if I'd initially turned Marco down with his whole fake-dating plan, this would have been the thing that would have gotten me to say yes.

Mixing, weighing, formulating, combining, baking, I missed this. My home lab was great, but I wanted to be back in a professional setting again. I'd sent out some more résumés but still hadn't heard anything back. One company had an automatic reply and said they'd be in touch, but so far nothing.

My alarm sounded, and with a sigh, I put my beaker back on the table. I'd have to clean all this up when I got back from Marco's house.

I took a quick look at myself in the mirror. I could practically hear Catalina's voice in my head telling me to make myself presentable, but he knew what I looked like. He had literally seen me at my worst. I did check out my armpits, though. Sometimes basic hygiene went by the wayside when I was in the middle of a project I loved.

Figuring I was good enough, I headed downstairs and ran into my grandpa, who was reading the newspaper. He lowered it to look over the top at me. "Going out again?"

His note of surprise felt so discouraging. "Yes. To see Marco."

He peered up at me from behind his paper. "Will you be out late?"

My grandpa tended to wait up for me. Not that I'd given him many opportunities to do it recently. "I don't think so. I'll call if anything changes."

He put his paper back up and told me to have fun, and I headed out to Marco's. I hadn't given myself quite enough time to get to his place. I had forgotten to account for Friday afternoon / evening Los Angeles traffic. When I finally arrived, I discovered that he lived in a nice, shiny condo building. There was even a valet to take my car. I felt a little embarrassed getting in line behind the luxury automobiles, but I handed off my keys with as much dignity as I could muster.

I took an elevator up to the tenth floor and walked to the end of the hallway to find Marco's place. The door was slightly ajar.

For some reason, this alarmed me. Why was his door open? Was he in trouble? I put my keys in between my fingers just in case he needed help.

Although what assistance I thought I could offer a man who could bench-press me, I wasn't sure.

I still couldn't believe he'd left his door open. Any random off the street could have just waltzed in. Didn't anyone in his life ever tell him he needed to lock his front door? Marco might have been smart, but common sense was like deodorant. The people who needed it most never had it.

But what if something had happened to him? I had to go in and see. So the random wandering in off the street was me. I pushed the door farther open and called out his name. "Marco?"

There was a rhythmic thump-thumping noise, and as I came around the corner, I saw Marco on a treadmill, running.

Without a shirt on.

I audibly gulped as my uterus skipped a beat.

I had guessed at his physique based on touching him and his appearance, but now I had to be sad about how poor my imagination actually was. He had the kind of perfect body that slow motion was invented for.

His big muscles flexed and moved as he ran, all sweaty and glistening, and the sight of him made my internal organs do a bunch of somersaults. He had a torso people should write poetry about or make sculptures of. Maybe they already had.

I could set up a carnival booth and sell tickets to get a look at him like this, and people would pay it.

He was so powerful and fast. There was a definite running-to-Isengard-to-save-the-hobbits thing happening here that I enjoyed.

So unfair. I had to pretend to date Mr. Sexy Chest and keep these ridiculous hormones in check. It was like the universe had decided I hadn't had enough bad things in my life and that I needed to be punished or tempted or something.

If Marco's plan worked and Craig wanted to be with me, I really hoped these pesky attraction issues of mine would go away. They had to, right? I couldn't still be lusting after him once Craig and I were official. I didn't need any additional awkwardness in my life.

Then I wondered just how long I'd been standing there ogling him like some mega creep.

"Marco?"

No response.

I walked over into his range of vision, and he noticed me. He looked very surprised, like he hadn't personally invited me over to his house or something. He pressed buttons on the console, and the treadmill began to slow down.

If he'd caught me running topless on a treadmill and surprised me, I would have fallen backward and knocked myself out. Marco, on the other hand, gracefully stepped off the machine as it came to a stop.

"Anna? Didn't we say five o'clock?"

I looked at my phone. At first I cursed my own stupidity for not getting a picture of him while he was running.

. . . for Catalina. Yeah, for Catalina.

Not any other reason.

But it was a little bit after four o'clock, and he definitely had said five. I felt so stupid as I realized what I had done. "Right. I set my alarm to remind myself to start winding down, but I mistook it for the 'leave now' alarm. I'm sorry about that."

He took a step toward me, apparently unaware of his partial nudity. To paraphrase Rey, couldn't he put a shirt on or something? He reached for a small towel and used it to wipe off the back of his neck.

My mouth went dry. Literally dry.

"And you just decided to let yourself in?" he asked with a small smile.

"Your front door was open."

"It was?"

"Yes. Are you trying to get murdered?" I was attempting to keep my eyes level with his, but they kept slipping back down to take in his chest and those abs on his stomach. I'd never seen a human who had real abs before. Marco seemed to have more than his fair share.

He smiled again. "My trainer was here. He must have left it open on his way out. So no, I wasn't trying to get murdered. Did anyone ever tell you that you worry too much?"

"Only my grandpa and a psychiatrist," I said absentmindedly as he reached for a water bottle and took a long drink of water. I felt so distracted by all the shiny, corded muscles on display.

Why was his neck sexy? That didn't seem like a body part that should be attractive.

I suddenly got hit with his scent and by all accounts, I should have been grossed out by how sweaty he was. Instead, it was like he was secreting pheromones directly into my bloodstream, and I felt powerless to resist. He was intoxicating.

Completely oblivious to what was happening to me, he threw the towel over his shoulder. "I'm going to grab a shower, and then we can talk after. Sound good?"

Was that a question? I wasn't sure. There was just so . . . much . . . chest. I nodded, hoping that was the right answer.

He left, and I watched him go clear up until the second he shut his bedroom door. I let out a frustrated little groan and turned away. I had images of Marco turning on the water, taking off those shorts, stepping into the shower . . . what was going on with me? I closed my eyes like that would stop me from visualizing what was happening behind that closed door. I needed some help.

When Catalina answered her phone, she said, "I'm glad you called. You have to stop me. I need one of those huge dog collars that will zap me anytime I try to shop online."

I didn't know what to say to that, so instead I asked, "What is wrong with me?"

"How honest do you want me to be? Also, do you want a list?" She paused. "Why do you sound weird?"

"I may or may not be at Marco's condo, and I need you to distract me."

"Why?"

I scrunched up my shoulders. "He's taking a shower."

"But why are you talking to me and not joining him?"

Good question. My body agreed.

"Please, let's talk about something else." Eyes shut, eyes open, it didn't seem to make a difference. I was either imagining him in the shower or running on his treadmill.

And I'd thought I had a weak imagination.

"You sound frantic. Are you going to lie to me again and tell me you don't have feelings for this guy?"

"It's not feelings." That wasn't a lie, was it? I mean, I liked him as a person. He was fun to hang out with and was nice and thoughtful, but that wasn't feelings. Just appreciating another kind human being. Who happened to have a body like an Olympic athlete. "He's just . . . attractive."

"Ding, ding, ding," she said. "Johnny, tell her what she's won!"

I did not need her pointed and correct sarcasm right now.

"Wait. Before we go any further, did you change out of whatever you put on this morning?" she asked.

I crossed my arms over my hoodie, as if she could see me. "Why would I change?"

"To hang out with Marco Kimball? You should put on a ball gown and a sash."

This was the opposite of helpful.

She let out a dramatic sigh. "The only other time I've seen someone lie this much and this badly, it was me to myself. And as the author of several cries for help, I know one when I hear it. Tell me the truth, Anna. You want that sexy beast of a man, don't you?"

I balled up my free hand. "I may or may not be in the midst of a hormonal Chernobyl," I finally admitted.

She let out a whoop so loud that I had to hold the phone away from my ear.

"I knew it!" she crowed.

"Just a second," I said. "I didn't say I had feelings for him. Just that he's attractive and that I acknowledge that very objective fact."

"Anna, mi amiga, I have just one ducking word to say to you." She paused for dramatic effect. "Kaboom."

CHAPTER FIFTEEN

"What is *kaboom* supposed to mean?" I asked.

"I told you this was going to blow up in your face. While I very much enjoy being right, you know gloating's not a good look on me."

"Nothing has blown up. I'm just saying I'm having a typical reaction to seeing a half-naked man—"

"Half-naked?" she shrieked. "What? When? How? Which half?"

"Which half? Do you really think he was Winnie-the-Poohing it with a shirt on and nothing else?"

"I wouldn't mind seeing that."

Neither would I.

I tried to shake that thought out of my head. There was nothing good that could come from this conversation because Catalina did not need to be encouraged. Or me, for that matter. "It doesn't matter because I'm still in love with Craig."

She moaned loudly. "Just admit the truth. You like Marco."

"This is entirely a hormonal thing," I said. "He's unnervingly handsome, and I'm responding to that."

"Or your body is just being more honest than the rest of you."

There was some kind of internal chemical compound at work here that could easily explain my attraction to Marco. Too bad I hadn't been paying closer attention in my college biology courses. Whatever it was, I wished I could examine it and distinguish all the elements. I'd study it, distill it, bottle it, and make a billion dollars.

I wondered if it would be wise to tell her that I found myself thinking about Marco all the time lately. So much so that he was edging Craig out of my brain entirely, and that concerned me. I couldn't let him push Craig out of my heart, too.

"Whatever it is, I'm feeling a little out of control over here. I don't know how to explain any of this," I admitted.

There was a long pause, and then she said, "You mean other than his hotness and kindness and hotness and intelligence? Because I've got to tell you, Anna, that would do it for most women. Myself included."

I didn't want to be pathetic like this. Marco had made it very clear that he was not interested in me. "How can I be in love with one man and be this attracted to another?"

"Have I never told you about the time when I dated Aidan and Hayden? At least Marco and Craig don't rhyme. That story didn't end well, by the way. But the point is, it is possible. I think it's even possible to be in love with two people at the same time. You'd just have to figure out which one you couldn't live without."

I actually found myself seriously considering her statement and couldn't believe that my brain had to even question which brother to pick. Craig. It was obviously Craig. Not having a good comeback, I said, "You do know you said 'hotness' twice, right?"

"Marco is twice as hot as other people."

"And the other words were stuff you threw in because all you care about is that he's hot?" I teased.

"Let me just say that it's a good thing I'm into Zhen now."

I found myself starting to declare, *You can date Marco*, but I choked after the first syllable. Like my body wouldn't let me say it. So I settled on, "Yeah, definitely. But I think this attraction thing is due to me not having dated anyone in so long. Like I'm in heat or something."

"That sounds excellent to me."

"It's not." It was making everything difficult. Especially given Marco's friends-only vibes toward me.

"You're single; he's single," she offered. "I say go for it."

"You're forgetting about Craig." He was the entire reason I was doing any of this.

"I'm trying to forget about him. I wish you would, too." She cleared her throat and then said, "Anna, I haven't wanted to tell you this, but I think you should move on from Craig. He is bad news."

"Not this again."

"I've done my research. Conducted surveys of the employees, did a deep dive on social media, and my conclusion is sound. He's a bad guy. He only cares about himself. He's a serial cheater who hooks up with women and never calls them again."

She sounded so sincere that it was hard to dismiss her words. "He's about to get married."

"You think cheaters don't get married?"

"No, I have to think that any self-respecting woman wouldn't marry a man who was cheating on her."

"Some women don't care," she countered.

I remembered Marco's dim view of marriage and knew he'd agree with her.

Catalina kept talking. "There are even rumors that he's the father of Tammy's baby!"

"Tammy from accounting? The married one who wouldn't shut up about her cute dentist husband? That Tammy?"

"Okay, so maybe that one rumor is wrong."

"Maybe they're all wrong." Craig couldn't be the way Catalina painted him. He couldn't. Because I wouldn't be able to love a man like that. He was good and decent and helpful. Not some slimy cheater.

I didn't know why my best friend had had it out for him since the beginning, but she seemed to be escalating.

Was that because I was on the edge of finally getting to be with him? Or I would be if Marco's plan actually worked.

"Anna, you have to see that—"

I cut her off. "We're not talking about Craig. We're talking about Marco." I looked over my shoulder just to make sure he hadn't wandered back into the room.

"But Craig directly relates to Marco because you mistakenly think that . . . you know what? Never mind. So you've finally figured out what every other woman in the world knows—Marco Kimball is hot. What are you going to do about it?"

"That's why I called you in the first place! I don't know!"

"Putting aside everything else, may I posit some things for you?"

This should be interesting. "Go ahead."

"First, there is the fact that I feel like you should willingly submit yourself to the very noble cause of feminine hedonism by enjoying Marco."

I rolled my eyes. While it was an argument, it wasn't a particularly good one.

Only some parts of me agreed with my assessment, though.

"Second," she went on, "he likes you."

"Untrue."

"He lights up every time he looks at you."

There was a hollowed-out feeling in my stomach that I couldn't define. "He does not."

"He really does."

"Then he's acting. That's the entire point of all of this." Of course he looked at me that way. He had to. Otherwise no one would ever believe our scheme.

"Okay, then somebody needs to give that man an Academy Award, because he is just that good. And you are not an expert on men's feelings. Let's not forget about the fact that you are completely clueless whenever a guy likes you."

I scoffed. "Not true."

"Oh yeah? What about that time we went out to the Moonlight Lounge and that guy flirted with you? He said you were beautiful, and your response was, *Thanks, but you just think that because I'm wearing this new lipstick shade called Rosy Dreams*, and then you described the ingredients, and he didn't so much walk away as he did run."

My memories of that event were completely different than hers. That man had not been hitting on me. "He was just being nice."

"He was interested, and you were oblivious. You can be aggressively dense sometimes. He asked if he could buy you a drink."

"But I already had a drink."

"I rest my case, Your Honor. Third, you and Marco have so much chemistry that I feel like I should be wearing lab goggles whenever I'm around you. And it's my job, so I know what I'm talking about."

"That's not—there isn't any—" Everything she was saying was wrong.

"He flirts with you."

"I'm sure Marco flirts with everyone," I countered. It was probably as normal to him as breathing.

"He didn't flirt with me, and men usually flirt with me. I saw him flirting with you at the party."

A little flutter filled my chest. He didn't flirt with Catalina? That was new, interesting information. "It wasn't real flirting. He was practicing."

"You think that man needs to practice how to flirt?"

"No, we had to practice me being used to it."

"Oh. I guess I can see that. You do freak out a lot."

It was true. I couldn't even argue with her. "Maybe this whole thing is like some kind of transference situation. I can't have Craig yet, so I'm transferring those feelings onto the hottest guy closest to me."

"Love the one you're with? I don't know if I buy that as an explanation, but okay. However, please allow me to repeat myself by saying that you are oh so very screwed."

Again, I was extremely concerned that she was not wrong. I was going to win this war with my hormones. I might have been down for a couple of battles, but I was the boss of my body. "Nobody's getting screwed." I paused as I realized what I'd said and then hurried to add, "It's just mind over matter, right?"

"We deal solely in matter, so you know that doesn't work."

"What about it being the thought that counts?"

"If that were true, then I would lose ten pounds today because I thought about eating healthier and exercising and instead I ate an entire bag of Fritos and had a two-hour nap."

I grit my teeth together in frustration and did another sweep of the giant living room / kitchen area to make sure he hadn't sneaked in behind me and was listening to every single humiliating word. All clear.

"I need your help in figuring out what to do next," I said.

"To be honest, I don't know," she said. "That caliber of man is above my pay grade. Give me a nerdy dude who thinks I walk on water any day."

I was about to tell her that I suspected Marco might be a secret nerd but figured this wasn't the time to add fuel to her quest to get me to hook up with him. "Tell me something bad about him."

"Okay . . . he'll probably cheat on you. Men who look like that usually do."

"That's not really fair. He's told me in the past that he doesn't do it and doesn't want to cheat in the future." I didn't tell her about his dad, which was weird. I usually told Catalina everything, but it felt like something personal he'd trusted me with, and I didn't want to betray him.

"The whole *tell me bad things about him* thing is not going to work if you keep defending Marco," she reminded me.

"Right."

"Um, he'll never choose you over that company. He's very dedicated to it. Neither will Craig, for that matter."

Oh. That was a slightly painful one. Was it true or was she just trying to come up with stuff?

"From what you told me, he seems very competitive. And sometimes that can be a good thing, and other times it's just annoying. Mark in the con column."

"Okay, but coming up with a list of things about him that annoy me, and there are many, isn't going to be enough to turn off whatever this is."

"Keep all hands and feet inside the vehicle at all times? Just don't act on it? I personally think that's a mistake and that you should stake a claim on Mount Marco as soon as is humanly possible, but here we are. The only way to not hook up with him is to just not hook up with him."

She made it sound so simple, and it wasn't feeling that way at all. Plus, I wasn't so much concerned about hooking up with him because I couldn't imagine that happening, especially given that he didn't see me as a potential hookup partner. He treated me like I was his kid sister or something.

And I didn't want to be a joke. Or someone he felt sorry for.

My biggest problem was that I didn't want to be in love with Craig and lusting after his older brother. I needed an off switch.

There was a crashing sound on her end, and she swore and then said, "I hope that helps. Rufus just knocked something over. I've got to go. Good luck, though. Call me if you need me."

Rufus was her dog, and he hated everyone in the world except Catalina. He never seemed to like it when she and I were chatting. I could only imagine how he treated the men she dated. I hung up the phone and put it back in my pocket.

Which left me alone in Marco's condo with my lascivious thoughts. I walked over to his bookcase and started going through his books. Some thrillers, some that looked like college textbooks, nonfiction business books. I ran my fingers across their spines, not really seeing the titles because I was again thinking about what he looked like when he showered. All that water running down that perfectly sculpted chest and—

"Anna?"

I shrieked and then dropped the book I hadn't realized I'd been holding. Marco was not helping my current situation—he looked like he hadn't even bothered to towel off. Droplets of water shone in his dark hair, and his clothes stuck to his skin, outlining some of those incredible muscles that were begging to be explored. Not by me, of course, but somebody should be doing it. It felt like a disservice to all women everywhere that it wasn't happening.

"You're like some kind of half-elf, sneaking up on me like that," I told him, putting a hand over my chest in an attempt to keep my rapidly beating heart in place.

"Did you just compare me to Legolas? I'm flattered."

"Unintentionally. I kind of see you as more of an Aragorn."

He somehow managed to move a little closer. "Even more flattered."

I was discovering that all kinds of Marcos were dangerous, but damp Marco was particularly concerning.

Then he bent over to pick up the book and put it back on the shelf, given that I was frozen in place. He leaned to put it away, in a spot behind my head.

Which brought our faces and bodies close together. My heart beat double-time in response to his nearness. And after he slid the book back into place, he didn't move. He stayed where he was, and I found myself mesmerized by his face. That jaw, those full lips, those dark eyes.

We stood there, my glasses fogging up while I tried to stifle my loud breathing so that I wouldn't sound like a wheezing cow, and I wondered if he felt even a fraction of the attraction I felt for him, then remembered that he didn't.

Friends only. Nothing more.

We were on a mission. For me to land the man of my dreams.

Whose name I'd completely forgotten for an entire eleven seconds as Marco's lips parted slightly, and I was so caught up in the soft sound he made and the gentle movement that I couldn't remember his brother's name.

"Can I just . . ." His words trailed off as he reached up to take off my glasses, his long fingers on either side of my head gently lifting them up and off my face. I held my breath the entire time.

Please don't let him say anything about them being fogged up, I prayed to whoever was listening.

"How can you see through these things?" he asked, sounding amused.

"They're, uh, the only way I can see."

I could only make out the blurry image of him lifting up the edge of his shirt to clean them, and I cursed the genes that had given me such poor vision that were keeping me from seeing that patch of abs he was currently exposing.

He finished, and instead of handing them back to me, he put them back on my face, so carefully and gently that it surprised me. My skin tingled in response to his nearness, and I fought off the desire to lean my head against his hand.

"Craig!" I practically shouted when it finally came to me. That was the name of the guy I was in love with and the reason I was here. Craig. Craig Kimball.

"What?" Marco asked.

"You brought me here to talk about Craig. I'm assuming."

His expression shuttered, and he moved away from me. "In a roundabout way."

It took all of my personal willpower not to grab him by his shirt and pull him back to where he had been just a second ago.

He walked over to his big sectional couch and sat down. He patted the cushion next to him, but I was still feeling jittery from what had felt like an almost-kiss (although I knew it hadn't been), so I didn't join him.

With him finally being out of the shower, it was like I could suddenly pay attention to the rooms around me. "This place is not what I was expecting," I told him.

"What were you expecting?"

"From you? An army of servants and an overinflated sense of self-worth."

He put a hand over his chest. "That flattered feeling is gone. You wound me."

"It's only a flesh wound," I said with a smile. "As to what I was expecting from your house? Chrome, steel, glass, and a whole lot of white." Instead, his condo had an upscale-dorm feeling. The furniture was nice and obviously expensive, but it was like he hadn't put any thought into design and cared only about his own comfort. There was a treadmill in one corner and in the other . . .

How had I not noticed this when I walked in?

There was a desk with four massive computer monitors, a chair rigged for sound and light, and a computer tower that glowed light blue.

"Marco whatever-your-middle-name-is Kimball, what is this?"

He crossed his arms defensively at my utter delight. "I told you I was a gamer."

"Uh, no, you told me you sometimes played video games. You did not tell me you had a setup that could program a spaceship launch." I ran my fingers across the back of his leather chair. Fancy.

"Because it was irrelevant."

"Right now it seems like the only thing that's relevant. A man who regularly squires supermodels around town likes video games."

"The two things are not mutually exclusive," he said. "And I don't squire people. I'm not a medieval knight."

That put an immediate image into my head of him in shining silver armor, and that somehow only made him hotter.

Still in defensive mode, he added, "It's not that much."

"Uh, it is. But that's okay. I know you're a secret dork at heart."

He rolled his eyes, and I couldn't help but laugh at his expression. There didn't seem to be much to tease Marco about, but this was definitely something I planned on giving him a hard time over.

"It's Ricci," he said.

"What is?"

"My middle name," he clarified.

"Your mother's maiden name."

He nodded. That was sweet. "What about you?" he asked.

"Duh, Urban Decay."

That made him laugh, and the sound gave me inappropriate tingles. I cleared my throat. "Seriously, though, I don't have one."

"Really?"

"Some people don't. We're not all like you rich people with your six middle names."

He put his feet up on his coffee table. "I only have the one."

"Maybe that's because you're not as rich as I imagined you would be."

This seemed to amuse him. "What makes you think I'm not?"

I waved around the room.

His mouth quirked up on one side. "Were you not just mocking me for my expensive gaming system?"

"Any software engineer worth their salt has a setup just like yours. Don't you have a yacht or something?"

"No. That feels like a waste of money to me. People in my life and my company waste a lot of money." He let out a ragged sigh. "That's one of the things I'm going to change at KRT Limited when I become CEO. I'll start with Minx and make it employee-owned with profit sharing. If everyone's contributing, everyone should profit. Then I hope to spread it to other divisions."

"That would be nice. I mean, it would have been if I still worked there. I probably would have had more saved up to start my own company."

Marco grinned. "You would have blown it all on some expensive piece of lab equipment."

I shrugged. What could I say? He was right.

He patted the cushion next to him again and this time said, "Have a seat."

This was making me nervous. I sat down on the couch, but I kept my distance. He gave me that weapons-grade smile of his where he knew he was being hot and charming, and I told myself not to fall for it. My heart softened at that smile, and I couldn't help but lean my head to one side with a slightly giddy smile in return.

So technically I did fall for it, but in my defense, I tried to prevent it.

"So, Anna no-middle-name Ellis, I wanted to know how you feel about surprises."

CHAPTER SIXTEEN

I had never really thought about it before. "I guess it depends on the surprise. Like when Grandpa had to do bird CPR on Wil Tweeton or when Catalina set me up with her third cousin who did not understand personal boundaries. Those were not great surprises." Or Marco Kimball appearing in my bedroom hadn't felt like a fun surprise at the time, but I was slowly coming around to it. "The mixer, though, that was a fantastic surprise, and I really enjoyed that."

"Great! So along that vein, and keeping in mind how much you love that mixer and that I am the one who sent it to you . . ." He trailed off, and now I was worried. Nobody brought up things they did for you unless they wanted something.

What more could he ask of me? Some nutso ideas ran through my head, including whether he might want me to be his surrogate to carry his heir.

That didn't freak me out as much as it should have.

"Remember how I asked you about hair, makeup, and clothes? How do you feel about me getting you some of those things? If I pay for them?" he asked tentatively.

A makeover? I hadn't expected that. He was right to be tentative. "You want to do a makeover. On me?"

"Yes?" Much more of a question than an answer.

"Pass," I immediately said.

"Like a montage from a movie," he said, as if that would convince me.

"It seems sexist and objectifying. I don't need to change the way I look."

"I'm not disagreeing with you. I just know my brother. He's pretty vain and shallow. Shiny things, remember?"

Surely there was more to Craig than that. Annoyed at what Marco was implying, I snapped, "I want him to love me for me. I want to be myself."

"You'll still be yourself, just enhanced. Isn't that your whole job? Enhancing women's best features?"

"Yes, but . . ." I let my voice taper off. He wasn't wrong.

"I don't know that you're in a position to argue when you're the cosmetic chemist," he pointed out unhelpfully. "Plus, attraction is about keeping the other person slightly off-balance. Craig has seen you one way—he needs to see you in another light. He won't know what to make of it."

Again, Marco might have had a point.

Before I could respond, he added, "And what if it works? You can take the empirical evidence and see if it makes a difference. If it doesn't, you can go back to—" He waved his hand in my direction. "To what you're more comfortable with. This is just about putting your best foot forward. When you did your science fair projects at school, didn't you make your presentation board look nice before you submitted it?"

"That's not the same thing," I said, even though it kind of was.

"My plan involves a lot of formal events. I thought doing something like this might even give you some extra confidence, and confidence is always attractive."

Confidence . . . there were things I felt very confident about. My intelligence. My ability to translate the ideas in my head into real, concrete objects. But if I were being honest, I'd never been very confident about my appearance. I just hadn't ever done anything about it because it seemed unnecessary.

Maybe now it was necessary. Although I didn't like what it was implying about Craig at all.

I had spent my professional career coming up with ways to make women feel better about themselves, more confident in their own skin. It would be a little hypocritical for me to back away from someone challenging me to do the same.

"Okay."

His face lit up. "I'm so relieved you said that because—"

We were interrupted by a knock at his front door.

"Did you finally figure out how to shut it?" I asked as he went to answer it. He gave me a look and then opened the door.

There were a bunch of female voices saying hello to him, and then three bright and happy-looking women entered the room, carrying cases and pushing a rack of clothes.

"Anna, I want you to meet Jen. She's a makeup artist." She was a tiny, dark-haired woman who reminded me a bit of a Disney princess come to life. "This is Andi—she does hair." Andi had a shock of vibrant purple hair put in a bun with chopsticks. "Gloria is going to be your stylist." She was older, dressed all in black, and cooler than I could ever hope to be.

Marco turned to tell them where they could set up.

I walked over to stand by his side. "Do you remember when you asked me if there was anything else you should know about me?"

He nodded.

"I might kill you for springing this on me. You should know that."

"Noted."

"Where did you even find them?"

"They've all done a lot of photo shoots for Minx, and they were happy to come over and help out. My assistant set everything up. I think she even called Catalina to make sure Gloria pulled the right sizes for you."

How Catalina ever managed to keep that quiet from me, I would never know.

"Over here!" Andi directed, pointing at a chair they had set up. I walked over with Marco.

"You owe me," I told Marco.

"I do," he agreed, far too cheerful for my liking.

I sat in the chair. Gloria was muttering to herself as she went through the clothes, and Jen took one look at my nails, gasped, and assured me that she was also an accomplished manicurist. Andi took my hair out of the messy bun I'd put it in.

"I'll be working in my room. Let me know if you need anything," Marco said, and he left.

Part of me wanted to call him back.

Andi was making tutting sounds as she walked around me. "When is the last time you had your hair cut?"

"Uh, two, no, three years ago."

"Three years?" she nearly screeched, trying to cover up her shock. "That's fine. It's fine. You're just long overdue for a cut. I'm guessing that I should be going for very low maintenance here."

"The lower the maintenance the better," I said.

She seemed particularly discouraged by my mousy brown hair. "I'm going to put in some blonde highlights, especially around your face. We'll leave your hair darker at the top and lighter at the bottom. That way you can go longer without getting your roots retouched. I'll be doing balayage and giving you a gradient look, if that's okay."

"I only understood about half of that, and I'm fine with whatever." If I was going to be like some nerdy girl from a 1990s teen movie, I might as well go all in.

Andi mixed product while Jen laid out a bunch of makeup cases on the table in front of me. She was holding Minx products up next to my face to find the right colors. I picked up a lipstick, eyeliner, and a bronzer from the table. "I made these," I told her.

"Very cool. And I'm going to teach you how to use them."

"Good luck," I said. People seemed to forget the artist part of makeup artist. Like being a cosmetic chemist and a woman meant I knew automatically how to make myself look good. That's why they were called makeup artists and not makeup spacklers. It would be like expecting the clerk in the paint department down at Home Depot to be Picasso just because he made the paint. One talent did not guarantee the other.

Time flew by as I discussed color theory with Jen and tried to avoid Andi's questions, since each answer seemed to horrify her more than the one before it. Gloria brought outfits and dresses over for me to say yes or no to, and that worried me. It felt like a test that I was about to fail by giving her the wrong answer.

The three women were all well acquainted and spent a lot of the time talking about photo shoots they'd done together, and it entertained me. I also found that I was enjoying being pampered. I could definitely get used to this.

Andi had me rinse off in the kitchen sink, where she washed, conditioned, rinsed again, and then brought me back to the chair.

"Do you own a hair dryer?" she asked.

"This seems like a trap."

"I'm going to take that as a no. You'll need to buy a big barrel curling iron. I think learning how to blow dry and roller brush at the same time might be a bit more involved than you're used to."

Jen showed me application techniques over and over again, and she would wipe all the makeup off and have me do it over until she felt satisfied that I could re-create what she had shown me. "I'm keeping it really basic. You have such great bone structure and pretty skin that there's no reason to pile it on."

"Are the compliments part of the service or do those cost me extra?" I asked.

That made her laugh. She had laid out twelve different brand-new Minx lipsticks for me. "There should be one for each of your new outfits." She and Gloria had been consulting on that for the last hour or so.

"Okay. How do I know which one goes with which?"

"Good point. I'm going to label them for you."

Andi turned on the hair dryer at that point and loudly told me how to re-create what she was doing by using the curling iron I was supposed to get. I wished I had a notebook to take notes.

Jen shouted over the noise, "I'll write down Andi's instructions for you," as if she could read my mind.

Or maybe she just recognized the necessity of doing so.

My hair was finished, and Andi turned me around to the small mirror that Jen and I had been using. It looked nice. Blonder at the bottom, but I didn't hate it like I thought I might. It actually made me feel a bit prettier. It hung down to my shoulders so that I could still pull it back if I wanted to.

"My turn," Gloria said, pulling me out of my seat. She had set up a screen and handed me clothes. "Try these on."

It took a long time to put everything on and listen to the opinions of the three women as to what should stay or go.

Then Gloria handed me a satiny red dress.

"It's a cocktail dress," Jen said. "Never mind. I'll write it down."

"That's an A-line, V-neck, knee-length chiffon dress," Gloria corrected Jen.

It took me a second to put it on. There were lines that made an X across my shoulder blades and a pretty bow at the back of my waist. I came out, and the three women smiled, even Gloria. Jen actually applauded.

"That's the one," Andi said.

"Clothes always hang so well on tall women," Gloria commented, like she was personally responsible for my height.

"Twirl around," Jen commanded, and I did. The dress spun out in a big circle around me.

"You'll want to make sure you wear underwear with this one," Gloria said, which concerned me. In what scenario would I be wearing this dress but not underwear?

"I wish I could see it," I said.

Andi pointed toward Marco's bedroom. "I would bet good money he has a full-length mirror in there."

Good point. I almost skipped over to his bedroom door and then knocked.

"Come in!" he called out.

I opened the door and stepped into the room. He was lying in the middle of his bed, and there was an infinitesimal part of me that urged me to run over and join him.

I refrained.

He lay there on his side with his laptop in front of him, holding a pen in his mouth.

The pen fell from his mouth a second later as he sat straight up.

"Anna . . . wow."

"What?" I asked, immediately suspicious that I had sat in makeup or gotten some hair dye on the dress.

"You look . . . nice."

Nice? *Nice* didn't merit a *wow*. Now I felt a little uncomfortable and put a hand over my stomach. Why say something flattering and then backtrack it to *nice*? "I didn't mean to intrude."

"I get it. You wanted to see what a clean bedroom looks like."

His room was very tidy. His bed was even made.

"Ha ha. Are you trying to tell me you did this all by yourself?" From his sheepish grin I guessed, "A housekeeper? I could keep my room clean if I had a housekeeper."

"Doubtful."

I had no comeback to that, as he was not incorrect.

"Did you want to show me your dress? If you're looking for my opinion, it's a yes."

"No. I came in to see if you have a full-length mirror."

"In the bathroom," he said, pointing toward a door. I walked over to open it, and he had a bathroom that could rival a day spa. Gleaming tile, a brilliant white soaker tub, a shower big enough to fit six people. Of course.

I found the mirror hung on the outside of his closet door and walked in front of it.

I smiled at my reflection. I swayed side to side, liking the way the skirt swished back and forth.

Marco had followed me, and I was glad. His bathroom felt safer than his bedroom.

"Do you like it?" I asked.

"My opinion doesn't matter," he said in a quiet voice, and I felt strangely disappointed. Maybe it was because I'd spent the last couple of hours with Jen as my hype woman.

"Well, I like it," I informed him, unwilling to let him rain on my parade.

"That's all that counts."

I noticed a tag at my waist and looked at it. "Six thousand dollars?" I gasped. "This dress is six thousand dollars?"

"I've been told that's how much dresses like that cost. It seems worth it to me."

"Easy to say when you're rich. I don't have six thousand dollars."

And then, honest to Obi-Wan's ghost, Marco leaned against the doorframe and folded his arms. It was a heart-stopping moment. "I thought we'd already agreed that I'd be picking up the tab for all this."

"I don't know. That feels like some kind of power imbalance."

"How? I don't have any power over you."

He was sorely mistaken there, but I didn't correct him. "Maybe it's that you have money and I don't."

"Then shouldn't you take it when I offer it to you? You need dresses for upcoming events. You can't buy the dresses. I can. So let me buy them."

"You're too logical sometimes."

"I'll try to work on that," he said with a wink.

"Do you know how many homogenizers I could buy with six thousand dollars? Four."

"What would you do with four homogenizers?"

"No idea."

"I could get you four homogenizers," he offered.

"That's not the point. It's just expensive," I said.

"Don't worry about that. I can afford it."

Figuring I'd protested enough to make my grandma happy, I decided I should head back to the main room before they sent out a search party. I came close to Marco, and he stiffened, standing straighter, tightening his arms so that his forearms flexed.

I didn't understand what his reaction was about.

"Thank you," I said. "It may be too much, but thank you."

It took him a second, and I watched as his Adam's apple bobbed twice before he cleared his throat and said, "You're welcome. I should, uh, get back to work."

"And I should get back to looking *nice*."

I twirled a bit toward the door and heard the sound of my skirt brushing against his leg. He was such a confusing man. I felt like I never really knew what he was thinking and remembered my grandma telling me that women spent twice as long wondering what men thought about as men actually spent thinking.

He was probably focused on his job.

And hoping that this now-very-expensive plan of his was going to work.

I rejoined the women, and Gloria had thought of everything—purses, shoes that actually fit my large feet, underwear to go with each outfit—and Jen was busy attaching pieces of paper to everything with notes. I changed back into my regular clothes, and Gloria took the pretty red dress and put it in a hanging bag.

Once everything was sorted and bagged up for me, they packed their belongings, and I walked them to the door. They all hugged me goodbye, even Gloria. Jen gave me her phone number so that I could call her with any questions, and then they were gone.

I was trying to figure out how I was going to get all this stuff down to Betty without making multiple trips when Marco came out of his room.

He walked over to me, and I couldn't help but feel a bit mesmerized as he came closer and closer. Like a large cat stalking its prey. Only if I were the prey, I'd lay down and pretend to be dead just so that he would catch me.

"We're alone?" he asked.

"Yep." The word unintentionally squeaked out of me.

"Good. There's something I wanted to talk to you about."

"There is?"

He nodded. "Seduction."

CHAPTER SEVENTEEN

All the blood left my brain and pooled in unspeakable places. If his plan was to seduce me, I found that I had no objections. "What?"

"You've got your armor, all ready to go into battle. Now you need a strategy."

He picked up a remote and clicked a button. It turned on soft music. He held out his hand to me. Holy Gimli's beard—maybe I really was about to be seduced.

Still no objections from any part of me.

Even though I knew he couldn't be talking about us.

"Wait. This is for me to seduce Craig?" I verified. I felt like I needed to make sure that I wasn't misunderstanding the situation.

Marco dropped his hand. "Yes."

Why was that disappointing? I couldn't speak for a moment.

Luckily, he filled in what felt like an awkward silence. "The reason I did all this was because there's a party next weekend. An engagement precelebration."

There was a pain from his words, but it was dull and faint. Not like the vivid sharpness I'd experienced every time before when I'd thought about Craig marrying someone else. "But they just got engaged."

"My stepmother loves any excuse to throw a party. Mostly so that she can drink without being judged. She says if you do it publicly, you're a happy drunk. Privately, you're an alcoholic. She does both and fails to see the irony. Anyway, this will be one of the many pregaming events leading up to the actual engagement party that will cost a fortune and be featured in gossip columns and online magazines across the country. And at this first event, there will be dancing."

"So . . . you're inviting me to a dance," I said, trying to ignore the rising flush of excitement. Finally, I was the girl being asked to the dance. That did funny things to my stomach.

"I guess, in a way. We should practice."

My whole being throbbed slowly at the idea that Marco was going to hold me in his arms again. "I know how to dance."

"I'm sure you do. But we don't want it to look like it's our first time."

He held out his hand again, and against my better judgment, I took it. He pulled me into his embrace, his right hand going around my waist. I put my arms around his still-sexy neck, and he took my right arm, tugging it down. Then he wrapped his left hand around my right one, and I dragged in a ragged breath.

"I know the last time you danced was probably at some farewell event at space camp, but you're not in seventh grade," he said teasingly. "This is how adults dance."

"Just because I enjoy nerdy stuff does not mean that I went to space . . ." My voice trailed off. "Okay, fine." There wasn't any point in arguing with him because I had gone to space camp, but I tried to hold on to that tiny bit of anger. Because despite his assurance that I was wearing armor, I felt way too vulnerable. I needed some kind of defense against him.

Then we were swaying to the music, moving slowly in a circle. And it felt a lot like a seventh-grade dance to me, but an updated adult version with a very hot man.

I willed my hands not to sweat again. It wasn't going very well, though. I was so aware of him. He was no longer damp, and he was emanating heat everywhere that was seeping into my pores, making my cells tingle in response.

It was nice to dance with a man who was taller than me. It wasn't something I'd experienced very often growing up.

I was so focused on him and his energy that I knew I needed to redirect myself. "Why do you think I need help seducing Craig?" It felt really odd to be having this conversation with him, given that Craig was his brother.

"You're the one who said you didn't have a lot of experience in this area." His fingers flexed against my waist, and it caused a burning sensation that started at that point of contact and radiated outward.

Marco was kind of acting like I'd never gone out with anyone. I mean, I had dated. Sporadically. I'd even had a few in the last couple of months with Catalina setting me up. But he didn't need to know just how minimal my experience actually was.

"I get that I'm like . . . not seductive, but what is there to know? Don't you just generally take off your shirt?"

"You don't get naked."

"Says the man who started this afternoon with half his clothes off."

He smiled down at me and looked like he wanted to say something, but he didn't. "It would be a little obvious."

"Obvious doesn't work?" I was a big fan of obvious things.

"It doesn't if it seems desperate. People like to chase. To want things that they know they can't have. It's human nature. So don't strip down. We probably just need to refine your flirting technique."

"That might be a good idea. I'm kind of like a hyperventilating walrus when I attempt it."

He laughed, and his hand tightened around mine. Which was still, thankfully, mostly sweat-free. My hairline and lower back? Not so much.

"You could practice on me," he offered. "I'm an attractive man."

"What makes you think you're attractive?"

"Most women I've met seem to think so."

Of all the conceited . . . "You've met me, and I don't think that about you."

That sly smile of his made him look mischievous. "I could say something really arrogant here, but let's just go with I know you think I am."

"Ha." So many lies were about to come out of my mouth. "I don't."

"Agree to disagree," he said, pushing me back slightly so that I could do a turn. I kind of wished I had my red dress on. "Plus, you've already told me you do."

Dang it. He was right. "The most attractive thing about you is your humility," I told him as I came back into his arms.

I misjudged the distance between us and crashed against his very firm chest. I stayed there for a moment, engulfed in electric flames, loving the feel of him against me when he said in a low voice, "That's not what you like best about me."

Okay, that just made everything worse.

Taking a step back, I tried to discreetly pull some air back into my lungs. He moved me into position so that we were dancing again.

"You are not my type," I told him. I didn't know which one of us I was trying to convince, but I didn't think either one of us was buying it.

"Not your type? I'm like ketchup. I go with everything."

"You eat ketchup? Don't your kind stick to gold-plated caviar and artichokes?"

"Artichokes? That's your insult?"

"Have you ever tasted one?" I asked him. It was a big insult.

"Come on, hit me with your best shot," he said. "Ask me if I'm tired because I've been running through your mind all day. Or if it hurt when I fell from heaven."

"Cheesy pickup lines? That's what we're relying on now? We are in real trouble."

"I'll have you know that cheesy pickup lines can work really well under the right circumstances."

"Are those circumstances the other person is so drunk that they don't notice?" I asked.

"Give it a try."

"Okay." I felt so ridiculously stupid. I could not use some dumb line on him. I'd never be able to get through it with a straight face. I let out a muffled groan. "This is what I like about science. If I add a precise amount of potassium metal to an exact amount of chlorine gas, then I get potassium chloride. Every time."

"I'm sorry life is more subjective than that."

"Me too. A well-ordered world would be so much easier to navigate."

He spun me again, and this time I came back to the right spot. Which was actually disappointing. I liked the accidental crash from earlier.

"I'll start you off. Marco, I dream about you at night." He said it in a high-pitched voice, like he was imitating me.

I smacked his right shoulder while he laughed.

"Fine. You are . . . nicely shaped. You have muscles that, um, are there and it works." So, so dumb.

"I would say more asthmatic otter than hyperventilating walrus," he said. "What else do you have?"

I tried batting my eyelashes at him. I remembered Catalina saying something about that once.

"Is there something in your eye?" he asked. "Or is that more of your flirting? Because I have notes."

"There's nothing in my eye," I snapped back at him.

"Hang on. You've got an eyelash on your cheek."

He reached up gently, and I held my breath. His finger touched my cheek so lightly, but it was like he'd pushed some detonator button inside me and everything had gone up in flames.

Marco got the eyelash and held his finger up in front of my lips. "Make a wish," he said softly.

I was afraid to. I should wish for this to work out and to end up with Craig, but I didn't. I made a wish that I had no intention of saying out loud. I wasn't even going to say it to myself.

I blew against his finger and fought off the instinct to kiss the tip while it was within kissing range of my mouth.

"So it seems like we've got a long night ahead of us," he said as he moved his hand back to my waist. His voice sounded a little off, but I didn't know why. "Because at some point you are going to have to have a conversation with Craig."

"We've had conversations, thank you very much." I was annoyed by how he acted like he knew everything and I was some idiot kid sister he had to help. "So, Mr. Expert, how would you seduce me if the situation were reversed?"

He came to a complete stop. He was still holding me in place, but we weren't dancing. He moved so that one hand was still at my waist, and with the other, he reached up to tuck my hair behind my ear, caressing the outer shell lightly with his fingers.

I was already a pile of putty.

"Women are different than men," he said, his fingers moving down my neck, onto my shoulder, my arm, until they joined his other hand at my waist. There were trails of fire everywhere he had touched me.

Everywhere he was still touching me.

"I would tell you how beautiful you look tonight. How my breath caught in my throat when you walked into my room. How I've been thinking all night how much I want to be alone with you, talk to you, be close to you. Touch you."

While he spoke in that low and mesmerizing tone, his voice rough and exciting, he was pulling me closer to him so that we were pressed together again.

Holy Treebeard. It was totally, one hundred percent working. I knew it was all a lie, but I was falling for it. Like a piano out of a twelfth-story window.

He leaned his head down so that his lips were close to my ear. "Then, because it's you, I would tell you my heart must be made of gallium because it melts when you're close to me."

The words tickled my ear, making me shivery and fiery. Turned out he was right about the cheesy pickup line, because I was ready to drag him to his bedroom.

When I realized that I was probably the only woman in the world who would respond to his science line, it showed me just how perceptive he was and that he understood women in a way that I would never understand men.

Or he understood me in a way that I would never understand him.

I also thought of how much I wanted this to be real. I was basically panting at his words, not able to breathe normally.

I noticed that he seemed to be breathing a bit harder, too.

"Should I tell you that I think the reaction between you and me would be exothermic?" he asked as he pressed his fingers into my back, still making me shiver and want his heat. Because anything that happened between us would be somehow exothermic and endothermic simultaneously, thank you.

Everything felt too tight, my throat, my chest, my skin, but at the same time like it was all about to burst.

"Wow, you are amazing at this. I almost believed you."

His expression shifted into something I didn't quite recognize, but then his smile was back. "See? Easy enough." He stepped away, letting go of me completely. It had only been a few seconds, but I already missed him holding me. He added, "It's a good thing we're friends."

"Yes," I said weakly. "This would all be really strange if we weren't."

Or maybe that was why this was weird. Friends trying to pretend to be lovers.

He stood there, and I realized that his smile didn't quite reach his eyes, so I attempted a joke. "You don't have to worry about whether or not you have game. If your game were any sharper, you could shave with it. If I learn how to do what you just did, Craig won't know what hit him."

But he didn't laugh like I hoped he would. Instead he said, "We should take a break. Are you hungry? We can order something in."

"Sure."

He went and sat on his couch, and not knowing what to do with myself, I did the same. He threw out a couple of options nearby, and we settled on a burger place. He used an app on his phone and passed it to me, where he had pulled up the menu of regular hamburgers for me.

"No cheeseburgers, right?" he verified.

"Yeah," I said, touched that he'd remembered. Although after our lengthy vegan discussion at the pizzeria, it shouldn't be surprising. I added what I wanted to the order and handed it back to him to finish it up.

"Thanks for dinner," I said. "In case I forget later."

"You're preemptively welcome," he told me.

Unsure what to do with myself and worried I might try to edge closer to him, I swung my legs sideways and knocked a manila folder off the coffee table. "Oh, sorry," I said, leaning forward to pick it up. I viewed a couple of the pages. It was a marketing discussion about names. "Is this for the new line?"

"It is." He nodded, putting his phone down.

I read the submissions out loud. "Vixen, Harpy, Tart. It's too bad you can't pick something nice and inspiring. Oh! Maybe Heroine."

"Like the drug?"

"No, not heroin. Heroine. With an E on the end. Like an amazing woman."

"Yeah . . . I'm not sure people will be able to hear the distinction. But I bet heroin cosmetics would sell for a lot. Maybe even find us a new audience."

I smiled, putting the folder and papers back on the table.

"Earlier . . ." He trailed off, and my heart came to a complete and total stop. Earlier? Dancing earlier? Wanting to kiss him earlier? A lesson in seduction earlier?

"With the team," he continued. "Did all that making over go okay?"

His question was both a relief and a disappointment. "They were great. But they had some requests that I was not okay with. Do you know where they wanted to wax me? I explained that we are mammals and that we're supposed to have hair."

At that he laughed, and it was nice to feel comfortable again after feeling awkward and unsure, so I kept going. "They also wanted me to get rid of my glasses. I told them it was nonnegotiable. I am not in a Superman situation. I don't suddenly become a sex goddess by taking my glasses off. My only superpower is poor vision. My eyes are basically just ornamentation at this point."

"I think your glasses are cute," he said. "But Craig is just . . . well, Craig. They've all worked with him before, so they know what they're talking about."

I didn't particularly want to explore or think too much about his statements. That Marco thought my glasses were cute, because that would just lead to a rabbit hole of *did he mean cute in an attractive way* or *cute like a blue-haired elderly lady walking her teacup poodle way*, and that Craig would not define it as cute with either definition, putting us back into that Craig-is-shallow territory that I was determined to steer clear of. By his own admission, Marco hadn't spent a lot of time with Craig since they were kids. People just didn't know him the way I did.

"I had to tell them that I can't do contacts because I will not stick things in my eyeballs, and they suggested Lasik. I'm not letting anyone point lasers at my eyes for any reason. Not even for your brother."

"Makes sense," he said. "I don't let people point lasers at my eyeballs, either."

I pointed at his gaming setup. "So do I get a demonstration? Or am I just going to have to imagine you doing it in the nerdiest way possible?"

"I can do better than show you. You can play with me." He got up and turned on his flat-screen TV. "I have just the game for you."

He grabbed a controller and handed me one. "I've never done this before," I warned him.

"In case you hadn't noticed, I'm a good teacher." Why did everything out of his mouth have to sound like the sexiest thing ever, even when he meant it in just a regular way? "I'll show you the ropes."

The game he chose started up, and I recognized the music. "Lord of the Rings?" I gasped.

"Yep."

He explained to me what each button did on my controller, but I was so eager to start that I wasn't really listening. He helped me create a character, and then we entered the game together.

Marco tried to show me what I should be doing, but I was enjoying twirling, taking in the landscape. He did get me to move forward, and we just kept slashing things with our swords.

After doing that for a bit, I announced, "I don't get this game. We're just running around and hitting anything that moves."

"Seems like you get it," he said.

We played until the food arrived, and then we sat at his table to eat. "Before we start, I have something," he announced.

He got up to go into his room, and I called after him, "I could make you a cream for that!"

Instead of responding to my joke, he came back with a large binder and put it on the table. "This is for you."

I took a big bite of my hamburger, pulling it toward me. "What is it?"

"It's a binder of information about Craig. Likes, dislikes, things like that."

I swallowed my food and said, "You made a binder with color-coded tabs about your brother?" He really was dedicated to the cause.

"My assistant made it."

"You should give her a raise," I said as I flipped it open.

"Sorry about the homework."

Not able to help myself, I immediately responded, "I love homework."

"I suspected as much," he said, popping a couple of french fries in his mouth. "There's ketchup here. If you want it. Because it goes with everything."

I did want it. That was the problem. I turned away from him and ran my fingers along the tabs of the binder, stopping at the last one. I read the title out loud. "Sports."

"He's a big fan of the Portland Jacks." He paused, like he was waiting for a response and then added, "They're a professional football team from Oregon."

"I know who they are," I protested, indignant. I did know that, right?

Marco didn't seem to believe me. "What do you actually know about sports?"

"There's balls and some type of head gear and butt slapping, from what I understand."

"I thought your grandpa was a big Dodgers fan."

"He is. But my parents were on their way home from a game that night and I've just . . . never really wanted to watch baseball since then."

"That's understandable."

"But you did the opposite. You run the company that your mom modeled for." He hadn't walked away from it, even though there had to be painful memories associated with Minx. Especially when they ran that retro campaign with his mother's image.

"Our situations were different. If your grandparents had owned the Dodgers, you would have still gone to the games."

I picked up my soda and took a drink. "You're probably right. You know, you have good insight into things."

"Spent a lot of time in therapy."

That surprised me. I put my cup back down. "Really?"

"It's not a bad thing."

"No, I agree with you. I'm just impressed. You don't seem like the therapy type. More of the put-everything-into-a-tiny-internal-box-and-cram-it-all-down-inside-you-and-never-speak-of-it-again kind of guy."

"I was that way for a long time until I realized how much it was messing me up. My dad wouldn't have wanted me to go, but when I turned eighteen, I started making decisions about the things that were best for me, and getting professional help was one of those things. Losing a parent is a lot, and it helped to have someone to talk to about it. Did you ever go to therapy?"

"I did a couple of sessions right after the accident. Then my grandma decided I was done and that all I needed was to work hard to deal with my feelings. But secretly I wanted to keep going."

"Why didn't you tell her?" he asked.

I shrugged one shoulder. "I don't know. I think I was afraid that if I spoke up, if I didn't do everything they wanted, that I'd lose them, too. I know that was irrational, but I was a kid. But I think that's one of the reasons why I don't always speak up for myself."

He considered this. "You stood up for yourself today with the Lasik thing."

"Yay! Point for me for not letting people cut my eyeballs open." I ate a few more french fries and then said, "It's funny. You would think you and I wouldn't have anything in common. We've had totally different upbringings. Different life experiences. But when I hang out with you—it's like none of that matters. Like you understand me."

"Maybe I do," he said. "Grief is a great equalizer. But then there's the fact that I just like hanging out with you, too. Speaking of, I gave you the binder, the hair, the clothes. Technically we're finished, but . . . do you want to stay?"

While I recognized the fact that I might have been mistaken, I thought I detected a hopeful tone in his voice.

Like he wanted me to say yes.

"Sure. Let me just make a phone call." I walked over toward the front door, out of sight. I dialed the number quickly and when I heard a "hello?" I said, "Grandpa? I'm going to be out late. Don't wait up for me."

CHAPTER EIGHTEEN

"Did you want to pick up where we left off with the video game?" he asked as we cleared our trash off the table now that we had finished eating. He had one of those fancy trash cans stored inside a sliding cabinet.

"Not really," I confessed. It wasn't as much fun as I'd assumed it would be. Maybe if there were some virtual-reality version where I could brush Legolas's hair, then I might feel different.

"Okay, so besides watching movies and creating makeup, what else do you enjoy doing?"

"I really like board games."

"Do you want to play one?"

Marco had board games? Interesting. "Do you have Monopoly?"

His eyes lit up. "I do. I got it as a present last Christmas. Hang on." He went into his room and came out carrying a black box, still wrapped in plastic. When he got closer, I saw that it was the Star Wars Complete Saga Edition. "I got it from my younger sister."

More shocking revelations. "I didn't know you had a little sister."

No wonder he treated me like one. This also meant that Craig had a sister. It reminded me how little I knew about the Kimball family before I'd met Marco.

"I haven't mentioned her before? Lindy. She's amazing. I think you'd like her." Marco set the game down on the coffee table and handed me a plastic tray that had all the playing pieces. He opened the board, and all the properties were planets from Star Wars, and we had to build X-wings and TIE fighters instead of hotels.

This was definitely my kind of game. All thoughts of his sister went out of my head. I grabbed the Kylo Ren figurine to play with. Marco took Han Solo, and that made perfect sense, given Marco's personality. I could definitely see him as a smuggler, captaining a spaceship and . . .

Cutting off my overexcited imagination, I focused on helping to set up the game. He said, "You're playing the Empire; I'm part of the Rebel Alliance. Which means I'm going to win."

"Famous last words," I said.

He grinned at me. "We'll see."

"Does Craig like board games?"

His eyes shuttered briefly, his smile slipping. "I don't know. We're not that kind of family."

Was he talking about playing the board games or spending time together? Knowing each other's likes and dislikes?

He added, "I'm guessing that means your family is the kind who sits around and plays board games."

"Yes, but my grandparents always crap out after three rounds of Monopoly. I've never been able to play it all the way through to the end."

"I'll be happy to introduce you to your first official defeat," he said.

"You think I won't beat you?" I asked as I moved my token to the starting point. "I think you're severely underestimating my competitive nature."

"And you're forgetting that I'm a CEO of a company and my real life is already like Monopoly. I even own a hotel on Park Place."

"You do not!" I gasped, in shock. Why did that make him even more attractive?

"You're right, I don't," he said with a smile. "But you believed me for a second, didn't you?"

"That's because I'm very trusting."

"Yes. You are," he agreed, his eyes glittering in a way I didn't understand. "I do own a house in Tuscany that my mother left me. I'll have to take you there sometime."

Why did he do that? Was he just making conversation? Being polite? Or did he envision me being in his future in some way? Married to his brother?

And why was I always reading so much into everything he said?

Shaking my head, I announced, "Since I'm your guest, I get to roll first. I'm sure you want to be a good host." I picked up the dice and tossed them onto the board.

"Cheating already?" he asked as I moved my Kylo Ren token eight spaces.

"Going first isn't cheating. It's just taking advantage of the opportunity when it presented itself."

"I'll remember that."

Landing on Kashyyyk, I said, "I'll buy it." I picked up my credits. "Wait. When did we decide that you were the banker?"

"Because of the two of us, I have a savings account in real life," he teased. "I think that qualifies me as the better person to handle the money."

"You better be honest," I warned him.

"I'm not the one who grabbed the dice first," he retorted.

"Then know that I'm keeping an eye on you." Not like that was a hardship or anything.

"What I know is what a stickler you are for rules." He paused. "Why are you such a fan?"

Shrugging, I took the property card from him and put it in front of me. "I like the idea that I can impose order on chaos. I know I can't control the world, but sticking to rules makes me feel like I can."

"I get what that's like," he told me.

There was a charged moment between us, our gazes locked, until I reached for the dice and handed them to him. "I hope you land on Kashyyyk."

At that, he laughed, and we teased and joked as we continued to play, in a race to see who could accumulate the most properties first. Marco was better than I'd expected him to be and definitely kept me on my toes.

Once the trash-talking died down, we settled into a comfortable rhythm, swapping stories as the night went on. We shared our childhood nicknames.

"Bird Girl or Bird Nerd," I told him. "You?"

"Brace Boy."

"Because you had braces? Unlike most people?" I questioned sarcastically. Kids were so unimaginative.

"Yes, but I also had leg braces because I was pigeon-toed."

That made him seem even more down-to-earth. "My grandpa would have thought your turned-in feet were adorable."

He laughed. "He would have been the only one."

"Not very popular with the ladies?" I asked.

"I didn't kiss a girl until I was a sophomore in high school."

"Wow. Even I got kissed before then."

"At space camp?" he asked with that grin of his.

Yes, but that didn't seem like information he needed to have. "So, what—you've spent the last fifteen or so years making up for lost time?"

"Something like that."

"Honestly, I find it hard to believe that every girl you met was too stupid to see . . ." My voice trailed off as I realized that I was close to making an idiot of myself.

"See what?" His tone was casual, but there was something there, just beneath the surface, that felt anything but casual.

Because how could those women have not looked beyond something temporary to see the amazing man underneath?

I bet when he got hot, they were all kicking themselves.

He shared with me why he never had a long-term relationship. "Every marriage I've ever seen has been about convenience. For status or money. I've never dated a woman who didn't expect elaborate gifts and expensive vacations."

"I want to tell you that I don't care about that stuff, but you gave me a mixer and I'm not about to give it back to you in order to seem noble or something."

He laughed.

I added, "I would offer to return it, but we'd both know that I wasn't serious. I should probably get credit for considering it, though."

"For the whole 1.2 seconds you thought about it?"

I moved my Kylo Ren token five spaces and gave Marco the rent money I owed him. "There are women out there who would think you're a pretty great guy, money or no money. You have a lot more to offer than your bank account."

"Thanks," he said quietly, adding my credits to his growing pile.

We talked about what we'd wanted to be when we were younger. I told him that I'd always wanted to be a chemist—that when I was little, my dad would do all kinds of home experiments with me. Hot ice. Elephant toothpaste. Alkali metals in water. "I thought he was magic. I still think of chemistry as being like magic."

"Why cosmetics?" Marco asked.

"My mom loved makeup. She really wanted to be an actress, which Grandma thought was a waste of time, so she ended up getting her degree in library science. That's how she met my dad—Grandma wanted to set him up with my mom, so he went to the library to 'check her out' as he liked to say, and they hit it off. When she got off work, she offered him a ride, but she had a flat tire. He came to her rescue and changed it for her, and that was kind of it. She didn't even mind that it had been sort of a setup. They got married really quickly."

"That's sweet," he said.

"Anyway, I was obsessed with her things when I was young. I would read all the labels for her moisturizers and lipsticks. I wanted to understand what the products were, to make those sorts of things myself. Like I could better understand my mom by understanding the things she used. She was so beautiful, and I wanted desperately to be like her."

Marco held the dice up in his hand, about to take his turn, but he stopped. "You are."

Unfortunately, I had chosen this moment to take a drink, as talking so much had dried my mouth out. I choked on my water. I coughed it out, and he looked concerned. He leaned forward like he was going to help me, but I held up my hand to stop him.

"I'm fine," I said when I could breathe again. "You don't have to say that. I'm going to read and study that ridiculous binder you gave me. I've said yes. You don't have to win me over. I'm going to help you."

"Anna, you are beautiful."

He sounded so honest, but it felt almost painful for him to say it. "Because I improved myself with some color on my face and in my hair?"

He shook his head. "You were beautiful before that. You didn't improve anything. You only made it a little different. And before you argue with me, you being beautiful, that's . . . what did you call it? Just an objective fact."

"No fair using my own words against me," I said softly, but he grinned, and I felt weak-kneed.

"If I was the man you were in love with, I wouldn't have wanted you to change a thing."

"But you're not."

"I know," he said in that cheerful way of his, only it didn't sound quite as authentic as it normally did.

"What about you? What did you want to be when you grew up?" I asked, returning my attention to the game. There was something going on here. Something one-sided, I reminded myself. I really liked him as a person—I didn't need to make this awkward.

"I never wanted anything other than being the CEO of Minx and then CEO of KRT after that."

"What little kid is playing with his trucks and says, *Someday I hope to be a CEO*?"

"The kind who grew up with my father," he said. "There was an expectation. Even when Tracie started pushing for Craig to take over, my dad still wanted me to follow in his footsteps. And if I'm being honest, there is some part of me that wants to spite Tracie. I felt like she took so much from me that I don't want her to have this, too. I know that isn't good or healthy." He paused, looking at me. For judgment? I wouldn't judge him for that. He added, "I don't think I've ever said that out loud before. And it's not the main reason I want the job. KRT Limited has been a family business for generations, and I don't want to be the weak link in that chain."

"Maybe you were meant to have a different kind of job. You could be one of those football guys who pushes people around."

"A lineman?" he asked, a little confused.

"Yes." If those were the big guys who stopped the other players, because Marco definitely had the physique for it.

"I'm probably past the point in my life where I could play professional sports. Also, do your sports homework."

"I'll do my sports homework," I promised. "You could do something else, though. Isn't there anything you'd like to try?"

He took my question seriously, pondering it. "I always thought I'd like to do what my great-grandfather did—start my own company and make it successful. But I won't. Like I said, my career's already been laid out for me."

"That seems a little sad," I told him as I took my turn.

"Enough about me," he said. "What about you and your secret project? I've really wanted to know what you're working on."

There was a burning desire to tell him. I knew I could trust him. So I did. "Keep this between us—I'm developing a lipstick that changes colors based on body temperature and pH."

"Doesn't that already exist?"

"The kind you're thinking of is static. They respond to an individual's pH, but the color doesn't change once it's applied. There's also one brand that changes from external temperatures. Mine will respond to temperature shifts, but it will also change colors depending on the person's physical reactions."

"A mood ring lipstick," he said, quickly putting our conversation from Catalina's party together with what I was talking about. "That's so brilliant. I can't believe no one's thought of it yet."

His words warmed me. "There should be an issue with toxicity from the thermotropic liquid crystals, but I've found a work-around."

He leaned forward, excited. "Are you going to tell me what it is?"

"No, Mr. Competitor. Because it will work due to a proprietary combination of ingredients. If I told you, it wouldn't be a secret." And then every cosmetic company in the world would copy me.

"You know, I could just reverse engineer it from that list you gave my assistant." At my expression, he hurried to add, "But I won't! I'm completely joking. Although, can you imagine a product with this level of innovation being undone by a shopping list?"

He sounded so impressed, and that made me feel ridiculously proud. "You think it will be successful? I haven't found the right solidifying agent yet, but I think I'm close."

"You will find it, and you're going to make a fortune, Anna."

Why did his approval mean so much to me? "Someday. When I save up enough."

"You know, you don't have to save all the money yourself to start a makeup company. You could find an investor." He took his turn, landed on one of my planets, and gave me the credits he owed.

"Where would I find an investor?" I asked, adding his money to my ever-growing pile. "Is there some Investors R Us downtown that I don't know about?"

"I happen to be related to one. Who already owns a makeup company."

"Your dad?"

"I could get you on his schedule."

I shook my head, unable to believe that this was actually happening. "What does that even entail? I'm pretty sure it's not showing up at his office and saying, *Hi, can I have some money, please?*"

"It is more detailed than that," he said. "But I could help you."

"Why?" I seriously didn't understand why he'd stick out his neck for me like that.

He frowned slightly, like now he was the one confused. "I want you to be happy, Anna. I want you to succeed."

But again I asked, "Why?"

He gave me this look, one that I couldn't have explained to someone else, but I felt it in my gut.

Then he said he was going to get another drink and asked if I wanted one. I told him I was fine, and he went into the kitchen.

Only I wasn't fine. Not even a little. That exchange left me shaky and unnerved, and I wasn't sure what to do with myself or how to process what had just happened.

Because much as I tried to deny it, something was happening here.

But when he came back, he was full of smiles and jokes again, and it was a relief. He started chatting about Craig, about his likes and dislikes. I asked specifically if Craig liked any of my favorite movies, and Marco shook his head.

"It may be better not to bring them up. He's never been into that kind of stuff."

I leaned against the couch, surprised. "I can't talk about some of my favorite things with him?"

He shrugged in a way that might as well have said, *Your fault for being the one in love with him*. What he actually said was, "It's your life, Anna. I'm just trying to give you the best chance for success."

We continued to have fun as the game went on, but that easy familiarity that had been there earlier in the evening had ebbed away a little, and he was definitely focused almost entirely on Craig and me being together.

Again, letting me know exactly where I stood with him. Friends only. Which was a good thing, I reminded myself. I needed to put aside my inappropriate crush on him.

We finally got to the end of the game, where I had mortgaged every property and had quite obviously lost.

"Go ahead," I told him. "I know you want to brag. You earned it."

"Without cheating," he said with a grin.

"Yeah, yeah," I muttered. A few hours ago, I might have attempted a slightly illegal move because I saw that I was losing, but eagle-eyed Marco had called me on it and of course he had to bring it up now.

"I'm just curious," he said. "Are there any games that you're good at?"

"Do you know what your problem is?" I asked him.

He folded up the game to put it back in the box. "I can think of a couple of women who could tell you."

"It's that you're not a good sport. I don't need you making snarky comments about my defeat like some elderly balcony Muppet."

He laughed at that, clearly getting my reference.

I added, "Gonzo is probably my favorite Muppet. In case you were wondering." I didn't know why that was pertinent, but I said it anyway.

"Maybe don't bring that up on your date with Craig," he said.

"So I can't talk about Lord of the Rings, Star Wars, or the Muppets? I hate to tell you this, but that's kind of my entire personality."

"I guess you'll have to think of it as another game."

"Relationship games suck," I said, crossing my arms against my chest.

"I don't disagree with you."

I glanced toward the window. "Hey, when did it get light outside?"

Blinking, Marco reached for his phone. "It's seven thirty."

"A.M.?" I clarified.

He nodded.

No wonder I'd brought up Gonzo. It was clearly due to my lack of sleep. "I can't remember the last time I did something like this," I told him. It might have been never. We'd had such a good time together, we'd stayed up all night and I hadn't even noticed.

And I'd finally completed a full game of Monopoly. I'd just forget about the part where I lost.

Marco stood up to stretch, lifting his arms above his head. I had my glasses on this time and was able to fully appreciate the part of his stomach he exposed. The abs were still there, safe and sound. I sighed happily.

"Do you want some breakfast?" he asked. "There's a smoothie place around the corner."

"Gross. I don't even like to eat vegetables. I definitely don't want to drink them, either."

He smiled at that. "There's a diner a couple of blocks over. I could load you up on some carbs and protein."

Very tempting, but I had to go home. "I had a curfew of midnight when I was in high school. As far as I know, it's never been updated, so I might be in big trouble when my grandparents realize that I was out all night."

"Can't you just tell them you got up early to go jogging?"

I laughed, and he looked confused, so I said, “Oh, you don’t know me well enough yet. They’ll never believe that. I don’t really like moving around a whole lot.”

“You can’t just sneak in?”

“They’re early risers. Not only that, but the birds will alert them.”

“Too bad the birds can’t be bribed.”

I stood up, realizing that I didn’t want to. I was happy where I was. I wanted to stay here. “Too bad,” I echoed, wondering at what point I was going to stop having this crush on Marco so that I could focus all my energy on Craig.

“My dad’s estate had some guard dogs that were big fans of steak. It’s definitely helpful when treats work.” The idea of a young Marco grabbing some filet mignons to tempt angry dogs with was an endearing thought.

Yep, definitely time for me to leave before I started daydreaming about that. “I should go and face the music.”

“Do you have your ticket from the valet? I’ll call them up and have them bring your car around.”

I took it from my pocket and handed it to him. I gathered up the glass and dishes I had used last night and brought them into the kitchen. I passed by the Craig binder, still on the table.

Putting the dishes in the sink, I walked back to the binder and again ran my fingers along the edges. I was surprised that I hadn’t spent a large chunk of last night reading it.

“Car’s on the way,” Marco said as he hung up his phone. “What do we need to take downstairs?”

I showed him the piles of clothes and makeup. He grabbed a couple of laundry baskets, and we were able to get everything down in one trip.

When we went out through the lobby, Betty was waiting there patiently for me out front.

“How do you know when it’s time to change the oil?” he asked. “Does it send you a message in Morse code?”

"I told you, no insults where she can hear you." I went to open the back passenger door, but it was stuck. I tugged on the handle. "See? This is why you don't upset her."

"Let me help." Marco leaned in, and I tried not to jump away from his nearness. I'd thought spending a lot of time with him would inoculate me to his potent brand of appeal, but I was finding that it only seemed to be exacerbating the situation. He yanked and wrenched the door open.

"Thanks." We started loading my stuff up in the back seat.

"So this probably isn't a good time to ask you, but I'm curious. When your modified lawn mower comes to a stop, do you have to stick your feet down through holes in the floor to make that happen?"

I just shook my head. "Don't listen to him, Betty."

Once everything was put away, I slammed the door shut. Marco had stepped back and stood next to the curb, his hands in his pockets.

Without thinking, I stepped forward and hugged him. I couldn't help myself. I felt his surprise, the way his body went rigid for a moment before he relaxed, his arms wrapping around me, holding me tightly.

Still wonderful, but a bit easier to manage this time. I didn't think I was going to injure him or myself.

Progress.

"Just practicing," I told him as an explanation. Total lie, but hopefully he couldn't tell.

"Do you want to go out with me tonight?" he asked against the top of my head. His tone indicated that he seemed surprised he'd asked me.

My voice probably sounded the same when I answered, "Yes."

Not a good idea, not a good idea, some internal voice said, but I ignored it.

Realizing that I'd been holding on to him for too long, I finally let go. It was most likely my imagination, but he seemed reluctant to release me.

"Okay. So, I'm going to head out. Thanks for last night." I put my hands down at my sides so that he hopefully wouldn't notice the way I was trembling.

He put his hands back in his pockets. "I'll text you about tonight."

I smiled and then walked around to get in my car. I said a quick prayer that she wouldn't die because after hugging him like that, I did not need more potential embarrassment.

He knocked on the passenger window, and I had to lean over to manually roll it down. I wondered if I'd forgotten something.

Marco leaned in on the passenger side, resting his forearms on the door. Then he flashed me that killer smile of his and said, "My favorite Muppet is Animal. In case you were wondering."

CHAPTER NINETEEN

There was no hope of sneaking in when I got home, as the birds erupted into a cacophony of sound the instant I walked in the door.

I couldn't even be too concerned about it, though, because I was still running the image of Marco's face through my head as he told me that Animal was his favorite Muppet. My grandpa was in the family room with his newspaper, and my grandmother came from the kitchen into the foyer.

"Where have you been?" she demanded.

"I told you not to wait up," I said as I kicked my shoes off.

She seemed so mad that for a second, she didn't register anything else about me. But then the observant scientist in her couldn't help but take in every detail of my appearance. "What did you do to yourself?"

"It's just a little bit of color," I said defensively. It was a good thing I'd left all my stuff in the car or else I'd be answering questions about that, too. I could only imagine how much she would freak out if she knew Marco was buying me things.

"Why did you have this makeover?" she asked, clearly wanting her question answered.

"So I would look nice, Grandma."

My grandpa piped up from behind his paper. "You know what they say—even an old barn looks better with a fresh coat of paint."

"Thanks, Grandpa. I think." I wasn't sure if he was trying to be helpful or if he thought I usually looked like an old barn.

My grandmother crossed her arms. "Are you trying to live up to some standard that this Marco has set?"

"That's not what this is about." It wasn't about Marco at all. I didn't think trying to introduce Craig into the conversation right now would be a good idea, though.

Because I knew she'd tell me that any man I had to change myself for wasn't worth my time.

She pressed her lips together so that they formed a thin line. I could feel the lecture coming on. Lecture Number 496—how there were so many other important things going on in the world that I didn't need to worry about frivolous things like hair color and painted nails.

It made me long for my mother again. She would have understood. She would have loved me changing up my look. She would have told me that it was okay to do frivolous things that made me happy. To want to feel pretty.

To my surprise, though, Grandma stayed quiet. "You can't come home so late. We didn't know if you were going to come home," she said in a soft, hurt voice.

It hadn't even occurred to me that staying out that way would be hard for her. Like the night my parents didn't come back. "I'm so sorry. I'd never want to worry you that way," I said, feeling terrible, but she hunched her shoulders and went back into the kitchen. I knew better than to follow her. She needed some time to process and work things out for herself.

I'd talk to her about it later and apologize again.

My grandpa had gotten up and came over to give me a hug. He kissed me on my forehead and then said the nicest thing in the whole world to me. "You look just like your mother."

He returned to his newspaper and his birds while I headed upstairs to take a power nap.

All in all, it had been a good morning. Nobody freaked out too badly, and now I had a secret that made me smile every time I thought of it.

Marco liked the Muppets.

~

True to his word, Marco sent me a text and asked if I wanted to catch a movie with him. I immediately replied yes and then, to ease my guilty conscience, I added, "For practice."

He didn't respond.

I met him at the theater because my grandma was still in a mood and I figured that was the safer bet. He was waiting for me outside. I'd considered myself to be a punctual person, but he always seemed to beat me to the punch.

His whole face lit up when he saw me, and I wasn't sure what to make of that. "You made it!"

"I almost didn't," I said, pointing at my forehead. "I burned myself."

"How?" he asked, looking and sounding concerned.

"With a curling iron! I just want you to know that I think it is ridiculous the amount of work women have to put in to look nice. I know that makes me a hypocrite given the industry I work in, but it is so stupid." I paused to take a big breath. "Why do we have to put hot things next to our foreheads?"

"I think the point is for it to go on your hair, not your face."

"Thanks for the update, Captain Obvious. I slipped."

He reached over and lifted the hair away from my forehead. I held my breath in anticipation of the moment when his fingers would make contact with my skin, but he only touched my hair.

"Poor Anna. Do you want me to kiss it better?"

Yes. Yes, yes, yes, yes. "No."

"It has glitter on it," he pointed out unhelpfully, letting my hair fall back into place when he took away his hand.

"I know. I think I burned it permanently into my skin. Like my own personal tattoo of shame."

He was grinning at me, and I didn't like it. "What?" I asked.

"You got dressed up for me."

I did. I wanted him to think that I looked nice. To say something. "It was for practice," I said, which was what I had told myself the whole time I was getting ready, including when I burned myself. Practice.

Too bad nobody here seemed to believe that.

Because he was wearing a pointed and knowing smile, and he was right. I could have left the makeup off and worn sweats and a hoodie, but instead I'd put on a nice pair of jeans and a pretty top with a black jacket that Gloria had picked out for me.

"Shouldn't we go inside?" I asked.

He held the door open for me, and we stepped inside. He asked if I wanted any snacks and, figuring he was paying and could afford to pay ten dollars for something that cost a dollar at the grocery store, I asked for Red Vines, popcorn, and a blue raspberry Icee.

"I'll be right back," he said.

My phone buzzed. I had a text from Catalina. I realized that I hadn't called her yet to fill her in on what was going on with Marco. She was probably dying. I dialed her number.

"I'm going to make you put that Find My Friends app on your phone so I can track you down," she told me. "What's going on?"

I tried to quickly catch her up and ended my recap explaining how I'd stayed over the entire night playing Monopoly, to which she made a sound like she didn't believe me.

"You played board games all night with a man who looks like that?"

"It's the truth," I insisted.

"You poor, wretched soul," she said. "All of that man going to waste."

She wasn't wrong. It seemed like somebody should be kissing him. It was then that I realized if that wasn't already happening, it would be soon.

With another woman.

That thought made me feel like somebody had dropped a one-ton anvil on my head.

"Where are you now?" she asked.

I pressed my hand against my chest, as if I could stop the way that my heart was aching. Which was dumb, because it was over something that wasn't even happening. He had told me he was single. "On a date with Marco."

Of course I realized my mistake a second too late. I tried to correct it. "Not a date. A hang. A friendly outing. A practice session."

But it was too late. "A date? With Marco? Banks and schools should close. There should be fireworks. People should barbecue in honor of this day."

"You can't see me, but I'm rolling my eyes. Nothing is going on with Marco and me. It's a business arrangement."

But that sounded hollow even to my own ears.

"It's too bad," she said. "Based on what you told me about his childhood, it sounds like he had to develop a personality because he couldn't just rely on his looks."

Why did that feel like a specific dig against Craig? I didn't want to get into that right now with her. "Marco is pretty great." Better to just agree with her.

There was so long of a pause on Catalina's end that I thought she had hung up. I was about to ask whether she was still there when she finally spoke. "I kind of feel like you owe it to us to see if this crush on Marco could turn into something more."

"Us?" I asked.

"Yes, us. All the women made to feel like they're less than. Not pretty enough, not thin enough, too smart, too ambitious. You have the chance to have a relationship with a gorgeous man who is obviously falling for you."

Why did I want that to be true? *Craig.* I said his name in my head. Repeating it over and over. *Craig, Craig, Craig.* Like that could force me to not consider Catalina's words.

"Marco and I are not in the same league," I told her. Even if there wasn't a Craig, Marco would still be himself and I would still be me. "We're not even playing the same sport."

"What did you just say to me?"

"Oh, I've been learning some sports stuff. I can make references now."

"Just think about it. By all accounts, and my own personal observations, Marco is a good guy, and I think you should give it a chance."

I wondered if she'd investigated Marco through the office grapevine, too.

He was walking back toward me with the food and I said, "I need to go. I'll call you tomorrow."

"You better," she said.

"Are you ready to go in?" he asked. I nodded, slipping my phone into my pocket. We walked over to the ticket taker, and Marco put his phone under a scanner. She told us to head to Theater 8.

"I probably should have mentioned this earlier," he said as we went into our theater, "but Marie-Angelique called a paparazzo to be here tonight during the movie. He's going to take pictures of us together."

"Okay. It feels a little creepy that we're going to be watched all night." I paused and then asked the question that was burning a tiny jealous hole in my soul. "Who is Marie-Angelique?"

"My assistant."

His assistant, whom he'd never referred to by name before. Marie-Angelique was not a name that you'd forget. "Is she French with flawless skin and dark hair, and five four?"

His raised eyebrows let me know I was close enough. She was probably gorgeous and good at her job and someday Marco was going to look across his office at her sitting perfectly at her desk and realize what a fool he'd been to let someone so perfect escape his notice before and . . .

"This is us," he interrupted my paranoid fantasy to say. "Seats eleven and twelve."

I glanced around before we sat down, wondering where the paparazzo would be sitting. How weird had my life become that I was currently concerned about this?

"What movie are we seeing again?" I asked.

"It's the Noah Douglas / Chase Covington buddy-cop comedy. It's getting really good reviews."

We settled in our seats, splitting up the food. I sat on his left. "It's kind of hard to get to know each other during a movie," I pointed out.

"It hasn't started yet. How would your friends describe you?"

At the moment, Catalina would say that I was stupid for not taking advantage of Marco. "Shouldn't you be asking me like, where I went to school or something like that?"

"You went to USC."

I kind of gaped at him. I didn't remember telling him that.

But he'd remembered.

"And you went to Harvard." He hadn't made a big deal about it when he'd told me, but apparently I'd mentally filed it away in my brain. "But if you want to know what my friends think of me, shouldn't you ask my friends?"

He shifted in his seat, his large frame not fitting easily into the stadium-style chairs. "I'm your friend. So maybe I should ask myself."

"What do you think of me?" Why did this feel so important?

"I think you are smart and loyal and passionate and dedicated to the things you love." He paused while I took all of this in. "How would you describe me?"

"Kind of the same, actually." Which was surprising, because on paper nobody would think we were the same kind of person.

I decided to leave out the parts about him being too charming for his own good and hotter than the melting point of tungsten (3,420 degrees Celsius).

"Good," he said gruffly, and I wondered what his response was about. Then he splayed his hands against his thighs, and I wondered if he'd try to hold my hand again. This time I would not hit myself in the mouth or sweat like I was trapped in a sauna. "Tell me about the last date you went on."

"It shouldn't be spoken of," I told him. "Let's just say he was much more interested in his food than he was in me. He didn't ask me anything about myself and wouldn't answer any of my questions except with some vague response. It was like going out with a Magic 8 Ball."

"My last date, she spent the entire night filming herself with her phone for TikTok. I'm not even sure she knew my name."

"You probably don't want to play weird-date poker with me," I said. "I'm going to win this one."

"Oh? Now I'm curious. What was your first date?" he asked.

"In junior high, a guy put his arm around my shoulders, and I punched him in the chest."

"When I was thirteen, a girl invited me over to her tree house. She tried to kiss me and so I climbed higher."

I took a sip of my Icee and asked, "So when you got over your irrational fear of girls, what was your go-to move?"

"I'll show you." He leaned back in his chair. "We should count shoulders."

"What?" Had I misheard him? I thought he was going to do something else.

Marco touched his right shoulder with his left hand. "One." Then his left shoulder. "Two." He touched my right shoulder. "Three.

"Don't punch me in the chest, okay?" he said. Then he had his hand on my left shoulder. "Four."

Only he kept his hand there. He had his arm around me. "Cute, but that seems like a lot of effort. Did women actually fall for that?"

That I was falling for it was beside the point.

"Like a charm." He stayed where he was, his arm in place, watching the movie with me, sharing food and laughing at the on-screen jokes like we were a couple.

It wasn't the hand-holding I'd been hoping for, but I'd take it.

I hoped the paparazzo was getting some good shots.

And that's how Marco acted for the entire following week. Like he was my actual boyfriend. He asked me out every night and I said yes. Every single time.

It was all under the guise of getting to know each other and being more comfortable together, and that's what I repeatedly told Catalina, but I knew it wasn't true.

So did she.

Marco took me axe throwing, and it turned out I was pretty good with the smaller axes. But every time someone said the word *axe*, which was a lot, he would turn and give me a mischievous grin.

We went mini golfing, to a sci-fi/fantasy trivia night at a local bar, to a concert, to dinner at fancy restaurants. Everywhere we went, our picture was taken. Catalina put an alert on her phone and would forward me a link every time a picture was posted. If what Marco had said about Craig's assistant was true, there was no way Craig didn't know about his brother and me.

I wondered if Craig had said anything to Marco, but Marco never indicated that he had. I was dealing with my own family drama—once my grandmother realized that I was going out every night with Marco, she said, "I don't know if I like the idea of you two spending so much time together."

"I am twenty-six," I reminded her. "I can decide who I want to spend my time with."

It was obvious she blamed him for the makeover thing, but that wasn't even his fault. I mean, technically yes it was his fault because he'd arranged and paid for the whole thing, but I hadn't done it for him.

I also had never really seriously dated someone before. Men were always secondary for me after schooling and my job. It wasn't that I didn't want to be in a relationship—I very much wanted to fall in love and have my own romantic fairy tale like my parents and grandparents. I'd just never made it a priority before.

I was proud of myself for sticking to my resolution in going after what I wanted and trying to be happy.

Marco and I finished out our week by going to an art museum for the debut of a new collection. There was a red carpet, and one of the Minx publicists was there to introduce us to the press.

"This is Marco Kimball," she said as we walked up to the first photo stop. I hoped I didn't look awkward and that there wasn't too much glare from my glasses from the flash. I felt pretty confident in how I looked, given how closely I'd followed Jen's diagrams, and I was wearing a sleek full-length black dress.

I was a long way from my Arwen debacle.

Someone asked who I was, and I expected the publicist to introduce me as just his date, but she said, "This is Anna Ellis, an up-and-coming cosmetic chemist. You should keep an eye on her."

Marco's hand squeezed mine. He had done this. He'd had her say that. No one here cared who I was or about my job.

It was things like that—those little things that he would do and say that made me think I was important to him.

I'd been worried that Marco was going to push Craig out of my heart, and I could feel it happening. I tried to conjure up that fantasy of Craig, walking together near the water, sitting on that bench, but it was always Marco's face that I saw.

Like I'd gotten over Craig completely.

And while Marco was attentive and fun and everything you could ask for in a fake boyfriend, it shouldn't have made my feelings change.

Because he hadn't done or said anything to make me think that he might feel the same. He called me his friend or his buddy often. He brought up Craig. Where I had once been desperate for any information about Craig and his life, now I found it annoying.

I had to keep my heart locked up. I just needed to spend time with Craig again. Let myself feel those feelings, remind myself why it was that I had fallen for him in the first place. Of course I was going to feel this way about Marco when I spent all my free time with him doing so many fun activities. Wouldn't I feel the same way if I'd spent that time with Craig?

Craig would find out that Marco and I were "together," he'd get jealous, end his engagement, pursue me, and it would be done.

I'd get everything I ever wanted.

And as I was having that thought, and ruminating about all the time I'd been spending with Marco in the past week, a timer went off. I was in my grandparents' kitchen, baking my lipstick and daydreaming about seeing Marco again tonight.

I took my mood ring lipstick out of the oven.

It was perfect. The texture, the appearance, the smooth glide against my fingertip. I had done it. I set a timer to let it cool, and it was the longest half hour of my life.

I put the lipstick on and ran to a mirror. It was a rose-pink color. I went into the kitchen and got ice out of the ice maker in our new fridge (which was, in fact, life changing). I put it against my lips.

My grandfather walked into the kitchen. "Why are you kissing ice, sweetheart?"

I pulled the ice cube away from my mouth. "What color are my lips, Grandpa?"

He peered over the top of his glasses at me. "A very faint pink?"

Yes! I ran into the bathroom and looked at my reflection. He was right. A soft bubble-gum pink. "I did it!" I shrieked with excitement.

"Good for you!" my grandpa said from the kitchen, even though he had no idea what he was commending me for. "Did you hear about the dyslexic ornithologist? He was a terrible word botcher."

I didn't have time for jokes. I had to tell someone. I ran upstairs to get my phone, and the first person I wanted to call was Marco.

So I did.

He answered quickly. "If you're asking for a Monopoly rematch, no can do. Tonight is my stepmother's party."

Tonight was huge—Craig would be at that party. The first time I was going to see him in person since Marco and I had tricked the world into thinking we were falling in love.

I found that I didn't really care about seeing Craig, though. I had one thing on my mind. "Marco, I did it. The mood ring lipstick. It works."

"That's fantastic, Anna! I'm so happy for you!"

I giggled with glee, so pleased with having finally figured it out, and just as thrilled by Marco's enthusiasm.

"You'll be able to show it off tonight," he said. "I can't wait to see it in action. I'll pick you up at seven, if that still works."

"It works! Bye!"

I hung up the phone and looked at my reflection again.

The shade had turned to a faint red.

But I didn't know what it meant. Was I excited about what I had accomplished?

Or did it have something to do with Marco?

CHAPTER TWENTY

I took a long time getting ready. Catalina texted me halfway through and asked me what I was going to wear. I responded back:

The red swishy dress and a healthy dose of irony.

Because no matter how I tried to spin all this, it didn't feel quite like me. It was fun to get all fancy, but it wouldn't be something I wanted to do every night for the rest of my life. That would be exhausting.

Catalina told me to stop, that there was no irony involved, and then demanded that I send her a picture. I did, and she responded with flame and thumbs-up emojis.

That made me feel a little bit better.

I got the rest of my makeup done, saving my new special lipstick for last. My lips were a neutral shade of pink, barely noticeable. I wondered how and why that would change tonight. I didn't have much by way of jewelry. There were the pearl earrings my grandma had given me as a college graduation gift. She'd gotten them from her own grandmother when she had graduated from college.

Then I took my mother's wedding ring and put it on my right hand. It would be like parts of my two favorite women were with me, and I figured I needed all the support I could get.

Then I headed downstairs, knowing that Marco would be on time.

But when I got near the front door, I realized that there were suitcases in the front hall. "Grandpa?"

"Yes?" he answered from another room.

"Where are you guys going?"

"We have that conference where your grandmother is doing a presentation down in San Diego. We're leaving for our flight in an hour."

I had been so caught up in Marco, our plan, and my lipstick that I had totally forgotten. "How long are you guys going to be gone?"

"Four days," he said, coming into the hallway with me. "And one of my grad students is coming by to feed the birds and give Chick Norris his medicine."

"I could have done that," I told him. Both of my grandparents passed out house keys to grad students like they were spare change.

He nodded. "I know. I just thought you might have plans with your young man. And I can see that you do. Don't you look pretty!"

"Fresh paint, right?"

"It's more than that."

Marco knocked then, and my grandpa managed to step around me quickly so that he could be the one to open it.

It had been so long since I'd seen Marco in a suit that the sight of him in a tux had me putting my hand against the wall so that I'd stay upright. Wow. He looked incredible. Was I allowed to say that? Maybe if he said it first and I could play it cool, I could mention it.

Although playing things cool wasn't exactly my strong point.

My grandfather and Marco exchanged greetings, shaking each other's hands. But Marco's gaze kept landing on me instead of Grandpa.

Did he like what he saw?

And why was it so important to me?

Say I look pretty, I silently willed him. He hadn't said it once, not since that time we'd stayed up all night together. And I had gone out of my way to dress up for him, no matter what I told myself and Catalina.

"Are you ready to go?" he asked me, and I felt my spirits wilt. My hand slid off the wall, and I grabbed my coat.

"Yes. Good night, Grandpa."

He kissed me on the cheek. "Have fun."

Marco had brought the Porsche, and I found it hard to walk quickly in these heels with the sidewalk so slippery.

"Here." Marco offered me his arm, and I was unreasonably angry with him. I didn't want to take it, but I wanted to fall even less.

"Are you okay?" he asked.

"Fine," I said. I couldn't sulk all night. We were supposed to be a couple. I couldn't be mad at him for something that wasn't even his fault. Maybe he'd just been trying to build me up during our game night. I shouldn't care so much about his opinion. So I put my hand through his arm, letting him walk me slowly to his car.

He was so warm. And so tall, even with me wearing these shoes.

"Your lips are light pink," he informed me. "They've changed color since you were inside."

I felt mollified that he'd at least noticed that. "That's what happens when I'm cold. That's the easiest reaction to provoke. I want to test some others but haven't had the chance yet."

"Maybe tonight will be full of ups and downs and you'll get your opportunity," he said as he opened the car door for me.

I kind of hoped not. I was in the mood for just ups. When Marco got into the car, he asked me about my formulation process, and we talked about the lipstick all the way to the country club where the event was being held. He asked such smart and intuitive questions that it surprised me. Maybe he knew more about makeup than I'd thought he did.

"What about the color scheme?" he asked.

Again, a good question. "A typical mood ring shifts through all the colors in the rainbow—black, green, purple, blue, red, orange, yellow. I didn't want that. There are some people who wouldn't care what color lipstick they were wearing, but I think most of our hypothetical users would prefer that I keep it in the pinks and reds so that it's more natural-looking. I could go more avant-garde going forward and make lipsticks that will have more variation."

"I think that was a good call," he said as he pulled up to the valet. The country club was large and intimidating-looking. A different valet opened my car door for me, and Marco was there, offering me his arm again so that I wouldn't fall.

I took it without hesitation this time. I was mostly over him not saying anything about my outfit.

Mostly.

"This is impressive," I told him. I didn't know anything about architecture, but it was obviously expensive.

"Yeah, this place is harder to get into than obvious joke here," he teased. "With my family, the more exclusive the better. Craig will be impressed that you're here tonight as my guest."

I hoped that wasn't true, but I was finding that I was a lot more willing to believe that Craig might not be the guy I'd thought he was.

Honestly, it was hard to compare anyone to Marco, because everybody was going to come up short.

Inside, there was a coat check, and Marco helped me remove my coat. I didn't know why that gesture was sexy, but it was. Oh. I realized that it was because he was helping me undress. My cheeks flushed as I imagined him finishing the job someplace private.

"Your lips are more of a hot pink shade now," he said. "What are you feeling?"

"Not really sure," I said, trying not to choke. There was no way I was going to tell him.

I looked at the crowd of people in the club for this party. They were dripping in diamonds and couture dresses. No one here would believe that Marco and I were together.

Some people had calm before the storm. I had panic before the nothing.

I took him by the hand and led him into a family bathroom and locked the door.

"You're not going to get drunk and cry now, are you?" he asked, sounding alarmed.

Feeling anxious, I started twisting my mother's ring around my finger. Marco, of course, noticed. "That's pretty," he remarked.

Oh, so the ring was pretty, but he didn't have anything nice to say about me? I fortunately didn't say that part out loud and rambled a little. "It's my mom's wedding ring. The gem's not real. My dad got a cubic zirconia because that's all they could afford. He wanted to replace it with a real diamond. Besides my earrings, it's the only nice jewelry I own. I mess with it when I'm nervous, and I don't usually wear it very often because I almost lost it once, but I wanted it with me tonight."

"Oh." He narrowed his eyes at me. "Did you eat today?"

It was a fair question. He knew that I tended to skip food when I was busy working on a project. "I had Pop-Tarts for breakfast because I'm in favor of supporting the American economy."

"Do you know what's in Pop-Tarts?" he asked.

I didn't bring him in here to discuss my ring or Pop-Tarts. Before I could change my mind, I blurted out what I wanted him to do. "Give me a hickey."

Long pause. "You want me to do what?"

"A hickey. I know you were a little behind in the romance department growing up and may not be as familiar, but if you . . . I don't know, mark me, then people will believe we're together."

This was it. Rock bottom. I was begging a man to touch me.

"Or we could just tell them that we're together. With our words," he said slowly, as if I was having some kind of breakdown.

Which was entirely possible. What if I hadn't protected myself from the toxicity of the lipstick the way I thought I had? I grimaced. That wasn't it.

I needed this. Something tangible so I wouldn't be made fun of. I knew it was ridiculous, but I wanted it to happen.

But I didn't want to explore the reason why I wanted it to happen. My surface explanation was good enough for me.

"You don't think it's a little tacky?" he asked.

"Are you worried about seeming tacky or are you worried about convincing your brother that we really like each other?" He put his hands in his pockets, and I was worried I was losing him. "This doesn't have to be weird."

"Yeah. I'm the one making it weird," he said sarcastically.

My heart had been pounding hard in my chest since we walked into the bathroom, and it only got louder. Because I could see from his expression that he was going to do it. His gaze was fixed on my throat, and my pulse there jumped.

This was about proving to other people that I belonged here. And had absolutely nothing to do with wanting to feel Marco's lips on my skin.

He sighed, taking his hands out of his pockets, and walked toward me. I tried not to bounce with excitement and anticipation.

"Dark red," he said as he put his right hand on the left side of my throat to hold me still. That pulse point beat even harder, and my brain was so fuzzy that it was hard to register what he was saying.

My lips. He was talking about the color of my lips.

"Where?" he asked, and it took me a second to register that he was asking where I wanted the hickey.

I fluttered my fingertips along the right side of my neck, too filled with anticipation to even speak.

"I feel like a vampire," he muttered just before he ducked his head and pressed his hot mouth against my cool skin. The shock of it was almost enough to knock me off my feet. I grabbed on to the lapels of his jacket, clutching him tightly. He sucked my skin delicately. That was never going to leave a mark.

"Harder," I told him breathlessly.

He used his hand to press me against his mouth, and the other went to my waist so that I was flush against him. He did as I instructed and sucked harder. He was so big and strong and overwhelming and I loved every second of it.

My entire body felt like one giant heartbeat, throbbing with want. My head went backward, too heavy to keep upright. I just wanted to go completely limp as hot sensations zinged through me. The spot where his mouth was fused to my throat, it was like he was pushing heat into my body, threatening to consume me.

His teeth nipped my neck; then I felt the warm press of his tongue against my skin, sending a jolt through me. I made a noise that was severe enough to make him stop what he was doing and ask, "Are you okay?"

I wasn't imagining anything—his breathing was uneven and unsteady. Less than mine, but it was still there.

Then I remembered that he'd asked me if I was okay. I wanted to say, *Yes, I'm just fine. All the blood has left my brain and is pooling in my gut, and there's nothing I want more than to grab your head and make you do that again, but just fine.*

Instead I said, "All systems go!" Which was stupid but true in more ways than one.

We stood there, staring at each other.

"Did it work?" I finally managed.

His gaze flicked hotly to my throat and then back up to my eyes. "Yes. Sorry if I got a little rough."

"No, I . . ." I had been about to say that I'd liked it. Probably not a good idea. I was not going to make an idiot of myself here and beg him to keep going. "I'm good."

The mirror was directly behind his right shoulder, and I glanced at my reflection. My lips were still a dark red.

So now I knew what that meant. I glanced back at him. Marco was too smart not to recognize it as well. Would he look at me with pity and sympathetically remind me for the millionth time that we were just friends?

In that moment, I didn't think I could handle that.

As if he recognized how I was internally freaking out, he offered me his hand. "Now that I've officially branded you, should we head inside and make some mistakes?"

Was he saying that the hickey thing had been a mistake? Or it hadn't been one and we should make some?

He was so confusing. I took his hand, though, ignoring how much I loved holding it. "Sure thing, James Bond."

Although in Marco's case it was more Double Oh Yeah.

"Don't you mean Double Oh Seven?" he teased with a wink, letting me know that I was still so discombobulated that I was saying things out loud that I had meant to keep in my head.

It wasn't my fault that he was so hot.

He opened the bathroom door, and I ignored the looks from people standing in the general vicinity as we went into the ballroom.

"Better James Bond than Arwen, though, don't you think?" he asked.

I appreciated his attempt to make me feel better. "You're not funny."

"I beg to differ." We entered the ballroom and honestly, I'd expected more. Like one of those heralds announcing our presence.

Rich people were disappointing.

"Are you ready for tonight? Did you read the binder?" he asked as we walked along the outskirts of the room.

"Yes," I told him, annoyed.

"Do you know how I know you didn't?"

"I'm a terrible liar?" I offered.

"It's still at my house."

How had I forgotten the binder? I hadn't thought of it all week. I'd done some homework on my own based on what Marco had told me, but the binder had totally slipped my mind.

That felt significant, because that binder was like the key to me possibly having a relationship with Craig. My own personal cheat sheet, meant to help me land the supposed man of my dreams.

Supposed? Where had that come from?

"I forgot. I've been busy."

"Yes, changing the face of the cosmetic industry."

That, and spending my free time either with him or talking to Catalina about spending time with him. She loved every single detail, and it was fun to share.

"Here," he said, reaching inside his inner suit pocket. He handed me a piece of gum. I held that shiny rectangle in my hand, looking at it.

"You brought me gum?" Could he hear the emotion in my voice? He was so thoughtful.

"I figured you might need it tonight."

A swell of emotion made me feel choked up. Like I could shed actual tears right now. "You're a really good man, Marco."

He grimaced and looked away. "If you knew what I was thinking right now, you wouldn't say that."

Mentally, I seized on his statement. What was he thinking? Was it about me? About our situation?

Deciding that ignoring it was probably best in order to keep this encounter embarrassment-free, I said, "There's nothing you could say that would change my mind. You're the kind of guy who would sit on the floor of a public bathroom to comfort a crying girl in a costume at a not-costume party."

He stayed silent for a moment and then said, "Anna, there's something I need to confess."

My lungs solidified in my chest, and I couldn't move.

"My dad thinks I'm not a serious person. Mostly because of the serial dating. I told you this arrangement was just about you and Craig and protecting Minx. But I realized that if I dated someone more . . . down-to-earth, he might see me differently."

"Oh." That wasn't at all what I'd hoped he would say. I felt like I should be offended, but it might be a bit hypocritical, given that he'd offered to let me use him to get Craig. "I wish you'd told me before. A heads-up that you had another ulterior motive would have been nice."

"You're right. I should have done that. I'm sorry."

"Thanks. And I would have still agreed. You just should have said something."

"I'm not always good at speaking up when I need to," he said in a way that felt like it was a loaded statement and something I so related to. "Can you forgive me?"

"Of course," I said, meaning it one hundred percent. I couldn't be mad at him for running a scheme when I was running my own.

He reached for my hand and held it, squeezing it gently. "Thank you." Another energy-filled moment passed between us. Then he said, "There's my brother and his fiancée. We should give them a show. Would you like to dance?"

I glanced over at Craig and Leighton. She looked stunning in an off-white dress, and he was handsome in his tuxedo. While I knew, obviously, that Craig was going to be here, I was expecting to have more of a reaction to us finally being in the same place at the same time. I had anticipated that I would be excited to see him. That I would be dying to talk to him.

Instead, all I could think about was Marco and the gum he had been carrying around in his pocket.

Realizing that he was waiting for me to answer his invitation, I nodded, unsure of what was happening with the way emotions were rolling around inside me. A detached part of my brain wondered what color my lips were right now. If they were changing like a chameleon to reflect all this inner turmoil. Was I still a little bothered by his confession? Touched by his thoughtfulness? Worried about talking to Craig? All those things at once? I unwrapped the gum and put it in my mouth. He automatically took the wrapper from me and stuck it in his pocket so I wouldn't have to worry about the trash.

How had we been friends for only a couple of weeks? It felt like it had been years, with us anticipating each other's needs. Him taking care of things before I even asked.

We moved into position, only this time, he pulled me in close, like he just had in the bathroom. When we'd danced at his apartment, we had left enough space between us that a person could have walked between us comfortably.

Now? Nothing was getting through, as we were pressed against each other.

My nerves were firing and misfiring anxiously, making me shaky. I was still feeling full of adrenaline after our bathroom encounter.

At least, that's what I blamed it on.

Which Marco definitely noticed. "Relax." He murmured the word against my earlobe, and my knees almost buckled. Good thing he was holding me. "You're supposed to be enjoying this. People are supposed to think we're falling in love."

That was the entire problem. I was enjoying it too much.

"I know," I whispered back.

"After all that time we've spent together, I thought you'd be more comfortable with me by now."

Me too. But if anything, I felt more aware of him, more afraid of what I was feeling.

Maybe I could make things more equal by putting some effort into this. I reached up with my hand to stroke the back of his neck with my fingers. I began to play with the hair at the nape of his neck. Soft. He nuzzled the side of my face in response, and it sent heat streaking through my veins.

"That did the trick. Craig's heading this way," he said.

"I can't believe your dumb plan is working," I told him softly, my eyes closed. I had kind of forgotten about Craig, being caught up in the chance to touch Marco.

"I'm more than just good posture and charm, you know."

He was definitely more than that. Marco stopped dancing, pulling away from me. I felt disoriented, like I was being yanked out of a world where only Marco and I existed, swaying together on the dance floor.

"Are you ready for this?" he asked.

"Ready as I'll ever be," I said and hoped it was true.

CHAPTER TWENTY-ONE

"Here comes your knight in rusting armor," Marco muttered, and I was sure that I had misunderstood him. He must have said something else, but I was too disheveled to have properly understood.

Craig joined us, and I waited to feel something. Nervous. Excited. Curious as to whether or not he'd take the bait.

Instead . . . all I could think about was Marco as he turned to face Craig while keeping one hand around my waist.

These feelings I had caught for Marco weren't okay. If for no other reason than I knew Marco wasn't interested in me, and I'd had enough unrequited crushes to last me a lifetime.

And what is Craig exactly? my subconscious asked.

I tried to tell myself that was an entirely different situation. Marco thought Craig and I could work out.

He did think that, didn't he? I couldn't really remember if he'd ever said as much. He'd encouraged me and seemed to believe this plan could work. But that probably had less to do with me and more to do with Marco's particular set of skills. Determination, passion, and total delusion.

Craig and Marco exchanged hellos that sounded terse to me.

I didn't say anything because I didn't know what to say. I'd been anticipating this moment and felt . . . empty.

"I'm going to grab you something to eat," Marco said. "You need something with nutritional value that isn't a Pop-Tart." He leaned in and said, "I'll try to find something as sweet as you taste."

I knew that had been entirely for Craig's benefit, but his words lit me up like a Molotov cocktail. I didn't need a mirror—there was no doubt my lips were a dark red.

Then he moved forward, like he was going to kiss me on the cheek. Which would be a normal thing for a boyfriend to do. My heart pounded in anticipation. But he stopped short. It felt weird. I was sure it looked weird.

Craig must have noticed. We couldn't let that happen again. Marco and I hadn't kissed, and we were going to fall into that rom-com trap. I would have to talk to him about it.

And we would have to kiss.

For no other reason than to keep this ruse going. Because now it wasn't just about trying to get Craig and Leighton to break up—it was about helping Marco get his dream job, too.

I wanted him to have it. In the competition for the CEO job, I had chosen a side. I wanted Marco to win.

That seemed significant.

"Be right back," Marco said and melted into the crowd.

Leaving me alone. With Craig.

What was I supposed to say? All that studying and learning about him, and I had no idea what to say to him. I finally blurted out, "Logan Hunt."

Craig looked very confused. "Excuse me?"

"I heard that Logan Hunt might leave the Portland Jacks. He's the quarterback." That was Craig's favorite team, and I had been reading boring sports gossip for this very moment.

"They'll throw more money at him. Plus, his wife works as an announcer at the stadium. He'll never leave."

Great. Now I had to know things about sports players' personal lives? Craig took his phone out and began scrolling. This was going extraordinarily well. Again, I was at a loss for words.

You never have this problem with Marco. That was the truth. Sometimes I felt like I talked too much. I'd even apologized for it once, but Marco had told me that he found the way my brain worked fascinating.

Meanwhile, the other Mr. Kimball found me so boring that he was on his phone.

"So, it's Emma, right?" he asked, still not making eye contact.

"Anna," I corrected him. He'd forgotten my name again?

"I was closer that time," he said with a smarmy grin that was like being doused in ice water as he finally glanced up at me. "You're here with Marco?"

His question surprised me—both the amount of disbelief in his tone and the fact that all our hard work getting photographed had apparently gone to waste.

"I am. Because I'm his date. Since we're dating." That didn't sound at all forced.

"Huh. I guess he doesn't have a type."

That felt painful. Maybe he meant it as a compliment and I was letting my own insecurities get in the way of that.

"You've changed some things about yourself," he continued on. "You look great! You're kind of like that . . . what's that fairy tale? Oh yeah. Like the ugly duckling."

This was it. It was happening. I did not consider myself to be a violent person, but I was going to throat punch a groom at his preemptive engagement party.

Maybe I should give him the benefit of the doubt. He might have been drunk, and I'd certainly made a fool out of myself the last time

I'd been wasted. This was Craig. He was a good guy. I had proof of it. I needed to calm down.

"How is work going?" he asked, probably as a way to smooth over what he'd just said. Which was good. I should give him points for trying to make the situation better.

"I'm actually not working at Minx any longer."

"Really? I didn't know that." He was the head of my department. How could he not know?

So much for my grand gesture.

"I'm sorry to hear that," he continued. "You were a valuable member of the team. Maybe you and I can get together later and discuss what happened and ways that we could possibly fix it."

My heart fluttered a bit at his invitation. Not as much as it would have in the past, but it was there.

"Sure. That would be great."

My phone buzzed, and I took it out of my purse to look at it. Marco was texting me, asking which of the desserts I could eat. He had included pictures. I shook my head, smiling.

Then I realized that Craig was looking over my shoulder, reading my texts. "Hot Bathroom Guy? Is that what you call my brother? Did you two hook up in a bathroom?"

"No." Then I remembered the plan. "I mean, yes. And it was hot. And sexy. And not at all unhygienic." Would that make him jealous?

Craig smirked at me. "Didn't know Marco had it in him."

What was I supposed to say to that? Also, he didn't seem jealous. Marco might have seriously misjudged this situation.

"It sounds like quite the whirlwind romance," he added. Was he digging? Trying to find out more information? That could potentially be a good thing.

"Yes. It was. Just a whirl of wind." I pressed my lips together. I sounded dumb.

"There you are." Leighton came over and gave me a friendly smile, inadvertently rescuing me from saying more stupid things. She looped her arm through Craig's. "I was missing you."

He kissed her on the cheek. "I always miss you. This is Anna. She's Marco's date."

Her smile brightened even more. She clearly hadn't seen me as a threat before and was now apparently happy to have any potential suspicions put to rest. "Good to meet you, Anna."

She held out her hand, and I shook it. I wanted to hate her but found that I couldn't be mad at this angelic creature. She seemed really sweet. "You too."

Now I was having guilt. Should we be trying to break them up? They looked happy together.

Shouldn't I want that? If I was really in love with Craig, shouldn't his happiness be the most important thing to me?

"My parents are looking for us," Leighton said. "Would you excuse us?"

"Sure," I said.

They walked away, and I glanced over at the food table. Marco was deep in conversation with someone, holding an empty plate. I realized that I hadn't texted him back what I wanted dessert-wise, so I sent him a response and shoved my phone back into my purse.

I looked for a place to sit down, but all the tables were mostly full. There was one off in the corner with a single person. As I got closer, I realized it was a teenage girl, and she was reading a graphic novel.

I didn't usually make conversation with strangers, but I was curious about a girl who'd come to a party like this and ignore everyone to read a story called *Beastars*. "Are you enjoying that?" I asked.

She looked over the top of her manga at me, and it reminded me so much of my grandpa that I almost laughed. "Why do you want to know?"

"I'm sorry, I was just curious. It looks interesting."

She was blonde with blue eyes and seemed familiar. "It is. I vastly prefer Eastern storytelling."

"Oh? Why is that?"

"Because they believe in redemption for their villains. And 'enemies to lovers' is that—true enemies to lovers. Western audiences want bickering acquaintances to lovers. Give me a situation where a villain has to change his whole world to be with the woman he loves, and I'm there." She said this with so much conviction that I liked her immediately and wondered whether it would be weird if I asked a teenager if she wanted to be my new best friend.

Not that I was going to replace Catalina, but it would be nice to have someone who loved the same kind of stories I did. I sat down at the table across from her. "Kind of like Han and Leia from Star Wars. They argued, but they were never enemies, and people cite them as enemies to lovers all the time."

She vigorously nodded. "Exactly. And their son had a real enemies-to-lovers relationship, and they ended that supposed fairy tale with a tragedy because he 'had to die.' Can you imagine the Beast dying after Belle confesses her love and kisses him?"

If we weren't so far apart in age, I might have guessed that we'd been separated at birth. "I'm Anna, by the way."

"Lindy. I'm Craig's sister."

The infamous Lindy who Marco thought I would like. He hadn't been wrong. "Nice to meet you."

She waved her hand, like she was brushing away my niceties. "How did you get into Star Wars?"

"My dad. He loved those movies. What about you?"

"My brother is obsessed," she said. "I think he even went to Comic Con one year with a Boba Fett helmet on so nobody would recognize him. He will neither confirm nor deny."

Craig was into Star Wars? I could work with that. That flame of love and attraction I'd always had for him flickered just a bit brighter.

"This conversation is much more my speed," she said. She had an intense gaze that reminded me of Marco. "Talking about things I enjoy instead of making stupid small talk. Which I always do wrong. Like, I think it's interesting that Greenland sharks can be over four hundred years old and eat reindeer and polar bears. Apparently that's not 'appropriate for company.'" She made air quotes with her fingers.

"I think it's cool." I did. Polar bears I could see, but how did they get reindeer? I was about to ask when she leaned forward and spoke.

"Who made you come?" she asked.

Like it had been some kind of punishment. I tried hard not to smile. "I'm here with Marco."

"Marco?" She blinked at me several times. "You're here with Marco?"

Why did people keep saying that with such a discouraging amount of shock in their voices?

"Yep!"

"How did that happen?"

She was so blunt that I wasn't sure what to make of it. "Marco rescued me. I was sad, and he helped me. He was so sweet."

"That sounds very unlike Marco. He cares about two things in life, and girlfriends are never one of those things."

That didn't sound at all like the man I'd come to know, and . . . I internally stuttered over the next line. The man I'd what? Admired. I'd been about to say admired. Nothing else. "What two things?"

"His company and me."

I did smile at her confidence, and it made me like Marco more to know that he adored his little sister so much that she was sure of her place in his life. But I also didn't want to lie to her. I had the feeling she was the kind of person who would see through it immediately. I reached for my purse. "I want to write down the title of that book on my notes app." I couldn't immediately see my phone and had to pull a couple of samples out in order to dig around.

Lindy grabbed one. "What's this?"

"A lipstick sample I'm currently working on."

Her eyes lit up. "You're a cosmetic chemist?"

It surprised me that she was familiar with that term. "I am."

"I want so much to go into the industry. My dad doesn't want me to work at Minx, though. He wants me to do something else."

I found my phone and pulled it out. "Like what?"

"Probably get married to some rich dude."

"That's . . ." What was I supposed to say? I was completely on her side, but I didn't need something I said getting back to her father. He might become part of my life. Especially if he invested in my hypothetical company.

"It's messed up," she said for me. "I do have a question for you, though. I've noticed with the skin-care products I've been using that it seems to be okay to mix AHA and BHA products with hyaluronic acid. Is that true?"

"Yes." I launched into an explanation as to why they worked together, but it felt like I didn't need to and she had already done her own research. Few people understood what I did as well as teenage girls on social media. They researched, studied effects over time, analyzed how products interacted with one another, whether the experiment was repeatable, and shared their results.

People who thought science was boring / not part of their lives didn't realize they were already engaging with it via their skin- and hair-care products.

Lindy asked about my current lipstick, and while I didn't share any secrets with her, I did give her the basics.

"Can I have one of your samples?" she asked, and I nodded.

"It always helps to have an additional user. You'll have to let me know what you think."

"I can't believe you're dating Marco."

"You keep saying that and it might permanently damage my self-esteem," I said in a teasing way, although it was the truth.

"Usually the girls he goes out with aren't very bright. You seem like your IQ is higher than your age."

"The first one who could construct a complete sentence?"

"You have no idea. You're definitely the first scientist. And a chemist doing interesting experiments? I'm here for it." She grabbed my phone and added herself as a contact before handing it back to me. "I will definitely follow up with you about the lipstick."

Her own phone buzzed. She glanced at the screen and then rolled her eyes. "My parental unit is telling me to come take a picture. I have to go."

"Okay. I look forward to hearing your thoughts."

She smiled at me and walked away. I noticed her opening the sample and applying the lipstick. I wondered what shade it was. I picked up a knife to look at the shade of my own lips. A neutral rose-ish pink.

I had just placed the knife back when a very tall, thin, and blonde woman appeared in front of me like some kind of apparition. I gasped in surprise.

"Who are you?" the woman demanded.

"Who are you?" I asked back.

"I'm Tracie Kimball. The groom's mother. I don't know you. This isn't an event you can crash. It's very exclusive."

Marco's stepmom. I'd heard so many bad things about her that I'd half expected her to have horns and cloven hoofs. She had that ageless look to her face like she'd had enough Botox and fillers that she could have been anywhere from thirty-five to sixty-five.

"I'm Anna Ellis."

She looked me over, head to my feet, and I noticed her eyes settling on my neck. I couldn't help but reach to cover up the hickey from her view.

"Why were you talking to my daughter?" she asked.

Okay, that might have seemed off with me being a stranger. "I'm Marco's date."

"My husband's son?"

I found her phrasing interesting. Not her stepson, her husband's son. Like there was no relationship between her and Marco.

"Yes?"

She narrowed her eyes at me. "Was that an answer or a question?"

I was starting to feel extremely uncomfortable and could feel sweat breaking out along my hairline. "An answer?"

I put my phone under the table so that she couldn't see me texting. It was an art form I'd perfected at work so that Jerry wouldn't know I was sending messages to Catalina.

Glancing down, I made sure I was sending the text to Marco and wrote:

Gondor calls for aid!

A few seconds later, I had a response from him.

And Rohan will answer.

CHAPTER TWENTY-TWO

I had only a moment to wonder how Marco had known the right response to give me before he joined us. He put down a plate in front of me with barely any food on it. Given how long he'd been away getting me something to eat, I'd been expecting a feast.

"Can we help you with something?" Marco asked in an impersonal way, like Tracie was a stranger who had gotten lost.

"Did you really think this was the sort of event to bring a random date to?" she asked with so much venom in her voice, I wondered if I was going to hear her rattle her tail with a warning.

"Anna is my girlfriend." He leaned down to kiss the top of my head, and I was so on his side in whatever this was that I barely registered that he had actually just kissed me.

Tracie crossed her arms. "The party is special. This is a once-in-a-lifetime kind of thing."

"Statistics and history would disagree."

She made a face that created an actual wrinkle on her forehead. I wondered if she knew about it.

"And Anna is special." Marco was a much better actor than I'd given him credit for. There was so much sincerity and warmth in his voice. Like he meant it. "There's no one I'd rather be here with."

My heart caught at his words, and I could only gaze up at him. He was looking down at me with what felt like affection, and if he'd asked me in that moment to give him the formula for my mood ring lipstick, I might have done it.

Most likely not, but I would have at least considered it.

A man approached us who looked so much like an older version of Marco that I nearly gasped again.

Tracie's entire demeanor changed from hard to soft. She smiled at her husband and wrapped her arms around him. "I thought I'd lost you."

Marco's dad gave one of those grimaces that was supposed to be a smile as Marco introduced us. "Anna, this is my father, Ken. Dad, this is Anna."

He held out his hand, and I stood up to shake it. "The chemist," he said. Lindy popped out from behind him, and I figured she had told him.

"She's the one making the cool lipstick, Dad."

He made another grimace-smile. "I'd like to hear more about it, if you wouldn't mind—"

"Actually," Marco interjected, "Anna has an investment opportunity that you might be interested in."

I was holding my breath. Literally unable to make my lungs work. Was this happening, right here, right now?

"Call Janine and get on my schedule. In the meantime, you should bring Anna to the house for dinner next week."

I couldn't quite make out Marco's expression, but he turned to me. "My family has a get-together planned, and you're welcome to come."

"That sounds like fun!" I couldn't quite parse out my own motivation here. Was it to spend more time with Craig? With Marco? Getting their father interested in helping me start up a company?

"It's in Vermont," Marco added.

Marco had been planning on going to Vermont and hadn't told me? That bothered me. Probably more than it should have. "Oh. Well, you know my schedule is clear."

"I guess we'll be there," Marco said in a happy tone that sounded completely false to me.

I didn't have a right to feel bothered. Marco was not actually my boyfriend, and I had to remember that.

After I flew to Vermont with him to hang out with his whole family.

"That's wonderful!" Tracie exclaimed, and I wondered if it was exhausting keeping up a front like that all the time. "Oh, there's the Hendersons. We should go over and say hello."

"Excuse us," Ken said.

Lindy looked like she'd been about to make a break for it, but Tracie got her by the forearm and dragged her along.

"Just so you know," I said, "your stepmom totally looked at my hickey. It worked."

Marco looked perplexed—like he was trying to solve a puzzle that didn't have a solution and my statement distracted him from figuring it out. "Apologies for all of that."

"It was fine. Tracie was interesting, but I've seen leeches that suck less. I'm surprised she had time to set up this party, what with her busy schedule of luring children into her gingerbread house."

That got me a half smile. "She's definitely interesting," he agreed. "She always has some fad she tries to get the family into. Right now she swears that essential oils will heal our physical and emotional issues and make us relax."

"The only way an essential oil is going to make you relax is if it's chloroform."

He gave me a full smile for that one.

"I'm just glad you were here," I told him as I sat back down. He took the seat next to me and bumped his knees into mine, and I tried very hard to ignore the tingly spikes spreading across my skin. "I was worried that I was going to say the wrong thing to her. I don't know anything about seersucker or polo ponies or whatever it is she cares about. It probably freaks me out because it's not easy for me to talk to Craig, and it would make things worse if I knew his mom hated me."

"Why do you have a hard time talking to Craig?"

"I don't know. I'm always worried I'm going to say the wrong thing and that I'll scare him off permanently. Or that I'll bore him." I glanced around the room and found Craig making out with Leighton. He had his tongue so far down her throat, I wondered if somebody would have to call an ambulance to get her some oxygen.

And I didn't feel jealous.

I was considering that realization when Marco said, "Anna, no one with half a brain would ever think you're boring."

"That's sweet." His words made me feel better.

"Do you ever feel that way with me? Like you have to worry about what you say?"

"Never." Marco was literally the easiest person in the world to talk to.

"Good," he said with a smile. He gestured toward the plate he'd gotten me. "Is that okay?"

"They would have kicked you out of a hunter-gatherer society."

"I didn't realize I needed to gather more."

"How often have we been hanging out?" I asked.

"True. Stay here. Keep eating. I'll get you more."

"That's the nicest thing a man has ever said to me," I replied with a sigh. Marco got up, laughing, and headed back to the food table.

This time, he returned much more quickly and was carrying three plates. I wondered if I should care what other people might think. Or if Tracie would try to charge me for eating extra food, but I was too hungry to care. Marco set them in front of me and then sat back down.

I got a handful of french fries. They were perfectly salted and crispy. "French fries is my favorite F word."

"That's sad."

"Why? What's your favorite F word?"

His hot, wolfish grin let me know I'd walked right into that one. He finally said, "Friday," but I got his nonverbal innuendo. I glanced around, wondering whose benefit that had been for, but no one was within earshot. He added, "And did you see that they have ketchup here? You know, in case you want any."

That took me a second, until I remembered that he had compared himself to ketchup in his zeal to convince me that he was my type.

I had to be blushing, but thankfully he didn't bring it up.

Grabbing a slider, I held it aloft. "Do you think they have this in a size for people who like to eat?"

He ignored my question and said, "I saw you talking to Lindy."

"She's great. I like how her brain works. She reminds me a lot of you." I took a bite of the slider.

"I've never seen her talk to anyone at events like this outside of family."

"Maybe you were right when you were lying about me to your stepmom and I am special."

"That wasn't a lie, Anna."

My breath caught, and I suddenly didn't feel quite so hungry.

At least, not for food.

"And you were chatting up Craig, too. You've hit the Kimball kid trifecta. What did he have to say?"

I suddenly found myself not able to remember much about what Craig and I had discussed. "He didn't know I quit Minx. Oh, and he said something about me being an ugly duckling."

A flash of anger crossed Marco's features. "Where is he?"

"Why?"

"I'm going to commit a little fratricide."

Having also wanted to punch Craig tonight, I got the impulse. And it was honestly a bit thrilling that Marco wanted to beat someone up on my behalf. I put my hand on his forearm.

"It's okay. I think it was supposed to be a compliment."

"You're too nice," he said, still sounding angry.

"I've been accused of a lot of things, but I'm pretty sure *too nice* was not one of them."

He put his hand on top of mine, his warmth and strength enveloping me. "You are one of the kindest, most considerate—" He cut himself off just as things were starting to get interesting. "I shouldn't be saying that."

"Why?" He was allowed to say nice things to me.

But he just shook his head. "It doesn't matter."

"It matters to me. You matter to me."

His gaze slid down my face to settle on my lips. I wondered whether I'd gotten sauce on my mouth, but that wasn't the expression he was wearing. My breath caught. "Dance with me," he said softly.

My stomach tried to protest that I was still eating, but the rest of me wanted to give in to his intoxicating invitation.

We walked onto the dance floor, a bit set apart from the rest of the crowd, and he took me in his arms.

I had a moment where I thought that I could happily stay this way for the rest of my life. Being held by Marco.

I really did have to get over this crush.

The problem was that I didn't want to.

Then, in an apparent attempt to conspire against me, the universe and the DJ put on the worst possible song.

"When I Fall in Love" started playing, and I said, "Oh no."

"What is it?"

"This was my parents' favorite song. Sometimes my memories come and go. There are days when I forget my mother's laugh or the color of my father's eyes. But then there are these memories that are so vivid, so light, that I don't think I'll ever forget. My parents would dance together, every night, to this song. I used to go out and sit on the stairs to watch them."

His grip tightened on me. "That's beautiful."

Craig and Leighton came around on my right side. He twirled her, like the song was fast instead of a slow one. She nearly smacked into me.

"Oh, sorry about that," she said, sounding out of breath.

"Are you okay, Anna Banana?" Marco asked, and it was like all the oxygen had been sucked out of the room.

"That's what my dad used to call me," I said in an almost-whisper.

"I know," he said while kissing the bridge of my nose.

Craig and Leighton danced away, but I was still in shock. He didn't know; he couldn't have. I hadn't even told Catalina about it. It was a reasonable guess considering the words rhymed, but it still was a jolt to my system.

Marco stopped moving, and we stood there, holding each other, gazing into each other's eyes.

I knew he'd said it for his brother's benefit, to imply a close connection, that he was pretending. The problem was . . . I believed him. I believed in that connection, even though I logically knew it wasn't real.

"I have a theory," he said in a low, deep voice that sent shivers racing across my skin. "Do you want to hear it?"

More than anything. "Uh-huh" was what I actually managed.

"When your lips turn that shade of red . . . I think you want to be kissed."

Another slam to my nervous system. "Say you're right."

"Let's. Since I am."

"Then . . . what do we do about it?" My head told me to stop. That I couldn't do this, but my ovaries were making a very convincing counterargument to keep going.

"We should test my theory, don't you think?"

"Here?"

"Not here," he said, and I wondered why when the universe was giving Marco brains, charm, handsomeness, and abs, it also felt like he needed the world's sexiest voice.

This was my chance. To tell him no, that we couldn't do this. That it was a mistake.

Because I was scared. Scared that these feelings I had for him were only going to get bigger, and then he really would push Craig entirely out of the way.

And Marco didn't like me that way. He was my friend. He'd told me that so many times. I was smart enough to know better. I couldn't be in love with him and have him sympathetically tell me he was sorry, but he just didn't feel like that about me.

Part of me was afraid that if Marco broke my heart, it might not ever heal.

I thought I'd hit rock bottom when I'd asked for that hickey, but I was about to take out the explosives and start fracking.

"Where?" I asked, feeling out of breath.

His eyes lit up. "Follow me."

He took me by the hand and led me off the dance floor, through the ballroom, and out into a hallway. I had the presence of mind to toss my gum in a nearby trash can. He tugged on a couple of doors until he found one that opened. It was a darkened conference room, with long tables and office chairs. He closed the door shut behind us and stood too close to me.

Obviously, not too close if we were going to kiss, but too close for my current peace of mind. This had to be meaningless. He couldn't know how desperately I wanted him to kiss me. All the times I'd daydreamed about it.

I tried to push those thoughts out of my head. This was about satisfying my curiosity. I would kiss him, and then I would know what it was like so I could stop wondering and move on.

That's what I would focus on. "This is a good idea. You never know when a well-meaning grandmother or surprise mistletoe would have forced us into a situation where we had to kiss. Better to get it out of the way."

A look of confusion furrowed his brow. "No one's going to make us kiss, Anna. My grandma is not here, and it's January."

"There could be leftover mistletoe," I said defensively.

He was so close. Not touching me but giving off all that masculine warmth that had the phantom feel of him against my skin. He reached down and took my hand, bringing it up to his mouth so that he could place a soft, hot kiss against it. I reached out with my other hand and pressed it against his chest to stay vertical, relying on his strength as my brain tried to shut off and let sensations take over.

"Anna, the only reason we should be kissing is because you want to."

"I do." The words were out of my mouth before I could think better of them. My whole body was aching with a thick, heavy desire. "For science," I added so that I didn't sound so pathetic.

"For science?" he repeated, his eyes dancing. He let go of my hand and put both of his hands on the sides of my face. "Should we be taking notes?"

I couldn't respond. Some tiny part of my brain told me again to leave, to not let this happen. But I didn't care.

When all of my blood returned to the correct spots in my body, I was probably going to care, but right now?

The only thing I cared about was his lips touching mine.

"So many things to research," he mused as he moved his head down toward me. I held my breath. If he didn't kiss me soon, I was most likely going to pass out.

Heck, that was probably going to happen either way.

"What does it taste like?" His lips were hovering over mine, tantalizingly out of reach. "Is it sticky? Smooth? How durable is it?" He shifted his head to the right. "Will it end up all over my lips?"

The suspense was both achingly sweet and maddening.

I put my arms around his neck, clasping my hands behind him. "If it did get on you, what color would your lips be?" I asked, feeling a little braver. Like he was lending me some of his confidence.

"Dark red," he said.

He was teasing me, and he was waiting. Every nerve ending I possessed was vibrating with anticipation and want. The air was charged around us, like lightning was about to strike. So I said what he wanted me to say. That it was just me, just him. This wasn't about any kind of experiment.

It was about me saying the truth.

"I want you to kiss me, Marco."

CHAPTER TWENTY-THREE

It was what he had been waiting for. There was a self-satisfied grin that I should have been outraged by, but again, I didn't care. I just needed him to kiss me.

Now.

I half expected him to devour me, like a starving man. That was how I wanted to kiss him.

Instead he moved in so slowly, drawing the moment out for what felt like an eternity. My lips were tingling in response to his nearness, and electric heat pooled in my stomach.

My whole body was pulsing with jittery anticipation.

"Anna." He breathed my name against my lips, and I sighed in response.

Then he finally kissed me, with the softest brush of his lips against mine, and I could no longer feel my legs. Jolts of crackling pleasure lit up synapses I didn't even know I had.

But as soon as it had started, it was over. The kiss was tentative, like he was asking a question and waiting for an answer.

It was like wandering in a desert for three days straight and then only getting one single drop of water.

It wasn't enough. I wanted to drink deeply. I was very thirsty.

"What are you doing?" I asked, hating how breathless I sounded. "Don't stop."

That weapons-grade grin of his was back, and instead of kissing me again, he said, "First test completed. Your lipstick is not sticky."

"I could have told you that," I grumbled.

"What are you feeling right now?" he asked, his eyes glittering intensely at me.

Frustrated. Annoyed. Like I wanted to kick him in the shin for giving me the barest taste of something I was dying for. "I . . . I don't know."

He saw it for the lie that it was. "Nervous? Excited?"

Completely turned on? Was that okay to say?

"Your cheeks are flushed." He touched one, and his fingertips were warm and smooth against my skin. "Is your pulse racing? Your skin is warm."

That was a lie. My skin was shivery and cool, and he was the one heating it up with his touch, but I couldn't quite form the words to tell him that. It was hard to imagine that a man this size could be so gentle and careful.

"Did you want me to keep going?" he asked in a voice rough with an emotion I couldn't quite identify.

"Yes." I pushed up on my toes to close the distance between us, but he moved his head back slightly, just out of reach.

"If this is going to be for science, we need to set up some parameters."

Screw the parameters. I wondered if there was a way to say, *I need you to pin me up against that wall and kiss me like you mean it* for science.

"Marco?"

"Polo," he responded, grinning at me.

"You've made your point. Would you please just shut up and kiss me?"

He returned his lips swiftly to mine this time, but it was a gentle press. He held still for a second, letting us both be in the moment.

Again those electrical flames lapped at my skin, demanding release. I needed a real kiss. I made a sound of protest against his mouth, and that seemed to change the situation.

Now he was moving against me, causing a delicious friction with our lips. It was still soft, gentle, teasing me. Promising so much more and only willing to give me this tiny fraction of it for now.

Stupidly, I had thought some small kiss like this would satiate the craving I had for him. We would kiss, I would get over it and move on, but that wasn't happening. It was making everything worse.

I pushed up against him, wanting more. He was being so careful with me, his kiss intense and gentle at the same time.

Only, the gentleness started to fade. Bit by bit, and the passion inversely increased, and he kissed me with a devastating slowness and thoroughness that had my limbs trembling, as if they'd been zapped and rendered useless.

His heart beat against my hands, hard and fast, his chest heaving like he'd been running. I realized that it was from keeping himself in check. Trying not to overwhelm me.

Didn't he know that I'd welcome it?

How could something be so slow and soft and yet intense and sensual at the same time?

"Taste. Good," he murmured against my mouth, and some part of my brain wanted to laugh—he sounded like a caveman. I liked the idea that I was having that kind of effect on him.

But then his fingers were tangled in my hair, cradling my head as he kissed me over and over again. My somatosensory cortex lit up like the Fourth of July.

Somehow, like he knew or was an actual mind reader, Marco moved me over to the wall. I was grateful for the support and the way that he had trapped me in place, kissing me like he had all the time in the world and planned on doing a thorough but sweet job of it.

And despite the fact that he was holding back and not ravishing me on that conference room table, the connection between us? That was real. It was almost . . . chemical. And I knew a little something about a chemical reaction.

On the outside, Marco and I seemed like two things that shouldn't go together. Like baking soda and vinegar. But when they were combined?

It created something new. Something powerful.

It made science fair volcanoes erupt.

His mouth slanted over mine again as he changed the angle of his head and the pressure on my lips, distracting me from my train of thought. Kissing him was like kissing an open electrical current but without any pain. Shocking and stimulating and exciting.

He shuddered against me and pulled back from the kiss. We were both gulping in air, trying to breathe normally. I had joked earlier that Leighton was going to need some oxygen, but if we kept going like this, I was the one who was going to need that ambulance.

Marco rested his hands on either side of my head against the wall. "How was that?" he asked.

"Nice?" It was literally the only word I could think of. But it felt imprecise, and as a scientist, I hated being imprecise. "No. Not nice. Something else." My brain was too fuzzy to concentrate.

He reached over to trace the outline of my lips with his index finger. "Electric?" he asked.

"Yes." How did he know that?

The smooth glide of his fingertip against my sensitive lips had me making a strangled noise and pressing back against the wall. His fluttery-light touch made my synapses fire and hum under my skin.

Then I did what I'd wanted to do before that day in my room—I reached out and kissed his finger. His breath hitched, and that small sound thrilled me in a way I didn't know was possible.

His lips quickly replaced his finger, and while he was still kissing me carefully, he was doing it thoroughly and I was enjoying the exploration. He pressed me against the wall, the hardness and strength of his chest pushing against my soft curves.

I felt a buzzing sensation that I at first wrongly attributed to whatever he was doing with his mouth and then realized it was his cell.

Pulling my head back slightly, I said, "I think your phone is happy to see me."

He seemed a little disoriented, his gaze unfocused. He reached into his pocket and pulled his phone out and checked the screen. "I've been summoned," he said. "We should go."

I think I nodded. I intended to nod, but my whole body felt lethargic and nonresponsive to my internal commands. There should be a sign that popped up on my forehead that read ERROR 404 ANNA_FUNCTIONINGBRAIN.EXE NOT FOUND.

Marco took me by the hand and led me out of the room. The hall lights weren't bright, but they felt blinding by comparison to the dark room we'd been in.

I noticed that he was grinning with that heart-destroying smile. "What are you smiling about?"

"The final analysis is completed. Your lipstick passes with flying colors." He wiped his mouth, but he wasn't wearing any of it. The lipstick had stayed put, like it was supposed to.

We passed by a mirror, and I yanked on his hand to stop. "Look at me," I said. My hair was all over the place, and my lips looked swollen. There was a blush still on my cheeks, like all my blood had rushed there to make sure it didn't miss out on the kiss. I tried to smooth my hair down.

He looked at me in the mirror and said, "People are definitely going to know what we were just doing. That's good. Come on."

My steps faltered for a second, and he had to wait for me to catch up. It was all part of a plan. Marco's plan. I had to remember that.

But he made it so easy to forget.

I thought his smile was a weapon, but I was wrong. It was his kiss.

And much like James Bond, Marco had a license to kill.

~

The rest of the evening flew by, and it was like I couldn't keep my eyes off Marco. Things had shifted between us. He was touching me constantly—he either had an arm around me or he was holding my hand. I loved every second of it, and more than anything, I wanted to ask him if he wanted to do a little bit more scientific research.

He drove me home, and we didn't really speak in the car. Not because I didn't have anything to say. I had too much to say and didn't know what to do. I needed some time to process.

We walked up to my front door, and I expected to say good night to him after I unlocked it. But he turned the handle as if he planned on going inside.

"That may not be a good idea," I said as I stepped into the foyer.

He flexed his hands and then put them in his pockets. "Still haven't vacuumed up the glitter?"

"I have!" I said indignantly. I hadn't, though. "It's just my grandparents aren't home."

He raised both eyebrows. "Oh?"

Why was that single syllable so sexy? "Yes."

Marco looked over his shoulder and said, "There might be a photographer out there with a long-range lens. I should come inside for a little bit. I promise to keep my hands to myself."

"Okay." I nodded, letting him come in and then closing the door behind him. Which was a huge mistake given that he was taking up all the space around us and I had to touch him to shut the door.

I thought of how at ease he seemed in my home and how much Craig probably wouldn't have been. Craig was a tame peacock. An exotic bird, full of gorgeous plumage and meant to be admired, kept as a pet and hand-fed. Marco was a wild hawk, out there getting the job done, strong and fierce. Going after what he wanted.

I had started to wish that I was the one he wanted.

We were alone. Well, mostly alone. The birds were all calling from the other room. "You should know, though, that the last time a guy came over while my grandparents were gone, it led to a bird maiming."

"Someone maimed a bird?"

"No. My grandpa was helping rehabilitate a goose named Geese Witherspoon, and she went after Richie because she didn't like anyone besides my grandfather. I had to take him to the hospital. We didn't go out again."

"Really? Maybe she went after him because he's a grown man using the name Richie."

"It wasn't that." Everything I was saying was unimportant, but Marco looked at me like it was the most fascinating thing he'd ever heard. It made my stomach feel like it was about to float away. "Geese are terrible jerks. They sound like a deranged french horn and will kick you like a mule and bite like a snake. They don't want you to feed them bread. They want to steal your wallet and your life."

"So I should steer clear of geese."

"Unless you want them to protect your castle. They're better than guard dogs."

"I'll let security know," he said with a smile.

"Wait. Does your family have a castle?" That might be a game changer.

"No. Just homes bigger than most castles."

"Aw. Because if you were a secret prince, it would make our fake relationship a lot more fun." And very rom-com tropey.

Something flashed in his eyes, but he said, "Sorry, I can't make you the next princess of Monterra."

"Bummer."

That felt like a natural conclusion to our evening. He'd been inside for a bit, and he should go because I really, really wanted to kiss him again, and I had so little pride left at this point that I was desperate to hang on to it.

"Why are all the birds named after famous people?" he asked. And again I might have been projecting, but it felt like he was asking not because he really wanted to know but because he didn't want to go.

But to be fair, that kiss of his had seriously scrambled my brain, and I didn't feel like I was operating on all cylinders yet.

"My grandpa. My grandmother doesn't have much patience for things she considers frivolous, but he's always loved pop culture. Half the time when he's reading his newspaper, he's actually going through his recent copy of *Us Weekly*."

Marco laughed at that, and I thought of how much I enjoyed sharing things with him.

"And because my grandma is unaware, she has no idea who the birds are named after. I think my grandpa does it because it amuses him to hear her yell *Jimmy Talon*, and then he'll add something like *star of The Tonight Show* under his breath."

He laughed again and leaned forward, like he intended to come closer. We stood there, gazing at each other intently, and I didn't care what was right or rational and just wanted to kiss him again.

But then he announced, "I should probably get going. I'll call you about the Vermont thing."

Before I could answer, he opened the front door and was on the porch, heading down the front walk.

He wasn't going to kiss me again. My inner voice reminded me that he'd said he'd keep his hands to himself.

Stupid Marco always doing what he said he would.

When he reached the end of the walk close to the driveway, he turned and said, "Hey, Anna?"

"Yeah?"

"In case you didn't know, the ugly duckling never had to change. She just needed to figure out that she'd been a swan all along." He paused, like he was waiting for a response. When he didn't get one, he said, "Good night."

My heart was pounding, my feet urging me to chase after him, my lips demanding that I do it now or there would be consequences. Instead, I closed the door and sank down to the floor. That man was going to be the death of me.

I got out my phone and called my best friend, who answered immediately. "He kissed you."

"How do you know that?" I demanded.

"I didn't! It was just a guess based on data and predictability and also me being awesome at knowing things. How french were the kisses? Like french vanilla ice cream or like riding a bicycle while wearing a beret and watching a street mime?"

"Honestly, it was like an out-of-body experience, only I was in my body and hyperaware and overstimulated all at the same time."

"That's the best kind," she said with a happy sigh. "Just know that I could not be more happy about this. No, I probably could, but then you would have to take me to the hospital because I'd be having a coronary. Tell me everything."

I recapped her on the entire night and this time gave her all the details. I did trust her judgment and I wanted an outside perspective. I felt too close to everything to know what I should do.

She was strangely quiet when I finished. "At what point are you going to realize that Marco is in love with you?"

That sent lances of shock through my chest. "What?"

"He is the CEO of a major international corporation."

Confusing. "What does that have to do with anything?"

"How does a man like that have so much free time to just hang out with you? Do you realize that he is rearranging his schedule to be able to spend time with you?"

"That's not—" But I stopped. What if that were true?

"And before you *but, Craig* me, you also have to realize that what you have with him is just a long-standing crush that is like a shadow that would disappear under harsh light."

What was I supposed to say to that? I suspected she was right. "I don't know how I feel." It was about as honest as I was willing to be in that moment.

"You do tend to crush on unobtainable men," she said softly, like she was afraid of hurting me. "You want your fairy tale. And I know you're waiting for your white knight."

"I'm not doing that," I immediately protested.

"You are. You love the idea of being rescued. Your grandma did it with your grandpa, your dad did it for your mom, and Craig rescued you in a parking lot."

"That's not the only reason."

"I would also like to point out that Marco kind of rescued you in that bathroom. And instead of leaving ten minutes later like Craig, he's stuck around."

It was extremely disconcerting to have someone close to you point out something you'd never even considered. Was this true? Was I so obsessed with fairy tales and happily ever afters and being rescued that I'd been waiting around for something to happen instead of going after what I wanted?

Like I'd resolved to do?

"Also, I would like to file a formal complaint that you haven't been kissing Marco this whole time. You should do it every chance you get. You can kiss him. You don't have to wait for him to make a move."

"I can't just kiss him." She was not understanding the situation. At all.

"Why not?"

"Because he doesn't actually want to kiss me."

"How long did he kiss you for tonight?" she asked.

I didn't know. Because time had basically stopped when his mouth was on mine.

"People don't actually go around kissing random other people for no reason," she added.

We had a reason. "Science?" I offered weakly, but I anticipated her response before she said it.

"Nobody kisses for science, either."

"That's not true. There are people who study kissing specifically as a field of study and—"

"You have put all your eggs into one poorly woven basket," she said. "For once in your life, be bold. Do something scary. Tell him. It doesn't bode well for your fake relationship if you can't communicate what you're feeling."

The idea of telling Marco that I had feelings for him was too much. "I've been bold. I went after Craig."

"You didn't. You and Marco invented some wackadoodle scheme to get him to notice you."

It was like she was forgetting all the scary things I'd recently done. "I quit my job!"

"And then had a new job a few hours later as a consultant. You've never been without a safety net. Start your company. Go get the man of everyone's dreams. Pitch your idea to an investor. Go for it."

I had the feeling she was right. And maybe I needed to spend an obsessive amount of time thinking about it. "What's going on with Zhen?" I asked and walked upstairs as she told me all about their date last night, and I smiled as I listened.

I wished, for the millionth time, that I could be more like her.

Because Catalina would be bold when it came to Marco.

Maybe it was time to be more like her.

CHAPTER TWENTY-FOUR

Marco kept being available to me in the evenings. During the day, I refined my mood ring lipstick, and at night, he and I hung out. We mostly stayed at his place—I supposed there was no need to keep getting photographed when Craig was a hundred percent aware that we were a couple.

We ate together, watched movies. We spent three days in a row watching all three Lord of the Rings movies. And during *The Return of the King* and Gandalf's speech to Pippin, I realized that Marco was mouthing the dialogue, probably unaware that he was doing it.

"You know all the words," I said, delighted.

"What? No."

"You do, you do!" I clapped my hands together. "You might love these movies more than I do."

"Not possible. I don't want to marry Legolas, so you win."

We spent a lot of time working on a business plan. He gave me a list of potential suppliers and manufacturers along with all sorts of projection numbers that I probably never would have been able to come up with on my own. He seemed just as excited about the prospect of pitching to his dad as I was.

"Do you have a name?" he asked the night before we were scheduled to fly to Vermont.

"I was thinking Aviary Cosmetics."

"That's pretty," he said as he reached for the first-quarter projections. A term I now understood, thank you very much. "Do you have a tagline for the company?"

"Beauty takes flight."

"Like you're trying to leave beauty? Fly away from it? That might come across negatively."

"Okay," I said, nodding. Fair note. "What about where beauty soars?"

"Sounds like sores. As in wounds. It's okay. We'll have a marketing department for that." He heard the mistake and corrected himself. "I mean you. You'll hire marketing. I can help advise you or . . . you could just do it yourself. I don't want to overstep."

It would be hard for him to overstep when he was taking care of so many important details for me. "You're not. Hiring a marketing adviser would be smart. More brain, less storm that way. I was also thinking it would be fun to have palettes that are named after birds. Like we'd have Peacock Blue. Canary Yellow. Oriole Orange. Cardinal Red."

That got his attention. "Cardinal? Like sin?"

My blood turned thick and heavy. "What? No. Like the bird."

"Too bad." He put the projections down, focusing all his attention on me. "Cardinal sins can be fun. I'm a fan of lust."

That made heat prickle up the back of my neck. "I'm more partial to sloth and gluttony myself."

He ignored my weak attempt at humor. "What color would that be? Cardinal red? Would it be a deep, dark red?"

We hadn't kissed all week. I had been longing for him so badly that I was literally dreaming about him. It was kind of torturous to spend so much time with him, be so close, but not be able to touch him.

Especially now that I knew how good he was at it.

But his question now—that felt like an opening to something that I was eager to seize. Because despite Catalina's sage advice, I had not taken a single bit of it. I should have. I should have made some kind of move before this.

"It would. A deep, dark red." I nodded, pushing the slideshow presentation to the side.

"I thought of a test we haven't run yet. Water."

"Water?" I repeated because suddenly this was not going where I thought it was.

"Is the lipstick waterproof?"

"Yes."

"This is something I have to see for myself." He took me by the hand and led me from his kitchen table and into his bedroom. I had one heart-stopping moment of unadulterated glee at our setting, but he took me into his bathroom.

He opened the glass door to his shower and turned on the water. He stepped under the stream, fully dressed, and turned to grin at me. "Let's see it."

I went with him into the water, and droplets landed on my glasses. I made sure to get a good look at him, though. He pushed his dark hair up out of his face, and it was like it was happening in slow motion.

If damp Marco had been dangerous, soaking wet Marco was downright lethal.

He reached over and took my glasses off, setting them on a shelf nearby. I started to shiver, and he incorrectly assumed it was because of the water. "Is it not warm enough?" he asked as he took me in his arms, holding me close.

I didn't know. I'd been so focused on him that I really wasn't registering anything else.

The water continued to fall on us, and I watched the way it lovingly traveled down his face, caressing as it went.

"You're my existential crisis, Anna. Do I kiss you or not kiss you?"

My pulse went triple time. "If I get a vote, I go with kiss me."

Only I didn't get to say the last word because he devoured it with his kiss. Our clothes were so wet, it was like I could feel every outline of his chest as he held me, each plane and sharp ridge that I wanted to touch and explore. To kiss and feel his skin beneath my palms.

I should have been freezing, but I couldn't feel anything besides heat. I half expected steam to start rising from the friction of our bodies as they intertwined. Water filled in whatever gap it could find, but there weren't many gaps. The sensations were overwhelming—that fiery heat from him and his kiss and the cold water surrounding us, covering us.

Still, he held back. I didn't understand why. I made it pretty obvious that I was enjoying myself and wanted more, please. But there was restraint. I could feel the tension in his shoulders, along his neck.

It was like he was making a dish, one where he was generally increasing the heat little by little. But I was ready for the main course.

Kissing him was like floating and falling at the same time. I didn't want him to ever stop. Electricity skated over my skin, across the water, until it landed in my veins, lighting my whole body up with desire and a need to somehow get closer, even though that wasn't possible.

What was happening in his shower was the most spontaneous and hottest thing I'd ever been a part of, even though we were both still fully clothed.

He brought the kiss to a stop, both of us breathing hard. He reached over and turned the water off. "What's the verdict?" he asked cheerfully as he pushed his soaked hair off his face again. We were so close that I could clearly see him, even without my glasses.

My mouth went dry, despite the fact that I was also drenched.

"It seems waterproof," I said when I could speak again.

"Good. Let me go grab you a towel and something to change into."

I stood shivering in the shower while he left, both from the cold and from the ache that tormented me. I crossed my arms and could hear Catalina's voice in my head telling me to go for what I wanted.

I knew I wanted Marco. I desperately wanted to climb that man like a tree. But despite my best friend's assertions, I didn't know if it was one-sided. If I was just a port in the storm. The woman he was spending time with and so convenient to kiss. Like he was some kind of serial kisser.

Regardless of how often he did or didn't kiss me, Marco never seemed affected the same way that I did. He seemed to enjoy himself, he was obviously intrigued by the science part of it, but it never felt like things changed in our relationship. He treated me the same way he always had.

He came back and handed me a towel and clothes that were going to be much too big. "I can throw your stuff in the dryer."

I nodded, and he left, closing the bathroom door shut behind him. As I started to pull my wet jeans off, I wondered at what point Marco was going to realize that his test was invalid because I hadn't been wearing any of my lipstick today.

~

I'd had to borrow a suitcase from Catalina, who threatened me under penalty of death if I didn't call her every night and tell her everything that happened in Vermont. During our plane ride, which was first class and now I didn't know how I'd ever go back to economy seats, Marco explained that the Vermont house had been his mother's favorite and that she had loved to ski. So every January, the family would go up for a week to ski and spend time together.

"My dad could only make it for like, three days tops and so we keep the tradition, but for a few days."

"That seems like a lot of effort." All these people packing and flying across the country when they lived near each other in California.

"Well, my family typically fights most of the year via texts and emails, so it's important that for a few days we put all that aside and fight in person."

I laughed, but I could tell that something about this bothered him. I hoped he would tell me.

The house was far from the airport, and Marco had rented an SUV to get us there. It had been a long day, and I ended up falling asleep in the passenger seat. I awoke to Marco gently shaking me.

"We're here."

I opened my eyes to a winter wonderland. Everywhere I looked, there was a blanket of sparkling white snow. I got out of the car and stood there, looking up. The snow was falling above me, and I twirled around in circles, laughing. Marco got out of the car and stood by the front, watching me spin.

"This is amazing!" I called out. "I've never seen snow before."

"You've never seen snow?" he asked incredulously.

"Nope."

He fell silent, and that's when I noticed how quiet it was. Like the blanket of snow was absorbing the sound. It was so beautiful.

"This," Marco said, and I turned to face him.

"What?"

"This is what you should show Craig. This part of you. Full of wonder and delight. You're . . . enchanting."

His words touched me, but he didn't want me for himself. He was ready to pass me along to his brother.

Because that's what he thinks you want, my inner voice chided me.

Ignoring it, I said, "Nobody's ever called me *enchanting* before."

"Really? Even with the D&D crowd you run with? I bet they have, and it was in some fantasy language so you didn't know it." He paused and then said, "Gi melin, Undómiel."

"What did you just say?" I asked. "What language was that?"

"Nothing. Forget I said it. It's not important."

I got the feeling it was very important, but I was afraid to risk looking like a pathetic idiot in that moment, so I said nothing.

"I'll grab the luggage," he said.

It was then that I turned and noticed the house. It wasn't so much a house as a massive chalet covered in snow. I wondered how I'd missed it. "Wow. I'm betting at one point there was a moat. You guys have some Scrooge McDuck money."

"We don't have a vault full of gold coins to swim in, if you were hoping to put that on the agenda," he said, carrying both of our suitcases. His phone buzzed, and he took it out of his pocket. "It's my dad. Their private plane was diverted into Philadelphia because of the storm. We're lucky we landed when we did. But that means we're on our own tonight."

If this wasn't the setup for half of my favorite rom-com movies. "Is this where you tell me there's only one bed?"

He made a confused face and gestured toward the house. "There's like, fifteen beds."

Now I was the one saying, "Never mind." I followed behind him, trying to step in his footprints because while the snow was gorgeous, it was also bitterly cold. A desert girl like me wasn't used to this, and I hadn't dressed appropriately. Marco stood in front of the door and waited for a second.

"I hope you're ready for this. You'd bat a pretty good average in assuming my family is the worst. Abandon all hope ye who enter here." Then he put in a key code and opened the door and I quickly went inside with him, trying to ignore the sense of foreboding he'd just caused.

The house was cold, too. I stood there shivering while Marco tried to flip the light switch. "The power's out."

"Oh." I edged closer to him. "That's not great."

"You're not afraid of the dark, are you?"

I paused before I answered. "I'm not afraid. But you should know that being afraid of the dark is a reasonable adaptive evolutionary reaction," I told him.

He laughed. "Let me make a phone call. The staff should know something about this."

I rubbed my arms while he paced back and forth, talking to someone.

He finished his call. "The housekeeper and the groundskeeper were snowed in earlier today. The storm is supposed to let up in a few hours, and everything should be good to go tomorrow. You and I are on our own tonight."

So maybe it was fifteen beds instead of just one, but I was definitely seeing the appeal.

I shivered again, hard.

"Why don't you go upstairs and get changed into some warm clothes and I will get the fire going."

"You know how to start a fire?"

He gave me a withering look. "It's not hard."

"Are you going to chop wood?" I asked hopefully. I would pay to watch that.

"There's already firewood."

"Oh. That's too bad." I grabbed my suitcase and asked, "Which room is mine?"

He'd started stacking logs in the fireplace. "Our room is the last door on the left."

I froze in place. "Our room?"

"My family will think it's weird if you sleep in a different room."

He was right.

And I wasn't just saying that because the prospect of sharing a bed with him was very, very appealing.

Huh. Turned out there was only one bed after all.

Despite Marco's assertion, I wasn't afraid of the dark. Just slightly uncomfortable with it.

Like now, as I had to go up the stairs and walk down a long, kind of scary hallway. I took my phone out and turned the flashlight on. I tried to think happy thoughts. About Marco.

I reached the end of the hall without incident and was so overrun with images of being snuggled up next to Marco that I couldn't remember if he'd said the room on the right or the left.

Picking right, I opened the door and walked into what looked like a teenage boy's room. I set my suitcase down and started to explore. This was probably an invasion of someone's privacy, but I couldn't help myself. The room was neat and had been cared for. Probably by the housekeeper Marco had mentioned.

There were tons of bookshelves, and I held my phone up to read the spines. I saw Tolkien's *Lord of the Rings* and *The Hobbit*.

Whose room was this?

I went over to a bulletin board, and there were pictures of a teenage Marco. Holding up a fish. On the back of an ATV. Playing outside in the grass with a dog. Sitting in front of a Christmas tree with Craig and baby Lindy.

In a Jedi costume with a plastic pumpkin on Halloween.

I knew it! I started scanning the room more earnestly and found another shelf that had a lightsaber, a stuffed Ewok, and a replica of Boba Fett's helmet.

On the shelf below that one were a number of trophies and medals, and I assumed they were for sports. But on closer inspection I saw that Marco Kimball had won the state science fair when he was thirteen years old. All the ribbons and awards were for academics. Science, specifically.

There was a diploma on the wall. It was from Harvard, and he had gotten his degree in biochemistry.

No wonder he knew so much about my job.

I would have bet good money that he'd majored in finance. Or business. Nope. Chemistry.

I took out my phone and texted Catalina because I had to tell someone or I was going to burst.

Marco is a huge nerd. I just saw his lightsaber.

She responded immediately.

Is that a euphemism?

I shook my head and wrote back:

No. An actual lightsaber. He's a dork. And he has a degree in biochemistry!!!

I saw the three dots at the bottom of my screen, and they stayed there for a long time, and so I was surprised when her answer was short.

It's like he was made just for you.

My heart fluttered at her words, and I looked around his room again. It was like that.

Another text.

Tell him.

I wanted to, but it was too scary. Not just because I was this close to turning Aviary Cosmetics into a reality but because Marco had come to mean too much to me. I didn't want to risk our friendship, and I was afraid that if I confessed that I cared about him, he would go running the other way.

Maybe I can test the waters, I texted her.

Do or do not. There is no try.

Shaking my head, I responded, Okay, Yoda.

"Did you get lost?" he asked.

I yelped when Marco came into the room. He smelled faintly of woodsmoke, and it was incredibly appealing and added to the whole rugged-outdoorsman thing I was currently picturing for him.

"I couldn't remember if you said right or left."

"Left." He came into the room, looking around like I had, but there was pain on his face. "I haven't been in here in years. The last time was to hang that." He pointed at his Harvard diploma.

That thought completely broke my heart. That Marco would come in here just to hang his diploma. Like he was trying to show that he mattered, that his accomplishments were worth paying attention to. "I thought you said your stepmom packed up your room and let Craig move in."

"That was at the estate in Los Angeles. Not the Vermont house." He said that like I was the strange one. Of course, at the Vermont house. How silly of me.

I picked up the lightsaber. "Lindy mentioned she had a brother who dressed up for a Star Wars convention, and I thought—"

He finished my sentence. "You automatically assumed she meant Craig."

I had. Because I had wanted it to be Craig so that we would have at least one thing in common.

"My brother calls Star Wars *the one with the big teddy bear and glowing swords*. Sorry to burst your bubble."

"Oh."

"Speaking of, the fire's started and I've got my laptop. Did you want to hate-watch *The Rise of Skywalker* again and tell me about how Ben

Solo is alive in the World Between Worlds waiting for Rey to rescue him?"

"I do." And I really, really did.

Marco showed me into the guest room that we were supposed to use. The room was luxurious but impersonal—like we were staying in a hotel. Which I guessed was the point. I preferred his nerded-out room to this one. It made me think about all the time we'd spent together, where he'd teased me for my obsessions, and he'd shared them all along.

I put my suitcase on the bed, and then I screwed up enough courage to ask him. "Why do you hide that part of yourself? All the fanboy stuff you used to love?"

He shrugged. "My dad thought it was a waste of time and that I needed to focus on other things."

"You should enjoy what you enjoy, Marco," I said, echoing the time he'd told me the same thing. "Especially with me."

It was dark, so I might have been mistaken, but I thought there was a heated, intense look in his eyes. He swallowed hard and then said, "Come on. It's cold up here."

I went back downstairs with him, and along the way, I thought of how he'd apologized for bursting my bubble with regards to Craig.

Only he hadn't. If anything, I was realizing that the Craig bubble had been burst a while ago.

Bubble was an apt term for my feelings for Craig, because they were very much like soap bubbles at the top of a mixture. Light, frothy, able to blow away with the slightest breeze. But with Marco? It was like a match striking flint—instant, combustible, roaring to life inside me with a burning hunger that I didn't know how to respond to. A ravaging fire with an unlimited fuel source.

One could float away without even being missed, while the other would consume me, making sure I would never be the same again.

Me coming to Vermont had nothing to do with Craig at all.

I had come here for Marco, and Marco alone.

CHAPTER TWENTY-FIVE

We had paused the movie and gone into the kitchen to find something to eat because my stomach would not stop rumbling.

"Why do women like Kylo Ren so much?" he asked.

"Because we have eyeballs. I mean, obviously there's more to it than that. He's the Byronic hero, the morally gray character who redeems himself out of love. Women like a man who is willing to burn down the world and change himself to be with her."

There was a picture of a boat on the wall with Ken and Tracie standing in front of it. I asked, "Is this your family's boat?"

"Yacht," Marco corrected me as he went into the pantry.

"Is there a difference?"

"Yes." His voice was muffled. "That's the *Tracie*." He came back out of the pantry, hands empty. "I told my dad that if he wanted to name it after my stepmom, he should call it the *Cirrhosis of the River*, but he didn't see the humor."

"Again you've failed to gather," I told him, pointing at his hands.

"The stove is gas, so it should work. I'm just not sure what you would want to eat. The staff haven't had a chance to stock the pantry yet."

"Poor little rich boy. Doesn't even know how to cook because you have a staff to do it for you."

"I don't have a staff at my place," he said defensively.

"No, there you have food delivery apps. Hang on." I went into the pantry to see what I could find. All my ideas weren't going to work because they required something like butter or milk, and given that the power was out, I didn't think it was a good idea to rely on food in the fridge.

"Do you think I can't cook?" he asked, leaning against the counter with his arms folded across his broad chest.

I grabbed a couple of cans of chicken noodle soup and brought them out. "If I had to guess, no. Let me teach you the basics. This is a stove. This is the knob you use to turn the stove on."

"I know how to turn things on," he said in a low voice that had me quivering. "Want me to show you?"

Yes, please, my body begged. His words made me feel like I was standing in a massive thunderstorm and being hit by every bolt of lightning at once.

"What?" I finally squeaked out.

"Did you want me to show you that I know how to cook?" he asked in a semi-serious tone accented by his teasing lilt. "My Sicilian ancestors would be insulted by your implication." He knew exactly what he'd just done to me, that innuendo of his that had nearly made me spontaneously combust.

"Okay," I said, still not quite sure what had just happened. He went into the pantry and started gathering up ingredients. I sat down at the counter to watch him work and to try to calm down.

But watching him cut, dice, open cans, gather spices, and put everything together in a big pot did not help. Because this was all too attractive.

"What did you just say?" he asked, and I realized I must have muttered something under my breath.

I also was not quick enough to censor myself. "I said there's something attractive about a man who knows his way around the kitchen."

He turned his head to grin over his shoulder at me. "And the kitchen's not even my best room."

I told my lady parts that it would be inappropriate to ask for a demonstration in his best room. Why did he flirt with me like that automatically, even when we were alone? I supposed it might be like method acting, where if you stayed in character all the time, it was easier to slip into the part when necessary.

"Tell me about Comic Con and the Nerd Who Was," I said. I needed the distraction. So while he finished up making us dinner, he shared stories with me about his past that was filled with the most delightful nerdery.

It was like stumbling across his bedroom had broken down a wall that he'd put up, and I liked seeing this side of him.

He'd made a soup with egg noodles. "Creamy chicken noodle soup without the chicken," he told me as he handed me a bowl. "Do you want to go eat this in the living room?"

"Sure." I followed after him, trying to be very careful and not spill because I knew Tracie would send me a bill and I couldn't afford to break so much as a candlestick in this place.

When we settled in, I got my first bite. "Wow! This is really good!" I told him.

"You don't have to sound quite so surprised. Did you want to watch the end of your movie?"

"Not really. The ending should be tried at The Hague. I need Lucasfilm to undo it and make a sequel. A cartoon, a novel, another actual movie, I don't care as long as they bring Ben back."

"Maybe I can make a call," he said with a wink.

My heart forgot how to beat. "Do you know someone there?"

"No, but my dad does. And as the heir apparent, maybe I could sway him a little."

If Marco got me Ben Solo back, I would marry him tomorrow. His connections reminded me again how different our lives were. "Are you going to inherit this house?"

"I hope so. My mom loved it here."

I was seeing the appeal myself. "You're part of this whole dynasty thing, which I do not get. The only things I'm inheriting are that barely functioning TV and Feather Locklear, who I'm pretty sure is going to outlive us all."

"It's not all it's cracked up to be," he said as he placed his empty bowl on the coffee table. "Sometimes I don't know where my father's demands end and where my dreams begin."

I put my bowl next to his. "I guess you'll have to figure that out."

He gave me a half smile and turned his gaze toward the fireplace. I thought of how we hadn't known each other all that long, but it felt like a lifetime.

How Marco seemed to remember everything about me and Craig couldn't be bothered to recall my name.

"Do you remember the first time we met?" I asked him.

If he was surprised by the randomness of my question, he didn't show it. "I don't think I'll ever forget it. It's seared into my brain."

"Your brother doesn't remember when he and I met."

"His loss. You would be a very hard person to forget."

That made my throat feel thick, like it was impossible to swallow. I would never, not for the rest of my life, forget Marco, either.

As if he sensed that I was feeling a little emotional, he turned the conversation to a neutral subject. "My family will want to go skiing when they arrive tomorrow. Are you up for it?"

"Ugh. I don't like doing things where I have to move my body."

"Yeah, we've met."

I smiled at him. A wave of tiredness crashed into me, and I leaned my head against the back of the couch. His leg brushed against mine, and I shivered from the contact.

"Are you cold?" he asked.

The fire had made the room very toasty, but I lied because of my own selfish interests. "Yes."

He opened his arms and said, "Come here."

Nobody had to ask me twice. I let him fold me into his embrace and nestled against his strong shoulder. I put my hand on his chest, loving his constant, firm heartbeat. I sighed happily.

"What kind of experiment is this?" I asked and then yawned.

"No experiment," he said, and I thought I felt his lips brush against my forehead. "And in addition to fifteen beds, there are eighteen showers in this house. In case you wanted to test the repeatability of that particular experiment."

I smiled and thought that I had never felt safer, securer, or more content in my entire life.

I'd never been happier.

We cuddled tightly, and he started stroking my hair. I wanted to purr like a cat and rub against him.

Instead, my breathing became slower, more even, as sleep clouded my thoughts.

The last thing I thought I heard him say before I drifted off was, "My brother is an idiot."

~

"Hi!"

I blinked several times, temporarily forgetting where I was. Sunlight streamed in through the massive windows.

Lindy stood over me. I had been sleeping on the couch at Marco's house in Vermont. And I was alone. I wondered where he had gone and at what point he'd left me by myself.

"Hey," I said to her, rubbing my eyes. "What time is it?"

"It's past noon. Everybody else went skiing, but I wanted to stay here with you." She started cracking her knuckles, and it was like fireworks popping.

I groaned, and she asked, "What's wrong?"

"I really hate that sound."

It took her a second to figure out what I meant. "The knuckle cracking? How have you not stabbed Marco yet?"

"What do you mean?"

"He pops his knuckles constantly. It's a Kimball family trait. We all do it, but Marco is the worst. He does it so much that it sounds like cannon fire."

That made me sit straight up. "Marco? He never does. I mean, there was that one time." At Catalina's party. When I'd asked him not to do it around me. "But he hasn't done it since."

Lindy looked impressed. "Wow. He must really like you. That's like the equivalent of a room full of roses. I'm really glad you're here, though. I have a report for you on the lipstick. I gave it to some of my friends to try out, and I wrote everything down. Then after, I wanted to go through every cosmetic I own and have you explain to me how they're made and what they do."

"Okay, but can I shower and brush my teeth first?" I asked.

"Sure. I'll come find you after!"

Not knowing how much time Lindy was going to give me before she tracked me down, I hurried to get ready. I wondered how many members of the Kimball family had seen me sleeping on their couch, most likely drooling.

Lindy made good on her promise, and I had just finished brushing my wet hair when she came into my room with an armful of supplies. I spent the rest of the afternoon discussing the science behind her favorite products, but what she seemed most impressed by was how easily I could re-create them for pennies on the dollar.

There was a knock at the door, and when I said, "Come in!" I was surprised to see Craig.

Not just surprised but distinctly not excited.

"Hey, Lindy—Mom's looking for you."

She rolled her eyes and gathered up her things. "We'll talk more later," she said to me.

Craig stepped into the room, and I felt self-conscious. "Excited for dinner tonight?"

Should I have been? I assumed it was just a family dinner. "Is this a big deal? Like I should dress up?" Were they celebrating Craig's engagement again?

"No. We usually dress casual. Which I'm sure you won't have a problem with."

I glanced down at my sweatpants and baggy shirt and then glared at him. He was a condescending jerk. I felt stupid. How had I ever imagined myself in love with this man? Because he was nice to me for ten minutes in a parking lot? Marco would have followed me home to make sure I got there safely instead of driving off.

I didn't know anything about Craig. His favorite sports team and video games didn't count. I never had known anything real about him. And the few things that I had learned? It had destroyed any pretend feelings I'd had for him. I'd been waiting for a rom-com hero. I wanted the fairy tale happily ever after that my parents and grandparents had. I'd made Craig be that hero even though he didn't fit.

He wasn't what I wanted. He never had been. I'd made up this person who didn't exist and put Craig's face on him.

But maybe that man, my ideal man, was the one I'd been spending all my time with.

I thought I'd wanted Legolas, but all along I'd been waiting for Aragorn.

"You seem to be settling in nicely," he said, and I noticed a venomous edge to his voice that reminded me of his mother. If I hadn't already been grossed out by his general demeanor, that one attribute would have pushed me completely over the edge. "This must be quite the upgrade for you."

"Did you need something?" I asked, not responding to his dig. Those things he'd said to me at the party—those hadn't been butchered compliments. He'd meant to insult me, and I had been, as Marco said, "too nice" to see it.

"Lindy told me about the lipstick."

That was unsettling. I was wearing it now. I reached up to touch my lower lip. "And?"

He came over and sat on the edge of the bed, close to me. "I thought we had an arrangement. That you'd bring that sort of thing to me first."

"Why would I do that? I don't work for Minx."

He reached for my hand, and I pulled it away from him. I didn't want him to touch me.

The door opened, and Craig jumped up, as if we'd been doing something wrong. Marco walked in the room and glanced between us, as if he'd interrupted something.

I rushed over to him and threw my arms around him. Not just because I wanted to get away from Craig, but I wanted to touch him again.

Marco kissed me hot and hard, making me dizzy, and then said, "I have to take a shower. Care to join me?"

Oh, I very much wanted that, but this time I knew for sure he'd said it solely for his brother's benefit.

Marco glanced over at his brother. "Close the door on your way out."

Craig did as instructed, but he looked frustrated and confused as he shut the door. I didn't know what that was about.

As soon as we were alone, Marco relaxed his hold on me, but I didn't let go. He smiled weakly at me. "I'm gross."

He most definitely was not. He was hot and sweaty from skiing, but I liked it. I wanted to pull him over to his bed and have him press me down and then see if his skin tasted salty and—

"It seems like things are going according to plan," he said, interrupting me.

There was no plan, as far as I was concerned. I didn't want Craig. But if I told Marco that, then what? Would he put me on a plane and send me home? He still needed me. He was trying to impress his dad by dating someone down-to-earth, right?

But if he wanted Craig and Leighton to break up, I was not the woman for the job.

What would he do if I told him that?

I knew I wasn't good enough for Marco, and it wouldn't take much for him to see it, too. I just couldn't let that wall down completely. I was caught in this limbo where I wanted to protect my heart and I was too afraid to lose him. I would stay in this pretense if it meant I got to be near him. So I just nodded and said, "Yep."

He gave me a sad smile. "I'm going to go shower. I'll see you after?"

Then he took off his shirt as he walked toward the door, and I was torn between shielding my eyes to give him some privacy and soaking in every second of getting to view his incredible chest and then his back.

He closed the bathroom door and ended my dilemma. I decided that I needed to go downstairs.

There was no way I could calmly sit here while he was naked in a shower with only an unlocked door between us.

CHAPTER TWENTY-SIX

I went to the library. So far it seemed to be the quietest room in the house, and I needed to be able to hear my own thoughts. The first thing I did was consider Marco's recent behavior. He'd felt a little off upstairs, and I wasn't sure why. Maybe the skiing had been strenuous and he just needed to relax a bit. Not to mention how cold it was outside. It would make me grouchy to have to spend a long time in it.

That made me think of last night, when we'd first arrived. Those words he'd said to me. Now that I knew he was fully certified in fandom, that actually made figuring out his words more difficult. I'd assumed it had been a foreign language. Maybe Italian?

But now it could be anything. Klingon. Orcish. Na'vi. Dothraki. There was no way to narrow it down. I tried phonetical spellings, but that wasn't yielding anything, either.

"There you are." Marco's rich voice filled the room and made my heart flutter with anticipation.

"Here I am," I agreed and turned to look at him as I set my phone down. Although I should have expected it, I didn't. Holy Kylo Ren's stupidly retconned reconstructed mask, Marco was damp.

Water and Marco combined were clearly my kryptonite. I cleared my throat loudly. "So . . . dinner. Which is happening soon." I inwardly cringed. "Is this like, a draping-ourselves-in-diamonds-and-couture-before-the-blood-sacrifice-starts situation?"

"Nothing like that," he reassured me as he sat down on the couch next to me. Much, much too close. He draped his arm across the back, and my skin tingled in anticipation.

"I was upstairs thinking about you," he said.

In the shower? Somebody was going to have to bring me the smelling salts. "Oh?"

"Yes. I was thinking that of the different experiments we've conducted, not one of them included a durability test."

"Durability?" I asked, my voice high and breathless.

I saw his Adam's apple bob in response. He nodded, as if he didn't trust himself to speak.

His suggestion was so, so reasonable and logical. We should absolutely make out. For science.

"A sustained, ongoing kiss." I nodded. But even in my hormonally intoxicated–like state, I recognized that it was a weak argument and the reason why. "This isn't about the lipstick, Marco. The only reason we should be kissing is because you want to."

His eyes darkened at my words, nearly black. His gaze flickered down to my lips. He obviously recognized his words being used, because he repeated mine back to me. "I want you to kiss me, Anna."

I leaned forward, eager and willing. I put my hand on his chest. Both because I wanted to touch him and to give myself an extra moment. We both were breathing hard and fast, and I was glad he was affected, too. Whatever his reasons were for this—to stop Craig, to save Minx, to participate in what was basically a leisure sport for him—I was glad he was here and wanted this.

Wanted me.

"Dark red," he murmured. The roughness of his voice made electricity zip through me, lighting up circuits I didn't know I possessed.

"Yes."

"And we're alone."

Technically, we were in a house full of people, but still I said, "Yes." That seemed to be the only thing I was capable of saying. I was going to be in big trouble if he started asking other things. Yes, I'd go upstairs with him to our room. Yes, I had forgotten all about his brother.

Yes, I'd fallen in love with him.

That last one was a revelation to me, especially given how hard I'd fought it. But it was true. I was in love with Marco.

That feeling overwhelmed me and compelled me forward. I had to kiss him. I couldn't tell him that I loved him. He didn't feel the same. I knew he didn't. But I could have this moment with him, this kiss, before reality had to intrude. Because I knew this would end. Probably badly, as Catalina had predicted. And not because we were caught or Craig found out about our plan, but because I had been stupid enough to fall for the best man I'd ever met.

He made a noise in the back of his throat when my lips pressed against his. I wanted to go for it, be reckless.

But, like always, I could sense how he was holding back. Like there was a bridge he wouldn't pass over, a line he wouldn't cross. I wanted it gone. The bridge blown up, the line washed away.

I pulled back so that I could look at him straight on. His eyes opened slowly, confused. "Could you kiss me like you mean it?" I asked.

"What would that look like?" It felt evasive, and it was annoying.

"I have to do everything around here," I grumbled, wrapping my arms around his neck so that our bodies were pressed together. I had, admittedly, been more of a passive but eager participant in the past. Mostly because he overwhelmed me, but tonight?

I planned on being incredibly active. I was more than willing to take the lead, and judging from his response, he was happy to let me. I set my glasses on the back of the couch and then climbed into his lap to kiss him like I meant it.

He groaned and opened his mouth beneath mine, and the amount of victory I felt—it was better than my first successful batch of the mood ring lipstick, and I didn't know I could feel more triumphant than that.

Whatever resistance he'd been holding on to for whatever reason—that quickly came tumbling down. He was intense, heated, wanting. His kisses were raw with a ruthless need that was shocking. I had known this was there—lurking beneath the surface—I just hadn't been prepared for how incredible it would feel. Knowing that he wanted me as much as I wanted him. The way it would send lightning singing through my veins.

I registered that we had shifted, and I was lying against the couch with him on top of me. But whether he'd pushed me back or I had pulled him down, I wasn't sure, but either way, neither one of us seemed to mind.

His kisses were fiery, demanding, and utterly consuming. It was like he had turned into a fallen electrical wire, buzzing and moving, too dangerous to touch, likely to overload my nervous system and destroy me. The electricity he sparked spread outward through me in a circular pattern, like a pebble being thrown into still water. The high voltage of his touch seemed to increase as those circles grew. He kissed and kissed me, in long, hungry strokes.

Then suddenly he stopped kissing me, and it was like being unplugged. I hated that he'd stopped, and I tried to protest.

But he had simply moved his lips across my cheek, up to my eyelid, down to my jaw, and then farther down to press soft kisses along my neck. Some perverse part of me wanted to remind him that there was no lipstick to test in any of these new locations, but the rest of me told it to shut up.

"Do you think we should pace ourselves?" he asked against my skin before he softly pressed the tip of his tongue against the pulse point in my neck, and my eyes rolled back in my head.

"Do you want to pace yourself?" I asked.

"Not particularly," he said before he kissed my pulse with his mouth. My erratic, unstable pulse that was liable to give out on me.

I wondered how it was possible to feel so charged and so hazy at the same time. While he continued to explore my throat with his mouth, I tugged on the back of his shirt to get my hands on some of the muscles I'd been dying to touch. When my skin made contact, it temporarily halted his movement, and he took in a sharp breath. His skin was warm and soft and oh, those rigid muscles of his. A girl could devote her life to this particular field of study.

Then he was kissing me again with that wild abandonment that made me feel like my brain was having a heart attack. Or a series of mini strokes. This wasn't butterflies that I was feeling in my stomach, though. It was eagles. Massive Lord of the Rings eagles flapping with their giant wingspan. And not just in my stomach. In every organ, under every patch of skin I possessed.

A tight electrical knot formed in my gut and begged to be released. Somehow, he deepened our kiss, making me feverish and frantic.

Simply put—a combustion reaction in chemistry was when something reacted with oxygen, and it released energy in heat and light as a result. That was my reaction with him. Completely combustible.

But a nagging part of my brain reminded me that Marco didn't know everything about our situation, and I felt like he should. Stupid guilt getting in the way of everything.

I pushed slightly against his shoulders. "I feel bad."

He grinned and then kissed me quickly. "That's the opposite of how you should be feeling right now. I can fix that."

"No, this is like . . . false pretenses." It was very hard to gather my thoughts enough that I could explain myself. "Because I'm—"

I'm in love with you.

I couldn't tell him. It would change everything. And fake relationship or not, I liked where we were. I was willing to accept crumbs if it meant I got to be close to him. I didn't want to scare him off. Plus, my traitorous mouth refused to form the words because it was much more interested in being fused to his.

He reached up to gently move some hair from my face, letting his fingers brush against my skin, and I leaned against his hand, wanting more of his fiery touch. There was something there in his eyes—something pure and strong—and it sent a rush of emotion through me.

"I wish you'd forget . . ." He let his voice trail off.

"Forget what?" I prompted, desperate to know.

"Nothing." He shook his head. "It doesn't matter."

I wanted to tell him that it did matter, but he was kissing my throat again, and apparently that made my voice box stop working completely. His hot mouth sent bolts of electricity shooting through me, sparkling and crackling until all I wanted to do was be lost in him.

When he returned his lips to mine, something had shifted. He turned over on the couch, pulling me so that we switched positions. Now he slowed our kiss, gentling it with a tenderness that made me ache even more. Those electrical flames he caused were still there, still making their concentric circles, just more slowly and going deeper.

I wished I could get closer to him and wiggled to make sure I was touching him everywhere. He groaned and shuddered at that, and again I was delighted that I had that effect on him.

Now it was his turn to run his fingers along the skin of my back, pressing his fingertips into me, definitely marking me. No one would be able to see it, but I was his and always would be.

"Your skin is so soft," he murmured next to my ear, his words scalding me. "Are you this soft everywhere?"

"I haven't done a thorough assessment," I said.

"I volunteer as tribute," he said with a grin.

I had just lowered my mouth down to his when I heard a strange noise.

"Ew. Why is everyone in this house making out?" Lindy's voice came through the room like a shot. I quickly disentangled myself from Marco, and it was like I was ripping off my own skin, leaving pieces of it behind.

I grabbed my glasses as I stood up, feeling uneasy on my feet, and wondered whether I should apologize to his sister.

"I am so traumatized," she announced. "This is gross. I'm supposed to tell you that dinner's almost ready."

"Thanks," I said breathlessly.

She left the library, and I couldn't help but reach up to touch my lips. They were so sensitive, and despite my considerable skills as a cosmetic chemist, I doubted that there was any lipstick left.

I didn't know what to say to Marco, after kind of abandoning all sense as we just had. We'd also been making out a really long time, and I hadn't realized it. That was probably because whenever he touched me, he made the rest of the world melt away.

"So, I should go and uh, get ready," I said, hoping that my legs were strong enough to carry me out of the room.

He was the picture of ease—lying there on the couch with his hands tucked behind his head—and the only thing I wanted to do in the whole world was go over and climb back on top of him. "I'll be up in a few minutes."

Right. We were sharing a room. A room where we could possibly be alone and lock a door so that no teenage girls would interrupt us.

Although, that would be bad. Not until I told him the truth. I'd tell him tonight. After dinner.

"Okay." I walked over to the doorway, feeling his eyes on me. "By the way, you lied."

He sat up slightly at my words. Was it my imagination or did he actually look a little worried? "About what?"

"About your heart being made out of gallium. I just did a pretty thorough analysis, and you seemed to be in an entirely solid state."

He grinned at me and then said, "You lied, too."

My heart seized in my chest. He knew. "What did I lie about?"

"You said you weren't seductive."

His words made my limbs feel heavy and thick with desire, and if I didn't leave the room right now, I was going to make a big mistake. "And I didn't even have to take my shirt off," I said primly and then left the room to the sound of his laughter.

I practically sprinted upstairs into our bathroom. My lips definitely looked swollen, the skin along my jaw reddened from his stubble. My hair was a total mess. I brushed through it quickly and realized I didn't have a good strategy on how to tell Marco. Talking it out always helped me process my thoughts.

I grabbed my phone and went into his old bedroom. Somehow, it was comforting to be surrounded by his favorite childhood things. I sat on his bed and called Catalina and told her almost everything—just not about my feelings. Because I knew what her reply would be.

When I said we'd made out a little, she gasped. "Where?"

"In the library."

"No, I mean where on your body?" she asked.

"The facial region mostly."

"Aw." She sounded personally disappointed.

And even without knowing that I was in love with Marco, she repeatedly urged me to talk to him, telling me that he wouldn't make out with me surrounded by his entire family unless there was something more there.

"Trust your gut, Anna."

That seemed like bad advice. "You mean the one that can't even tolerate dairy?" It shouldn't be the judge of anything.

I glanced up and saw that it had started to get dark. I told her I had to go and then went back into the room I shared with Marco. I heard him humming a song to himself in the bathroom and the sound of a buzzing razor. I knocked on the door.

"I'm going downstairs," I told him.

"I'm right behind you," he said.

I went down to the first floor, my head still a muddled mess, and faltered on the last step. Marco's entire family stood there, and despite Craig's assurance, no one was dressed casual. The women were in nice dresses, and the men had button-down shirts and sports coats on.

I was woefully underdressed and couldn't even go and change because I hadn't had the foresight to pack anything for this kind of occasion. I thought it was going to be a regular dinner. I didn't know they were planning on having the queen of England join us.

They all turned to stare at me, and I felt incredibly self-conscious.

Marco came to the top of the stairs, dressed appropriately and looking dashing, but stopped short when he saw me. His expression changed, and he turned around and left.

Great. I had embarrassed him so badly, he was now fleeing the scene. I had the urge to follow him, but I stayed put. I could do this. Leighton came up to me with a kind look in her eyes and said sweetly, "I think I have a dress you can borrow."

Unless she had two dresses I could tear apart and stitch back together, that wouldn't be happening. "Thanks. I'm okay."

Tracie began to talk loudly about a vacation they'd taken with people named Bud and Mitzy who had been ridiculously drunk, and that sounded like a pretty great idea. I'd drink, and then maybe I wouldn't remember any of this.

Although I never wanted to forget the way Marco had kissed me.

I had walked over to the man standing by the bar and asked him for whatever he had that would make me drunkest the fastest. Then Marco's arms were stealing around me, and he kissed me on the cheek. "Sorry, everyone," he announced. "Should we go in?"

When he took a step back from me, I realized that he had changed into a T-shirt and jeans.

If his heart wasn't gallium, mine was, because it completely melted. He had done that for me. So I wouldn't feel uncomfortable.

How could I not be in love with him?

And how could I not tell him?

CHAPTER TWENTY-SEVEN

"Marco, there's something—" But I was cut off by everyone else leaving to go into the dining room.

He smiled at me and took me by the hand to lead me into dinner. I was seated between him and Lindy, and that was a pretty great place to be. Talk of Ken and Tracie's recent vacation continued as the first course was brought out. It was a cold, spicy soup, and although I didn't normally do well with a lot of heat, it was delicious. That was followed by a salad, which felt familiar, but it reminded me of Chinese food, given the ingredients.

"My mom is doing a theme," Lindy said as they cleared the plates. "Places she and my dad have traveled in the last year. So Mexico, China."

Servers came out with the next course, and Lindy said, "Here's France."

Snails. They put a plate of cooked snails down in front of me. I gaped at Marco, but he didn't seem to notice.

Maybe I could skip this course. But everybody else was diving in, and I didn't want to be the odd person out. Plus, I had always followed my grandpa's rule about trying everything put in front of me.

"You don't have to eat it," Marco said, but it was okay. I could do this.

I tried it. It was chewy, rubbery, and salty. I leaned over to Marco after I managed to swallow some and said, "At the very least, I should get a superpower after eating that."

He smiled and said, "I don't think it has radiation, but with my stepmom, you never know." Then he added, "I'm sorry I didn't tell you about the dress code."

"It's fine. Thanks for changing."

"You're welcome."

I took a very big drink of water and started pushing the shells around my plate. Marco's dad addressed Marco and said, "Janine just confirmed that I had a cancellation five days from now, so I'll be able to fit you and Anna into my schedule."

Five days. That was both exciting and scary.

"Thanks, Dad," Marco said.

Ken folded his hands and pointed his gaze at me. "You should tell me a little about yourself, Anna."

"Oh. I'm not really sure what to say." I hated being put on the spot.

"Anna is brilliant," Marco interjected. "Very talented. Very sweet and kind."

His words were warming me, sparking through the air toward me. I was sure he was just being nice, but I was ready to buy into whatever he was selling.

"She's funny, too," Lindy said.

"She is?" Tracie interjected. "Such as?"

I never thought of myself as funny, and I wasn't sure how I was supposed to prove it. Other than telling one of my dad's jokes. "A man walks into a bar and says, 'I'll have H_20.' His friend says, 'I'll have H_2O, too.' The second man died."

Marco laughed, but he was the only one, and I felt like I had to explain. "H_2O_2 is hydrogen peroxide, and if you drank it . . ." My voice died off as the next course was brought in.

"Do you know what you should do if nobody laughs at your chemistry jokes?" Marco asked me quietly. "Keep telling them until you get a reaction."

That made me feel slightly better, and I reached under the table to hold his hand. He squeezed it in solidarity.

"Should I be spending this weekend trying to butter your dad up?" I asked.

"He's not butterable. But I can help you if you want."

I squeezed his hand in return. Thankfully the conversation turned to another topic, and I was able to eat the rest of my dinner in relative peace and didn't mentally relive my dumb joke too often.

Marco's phone rang, and he glanced at it. "Excuse me a moment. This is the office."

He got up and walked out of the dining room. The last dish was served.

"This is a mango shrikhand," Tracie said. "We had it on our last trip to India."

They set a bowl in front of me, and I took a small taste. It was delicious—light, creamy, sweet. I started shoveling it into my mouth. The texture was amazing, the spices and nuts such a great contrast to the cool dish.

Marco came back in the room and sat next to me. He put his hand over mine and said, "What are you doing?"

"Eating?"

"That's made with yogurt," he told me. He glared across the table at Tracie. "I told you she was lactose intolerant. Why would you serve this?"

Lindy looked shocked, as if Marco didn't usually speak this way to her mom.

The dish had yogurt in it? I couldn't even tell. I kicked myself for not asking. I should have. I had just wanted to fit in so badly.

"I forgot," Tracie said defensively, and even I could see it was a lie.

A server came over to take the mostly eaten dish from me, and I tried to hand it to him and I missed. The bowl fell to the floor and shattered.

There was a moment of thunderous silence, and then Tracie said, "My china!"

"My mother's china," Marco quickly corrected.

"Do you know how impossible it is to find a match for this set?" she asked, oblivious to Marco's statement.

"I'm so sorry," I said, turning toward Marco. "That was your mom's? I feel terrible. I can pay for it."

"It's fine," he said. Dinner was obviously over, and Marco took me by the hand and led me up to our room.

"Do you have something?" he asked. "Or should I send someone out?"

"I have medicine." All of that was bad. So, so bad. How was I going to fit in with the Kimballs when I was ruining their things and getting sick during their vacation? I dug through my purse until I found my Digestive Advantage pills. Ken wasn't going to want to meet with me now. I had wrecked everything. I took a couple of pills and lay down on the bed. "I certainly made tonight interesting, didn't I?"

He sat on the bed next to me and took my hand. "You really stuck that crash landing."

I smiled. "I didn't even have time to return my seat and tray table to their upright positions. Your dad's going to hate me, isn't he?"

"He won't care."

"Won't your stepmom make him care?"

"Money always trumps family." He sounded so sad that it made me tear up.

I cleared my throat. "I'm like that china. Broken and difficult to match."

"Broken things can be mended. And there's more than one person out there who will be a match."

But not him. He didn't see himself as a match for me.

I looked up at the ceiling so that I wouldn't cry. I'd wanted to impress Marco, for his family to like me. I'd wanted his dad to see me as a serious scientist and businesswoman. Instead, we were here. "This is the most predictable thing I've ever been a part of."

"How?"

"I wore the wrong thing and broke something valuable and now I'm going to spend the rest of the night with gas pains and diarrhea because I ate something I shouldn't have. On the bright side, the mango shrikhand didn't kill me, so it's only going to make me stronger, right?" I joked.

"What can I do for you?" he asked.

"Pretend you don't hear what's happening in there?" I said, pointing at the bathroom door.

He smiled and then leaned down to kiss me on the forehead. His lips again felt like he was branding me, burning me.

"It's a deal," he said against my skin.

~

I spent most of the night in the bathroom. Marco brought me cold washcloths for my face and neck, but I was miserable. It took a few hours, but I finally started to feel human again.

I needed a drink of water, but I wanted it in a glass. I went into the bedroom, and Marco was passed out on the bed. He looked so boyish in his sleep, so carefree. I couldn't help myself. I leaned over to kiss his cheek softly. He stirred in his sleep but didn't wake up.

How different this night might have been if his stepmother hadn't basically tried to poison me.

Closing the door quietly, I went out into the hallway. I was close to the stairs when I realized there was something under my feet. I blinked a couple of times. It was red rose petals. Everywhere.

Like someone had murdered the host of *The Bachelor* in the hall. I heard a noise, and I turned, expecting to see Marco.

But it was Craig, coming out of his bedroom.

"I wanted to talk to you," he said. "I heard you get up."

"At three in the morning?" That seemed kind of creepy.

He came closer to me. "Let's cut to the chase. I know that you have serious feelings for me. That you might even be in love with me."

What? How? What?

"Had," I corrected him. "And I was seriously mistaken."

He tried to reach for my hand, but I pulled away from him. "Don't you think we should explore this?" he asked.

"With your sweet fiancée in that room right there? In the middle of what I can only assume was a romantic gesture on your part?" I asked. "Catalina was right about you. You are the tooliest tool ever." She was also right about him being a cheater. There would be no living with her after this.

"Leighton understands how things are." He moved closer again.

I saw a shadow approach us. Marco.

Immediately, I thought of how this must look. Like I had some secret midnight rendezvous with his brother. That I was making out with Marco in the library and then meeting up with Craig late at night. Craig didn't know that Marco and I weren't really together. Craig was willing to cheat on Leighton, and it must have looked like I was willing to do that, too.

It was going to make Marco think less of me. My heart pounded hard as I realized how scared that made me. His opinion mattered so much to me.

"I'm going to get a drink," Marco said in a neutral tone, and I was too afraid to offer to go with him. Because honestly? I felt a little like I had just cheated on him, even though nothing had happened.

And never would.

Marco silently walked past us. I wanted him to make eye contact with me so that I could show him nothing was going on, but he didn't. He went downstairs, and when he was safely out of earshot, I said to Craig, "Leighton deserves better."

"So does Marco," he snapped back, and his shot was true and lodged itself right in my heart. That was painful.

And correct.

I went back into the bedroom and curled up on the bed, waiting for Marco to return. I wanted a chance to explain. To tell him how my feelings had changed. That I wanted him, not his brother.

But then I went back to the place I always did—my fears and insecurities. Just because Marco was nice and liked kissing me didn't mean he had feelings for me. What would he do when I told him?

If I told him. Despite my earlier decision, I didn't think I could go through with it. I wouldn't risk losing him. He was too important to me.

Catalina was right. Given enough time, I would talk myself out of almost anything.

I was broken, not sure how to mend myself or my relationships. I didn't know how to navigate a conversation with him where I was messy and vulnerable and myself. Science had rules. You followed them, and things turned out the way they were supposed to. But I didn't know the rules here. How to keep Marco in my life, even if he didn't feel the same way that I did.

That was my main fear. That Marco could never love me like I loved him. And him saying that to me, that would destroy me. Utter destruction, laying waste to my heart and soul.

I didn't know what to do. And I hated this feeling. Not sure how to move forward, not able to go back. Just stuck.

While I was still wrestling with my choices, trying to figure out the right thing to do, I wound up falling asleep.

The next morning, I woke up to him coming out of the bathroom. His expression was flat.

"Marie-Angelique called last night. There's an issue with one of our suppliers. I'd hoped that it would work itself out, but it hasn't. I have to go back to California today."

"Oh. Okay." I thought of how awful I must have looked and tried to pat my hair down.

He seemed so serious, so unlike my Marco. This must have been what Catalina had initially been referring to, when we first started talking about him. I'd never known this guy. Was this solely about work? Or did it have something to do with Craig and me last night?

Was he jealous?

That was a good thing. It meant that there might be something else there.

"You're welcome to stay," he said.

"No, I don't want that. I want to go back. With you." There was zero chance I was going to stay in the Kimball house without him.

This seemed to surprise him. "Good. Well, get packed. The car is going to be here in about twenty minutes."

That wasn't enough time, but I was eager to put all of this behind me. Maybe when we got back to Los Angeles, things would go back to the way they were. Not entirely as they were, because I didn't want to forget about that kiss in the library, but I did want things to be easy and comfortable between Marco and me again.

But that's not what happened.

~

Marco was polite but distant the entire trip home. In the car, on the plane. He dropped me off at my grandparents' home and didn't even get out to say a proper goodbye to me.

The whole rest of the week, he was too busy to meet with me. I hated this. I missed him so much that I physically ached. Catalina had been right again—he had obviously been clearing his schedule to spend time with me.

Or he was filling it up now so as to avoid me. Either way, I didn't like it.

He always answered my texts, polite and encouraging for the upcoming pitch, but what we had was gone.

I had no idea how to get it back. Why things had changed. I needed my Marco back.

Was he angry about the Craig thing? Catalina kept encouraging me to just talk to Marco, but I couldn't when he was being distant like this.

Not to mention that I couldn't have him turn me down and then still manage to pitch my company to his family. It was better to be in this in-between state than risk everything that both he and I had been working toward. If Marco was going to break my heart, he could do it after we got a decision on the company. I didn't want to ruin it for me, but I didn't want to ruin it for him, either.

But that didn't stop me from thinking about him constantly, wanting to be close to him again.

One night, while I was sobbing, watching Aragorn and Arwen reunite, I called Catalina.

"Who do I need to stab?" she asked when she heard my voice.

"I'm in love with Marco." It was the first time I had said it out loud.

"And Bingo was his name-o," she said sarcastically. "Let me translate that for you. Duh."

"You're not going to say you told me so?"

"Nope. Just kaboom, like I promised you."

"When you said this would blow up in my face, I thought you meant that Craig would find out and that was how I would get my heart destroyed."

"No. I could see what was happening between you and Marco, even when you couldn't."

"Then why is he being this way?" I whined, feeling pathetic.

"My theory is because he loves you and he thinks you're in love with his brother."

"How could anyone think that? Craig sucks."

"Uh, I don't know, because you've spent the last two years saying you were?"

This was an excellent point. I hadn't told Marco that my feelings about Craig had changed. He was still operating under that assumption. Would it make a difference? "But why do you think Marco loves me?"

"Anna, you're an amazing person. Everybody should be in love with you. Even that jerk Craig. You need to tell Marco how you feel so that he can make a choice after he has all the facts."

I shook my head. "I just can't believe that someone like him would feel that way about someone like me."

"That is literally the stupidest thing I've ever heard, and I once had to listen to Steve explain how the WWE is real."

That made me sit straight up in my bed. So far, Catalina was batting a thousand. An expression I only knew because of Marco. Maybe I should trust her over my own insecurities. "Aren't you the one who is always telling me not to say *I love you* first? Never pull that trigger unless fired upon first?"

"That's advice for me," she said, exasperated. "Not you. I think he needs to hear it."

He needed to hear all of it. I was afraid, but my grandma had once said that bravery wasn't the absence of fear but pushing on in spite of it. I had to tell him how my feelings had changed. He didn't have all the facts. He couldn't make choices if he didn't have all the information.

There was a giant lump in my throat, but I could do this. I could. "Right. So I'll tell Marco. I'll do the presentation, and then his dad is going to make me an offer, and I'll pull him aside and tell him everything." It seemed like a good plan. Mostly because there was no way I could confess my love to him, have him tell me he wasn't interested, and then keep it together long enough for my pitch.

And if he didn't love me back, well, I would blow up that bridge when I came to it.

CHAPTER TWENTY-EIGHT

It was the morning of the pitch, and it had been arranged to be at Minx Cosmetics. I'd spent my solitary week practicing it in the mirror and refining my formula. I felt confident in both. I paced back and forth, going over the words. "Good morning, gentlemen. I've come here today to share with you the newest innovation for the future and how I hope to build a company based on the science of neurocosmetics."

Glancing up at the clock, I saw that it was almost time to start. Marco wasn't here. Maybe he wasn't coming. It wasn't like him to be anything but early. I kept running the pitch through my head, focusing on that. I would get through the next hour, and then I'd worry about Marco.

"I'm here." Marco walked into the waiting room, and I nearly collapsed in relief at seeing him. Without thinking, I went over and hugged him. His body was stiff, but it was so good to see him and touch him again that I didn't care if he hugged me back.

"I've missed you," I said. I wanted to tell him everything right then, right there. Not yet. I would tell him after. Right now, it was enough just to have him close to me.

His arms went around me, and he returned the hug. "I've missed you, too."

I rested my head against his chest. His body still felt tense, anxious. I looked up at him. "Are you nervous?" Heaven knows I certainly was.

"A little," he confessed.

"Crack your knuckles," I told him as I let go of him and covered my ears.

He gave me an odd expression, but then he did it, giving me a half smile while he did so.

"Better?" I asked when he was finished.

"Yes."

That look of his was back, the one that made me want to tell him everything. Or maybe that was just how much I needed to tell him that I loved him. "There's so much I want to say to you," I said.

This wasn't the plan, but he was here, and that was all I cared about. But before I could say anything else, a middle-aged, no-nonsense woman came over to us. "Mr. Kimball will see you now."

This must have been Janine, Ken's assistant. Marco thanked her and turned to me. "Shall we?"

"I'm nervous, too," I confessed. For so many reasons.

He ducked down slightly so that our gazes were level. "I believe in you, Anna. You've got this."

It was the perfect thing to say, and it filled me with an optimism I wasn't used to feeling. We went into the conference room. Craig and Ken were waiting for us. I had a momentary flashback of the last time I'd been in a conference room with Marco, but I told my ovaries that now was not the time.

"Anna, good to see you again." Mr. Kimball shook my hand, but Craig sat at the table with a smug smirk on his face. Marco and his father took seats next to one another, and I went to stand next to the whiteboard. This was it. I had this. I knew my stuff, backward and forward. I could do it. I shook off the nervous energy I was feeling and launched into my presentation. "Right. Good morning, gentlemen. I've come here today to—"

Ken held up his hand, indicating that he wanted me to stop. Oh no, had I messed up already?

Then he said, "There's no need to hear your pitch."

"What?" I had spent a lot of time working on this. "I have charts and graphs."

Marco looked furious. "What's going on?" he demanded.

Craig apparently decided now was the time to speak. "What's going on is that your little girlfriend is an employee of KRT Limited. She signed a standard consulting contract. Which means we own her lipstick. Any intellectual property she develops as a consultant belongs to us."

What? Was that true? I cursed myself for not reading that contract. It was like Craig had just lobbed an anvil across the room that had struck me square in the stomach. They owned my mood ring lipstick? This was going to be the mark I made on the cosmetic industry, the thing I would be known for.

And Craig acted like he was about to take it all away from me. My dream.

Given the looks he was exchanging with his dad, they'd been in on this together. They could have called anytime during the week to destroy my life, but no, they'd apparently wanted to do it in person.

Marco looked scary. "Did you bother to read her contract?"

Craig's smug expression finally faltered. "Why does that matter?"

"Because Anna didn't sign the standard contract. I made some alterations. Including the fact that any products she developed would remain her intellectual property and specifically did not belong to Minx or KRT." He glanced at me and gave me a sad little smile. "You didn't read the contract, did you?"

No, I had not. I put my hand over my heart.

"Why would you do that?" his father asked, clearly annoyed. Craig's face turned red, and he sputtered in protest.

Why would Marco do that? My heart leapt with hope. Why would he put a clause into my contract unless . . . unless . . .

He had always been trying to protect me. He was always looking out for me and my best interests.

What did that mean? I knew it meant something, but it was like I couldn't process all the thoughts zooming around in my head into something meaningful.

I knew what Catalina would say. She would say that Marco had done it because he had feelings for me, too.

And I'd been too stupid to see it.

Marco stood up, buttoning his suit coat. "Anna, my recommendation is that you not listen to anything that these two have to say. There are hundreds of investors who would see what you're offering and want to invest in you. You have such a bright future." He paused and then glanced at his brother. "I hope you are happy and get everything you want."

He gave me the saddest look, and then he walked out of the room.

And I just stood there, frozen with fear.

Because the only bright future I wanted had just left.

No. Things were not going to end this way. I wouldn't let them. I started gathering up my things, intending to chase after him. I had to tell Marco everything. His words had sounded so final. So over. I couldn't let this be it.

But then Craig was standing in front of me. "Wait. We're not finished."

"We most certainly are," I said.

But then Ken was there, too. "We can make you an investment offer. We will give you whatever cash flow you need for facilities, equipment, and a staff. But in exchange we take eighty-five percent of your company."

Did they really think I was that stupid? "I'd rather run this out of my grandparents' garage than hand it over to you." I did believe in myself. Marco believed in me. And those two things were enough. The money would come eventually. I didn't have to sign my dreams away to make that happen.

Ken's phone buzzed, and he looked at his screen. His expression changed, shocked. "Marco just emailed his resignation." He started angrily pushing buttons, and apparently Marco's number went straight to voice mail. "You will call me back. I don't accept your resignation. This is unacceptable behavior."

Craig's entire demeanor changed. "You don't have to do that, Dad. I'm here. I can take over Minx."

He was such a weasel. How had I been such an incredibly bad judge of character? Not only of Craig but of Marco, too. Why hadn't I told him sooner? Why had I waited?

Ken looked his second son over and dismissed him. "No, you can't."

Marco quit? Why had he done that?

The realization hit me hard. It was for me. He had left his mother's beloved company and his dream job as CEO of KRT for me. Because his dad and brother had tried to screw me over.

It was the grandest of gestures.

I had to find him. Why was I still here listening to Ken and Craig fight? I ran out of the room and heard Craig calling after me, "That contract was not valid! We'll sue!"

I realized I didn't know where Marco's office was. I asked the receptionist on this floor, and she told me it was five stories up. I thanked her and made my way to the elevators. I kept pushing the button, but it was taking too long. I opened the door to the stairs and started running.

Up.

Five flights of stairs.

By the time I'd reached the top, I was so winded, I was worried I was going to pass out. This had been a bad idea. I asked the receptionist which way to go, and it took me a couple of tries, but she eventually understood my question and pointed me in the direction of Marco's office.

I ran past a small, dark-haired woman who asked, "Can I help you?" I went into Marco's office, pushing the door open.

It was empty.

I turned around and went back to the woman. "Are you Marie-Angelique?"

She looked confused. "I am."

"Marco quit?"

"He did." Her sad expression made my heart twist in my chest. "He told me right before he emailed his father."

Which meant he'd been here. I must have just missed him. "Where did he go?"

"I don't know if I'm supposed to say anything."

"Please." I was ready to get on my hands and knees if need be. "I have to find him."

"He said something about going to his mother's house in Italy. I think he went home to pack."

"Thank you." I hugged her and then made a run for the elevators. I assumed running downstairs was easier, but I was already a sweaty, gross mess and did not need to add to it.

The elevator came quickly, and I ran through the lobby and out to the parking lot. I got into my car and started it up.

And nothing.

The engine didn't turn over.

"Come on, Betty. Not now. You can't do this to me now," I said. I had no idea when his flight was leaving. Catalina was here in the building, but she was working. I didn't know how long a rideshare would take, and I couldn't risk not getting a ride right away.

Marco's stupid Porsche was probably so fast that it could basically teleport him back to his condo. And I was stuck.

I worried that I'd never catch up with him.

I called my grandfather. "Grandpa? Betty died."

"Who died?" he asked, sounding concerned.

"My car. I need you to come get me at Minx."

"I thought you quit that job."

I closed my eyes. "Yes, but I had that presentation here. There's a lot to explain and I will, but right now I have to go to Marco's house, and my car isn't working, so I need you to come get me."

"Okay. I'll be there as soon as I can."

Waiting that half hour for him to arrive was pure torture. I worried that Craig would have me escorted out of the parking lot or something else horrible or that Marco was already on his way to LAX and I was never going to see him again.

Not knowing when he was leaving, I tried to call and text him. There was no response to my texts, and the calls went immediately to voice mail. Was he screening me? Or had he just turned his phone off?

I called Catalina for reassurance. I told her what had happened. "Do you want me to take the day off and drive you?" she asked.

"No." I couldn't put her job in jeopardy. Especially now that I wasn't going to be in a position to offer her a new one. "My grandpa's coming. I'm just . . . so scared."

"Scared of what?"

"I'm scared he'll be gone before I can reach him. I'm scared that he won't feel the same." And that I would never recover if he rejected me.

She made a sympathetic sound. "I know you have suffered some unimaginable losses in your life, and it makes sense that you'd be afraid of another one. But love means risk. It will be scary, but I know you can do it. And regardless of what happens, I'll always be here for you."

I did know that. I thanked her and promised to update her when I got the chance.

I hoped there would be a happy update.

"Also, you should slash Craig's tires on your way out. Screw being the bigger person."

That made me smile, and we said goodbye.

My grandpa finally arrived, and I climbed into the passenger seat gratefully. Chick Norris and Feather Locklear were in the back seat, and I heard again that the Yankees sucked.

"Thank you so much," I told him. We drove about twenty feet, and his car started making a clunking noise, and the engine went silent. He directed the car over to the curb and then came to a stop.

"Uh-oh," my grandpa said.

I braced my hands against the dashboard. This could not be happening. That was it! I was taking that consultant money and I was going to buy everyone in my house a new car.

"I'm out of gas," he said apologetically. "I'm sorry. I should have checked it."

"It's fine," I said. I couldn't be mad. That was just the sort of thing my grandfather did.

"I'll call your grandma. She has today free."

Which meant another half hour. I felt time slipping away from me, and it was so frustrating that there was nothing I could do. Marco could be making his way to the airport at this very moment.

The problem was that sitting here, I had nothing but time to consider how badly this could all go. Marco wouldn't laugh in my face. I knew him well enough to know he'd never be so cruel. He would be kind if he had to let me down, but the idea that I would bare my soul to him and he would say *no thanks*? As Catalina had pointed out, I had suffered a lot of loss. I didn't want to lose him, too.

When my grandmother got there, I was tempted to tell her to take me home and forget the whole thing. It would hurt, but I'd get over it, right?

"What's wrong?" my grandfather asked.

"I'm in love with Marco, and I'm terrified. What if he doesn't love me back?"

There was so much kindness in his eyes that it actually made me feel worse. "My sweet girl, what if he does? Be brave."

"I don't want my heart to be shattered."

"Nobody does. But life isn't worth living if you hide away in your grandparents' house and never chase after your dreams. Chase after this one."

It was the most profound thing he'd ever said to me. It also made me feel resolved again. I was going to tell Marco. I wanted a life with him. A company that we'd start together, to adopt some birds and have some babies and wake up every morning with him.

If that scared him away, well, then he wasn't the man I thought he was.

My grandpa added, "You don't want to have any regrets. Or egrets. Egrets are terrible to take care of."

That didn't quite distract me in the way that he'd probably hoped. "This is all happening really quickly, though." One last protest from my scarred psyche.

"Do you know how fast it happened for me?" Grandpa asked. "The second hour in the hospital after I'd broken my leg. I knew your grandmother was the one for me and that I'd never love anyone the way I already loved her. It was the first night for your parents, too."

Maybe it hadn't been the first day, but it had happened quickly and without me even noticing. I'd been falling for Marco every day and had been so distracted by shiny, fake Craig that I hadn't realized it.

My grandmother arrived, and my grandpa patted me on the hand and said, "Let's make like flamingos and get the flock out of here."

That made me smile, and I got out of his car and went over to my grandma's. I slid into the back seat with the two birdcages. I strapped both cages into the modified dog harness and announced to my grandmother, "I'm in love with Marco."

My thinking was the more people I told, the easier it would be to tell Marco. I probably should have told him first, but apparently I was a stupid person.

"Polo?" she asked, confused as she pulled into the street.

"No, the Marco who you didn't want me to spend time with."

"The one trying to make you change yourself?"

"That's not what he was doing," I said. "Marco always liked me for me. He didn't want me to change. But I love him so much that if he wanted me to wear a purple wig every day for the rest of my life, I would do it."

"I knew this was going to happen," she said. "I saw him give you gum."

"What?" That seemed like such an oddly specific thing to say.

"I hate getting up in the mornings. Always have. Your grandpa always gets up early to start the coffee for me because he knows I forget half the time, and I should not be walking around in the world uncaffeinated."

Boy, was that true. And how had I not known that my grandfather did that every morning for my grandmother?

"He thinks of me, of what I need. Your Marco does the same thing. You just make sure that he treats you right," Grandma said, wagging her finger at me in the rearview mirror.

We finally made it to Marco's building, and my grandparents offered to stay and wait. I think my grandpa in particular was very interested in seeing how things turned out.

"No. It's okay. Go. I'll be home later."

I watched as they drove off. Knowing they were outside waiting for me would just be another safety net, and I had to do this without one.

It was the only way I'd be honest.

CHAPTER TWENTY-NINE

When I got to his condo, the door was shut. I knocked on it and prayed that he would answer. That I wasn't too late. My heart was in my throat, pounding so hard that it was hard to hear. I couldn't tell if he was inside or not.

Relief flooded through me when the door opened and there he was. He had changed into comfortable clothes, and I saw a suitcase behind him in his hallway. I loved him so much that my heart ached from it, and again I thought of how everything that mattered to me was riding on this moment.

"What are you doing here?" he asked.

Be brave. I took a big breath. "I need to talk to you." I hesitated when he didn't let me in. My voice broke slightly. "Please."

His face looked weary but concerned. He nodded and stepped aside, closing the door behind me. He walked into the living room, and I thought of all the times we'd spent here together. All the fun we'd had. Why had it taken me so long to figure all of this out?

Marco sat on the couch, but I was too fidgety to sit still. I stayed standing. I'd built this up so much, had so much encouragement, had made my resolution over and over again, but now that I was here, I found it nearly impossible.

"Why did you leave? Today?" I asked.

He looked down at his hands. "I realized what a terrible person I was being."

That was about the last thing I'd expected him to say.

"I saw the way they were all ready to play games with your life. Ready to ruin your dreams. All I could think of was how I'd been willing to do the same thing. How I was willing to use you to impress my father. For a job."

"Your father and brother trying to steal my lipstick is not even close to you trying to date somebody down-to-earth to impress your dad."

"I'm still ashamed."

This made me sit next to him. Why was that such a big deal to him? We'd been in it together. I remembered how he said he was afraid of ending up like his dad. "You're not like Ken."

Marco swallowed hard. "I took those first steps. Trying to break up Craig's relationship, being willing to use you for that."

"I was fully aware of what I was doing. You didn't trick me or use me." I was too afraid to touch him, but I still wanted to reassure him. "I'm the one who should be apologizing to you."

He looked surprised. "For what?"

"Do you remember when I told you that I wanted Craig more than almost anything?"

"Painstakingly."

I took that as an encouraging sign. "That wasn't true. I don't love him. I never did."

Whatever I was expecting, it wasn't Marco folding his arms across his chest and sitting back. Closed off. "You put on a pretty believable show."

This he believed? "He's not the person I thought he was. I've known for a while that I didn't have feelings for him. You know that I'm a terrible liar. You've always been able to see through me, even when I was lying to myself. And to you."

Marco said nothing. My mouth went dry, and my heart beat so hard, I was afraid it was going to give out completely. Some animal part of my brain urged me to run, but this was my chance to tell him everything. I would put my cards on the table and be honest with him. The way I should have been a long time ago.

So I kept talking. "I should have told you. But I was afraid."

"Of what?"

"Of not seeing you again. Of you ending our deal because I'd broken our rule."

The silence was overwhelming. But then he finally asked softly, "What rule, Anna?" even though I felt like he knew.

There was hope there. I heard it, even though part of me wanted to deny it. Even now. I had to stop letting my insecurities rule me. I couldn't let fear make decisions for me.

This was it. I could do this. The words rushed out of my mouth. "The one where I wasn't supposed to fall in love with you."

His arms relaxed, and he looked stunned. Still hesitant, still distrusting, but willing to listen. "Slower, and with more specific words."

He hadn't run away screaming. I took that as a good sign. My adrenaline still spiked with that ever-present fear, that worry of what he might do. But I had to say it. "I love you, Marco. I have for a long time. And I understand if you don't feel the same way. I also know that you have a hard time trusting people. That nearly everyone you care about lets you down. But this is real. I love you, and I'm always going to love you."

He stayed silent, and I could see the emotions flitting across his face, one after the other.

"When I shattered that bowl, remember how you said it would be easy to match me, that I was mendable, even though I'd been broken. But the thing is, I think we're both broken and that we can mend each other. Our pieces fit together, and we'll make something whole. Something beautiful. I love you, and if you don't feel the same, that's fine." No, now was the time for total honesty. "I take that back. It wouldn't be fine. I don't just love you. I want a life with you. A company, pets, kids, the whole thing."

There. I'd put myself out there as much as possible, and now it was going to be up to him.

The ball was in his court.

"You love me?"

"Yes, I love you. Infuriating, charming, wonderful, intelligent, kind you." I took another deep breath. This was the bit I needed an answer to. "Do you think you could ever feel the same way about me?"

Then his lips were on mine, swallowing my words. He kissed me hard and thoroughly and I could feel his emotions, that he felt the same way as me. Pure joy blossomed inside me. Marco loved me, too. There was no denying it this time. Kaboom. I was going to buy Catalina a very pretty present.

When the kiss ended, he leaned his forehead against mine, his hands on my face. I clung to his wrists, relying on his strength. "That wasn't an answer," I chided him, not able to suppress my blissful smile.

He grinned, my favorite thing in the world, and said, "Wasn't it? I have a hypothesis that actions are better than words."

"I need the words."

He stroked the side of my face so lovingly and tenderly that I wanted to melt into him. "I have felt so selfish. Wanting to kiss you, touch you, be close to you, and the whole time I thought you were in love with my brother. Do you know how hard it is to be in love with someone who loves somebody else? I tried hard to be respectful of you and your feelings, Anna. And there were so many times that I felt like I was taking advantage of you."

"You never once did that," I told him, pressing my cheek against his.

"I struggled so much with guilt. I used that flimsy experiment pretense to be able to kiss you when I was so desperate for you that I could barely stand it. In Vermont, I felt like I had taken things too far. I wanted to take them further. If you hadn't gotten sick that night . . ." He trailed off but then pressed a kiss on my cheek. "I knew I had gone too far over that line. That I had to respect you and the feelings I thought you had for Craig."

"Feelings I never had," I corrected him.

He kissed me gently. "I know that now. I wish I'd known it then. Because I used to be a love atheist. I never believed it was real. But you turned me into a believer. Because what other way is there to describe what I feel when I look at you? Of course I love you. I love everything about you, every perfect and broken piece. I think I loved you from the first time I saw you in your cosplay dress at that company event. I thought, *Here's someone who needs me*. But that wasn't true. I needed you. I didn't realize what was missing from my life until you came barreling into it. I love you, and I want everything you want. A life. A family. A business. Whatever you want, just so long as we're together. I do want you to be happy, but I want you to be happy with me."

My heart leapt and jumped in celebration, the joy I was feeling threatening to make me burst into song. I couldn't remember ever feeling this happy. I'd been so worried he wouldn't love me, and to find that he did? That he always had?

Then it was my turn to kiss him, to show him what his words meant to me. Maybe a little bit of action was better than words. When we were both breathing hard, I said, "I would let someone put lasers in my eyeballs for you."

"Gi melin, Undómiel."

"That's what you said to me in Vermont. What does it mean?"

"It's Elvish. Well, technically it's two different dialects of Elvish. But it means *I love you, Evenstar*."

Evenstar. That's what they called Arwen in Lord of the Rings. He was such a giant nerd, and I loved that about him. I loved everything about him.

This time, I tackled him, and he was laughing as he fell back against the couch, until I made sure that he wasn't laughing anymore.

"I should have told you sooner," I said when I broke off for some much-needed air. "I should have spoken up and said how I felt. What I wanted. It's always been so hard for me. I thought I would lose things if I spoke up. But I've found the opposite to be true. I regret not doing it sooner."

"It's okay," he said, tracing the outline of my face with his fingertips, like he wanted to memorize it. "We'll make sure that we always tell each other what we need and how much we mean to each other. Because now that I have you, I don't plan on ever letting you go again."

"Good. Because I don't plan on going anywhere. You're my eyelash wish come true."

He kissed me gently, tenderly. I loved him so much. "You wished for me?"

"I did. And I wouldn't even admit it to myself. Today I ran up five flights of stairs at Minx to find you."

"That is love. Why didn't you wait for the elevators? They're actually really fast."

"Do you think you could please shut up and go back to proving your hypothesis correct?"

"I'll do anything for science," he said with a smile and then kissed me in a way that let me know everything I needed to.

EPILOGUE

Six months later . . .

"You're going to call him tomorrow?" Catalina asked me, her voice crackling slightly on her end of the phone. Marco stopped at a red light to make a left turn. I wanted to ask him again where we were going, but he had been strangely silent on the matter.

Catalina let out an impatient sound that made me respond. "Yes, I am going to call Zhen and offer him the job. But only if you promise that you're not going to sexually harass him at work."

"I make no such promise. Plus, that would be highly hypocritical given that whenever you and Marco are in the lab together, I'm concerned about everything around us spontaneously combusting."

Zhen and Catalina had been dating for nearly as long as Marco and I had. Now that Aviary Cosmetics had all its funding lined up, I'd promised I would hire him away from Minx.

Catalina had, obviously, been my first hire.

Well, after Marco. But he was my partner, working as CEO, so I didn't count that.

"And what do we say to our best friend?" she asked, and I rolled my eyes.

"Catalina is always right. And I will never doubt her again. And I will name my firstborn child after her." This had started after I'd found out just how much I owed to her. Marie-Angelique and Catalina were friends, and when the whole pitch-meeting-gone-wrong fiasco had happened and Marco quit, Marie-Angelique had immediately called Catalina to fill her in.

At which point Catalina had told her to make things seem urgent, as if Marco were planning to leave right away, so that I would be motivated to act. Marco's flight to Italy had actually been scheduled for four days later.

"But if you'd known that, you would have talked yourself out of it, and then you wouldn't be so happy right now!" she had insisted. "It's not a rom-com ending unless you stop him from going to the airport," and I was inclined to agree with her. I figured a little lie was okay if things turned out so well in the end.

Catalina said, "Okay, well, have so much fun on your date tonight. With whatever it is that you have planned."

It was an odd thing to say. "Okay, weirdo. See you tomorrow."

When I hung up my phone, he reached over to stroke the back of my head, and I smiled at him. "What did Catalina have to say?" he asked.

"She was verifying that we were going to make that offer to Zhen tomorrow. I think he'll be a good fit. He's a great chemist and a nice person."

"I meant before. That thing about Leighton."

"Oh! Catalina follows Leighton on Instagram, and apparently she eloped with that kindergarten teacher she's been dating." Craig and Leighton had broken up not long after the Vermont trip. Catalina's direct message to Leighton might have played a part in that, but we weren't sure. Craig had claimed that they'd broken up because Leighton had "issues," and I assumed one of those issues was that she didn't want to marry a lying scumbag cheater.

Anyway, she'd met a great new guy who her family didn't approve of, and they'd disowned her, but she seemed ridiculously happy. It turned out that Marco wasn't quite the judge of character he had believed himself to be. I delighted in teasing him about that.

Craig, meanwhile, was apparently working his way through all the sorority houses of Southern California. Each girlfriend seemed to be younger and blonder than the last. Ken had not made Craig CEO of Minx and had brought in someone new. Tracie was apparently livid but hadn't done anything beyond express her anger. There was no way she would ever leave her husband or her lifestyle.

Lindy told her father that she planned on becoming a cosmetic chemist and was currently working this summer as an intern at Aviary. Her love of chemistry was contagious, and she was so great to have around.

It was also nice that she could work for free. Marco had lined up several investors, but we always seemed to be worrying about money. He was sure that once our first product line launched, we would be ridiculously successful.

And I'd learned a long time ago to not doubt Marco.

"Are you ever going to tell me where we're going?" I asked.

"Nope. It's what we in the industry like to call a surprise."

"So annoying," I said, but there was no conviction behind my words. I kissed his palm, and then he threaded his fingers into my hair so that he was massaging my scalp. He knew how much I loved that and that it would most likely keep me from asking too many questions.

He was right.

I held up my phone to show him the text my grandpa had just sent me. "Grandpa's got a new rescue. Meet Eggolas."

He glanced at the photo. "Tell your grandfather that I'm disappointed in the name. He should have gone with Orlando Plume."

I laughed and sent the text. Grandpa sent back a thumbs-up emoji. "I think you convinced him."

Marco pulled the car over. We were in a nice neighborhood—the kind with big houses and tree-lined sidewalks. "Where are we?"

"So many questions." He shook his head. "Come on. There's something I want to show you."

I was thoroughly confused and curious at the same time, which I loved. I got out of the car and followed him. He put on a backpack and took me by the hand. There was a sidewalk that led between two houses. "Are we allowed to be here?" I asked. This definitely seemed like a HOA type of place, and with our line about to launch, we did not need a headline that the owners of Aviary Cosmetics had just been arrested.

Maybe that was the point. Marco was trying to drum up some extra publicity. He was willing to do whatever he had to do to make our dream a reality, and I loved him for it.

We got to a locked gate, and I decided that if Marco wanted me to climb it, I was probably out. "That's trespassing, right?"

"Not if you have a key." He unlocked the gate, and it led into a massive park. There was an expensive-looking playground that resembled an actual fort. Trees everywhere, lush green grass, gorgeous flowers in every hue.

I had to shade my eyes as we walked toward the middle, and I realized that in the center of the park there was a large man-made lake. The path we were on wound around it.

"This is so pretty," I told him.

He nodded. "I thought you might want to go for a walk."

I wrapped my arms around his right arm, resting my head against his shoulder as we walked. We talked a lot about the launch and about the head of marketing for the company. Prisha was worth her weight in gold, and I told him that we were probably going to have to offer her a raise soon if we wanted to hold on to her.

He interrupted our conversation to point to our right. "Hey, a bench. Want to sit down?"

It was then that I realized what was happening. This was my fantasy. The one I'd used to have about Craig that quickly became about Marco. I'd told Marco about it the day I'd confessed that I was in love with him, but I hadn't thought about it in so long, as I had the real thing and didn't need to pretend.

We were together in a beautiful park, walking alongside a body of water, sitting on a bench to talk.

I sank down on the bench while he took off his backpack. My heart was already going a mile a minute, but I didn't want to jump to any assumptions. This was enough. Being with Marco was enough.

I didn't need more.

Even if I secretly wanted it.

He reached into his backpack and pulled out a large box. "Today the first shipment of palettes arrived, and I wanted you to be the first person to see them." Our logo was on the side of the box, and I didn't think the sight of that would ever grow old.

I opened the box slowly, and there were the palettes, just as he'd promised. I tried not to be disappointed, but I couldn't help it. We had been talking marriage since we became official, but we'd agreed to focus on launching Aviary first. It would be too much to try to start a company and plan a wedding.

The palette on top was wrapped in plastic, and I undid the plastic carefully. Our logo was embossed on the top, and I ran my fingers across it. "So pretty."

"Like you."

I smiled at him and then flipped the lid open.

There was a ring in one of the containers where there should have been a blush. I picked up the ring. Not just any ring.

My mother's ring.

I looked up at him, and he had gotten down on one knee. "I've been planning for this moment for a long time. The day you came over and told me you loved me? I wanted to ask you then. Which means

I've had plenty of time to think about what I wanted to say. To tell you how much you mean to me and how excited I am about the life we're building together. How deeply in love with you I am. But I couldn't think of anything perfect. And that's what you deserve. Perfection. So I thought I'd go for simplicity. Anna Urban Decay Ellis, would you please do me the honor of marrying me?"

I sat there, my mouth open, temporarily unable to respond. He took the ring from me and slid it onto the ring finger on my left hand. He said, "By the way, I did what your dad always wanted to do and replaced the cubic zirconia with a diamond."

Oh. That put a lump in my throat and made it hard to breathe.

"I can't believe you thought this wouldn't be perfect," I said, my eyes filling up with tears. "This is perfect. You're perfect. I love you so much."

"You haven't actually answered."

"Yes! My answer is yes!" I threw my arms around his neck and kissed him. A few moments later, I lifted my head up, the tears now falling down my face. "When we get married, can we have a theme wedding and dress up like Aragorn and Arwen?"

He laughed, wiping my happy tears from my cheeks. "We can talk about that later."

I held my hand up, admiring the ring. It made me feel like my parents got to be a part of this moment, and I loved him more for it. "You did so good," I told him.

"I do try," he said smugly, sliding onto the bench next to me. He put his arm around me and pulled me in close. The sun began to set, reflecting off the lake. Everything around us took on a golden sheen. Marco couldn't have arranged it better if he'd tried.

"Someday I want to be ninety years old and sitting here with you," I told him.

"I'm in. I can't think of anyone I'd rather grow old with than you." He kissed the tip of my nose. "But before we're too old to enjoy ourselves, I do have some experiments I'd like to run. Of a personal variety."

"Such as?"

"I'll show you later," he said with a waggle of his eyebrows that made me giggle. "Just promise me you'll always be my lab partner."

I put my hand in his. "I will. Now you're stuck with me."

He kissed the back of my hand, my new diamond ring sparkling in the golden sunlight. "So you're promising that I'm your adenine."

"Why is that?"

"Because it means I'll always be paired with U."

I laughed. "Please never stop making science jokes."

"We'll put that in our vows. But before we get that far, I have one more rule."

"You know how much I like rules," I said.

He laced his fingers through mine. "You have to always be yourself, let me love you forever, and live with me happily ever after."

I kissed his cheek softly. "Technically those are three rules. But my answer is yes. It will always be yes."

AUTHOR'S NOTE

Thank you for reading my story! I hope you liked getting to know Marco and Anna and enjoyed them falling in love as much as I did. If you'd like to find out when I've written something new, make sure you sign up for my newsletter at sariahwilson.com, where I most definitely will not spam you. (I'm happy when I send out a newsletter once a month!)

And if you feel so inclined, I'd love for you to leave a review on Amazon, on Goodreads, with your hairdresser's cousin's roommate's blog, via a skywriter, in graffiti on the side of a bookstore, on the back of your electric bill, or any other place you want. I would be so grateful. Thanks!

ACKNOWLEDGMENTS

For everyone who is reading this—thank you. When so much in the world has been dark and difficult, it has meant the world to me that I can craft some light, fun, romantic stories that lift up both you and me. Thank you for your support and for cheering me on. It means so much.

I have to thank my editor Alison Dasho first—for believing in me, for loving my stories and my ideas, for always having such good insights and suggestions, and for being every bit as excited as I am about stories and movies and shows. I'm so grateful that we get to work together. I'm thankful to everyone at Montlake who has worked hard to make this book a success (Anh Schluep, Tricia Callahan, Cheryl Weisman, Stef Sloma, Jillian Cline, Erin Calligan Mooney, Kris Beecroft). And to Charlotte Herscher—edits have always freaked me out and made me doubt myself, but you've somehow mastered the art of giving suggestions that don't feel scary and/or overwhelming while still making me feel so great about what I've written. I consider it a huge privilege that I've been able to work with both you and Alison for so long. I hope the movie quotes get to stay!

Thank you to the copy editors and proofreaders who find all my mistakes and continuity errors and gently guide me in the right direction. A special shout-out to Philip Pascuzzo for the gorgeous cover for this book. We've done so many books together that I no longer have to look up how to spell your name correctly. Thank you for all the beautiful artwork you've done over the last few years for me.

For my agent, Sarah Younger—you are the person I count on for so many things, and you always come through flawlessly. Protecting me, encouraging me, pointing me in the right direction, being my number one advocate and champion. I'm very grateful for the series of events that brought us together.

Thank you to Dana, Julia, Jordan, and Hailey of Dana Kaye Publicity for everything you guys do and the way that you keep me on track (especially the gentle nudging/reminding) and all of your fantastic advice.

I have to send a huge thank-you to Krissie Gerrard of Envy Cosmetic Consulting (@bak2thelab). You were so generous with your time, with your explanations, for breaking things down in a way that even a nonscience person like me could understand them. Thank you for allowing me to share some of your personal/professional experiences with the readers—the self-tanner incident happened to Krissie, and it made me laugh, so I knew I had to include it. She helped make this book possible and taught me a lot about cosmetic chemistry!

Thank you, Jen Springer, for talking all things makeup with me and giving me advice and tips.

Rian Johnson—I'm trying hard not to make my social media be all about how much of a fan I am of yours, but it's true. Everything you do is brilliant, and it inspires me as a writer, so thank you for that. And I'm dedicating this book to you and giving you my eternal gratitude for being the father of Reylo, a true enemies-to-lovers romance that should have ended happily ever after. #BenSoloStillDeservesBetter #SoDoesRey

Peter Jackson—you made me love Lord of the Rings. I've tried reading the books and I just can't, so it's a testament to your talent that you made me care so much about those characters and their stories. I'm sure somebody will try to remake your movies, but I can't imagine that it will be anytime soon. They are classics.

Jim Henson—I really, really love the Muppets. I have ever since I was a little girl (*Sesame Street* was my jam and taught me how to tie my shoes). I'm so grateful that your company continues to carry on your legacy and bring more joy and happiness with the Muppets to a new generation (I can hardly wait to introduce my new grandson to my favorites).

For my kids—there have been dark and hard days, but I know we'll get through all of this together. I love you more than words could ever say.

And Kevin, who never reads a word of what I write, I love you so much that I'd let someone put lasers in my eyeballs for you.

ABOUT THE AUTHOR

Photo © 2020 Jordan Batt

Sariah Wilson is the *USA Today* bestselling author of *The Paid Bridesmaid*, *The Seat Filler*, *Roommaid*, *Just a Boyfriend*, the Royals of Monterra series, and the #Lovestruck novels. She has never jumped out of an airplane, has never climbed Mount Everest, and is not a former CIA operative. She has, however, been madly, passionately in love with her soul mate and is a fervent believer in happily ever afters—which is why she writes romance. She grew up in Southern California, graduated from Brigham Young University (go, Cougars!) with a semi-useless degree in history, and is the oldest of nine (yes, nine). She currently lives with the aforementioned soul mate and their children in Utah, along with three cats named Pixel, Callie, and Belle, who do not get along (the cats, not the kids—although the kids sometimes have their issues, too). For more information, visit her website at www.sariahwilson.com.